Unholy

"What are you saying?" Weinerbaum asked the alien. "If I could get you access into the Earthlink, you'd be able to disrupt the *Orion*'s pre-launch schedule?"

"Is so. Delay *Orion* departure until saner minds control. Meanwhile, brothers in science free to explore mysteries of Titan."

Weinerbaum's first reaction was to balk. But fate was daring him to accept the challenge—to recruit the aid of aliens whose scientific methods were advanced far beyond Earth's. It could be the dawn of a new Age of Reason.

Then a flicker of doubt clouded the vision. "I would want your assurance on one thing," Weinerbaum said.

"Brother in science has only to ask."

"You will confine your attention strictly to the *Orion* launch. No other aspects of the global net are to be interfered with. That is clearly understood?" Weinerbaum felt foolish. This was an intellect from an ancient, spacegoing culture, and he was addressing it as if it were a sneaky student.

"Trust me," the alien said.

FIRST TIME IN PAPERBACK

By James P. Hogan
Published by Ballantine Books:

CODE OF THE LIFEMAKER
THE IMMORTALITY OPTION

THE GENESIS MACHINE
THRICE UPON A TIME
THE TWO FACES OF TOMORROW
VOYAGE FROM YESTERYEAR

The Giants Series:
INHERIT THE STARS
THE GENTLE GIANTS OF GANYMEDE
GIANTS' STAR
ENTOVERSE
THE GIANTS NOVELS (Omnibus)

Books published by The Ballantine Publishing Group
are available at quantity discounts on bulk purchases
for premium, educational, fund-raising, and special
sales use. For details, please call 1-800-733-3000.

The Immortality Option

James P. Hogan

A Del Rey® Book
BALLANTINE BOOKS • NEW YORK

A Del Rey® Book
Published by Ballantine Books

Copyright © 1995 by James P. Hogan

All rights reserved under International and Pan-American Copyright Conventions. Published in the United States by Ballantine Books, a division of Random House, Inc., New York, and simultaneously in Canada by Random House of Canada Limited, Toronto.

Library of Congress Catalog Card Number: 94-29296

ISBN 0-345-39787-8

Manufactured in the United States of America

First Hardcover Edition: February 1995
First Mass Market Edition: December 1995

10 9 8 7 6 5 4

TO JUNE, YVETTE, AND LUCY

Acknowledgment

This is to thank Hans Moravec of the Robotics Institute, Carnegie Mellon University, for his help and fascinating thoughts on minds, machines, and where they could all be leading. And for some very enjoyable company.

Prologue

B Y THE SECOND DECADE OF THE TWENTY-FIRST CENTURY the nations of Earth, while as prone as ever to the localized squabblings that would probably be a part of the human scene for as long as humanity endured, had receded from the specter of global doomsday that had tied up entire industries of creative talent and stifled vision for over fifty years. After a period of indecision while governments absorbed the new realities and former defense-satiated contractors searched for a new direction, the leading-edge technologies that the years of confrontation had stimulated became the driving force of a revitalized, multinational space program.

An early object for further investigation was Titan, the giant moon of Saturn, perpetually cloaked in high-altitude clouds of red-brown nitrogenous oxides. The first probe to attempt a surface survey was the European *Dauphin*, which arrived in 2018. Data acquired previously from astronomical observations and the probes sent to the outer planets in the 1970s suggested surface conditions close to the triple point of methane, raising the intriguing possibility that it might exist as a gas in the atmosphere and in its liquid and solid phases on the surface, thus playing a role comparable to that of water on Earth. Some scientists speculated that the hidden surface of Titan could consist of methane oceans and water-ice continents covered by nitrogenous hydrocarbon soil precipitated from the upper atmosphere, with methane rain falling from methane clouds formed below the aerosol blanket. It was even possible that radioactive heat released in the interior might maintain reservoirs of water that could escape to the surface as ice "lava" and perhaps provide a fluid substrate for mountain building and other tectonic processes.

And, indeed, radar mapping by the *Dauphin* orbiter revealed vast oceans, islands, continents, and mountains below the all-enveloping clouds, the details of which were published and caused widespread excitement. The public account, however, left out the highly reflective objects—suggestive of huge metallic constructions—which in some cases extended for miles, along with the glimpses of strange machines transmitted back by the *Dauphin*'s short-lived surface landers.

The Europeans shared their knowledge of what was presumed to be an advanced alien culture only with the Americans, who at that time were alone in possessing a large, long-range craft in a sufficiently advanced stage of development to follow up on the discovery. This was the pulsed-fusion-driven *Orion*, the development of which had been partly funded by a private consortium centered on the General Space Enterprises Corporation (GSEC) specifically for manned exploration of the outer planets. Launched, crewed, and managed operationally by the newly formed North Atlantic Space Organization (NASO), the *Orion* mission to Titan departed two years later.

In addition to NASO personnel, the mission included scientists from a wide range of disciplines, linguists and psychologists because of the prospect of encountering some form of intelligence, and a force selected from elite American, British, and French military units to afford a measure of protection, since the probable reaction and disposition of that intelligence were unknown. In this age of mass culture the GSEC directors were mindful that any future policy toward Titan that they might consider beneficial to their interests would need strong public support to be viable. Accordingly, at their instigation, the mission also included a major celebrity from a field that the antiscience reaction of recent times had endowed with significant public influence, which GSEC hoped to be able to exploit to its advantage: the super-"psychic," Karl Zambendorf. Along with him went the team of assistants that accompanied him every-where.

What the mission found on Titan was more astonishing than anything that even the most fanciful interpreters of the *Dauphin* data had imagined. Below the cloud cover, Titan was inhabited by a living, evolving biosphere of machines. Sprawling tangles of self-reproducing industrial technology proliferating out of control extended across huge tracts of the surface. And roaming around this mechanical "jungle" were various kinds of freely mobile machines that apparently formed part of a weird yet apparently functional ecology.

The only explanation the bemused Terran scientists could conceive was that it had all somehow mutated from an automated, self-replicating industrial complex set in motion by some alien culture long before. What alien culture? Where were they now? What had gone wrong? Why Titan? Nobody had answers.

But perhaps the most amazing find of all was that this unique form of life had evolved its own bizarre brand of intelligence. The scientists dubbed the beings the Taloids, after an artificially created bronze man in Greek mythology. They were an upright, bipedal species of self-aware robot that wore clothes, tamed and reared mechanical "animals," grew their houses from pseudo-vegetable cultures, and worshiped a mythical nonmachine machine maker, which they reasoned must have created the first life. They saw the miles of proliferating machinery as "forests" and quarried ice to build their cities. As nearly as could be approximated, the Taloid culture was comparable in its level of progress to Europe's at the time of the Renaissance; accordingly, the Terrans dubbed the Taloids' geographic political groupings after the medieval Italian city-states.

In terms of advancement and productive potential, the technology running wild all over Titan surpassed anything that existed on Earth. The backers of the *Orion* mission quickly realized that whoever could gain control of that potential would cease to have any effective competition on Earth, commercially or politically. Therefore, just when the

Taloids were beginning to challenge the old feudal tyrannies and experiment with more liberal ways of governing their affairs, the mission's GSEC-backed leaders adopted an interventionist policy aimed at keeping the traditional rulers in power as local puppets to run the intended neocolony.

Public opinion back on Earth was misled by distorted accounts of what was going on, and for a while the future of the Taloids looked bleak. But then, more by accident than through any deliberate design, Zambendorf and his crew became the instigators of a new "religion" that swept through the Taloid nations, causing them to throw out the old, authoritarian powers and their teachings, and hence to reject the intervention of the powers from Earth that were trying to prop up the old system.

The resulting exposures became the subject of an international scandal, causing GSEC to be relieved of its control and NASO to assume full command of the Titan mission. The GSEC representatives and associates left ignominiously with the *Orion* when the time came for it to return to Earth. Zambendorf and his team, however, remained as part of the mixed complement of NASO personnel, scientists, and a small military detachment left behind to carry on the work at Titan until the arrival of the newly completed Japanese ship *Shirasagi*, due five months after the *Orion*'s departure.

1

The Psychic
Who Valued
Reason

1

ACCORDING TO THE COMPUTERS THAT PROVIDED A RUDImentary translation between English and the strings of ultrasonic pulses via which the aliens communicated, the Taloids called it a river. And, indeed, its functions were comparable to those of a river: It flowed through the forest, attracting and sustaining life; it brought nutrients down from distant sources; and it carried away the debris, detritus, and wastes that were inevitable products of life in action.

In reality, the "river" was an immense conveyor line rolling through miles of machines and assembly stations, all thumping, whining, pounding, and buzzing on either side beneath an overhanging canopy of power lines, data cables, ducting, and pipes. The river came from more thinly mechanized regions, forming gradually out of the mergings of lesser transfer lines serving local material-processing centers and clusters of parts-making machines. Farther down it broadened, fed by incoming tributaries bringing ever more complex subassemblies and recycled parts. These flowed onward to fabrication centers lower down, which included the assembly sites for the peculiar machine "animals" and, at a number of specialized locations, for the Taloids themselves. And finally, everything that had not been utilized— components rejected by the sorting machines, substandard assemblies, unwanted pieces and parts picked up by the roving scavenger machines—was consumed in reduction furnaces and recovered as elementary materials for reprocessing.

The waste and inefficiency were enormous. In some

places masses of jammed and defunct machinery stood in idle decay, partly dismantled by the scavengers. Piles of nuts, bolts, strands of wire, cuttings, and stampings covered the ground everywhere like a layer of forest humus. Entire lines of design died out, while others appeared in their place. But amid it all, as with the carbon-chemistry variety of life that had taken possession of distant Earth, the common thread that bound them all together as descendants from the same remote ancestral event managed somehow to sustain itself and endure.

It was like trying to find your way through a General Motors plant in diving gear with the lights out, Dave Crookes thought, perspiring and cursing inside his dome-helmeted extravehicular suit as he clambered over a gap in a line of pumping stations thick with hydraulic-line couplings. The Taloid in the lead—known as Franklin among the Terrans—waited a couple of paces ahead, while Armitage, the military escort assigned to the party, held aside a web of cables hanging like vines from the supports of a rotor housing dimly outlined in the gloom above. The party included an escort more as a matter of form than from any real need for protection against anything. And the troopers were always happy to get away from the base and see something new outside.

The beam from Crookes's flashlamp revealed pipes running across concrete foundations ahead, with steel pillars and a construction going upward. To the left of the construction, cables radiated away from an arrangement of protruding columns of stacked disks that looked like the insulators of a power transformer. On the right, a pile of scrap overflowed from a recessed space beneath the concrete foundation. A spindly six-legged machine that had been rooting with its tapered snout around the base of the pile scampered away into the darkness.

"Watch yourself above, to the right," Armitage's voice warned through the speaker in Crookes's helmet.

There was a piece of pipe sticking out with a valve on the end. "I see it," Crookes acknowledged.

The voice of Leon Keyhoe, the signals specialist accompanying Crookes, came over the circuit. "How much farther to the tower? This is getting to be like an obstacle course across Osaka." Keyhoe had put on weight during the voyage out from Earth with the *Orion*, and he sounded breathless even in Titan's low gravity. Being cooped up in the base at "Genoa" for most of the time since the ship's departure over two months previously hadn't helped matters.

"By my reckoning we should be practically there," Crookes answered.

"Men!" Amy Rhodes exclaimed as she followed Crookes over the wall of hydraulics couplings. "Just no spirit of adventure, that's your problem. No wonder it took thousands of years for Earth to get explored." Deigning to step down, she jumped the four feet from the top casing to the steel mesh plates covering the ice below.

Crookes turned away to resume following Armitage and Franklin. Behind Rhodes, Keyhoe heaved himself up and paused to wheeze for a moment before lowering himself down the other side of the obstacle. He was followed by "Charlie Chan," the Taloid bringing up the rear, so called on account of the golden hue of his metal hands and the facial parts not covered by his rough black hat and clothes of what looked like tire tread and woven wire.

The closest they had been able to land the flyer had been about half a mile back, among the remains of some kind of derelict construction beside the main conveyor line that ran through the area. The flyer's two-man NASO crew and the party's other military escort had remained to guard the craft—necessary, since certain types of Titan's metal-searching animals had developed a liking for Terran alloys—while the scientific party continued the rest of the way on foot.

The "tower" was in fact little more than a protuberance of girder frames capped by a circular platform, standing thirty feet or so above the general level of the structures in the vicinity. What made it interesting to communications engineers like Crookes and Keyhoe were the shapes on top that pictures from low-flying reconnaissance drones had revealed, suggestive of communications antennas. The pictures were low-resolution infrared, however, which made positive identification difficult, and no actual transmissions had been detected. Hence, the only way to find out for sure what the shapes were had been to go there and look.

If the whole Titan scene was indeed a result of some vast, alien, self-replicating industrial operation gone wrong, as supposed, it seemed likely that it would originally have used radio communication. A number of scattered and intermittent transmission sources existed, seeming to support such a conjecture, and some of the Taloids possessed what appeared to be a residual reception capability by which they could, on occasion, "hear" the transmissions. Traditionally, these latter were considered by the Taloids to be mystics who interpreted voices from the deity.

The prevalent opinion among the Terran scientists was that radio had formed the primary means of communication early on in the alien project but had become impracticable for some reason after the whole scheme messed up. So the system had reverted to the backup communication modes that the aliens would surely have provided if they had been any kind of engineers at all, and the isolated signals still being picked up were simply a remnant of something that was in the process of dying out. Thus, the scientists reasoned, there ought to be "fossil" radio facilities, recognizable in form but no longer functional, such as antennas, like vestigial limbs, still being built the way they always had been but no longer capable of doing anything. Verification of the prediction would go a long way toward advancing the theory. Hence the expedition to the "tower" in the part of Titan the Terrans called Genoa.

It was all a long way and very different from Denver. Crookes had signed up as one of the mission's scientists in the aftermath of a divorce to get away and find freedom in totally new surroundings for a while before returning to begin a new life. And he had done so in an unexpected way. On the face of it, "freedom" seemed a strange way to describe life in the confines of Genoa Base, lived according to the strict code of NASO's offplanet regulations. But the sense in which the word meant more to him was the release from the worldly obligations of bills, mortgages, departmental budgets, and dreary social chores, and the ability to concentrate in the company of his intellectual peers on the mysteries of Titan and the Taloids without distraction. For once in his life it was the job of others to take care of all the necessary things that didn't interest him, letting him enjoy the things that did, even if that did entail blundering around in mechanical jungles, encased in a claustrophobic EV suit.

Whatever had stood on the concrete foundation was gone. A line of supports carrying pipes now crossed the area above a pair of rectangular pits, one containing reciprocating machinery driven by gear trains, the other half-filled with a stagnant liquid, probably methane. A pair of thick, vertical stanchions, with a partly solid metal wall filling the space between, rose out of the clutter to support an arrangement of girders and platforms above. Armitage's hand lamp picked out more braces and structural ties above that. Consultation with a map sketched from the reconnaissance pictures showed that they had reached the tower.

Franklin pointed at the box attached to Crookes's belt. At the same time a red light on it began flashing, indicating that it was receiving high-frequency Taloid sonic pulses. Crookes unclipped the "transmogrifier"—a much improved version of the device he and Keyhoe had improvised after the first Terran-Taloid contact, though the name they had given it then had stuck—and touched a button with a finger of his gauntlet to interrogate. The message on the miniature screen read: OKAY TERRAN (CLIMB TREES?) OWN BACK WORLD-PLACE?

Crookes nodded and switched in the channel of his suit radio that was set to the transmogrifier frequency. "Sure. We do it all the time." The device emitted an inaudible stream that Franklin seemed to understand.

I FIRST LEAD IF IS GOOD. TALOIDS (USED TO/TALK WITH?) FOREST.

"Fine."

"Why don't I go next after Franklin?" Amy Rhodes's voice said in Crookes's helmet. Her tone of voice wasn't so much a suggestion as a demand. Technically, Crookes was in command of the party, and it seemed to rile her; her attitude had been belligerent ever since they had set out. He shrugged inside his suit and made a nonchalant face.

"Sure. Go ahead." He caught Armitage's eye behind the face piece of his helmet. The soldier raised his eyebrows and turned away. It wasn't something that was worth getting into an argument over.

A long platform resembling a catwalk spanned the gap between the two stanchions about ten feet above where the group was standing. There was no access ladder, but Franklin reached the platform without much difficulty, climbing first to a run of hoses topping a line of cylindrical tanks, and from there up a series of stays and struts that provided holds. Amy followed, making a show of gliding on her feet and using her hands lightly for balance like a rock climber. Armitage went next, moving solidly and unhurriedly, and then Crookes. After a short delay and more huffing over the intercom circuit, Keyhoe appeared from the shadows below, with Charlie Chan following immediately behind.

They could now see beneath the tower over an incomplete section of the wall. Instead of the derelict lower levels they had expected, they found themselves looking down onto a fast-moving conveyor carrying an assortment of assemblies and components, which from its direction would join the main "river" not far from where the flyer was parked. Whatever installation had once existed in the base of the tower was gone, and a subsequent phase of construction had seen the conveyor run straight through where it had stood, leaving the skeleton of the former structure, with its tower above, straddling the banks like a bridge.

From where they now stood, there was no easy way farther up. The pillars at the right-hand end of the platform supported banks of switchgear boxes that gave moderately easy access for the next twenty feet or so, but the structure above was stark and bare, with little prospect of much to stand on. The center section held nothing but the support frame for the upper platform, high above them and way out of reach. That left only the pair of I-section girders standing cornerwise to each other at the left-hand end and forming a vertical right-angle channel about three feet wide on each side. Crookes and the others moved to that end and inspected it with probing flashlamp beams. The channel carried runs of heavy cables secured at intervals by fastenings that could, in a pinch, serve as a makeshift ladder. Awkward but not impossible, Crookes thought. After about thirty feet the channel reached the frame beneath the upper platform, and from there on the rest would be easier. Franklin was already experimenting, driving his straightened steel fingers between the cables like a wedge and walking himself up on his toes until he found a stance.

Hell, this is supposed to be a scientific investigation, not a display of heroics, Crookes thought. One rip in a suit at Titan's surface temperature would be lethal. Why risk it? They could be back with the right equipment in a matter of hours.

Amy seemed to read his mind—or, more likely, the expression through his faceplate. "Oh, I'll go," she said in a tone of exaggerated weariness, making it sound as if he were suffering a failure of nerve. "I led the Eiger a couple of years back. This is a cinch. I'll take a line up that you guys can hook on to." Armitage's sigh came heavily over the intercom circuit, but he said nothing.

Dave Crookes reflected later that that would have been the time to settle things. He should have pulled rank right then and declared that they were going back to the flyer, and that was final. The French had a phrase, *esprit de l'escalier*, which could be roughly translated as "staircase wisdom": the feeling that practically everyone experiences from time to time of belated realization only when halfway down the stairs and on the way out of the building, after the interview is over, of what one *should* have said. Or sometimes it happens ten seconds after putting down the phone.

But the way the situation felt to Crookes at the time was that making an issue out of it would have been overly defensive in just the kind of way the taunt was intended to provoke. Keyhoe was giving him a ready out if he needed one, holding both hands up protectively and shaking his head inside his helmet in a way that said emphatically, "Not me. No way!" But Crookes moved a couple of paces back and swung the beam of his lamp past Franklin, who was already six feet above their heads, and followed the channel upward to pick out the rest of the proposed route.

"It's what we came here for," Crookes said, making his voice matter-of-fact. "Okay, Leon can give us some light from down here. Charlie Chan had better stay with him. The rest of us can go take a look." He looked at Amy and couldn't resist adding, "Okay, if you want to play mountaineer, you go first."

Amy uncoiled a line from the gear they had brought with them and treated Crookes and Armitage to a minilecture on safety procedures. Then she set off, bracing a foot on each side of the channel and finding handholds among the cable restraints. The others watched as her legs, her backside, and the bottom of her pack receded upward in the light from their lamps, with Crookes holding the trailing line clear from obstructions. Then her voice over the intercom announced that she was at the platform and was securing herself. She pulled in the line; Crookes called to let her know when it was taut, and then followed.

There really wasn't a lot to it. The EV gauntlets afforded a good friction hold between the cables in the same way Franklin's Taloid fingers had, and there were more brackets and bolts to stand on than had been visible from below. Macho-jerk men could be a pain, Crookes reflected as he moved upward, falling quickly into a rhythm. But macho-jerk females were worse to deal with. No sense of how much force was appropriate; they went for the throat over trifles. Maybe it was because nobody had ever taught them when it was chivalrous or just plain smarter to hold back.

He joined Amy and Franklin on the upper platform and clipped himself to a loop she had made around a brace. Then Crookes brought up Armitage, who appeared a couple of minutes later, his M-37 slung along the side of his backpack. They stood up and surveyed the surroundings.

The four figures and the parts of the structure immediately around them stood out white in the light of the beams being directed from below. All around, the daytime twilight of Titan—about as bright as a moonlit night on Earth—showed the jungle of metal shapes extending away in every direction, highlighted intermittently in places by bursts of sparks and flashing electric arcs. The platform itself formed a terrace ten feet or so wide around a central superstructure continuing upward to the circular base visible in the reconnaissance pictures, which supported the antennas. The superstructure looked as if it should have been rectangular. However, two of its sides were missing, leaving the terrace on the far side as two narrow strips at right angles forming an exposed corner projecting precariously into space. Girder lattices sloped up to the circular base at an easy angle and would be no problem to climb.

"Well, this is my department," Crookes announced. "Let's see what we've got."

He began picking his way up the nearest lattice, using the cross-trusses as a ladder. Franklin came after him, while Armitage watched from the platform below and provided light. Amy wandered off to explore the far side of the terrace.

A parabolic dish and a helical antenna shared the base with what looked like part of a rhombic array, as well as other forms that Crookes was unable to identify. The first odd thing that struck him was that none of them possessed any electrical connections. They were mechanical assemblies only. Then he noticed that even the mechanical constructions were incomplete. Parts of the mounting for the parabolic dish, vital to allow it to rotate and elevate, were absent. Instead, the mechanism had been welded, rendering it totally immobile.

He was, indeed, looking at what they had suspected: a collection of fossils. Somewhere long in the past the instructions for making them operable had been lost, but a vestige of the form had remained. Whatever machines had erected this place had followed blindly directions contained in the blueprints passed down, possibly for millions of years, from the unknown origins from which the strange landscape below and all around him had sprung. As he gazed at the shapes, he wondered how long they had stood like this, staring mutely upward, waiting for messages they could never hear. And how many similar generations before them? . . .

Less than a scream, a short, sharp cry of alarm cut through the silence in his helmet. Then, almost in the same instant, he heard Keyhoe's voice from below: "What was that?"

And Armitage: *"Oh, Christ!"*

Crookes moved to the edge of the antenna base and held on to a mast to look down. Armitage was on one of the projecting sides of the terrace, scanning the area below with his lamp, while Franklin stood a few feet away, pointing downward with frantic stabbing motions—it was daylight to the Taloids. The red light on the transmogrifier at Crookes's waist was flashing. There was no sign of Amy. A few seconds later Crookes saw the light of her flashlamp as it was carried away on the conveyor below.

Whether she had slipped or a part of the structure had given way beneath her, nobody ever knew. From the catwalk where he had stayed with Keyhoe, Charlie Chan saw her fall, and he was back down to the floor level and through a gap in the wall to the conveyor line before those above had exchanged another word. But quick as he was, there was no trace of her when he got there. Crookes radioed the crew of the flyer, who switched on floodlights to watch for her at the larger conveyor, but nobody was sure if the tributary joined it upstream from where the flyer had landed, or down.

In any case, they saw nothing.

2

WEARING A MAROON ROBE, WITH A TOWEL HANGING loosely around his neck, and carrying his toilet articles in a plastic bag, Karl Zambendorf came out of the men's shower room in the Terran base on the outskirts of the Taloid city called Genoa and made his way along the corridor leading back to his cabin. The original base, built from prefabricated parts brought by the *Orion*, had been extended since then by the adaptation of materials from Titan itself. With its mesh floors, its utilitarian fittings, and the starkness of its metal walls barely relieved by ubiquitous cream-yellow and lime-green paint, it was cramped, sweaty, smelly, and stuffy; but to those who had been its occupants through the two months since the *Orion*'s departure, its oasis of light, warmth, and companionship, in the minus-180°C cold of Titan's cloud-covered darkness 800 million miles from Earth, evoked feelings of fondness and security that only their visions of home itself could match.

Zambendorf's cabin was a standard two-man NASO affair with twin bunks, a small desk with chair and computer terminal, a hand basin and utility worktop, and a toilet through a narrow door at the rear. Otto Abaquaan, who shared it with Zambendorf, was elsewhere. Zambendorf replaced the towel and other things he was carrying and finished dressing.

He was in his early fifties, somewhat portly but with an erect bearing, his graying hair worn collar-length and flowing, bright eyes and hawklike features made all the more patriarchal by a pointed beard that he whitened for effect. AUSTRIAN PSYCHIC PICKED FOR NASO MISSION, the headline

17

of one of the prominent East Coast dailies had blared before the mission's departure, while the host of New York's most popular Saturday night talk show had introduced him as "the man who reads minds, foretells the future, sees without the senses, and makes the impossible happen routinely. The walking enigma that scientists the world over are at a loss to explain."

The official reason given for including Zambendorf in the mission was that because he was a popular cult figure, his presence would help popularize space and hence advance GSEC's longer-term interests. The faithful naturally believed that the authorities had at last recognized Zambendorf's telepathic abilities as genuine, and he was being sent as Earth's principal ambassador.

In fact, Zambendorf himself hadn't been sure of the real reason until after the *Orion*'s arrival at Titan. GSEC was interested in the fabulous industrial capacity spread over the moon's surface. If even a fraction of that potential could be organized and directed to profitable ends, Earthly competition would effectively cease to exist. And it hadn't taken GSEC long to find support in Washington and the capitals of Europe, where others were quick to note that a commercial monopoly of such dimensions would confer virtual world domination politically as well. But the success of their plan would depend to a large degree on creating favorable public opinion. Zambendorf was a world celebrity with high emotional appeal and hence could influence public opinion. So "owning" Zambendorf—an unlikely eventuality, given his personality and disposition, but that was the way corporate minds thought—and associating him with Titan in the public mind would create a powerful means for steering official policy regarding Titan in whatever direction GSEC might find it expedient to desire. But ironically, Zambendorf and his team had played the biggest part in causing that scheme to come undone.

While Zambendorf was buttoning his shirt, the door opened and Otto Abaquaan came in. He was an Armenian, handsomely lean and swarthy, medium in height, with a droopy mustache, thick eyebrows, and deep, brown liquid eyes that moved lazily but missed nothing.

The two men had met almost twenty years previously in West Germany, when Abaquaan had been working a stocks and bonds swindle. Overconfident after three months of easy pickings from wealthy dowagers, he had failed to check out Zambendorf thoroughly enough before selling him a portfolio of phony certificates. Only when Abaquaan's contact man was arrested and Abaquaan himself was forced to flee the country hours ahead of the police did he discover that Zambendorf had seen through the scam and paid in phony money. But Abaquaan had displayed a masterful style, and after administering the due comeuppance, Zambendorf had tracked him down again later to recruit him as a working partner.

Zambendorf had no word corresponding to "can't" in his vocabulary and was optimistic about everything; Abaquaan, by contrast, worried. Which was just as well, since somebody had to be realistic about the difficulties inherent in the schemes Zambendorf dreamed up in his enthusiasm and attend to all the details if the schemes were to be made workable. Their opposition of temperaments suited them to each other admirably, and Abaquaan had become the first of the strange mix of individuals who had gravitated into Zambendorf's orbit over the ensuing years.

Abaquaan propped himself on the chair by the narrow writing desk. "I was talking to one of the troops who were over in Padua," he said. "It's beginning to sound as if Arthur's guys are right—there's some kind of a fundamentalist revival movement being fanned up over there. The old days were better and all that kind of stuff. There could be more trouble brewing if it catches on."

"Padua," situated on the far side of an ice and rock desert from Genoa, where the Terran base was situated, had been the scene of the failed intervention attempt by the mission's politicians. "Arthur" was the Terrans' name for the Taloid leader of Genoa. He had evicted the old feudal-style regime and formed a liberal breakaway state before the arrival of the *Orion*, and his followers were the most recep-

tive of all the Taloid nations when it came to compre-
hending and absorbing the new Terran sciences.

Zambendorf began combing his hair and beard in the
mirror above the washbasin. "Oh, something like it was
bound to happen sooner or later," he said airily. "In physics
rapid changes in anything invariably give rise to forces that
oppose the changes. Social laws are no different. History is
full of examples of reactions against change that some people found too sweeping. But it's all evolution, Otto. You
can't stop it."

Abaquaan was a pragmatist. Philosophical observations
on the nature of evolution were not among the habits that
had characterized his life. "Five dollars to a dime says that
Henry's behind it," he said. "I never believed that he'd just
go away. And he won't have any problem getting backing
out there."

The Terrans had given the Taloids somewhat arbitrary
names. "Henry" was the deposed king of Padua, who had
gone into exile along with most of the former nobility and
high clergy after Zambendorf had accidentally created a
new cult of brotherhood and nonviolence that had toppled
the official religion.

Zambendorf turned from the mirror and took a red
woolen cardigan from a hook on the back of the door. "Oh,
I have no doubt that reason will prevail in the end," he assured Abaquaan. "You know, Otto, I used to be cynical
about the ways of things, too. But it is true that the mellow-
ness of advancing years reveals the world in a more agree-
able light. Or maybe it's the new perspective that one
acquires of the universe, contemplating Earth from this distance. You really ought to try making the effort to adjust to
it. I feel revitalized: able to face the future with complete,
unswerving confidence."

Abaquaan had been hearing something like this about
once a week for nearly twenty years. It still filled him with
the same forebodings. He turned his eyes briefly toward the
ceiling. "Confidence, Karl, is what you feel when you don't
understand the situation."

Zambendorf heard something like that about a dozen

times a week. He picked up his watch from the shelf where he had left it when he had gone to take his shower and checked it as he slipped it back on his wrist. "Anyway, it's about time," he said. "Is Drew ready in the mess?"

Abaquaan had returned from checking the situation in the general personnel messroom. "He's there," he confirmed, nodding. "You're all ready to go."

Demonstrations of Zambendorf's powers had become a welcome feature of life at Genoa Base. The scientists were particularly intrigued, and one or two of them were wavering on the verge of becoming believers. This evening a spectacular event had been scheduled to put Zambendorf to the test yet again.

Zambendorf cocked an inquiring eye. "How was the mood out there?" The flippancy of a few moments ago was gone from his voice. "In the circumstances, do you think this might not be the best time for it? We could kill the transmission and set it up again later." He was referring to the news about Amy Rhodes, which had been announced only earlier that day. Hers was the first fatality the mission had suffered. Although nobody had been under any delusions about the risks inherent in an operation involving so much that was previously untried, nevertheless it had come as a shock to all of them when the inevitable eventually happened. It was as if the charmed phase, in which the mission had been protected against the odds, was over and now anything could happen.

But Abaquaan shook his head. "That wasn't the feel I got, Karl. Calling off the show would only make the atmosphere heavier. What they need right now is a distraction. I think you should go ahead."

It was what Zambendorf had hoped. But part of the charisma he had with his team lay in letting them know that he trusted their judgment. He nodded and checked himself in the mirror before moving toward the door. "Then let's see how we do. I do hope that Gerry Massey gets his end of it right."

3

THE GENERAL PERSONNEL MESSROOM WAS THE FOCAL point of off-duty life at Genoa Base. It was about forty feet long and half as wide, with ribbed metal walls painted lime green up to chest height and peach above that. A large mural display screen halfway along one sidewall could be driven locally or hooked into the general communications net. An always-open serving counter faced the room from one end, from which one or more white-jacketed NASO chefs dispensed such delicacies as NASO eggs, NASO beans, NASO chicken legs, and dried soups and vegetables reconstituted with recycled NASO water. Three long, scratched plastic-topped tables stretched most of the way to the other end, where there was a smaller counter that served as a bar for twelve hours of every twenty-four. The open area of floor beyond the tables had accommodated performances by the dramatics group and a string quartet as well as providing space for nightly dancing and the Saturday amateur-night cabaret.

Drew West had a clean-cut college look, and he continued keeping his appearance spruce and neat in a relaxed kind of way even after months at Genoa Base, where T-shirts and jeans tended to be the order of the day and even the military had drifted to wearing fatigues most of the time. Today he was in gray slacks and an open-neck white shirt with sleeves turned back to the elbows, sitting at one of the long tables roughly opposite the mural display screen. A mixed gathering of scientists, NASO personnel, and off-duty military types occupied most of the space on the benches around him.

Drew was the team's business manager. He had started out long before as Zambendorf's accountant and then had become his next full-time partner after Abaquaan as each recognized the talent of the other as a solution to a need that life at the time was failing to supply. West's contribution was a genius for causing money to disappear from places of visibility where it was likely to attract unwelcome attention from taxation and other authorities, while at the same time keeping its earning ability intact. Zambendorf, in return, offered a life of variety and excitement beyond the usual accountant's fare, although even West in his wildest imaginings had never guessed that it might one day lead to traveling almost a billion miles from Earth to find living machinery and a race of intelligent robots. Since those early days he had developed the additional skills that came as part of the graduation to full accomplice. For the Zambendorf phenomenon was, if the truth were known, very much a team affair.

"I'm just the business manager," West said, mustering his most practiced expression of innocence and showing his palms to the dark-haired young woman in an olive tank top sitting opposite him. "I don't know how Karl does any of it. If you say he's a fraud, then okay. A lot of other people think so, too. I just worry about arranging appearances and getting paid. It's a job."

Sharon Beatty worked with Dave Crookes and Leon Keyhoe in the electronics section. She had never understood why Zambendorf was there, and it disturbed her that so many seemingly rational people should take his antics seriously. She had wasted too much of her life being sidetracked by zany beliefs while she was a student, and, with the staggering nature of the recent discoveries on Titan, there were better things to occupy her time. It mystified her that everyone else didn't feel the same way.

"Gerry Massey can duplicate anything that Zambendorf has ever done," she said. It was hardly the first time West had heard this. "And Gerry never claimed to be more than a good conjurer." She directed her words not at West particularly but to the company in general.

Malcolm Wade, a Canadian psychologist and also an incurable Zambendorf believer, answered from the next table. "Mimicking an effect by a conjuring trick doesn't prove that it's a conjuring trick every time. Just because you can produce a rabbit from a hat, it doesn't mean that all rabbits come from hats, does it?"

"If a simple explanation will suffice, there's no justification for invoking a more complex one," Sharon replied tiredly. She didn't know how many times they had been through this. Conversation became repetitive when people were shut up in a place like this—especially with someone like Wade, who continued asking the same questions no matter how often he was given the same answers.

Behind them, Andy Schwartz, captain of one of the *Orion*'s surface landers that had been left as part of the transportation pool, was lounging with his back to the wall, flanked by a couple of his flight crew. If Zambendorf really could receive information faster than light, why, he wondered, had nobody ever suggested checking him against long-range radar probing of a selected region of the Asteroid Belt? But he kept the thought to himself. Watching the experts at odds with each other relieved the off-duty boredom, and he figured that Zambendorf was encouraging the spectacle in order to entertain. Letting it all get too serious would have spoiled things.

At the table in front of them a beefy, straw-haired, pink-complexioned NASO sergeant called O'Flynn was talking to Graham Spearman, one of the biologists, over a plate of sausage and fries. "Ye'd think, now, that one way of testin' an ability like that would be by callin' a horse race or one o' the big matches before the results come in on the laser link. And there'd be money to be made from it, too."

"Hmm. And without needing to set up this Massey business at all," Spearman agreed. He was in his late thirties, with thick-rimmed spectacles and a droopy mustache, and he wore a tartan shirt with jeans. Spearman was generally known as amiable and totally apolitical, which meant that practically everyone was able to get along with him.

O'Flynn quaffed from a pint mug of hot, sweet tea and nodded. "Me point, exactly."

"It needs a tuned mind at the other end," Wade chimed in, turning and gesturing with the stem of his pipe. "Massey has the beginnings of real ability, too, you know. He just doesn't realize it himself yet."

"Is this a fact, now?" O'Flynn said.

Harold Mackeson, NASO's British commander of Genoa Base, was present with an aide. A portable communications pad lay on the table in front of them. Mackeson regarded the whole thing as part of the diversions it was his job to promote for the good of morale, and he had agreed good-naturedly to oversee the proceedings. Farther along, past the mural screen, Werner Weinerbaum, the mission's chief scientist, sat with a group of his senior specialists, talking loftily about the latest analyses of alien software from what appeared to be one of the control nodes out on Titan's surface. Their manner showed that they were above even acknowledging the existence of this Zambendorf nonsense, let alone having any time to involve themselves in it. For anyone who might be wondering, they just happened to be in the messroom purely coincidentally.

Gerold Massey was a professor of cognitive psychology at the University of Maryland, as well as being an accomplished stage magician. One of his special interests had long been the exposing of fraudulent claims to paranormal powers. Massey was also a personal friend of one of the NASO directors involved in organizing the mission and had been sent with the *Orion* ostensibly as an official psychologist. In reality, he had been there to act as an on-hand observer of what Zambendorf was up to and if necessary to provide a counterforce if whatever stunts GSEC involved him in started going too far.

The impossible had happened, however, when they had become allies in the common cause of preventing the Taloids from being exploited. Called by commitments back home, Massey had left with the *Orion*. But his improbable compromise with Zambendorf had not only endured, but reached the point where Massey was now cooperating in one of Zambendorf's demonstrations. Even Drew West, who was used to the spell that all who came within Zambendorf's range seemed to fall under, felt that Zambendorf had outdone himself this time. Those like Malcolm Wade, of course, took it as evidence of Massey's conversion. In fact, Zambendorf was as good a psychologist as Massey was an illusionist. He had known that any stage magician would have found the prospect of a ruse involving separation over interplanetary distance—unlike anything that had been tried before—irresistible.

"Here he is now," O'Flynn said, looking up as Zambendorf came in through the door midway between the screen and the serving-counter end of the room.

"Ah, right on time," Mackeson said. He surveyed the display on his panel. "We're hooked into the beam from the *Orion*. If Massey was able to respond immediately, his transmission should be coming in any time now." He keyed in some command characters. The large screen on the wall flickered into life with a caption giving the current date and time in the *Orion*'s local units, along with a message that read: CHANNEL PRIMED AND HOLDING.

"If Karl pulls this one off, the drinks are on me tonight," a voice somewhere murmured.

"Wait and see," Malcolm Wade prophesied confidently.

Zambendorf let his gaze drift casually around the room. In the split second while it passed over Drew West, West signaled with the scratching of an eyebrow that nothing untoward or unexpected had occurred while Zambendorf had been away. Zambendorf ambled across to look over Mackeson's shoulder. The screen on the portable panel in front of Mackeson showed the numbers 53, 17, 7, 68, and 90 in a line across the top. The same numbers had been written in large numerals on a strip of paper fastened to the wall below the room's large mural screen.

The distance to the *Orion* was by now such that the propagation delay for electromagnetic signals was fifty-two minutes. Almost that amount of time ago, Zambendorf had been there in the messroom to try something that one of the communications engineers had dreamed up—or thought he had; Otto Abaquaan was very good at suggestion. In a series of messages exchanged between Titan and the *Orion* the previous day, Massey had agreed to participate.

Less than an hour earlier, five members of the company, chosen by lot, had drawn the numbers randomly from a set of bingo disks shaken in a box. Then Zambendorf, presuming that Massey had prepared himself, had endeavored to transmit the selection to him telepathically. The arrangement agreed on the previous day was that as soon as Massey received the numbers, he would send them back over the communications beam linking to the *Orion* via relay satellites that had been left orbiting Titan. That response would, of course, take fifty-two minutes to reach Titan, even with the instantaneous outward transmission Zambendorf had claimed. Or, to put it another way, if Massey was able to return the numbers after fifty-two minutes or thereabouts, then he must have been aware of them virtually as soon as they were chosen. To kill time while they were waiting, Zambendorf had then announced that he was going back to his quarters to take a shower.

The legend on the large screen changed to CONNECTING, which meant that the message processors at Genoa Base had picked out an incoming packet with the identifier Mackeson had instructed them to watch for. A moment later Massey appeared: fiftyish, his forehead accentuated by a receding hairline, with rugged features setting off a full beard starting to show gray streaks. He was wearing a short-sleeved navy shirt and sitting sideways to the camera at a desk console in what looked like one of the *Orion*'s cabins. As if cued, he swiveled his seat to face the screen more directly and began speaking.

"Well, hello, all you people back there. We're getting close to Earth now, although to look outside, there isn't much difference to be seen—the sun's bigger, and that's about all. I must say, this old tub that you perhaps remember fondly is bearing up remarkably well ..." He looked away for a moment. "I see we're slightly early here. Vernon, why don't you put that thing down for a moment and come around and say hi to our friends?"

The view on the screen tilted and slid sideways, then came to rest with the view captured from a different angle as whoever had been operating the camera set it down. Seconds later a younger man in his twenties, lithely built and with wavy brown hair, moved into the viewing angle. Everyone in the messroom recognized Vernon Price, Massey's assistant who had accompanied him to Titan. Price grinned and raised a hand.

"Hi, guys. Well, I plan to be splashing around on a Florida beach just a couple of weeks from now. It just tears me up to think of all that science you're doing back there that I'll be missing." Ribald mutterings ran around the company watching on Titan. "Seriously, though, I'll be interested to see how this thing of Gerry and Karl's works out. By the time you see this, everything will be over where we are. So nothing can change whatever has happened."

"We're almost due now, Vernon," Massey interrupted beside him.

Price glanced offscreen, presumably at a clock somewhere. "Oh, right . . . So, I guess, just sit back and enjoy the show, eh?" He disappeared from view. The image on the screen gyrated again, then stabilized to center Massey in the frame. Massey settled himself down in his chair, head against the back and arms draped loosely along the rests.

"Well, if you're on the schedule that we fixed yesterday, something should be due just about now." Massey closed his eyes and exhaled long and audibly. "I'm ready here, making myself relaxed and trying to be as receptive as possible. If nothing strange happens to prevent me, I'll try and give you a commentary of my impressions. Right now there isn't very much to comment on, though. I do feel unusually aware of the depths of space extending away in every direction outside this ship, but that could be purely subjective, of course—" Massey had seemed to be about to say something more, but his brow creased suddenly, apparently in surprise and not a little puzzlement. The atmosphere in the messroom tensed expectantly as everyone watched what had taken place hundreds of millions of miles away almost an hour before.

"What is it, Gerry?" Vernon Price's voice asked from off camera.

"I'm not sure. I feel more than just aware of the space outside. It's as if part of my mind is reaching out into it . . . being touched by something. My God, I'm getting something! Suddenly I'm flooded with an image of Karl, and yes, the feeling of a number. It's . . . let me see . . ." Massey brought up a hand, touching his fingertips to his brow. "Fifty . . . fifty-three. Is that it?"

Astonished gasps went up among the company gathered in the messroom. Mackeson tapped at the keys on his pad, and a 53 appeared superimposed in red on the image, high and to the left. Zambendorf watched impassively from behind, while to the side Malcolm Wade emitted satisfied puffs from his pipe. Weinerbaum looked on from the center of his group, disdainful but now silent.

"Yes, and I think I'm getting the next." On the screen, Massey was sitting forward in his chair, his hand gripping the armrests with the apparent effort of concentrating. He leaned back to stare up at the ceiling and announced, "Seventeen."

Smiling, Mackeson shook his head in a way that said he couldn't buy this even if he was unable to explain it. He added 17 to the top of the screen. Sharon Beatty was looking tight-faced. "I guess it's beers on me," the voice that had spoken earlier concluded glumly.

Now the screen was showing Massey in close-up. He was frowning and biting his lip and seemed to be having difficulty. "This one's not coming through very clearly at all . . . No, just a blur, I'm afraid. It has a feel of 'threeness' about it—thirteen, maybe, or thirty-something, but I think I have to pass."

He seemed restless with the next one also, shifting his gaze and looking around as if he half expected the answer to appear on the walls. But just when the audience was convinced that he was about to confess a second failure, still with his head turned toward the back of the cabin, his voice said, "Sixty-eight." Then he picked up a glass of water from the top of the unit beside him, took a long and evidently much-needed drink, and as he wiped his beard with a hand declared, "And the last one is . . . ninety." Massey faced the screen fully again and shrugged, showing his empty palms. "Well, there it is. That's what I got—or thought I did. Right at this moment only you know how well we did. I'll be curious to find out. Until then, so long from Vernon and myself on board the *Orion*." The image blanked out, leaving displayed the four numbers and one blank.

Four out of five—a score against odds of millions. Applause and appreciative comments came from all around. Zambendorf remained as he had stood all the way through, acknowledging them only with a faint bow. It was one of his strong beliefs that when events spoke for themselves, it was wisest not to interrupt.

"Well, then?" Wade challenged, looking smugly at Sharon Beatty.

"I'll have to think about it," she returned curtly.

"Well, it's going to have me doing a lot of thinking tonight, that's for sure," Graham Spearman told the room, shaking his head.

"It's gotta be real," Andy Schwartz said, looking from one to the other of his crewmen for support. "What other way could there be to explain it?" Neither of them could offer an explanation.

"If you will excuse me, I have more important matters to attend to than these antics." So saying, Weinerbaum rose and conveyed himself aloofly from the room. Most of his retinue of scientists followed. The others left in the room exchanged grins. It was as good a way as any for the mission's chief scientist to admit that he had no explanation, either.

4

THE FARMING VILLAGE OF UCHAL WAS SITUATED IN THE border region to the west of the great forests of southern Kroaxia. Its cluster of houses, including the central church and village hall, the headrob's manor next to its private plot of land, and the outlying barns and animal stables, were grown from foundations that had started as artisan-produced seed cultures. The growing walls were trained to merge into enclosed structures, and the doors and windows formed at the same time by pruning and shaping. In the surrounding fields, rows of tube-forming machines and frame welders supplied a steady harvest of basic body parts for a variety of domestic animals, while orchards of crystallization furnaces extruded purified silicon to supply the assembly centers of new robeings as well as animals. The village also kept herds of wheeled glass crushers and three-legged hole tappers, as well as free-range oil siphoners that brought back mixtures to feed the separation columns at the communal dairy.

This prosperity was due in no small part to the remoteness of the district, which generally left it untouched by the wars and squabbles between Kroaxia and the neighboring nations. The attentions of the royal tax collectors were another matter, but even that burden had eased considerably in the course of the last eight bright periods. Eskenderom, the former king of Kroaxia, had fled into exile, along with his court and priests, after the people had rejected their outmoded doctrine of the Lifemaker and adopted the teachings brought by the "Lumian" gods from their world of light beyond the sky. Now the new ruler of Kroaxia, whose name was Nogarech, was changing to ways modeled on those the rebel leader Kleippur had instituted in his breakaway state, Carthogia, which he had proclaimed independent and had defended successfully even before the Lumians had arrived. In Carthogia no robeing was enslaved to another; all citizens were free to own property and to trade or work for their own profit; the rulers could be dismissed by the people; and knowledge was regarded not as a sacred mystery to be revealed by the Lifemaker's chosen priests but as an understanding that could be gained by anyone through diligent observation, inquiry, and reason.

Thirg was a Kroaxian who now lived in Carthogia. Before the fall of Eskenderom's regime, he had been known in Kroaxia as Asker-of-Forbidden-Questions. He had lived as a recluse in order to pursue his inquiries after truth in peace, without interference from priests and free from the scrutiny of the Holy Prosecutor's informers. Now he was an adviser on philosophy and science to Carthogia's ruler, the former general, Kleippur, outside whose capital city of Menassim the Lumians had erected their camp. Thirg's prime task was to study—and, as far as was possible, adapt for the use of the Carthogians—the awesome knowledge of the Lumians: knowledge that enabled them to ride in huge, wheeled, animallike vehicles that were not alive, to command weapons capable of annihilating whole armies, and to actually rise up into the sky in strange craft that the robeings had at first thought to be dragons.

Thirg had come to Uchal to visit an old friend of his called Brongyd, who in former days had also entertained thoughts that it was wiser not to talk about and had conducted his own unauthorized researches. Brongyd's fascination had always been in trying to understand how it was possible for a suitably arranged combination of nonliving parts to take on the quality that was called life. He had spent hundreds of brights cataloging and classifying the thousands of species of immobile sorters and roaming collectors, the scavengers, metals extractors, plastics strippers, and chip recoverers, trying to piece together the puzzle of intricate, interdependent pathways by which nature recycled its materials as it constantly renewed the living world. He had followed components through miles of forest conveyors and transfer lines and had constructed charts of the merging and branching patterns by which assemblies grew and flowed uncannily to their destinations. And he had dismantled hundreds of dead animals and static machines to trace where their component parts and raw materials had come from. It had amazed him to think that a bearing lining picked out of the undergrowth by a forest browser in Kroaxia might end up twelve brights later in the rotor of a centrifuge on the far side of Carthogia. And now Brongyd was wondering if he need have bothered. For the Lumians, by the sound of things, created life as routinely as Robia's wagon makers directed the growth of racing bipeds or a noblerob's four-legged carriage.

"So art thou saying 'tis true what I have heard?" Brongyd asked. The surface thermal patterns around his imaging matrices formed flickering whorls of wonder. "The beasts that live yet are not alive, the Lumians *make* in farms created for the purpose?" He and Thirg were standing at the edge of the village, beside the lane leading to the headrob's manor, watching laborers clearing metal shavings from workheads in an adjacent field. Rex, Thirg's mecanine that had journeyed with him to Carthogia and now back into Kroaxia, sat on its haunches a few feet away, sniffing the breeze and occasionally twitching one of its collector horns.

"So it would appear," Thirg affirmed. "And the farms were not cultivated by clearing forests and seeding deserts, but assembled by machines that the Lumians made with other machines, which in turn were shaped by means of simple tools fashioned from metals that they melted out of lifeless rock."

"So on their world *they* made the first machine!" Brongyd concluded.

"They regard it as no more than an elementary craft," Thirg said. "The feats of the armorers in Menassim, who merely cause self-repairing hydrocarbon mail to grow in methanated soils and coax it into assuming robody contours, impress them more."

The vanes around the coolant outlets of Brongyd's lower face ruffled in bemusement as he thought through the implication. Allegedly, the Lumians were composed of glowing jelly that needed to be bathed constantly in hot, corrosive gases inside their flexible casings. Such gases formed the natural atmosphere of the Lumians' home world, which had oceans of liquid ice and was hot enough to melt mercury.

"But the Lumians are formed from organics, even though they be of a kind unknown to us," he finally said. "If there were no machines on Lumia originally, Thirg, then what form of intelligence grew the first Lumians?"

It was the same question, turned upside down, that generations of robeing thinkers had asked themselves when they pondered on what had built the first machine. By now Thirg was getting used to thinking from the Lumian viewpoint, where everything happened upside down or inside out. Instead of their offspring being put together naturally at assembly stations that all shared and maintained in common, the Lumians *grew* them individually inside their own bodies, with all kinds of attendant problems when the time came to eject them. They replaced their worn parts in the same way, by assembling them from the inside out of molecules circulated in fluid solutions—how the molecules knew to attach where was something Thirg had never understood. But things like roadways and bridges for their nonliving "animals" to move on, and the homes they lived in, they assembled laboriously, piece by piece, from the outside. Impossible as such a scheme of things sounded at first mention, from his dealings with the Lumians on behalf of Kleippur, Thirg was getting an idea of how they believed it could all have started.

He replied, "They speak of origins long ago, under conditions far hotter and more violent than exist in Robia, in which chemicals borne in liquids were able to assemble themselves into forms that, though beyond any experience or indeed powers of imagination of ours, acquired that ability to manufacture replicas of their kind which is designated as possessing life. From that life that was not aware, there emerged the aware form of life that was not machine yet could create machines."

"So this 'chemical life' of which you speak was able to appear of itself, out of no life?" Brongyd asked.

"Thus we are assured."

"And it was the descendants of this chemical life who built the machines on Lumia and have now traveled thence from beyond the heavens?" Brongyd went on. "They are not gods, nor do they have need of any Lifemaker doctrine to render comprehensible the fact of their existence."

"It seems a failing of robeings to invent fanciful explanations that lie beyond comprehensibility rather than to make the effort of expanding their powers of comprehension," Thirg replied.

Brongyd frowned at the obvious question that statement left unanswered. "Thus are the Lumian machines and flying beasts explained," he agreed. "But thou canst not proclaim that in similar fashion did these strange chemical intelligences of which you speak bring forth the life that abounds on Robia. If no Lifemaker created robeing, but it was the mind of robeing that created Lifemaker, whence, then, Thirg, came we?"

Thirg sighed. "Of that even the Lumians confess ignorance," he admitted. "They conjecture that we, and all the life of Robia, emerged from simpler ancestors, built by another race still and sent hither from a different world whose distance defies even the comprehension of the Lumians. Why to this place, and how many twelve-times-twelves of twelve-brights ago, are questions to which perhaps none, neither Lumian nor robeing, in the remainder of the course of time will ever know the answers."

Suddenly Rex began gnashing its cutters and sprang to its feet, tense and alert. Thirg and Brongyd stopped talking and looked around, aware now of the sounds of voices and general consternation growing louder. The villagers nearby had stopped work and were staring, too. Along a track leading from the edge of the forest a double line of armed riders was approaching, followed by a growing crowd of curious, chattering workers and children from the surrounding fields.

The weapons the newcomers bore were mostly a mixture of traditional carbide-edged swords, axes, and lances. In addition, however, some carried the newer "hurlers" developed by Kleippur's artisans in Carthogia: tubular in form, that used explosive gases to shoot a projectile capable of shattering a slab of ice a finger's breadth thick at over a hundred paces. The Lumians possessed weapons that seemed to function in the same general way, although capable of operating at speeds that staggered the imagination and with immensely greater power. They could also call down heat darts from the sky that detonated with furnace light, one of which was enough to demolish everything within a circle of forest twenty paces across.

The riders wore cloaks of laminate mail or heavy woven wire over body armor made of acid-resistant and heat-absorbing organics. Their expressions were harsh, and they ignored the shouts from the villagers on either side. At their head was a thick-bodied figure with a red beard of accumulated cupric plating and a grim set to his cooling louvers. Although this was clearly not a military force, he was wearing a Kroaxian army helmet of wheelskin with a plume of bronze threads. The rider beside him carried a pennant with a design that was new to Thirg, of three circles interlinked. Halfway along the column of horserobs was a six-legged cart being drawn by a pair of spring-wheeled tractors, with several figures riding in it. Thirg looked uneasily at Brongyd. They moved to follow the growing throng, with Rex staying suspiciously at Thirg's heel.

In the center of the village the leading riders parted below the steps leading up to the communal hall and drew up into two lines facing outward across the square while the cart halted in front of them. It was carrying a long bundle, Thirg could now see, wrapped in a sheet of metallic braid and fastened with cord. The way the rest of the riders fanned out to station themselves like guards at the ends of the streets entering from among the surrounding houses added to his rising apprehension. The crowd, which had grown quickly, seemed similarly affected and became subdued. Ol Skaybar, the village headrob, appeared from the direction of the manor house, accompanied by a number of his helpers and lieutenants. They looked bewildered, shaking their heads at one another and gesticulating among themselves. Nobody seemed to know what was happening.

The leader and the standard-bearer dismounted in the space in the center, between the horserobs facing the crowd, and climbed the steps in front of the hall, which was the customary place for addressing gatherings. Two henchmen who had been riding behind followed them. While the leader and the standard-bearer turned to face the crowd, the other two moved behind them and unfurled a banner showing the same three interlinked circles as had appeared on the pennant. They fastened it to the doors of the hall as the leader began speaking.

"My name is Varlech, Avenger-of-Heresies. We have been sent to this place by the defenders of the Lifemaker's True Faith, who even now are organizing to protect the sacred teachings that have guided Robia for uncounted generations against the blasphemies being spread by the Dark Master's agent, Kleippur." Alarmed mutterings broke out anew around the square. Several villagers started to protest but were quelled into silence by threatening gestures from the mounted guard. Varlech continued:

"Kleippur will destroy all that was handed down by your fathers as holy. He will steal away the minds of your children. Even as I speak, robeings in the service of Kleippur take Lumian desecrators into the deepest parts of the forest to violate the assembly shrines that are the very sources of life. Even now, Carthogia's schools reject the wisdom of ages to disseminate alien falsehoods that deny the existence of Lifemaker Himself."

Now the assembled crowd was quiet and less sure of itself. Varlech gestured with his arms, turning from one side to the other to take in all of them. "Can you not see what this means, O brothers and sisters of Uchal? Nogarech has been beguiled by the sorcery of these impostors from beyond the sky. He is selling the souls of Kroaxians in return for the temporal power the Lumians can confer upon him for a while. Even as I speak—and this have I seen with my own matrices—Lumian and Carthogian sorcerers conspire in vile experiment to devise methods whereby the life process of Robia shall be perverted to produce aberrant, unnatural forms to satisfy the covetousness of Lumians.

"But . . ." Varlech raised a steel finger in warning. "It shall be only for a while. The Lifemaker will not forget or forgive, for do the Scribings not tell that the transgressors in heresy and blasphemy and those who follow false doctrines shall be consigned to the great reduction furnace? But it is not too late to renounce thy errant ways and return to the path." He turned to indicate the banner hanging behind him. "There you see united the true power that shall protect thee, spiritual, moral, and temporal: the forces of Lifemaker, clergy, and nobility intertwined as one trinity. This is the message that we have brought."

As if on cue, several voices among the crowd began shouting.

"He speaks truly. We have strayed!"

"To serve aliens, Kleippur would have us melt?"

"Loyalty to the trinity!"

Thirg leaned close to murmur to Brongyd. "Who are they who call out thus, so promptly?"

Brongyd shook his head. "Strangers here. I know them not."

"Were they sent ahead secretly by this Avenger to perform thus, thinkest thou?"

"Possibly, Thirg. It is possible."

Nevertheless, some of the villagers were already showing signs of wavering. Ol Skaybar, the headrob, however, was less easily swayed. Followed by Izonok, one of his cousins, who was also the bailiff, and two more of the local officials, he strode up the steps and confronted Varlech in a loud voice.

"I know not what powers have sent thee hither, Reviver-of-Faith-That-Is-Baseless. But an enemy of robeings,

Kleippur is not. For I have traveled widely in Carthogia, and *I* have seen. Kleippur is the true servant of his people, not of any Dark Master that inhabits only the unlit recesses of thy own imaginings. The Carthogians live in freedom and dignity, untrammeled by priestly superstitions or the terrors visited by inquisitors. Lumian knowledge is truth, for by its power do not Lumians travel hence from distant realms? By Lumian truth do the Carthogians prosper, and Lumian power protects them—"

To the horror of Thirg and the watching villagers, Varlech calmly raised his hurler and fired it at Ol Skaybar's chest. The headrob staggered backward, his front casing pierced by a jagged hole from which violet sparks poured, and collapsed. A shriek came from one side of the square. Thirg turned his head and saw Ol Skaybar's wife and several others of his family standing with more guards, who must have brought them from the manor house. But even as the first shouts and screams started coming from the rest of the crowd, Varlech produced a smaller, hand-held hurler and before their eyes dispatched Izonok in similar fashion, while the two villagers who had gone up the steps with them were cut down by Varlech's other lieutenants.

"Silence!" Varlech's voice lashed around the square like a wagoner's tractor goad. All pretense of this being an attempt at persuasion vanished. The villagers cowered as riders leveled hurlers to cover them, and the rattle of weapons being unsheathed came from around the square. "Kleippur's words would render you as helpless and defenseless children to be delivered to the Lumians. A people worthy to preserve themselves need strength and discipline as were provided by the ways of old." He half turned and pointed scornfully at the four corpses lying at the top of the hall steps. "What use was the power of the Lumians to *them*? . . . And do you imagine that these skybeings themselves are served any better? Do you believe those who tell you that the Lumians are gods? Pah! Fools!" Varlech nodded down to the attendants who had ridden in the cart, and they began uncovering the wrapped bundle. "The Lumians are as mortal as robeings," he told the crowd. "And as sub-

ject to the Lifemaker's wrath. Witness the fate of even skybeings who displease Him!"

Varlech pointed. Gasps of awe went up as the attendants uncovered and raised into view a form that was like a robeing yet not robeing, with an outer casing that bent like organically grown polymer and a transparent outer head shaped into a dome. But the dome was shattered, and the grotesque inner head it contained, instead of writhing with the violet radiance that signified Lumian life, was still and cold. An attendant prodded through the outer head with his sword, and all heard the scraping sound it made. The face was as hard and lifeless as a rock lying in the desert. It was the body of a dead Lumian.

Thirg watched in dismay. He knew that the Lumians were not gods, nor had they ever claimed to be. What he was seeing changed nothing that he had previously believed. He had never doubted that mishap could strike Lumians, too, and was bound to, in some form or other, sooner or later. But the effect on others, even if merely confuting what had never been more than a product of their own gullibility, would be very different.

"We have not come here to ask agreement or beg favors," Varlech announced in a loud voice. "The village of Uchal and its surrounding holdings are placed forthwith under the law handed down by the Lifemaker to the protectors of the True Faith. They have directed that a force be formed of Redeeming Avengers to take up arms against the heresy now loose across these lands. Accordingly, it is decreed that in support of this holy mission, a tax of one-sixth of all produce and revenues shall be delivered every four brights. Further, a force consisting of one in six of all males of military age shall be raised to train as fighters with the Redeeming Avengers. And furthermore, the district of Uchal will render such accommodations, supplies, and other support as are deemed necessary to the success of the Redeeming Avengers' mission. To facilitate compliance, an officer of the Redeeming Avengers and a supporting staff will be installed here in place of the treacherous headrob who was in league with the dark powers. But the Lifemaker in his compassion will spare the others of his kin, who will be taken hence as guarantees of the people of Uchal's good faith."

A number of the Avengers turned out to be Kroaxian priests. When Varlech had finished speaking, they moved with soldiers through the crowd, picking out other individuals they perceived as threats, to be taken away also. These included more of Ol Skaybar's helpers and officials, the village schoolteacher, and two students who had visited Carthogia's university of learning. They took Brongyd, being an independent inquirer after truth like Thirg. But when one of the priests questioned Thirg, Thirg described himself as being an emissary from Menassim, the principal city of Carthogia. The priest seemed less certain what to do with him and sent for Varlech.

Rex snarled, coolant vanes bristling, as the leader approached. One of the Avengers drew back his spear threateningly. "Easy, Rex," Thirg commanded.

Varlech looked Thirg over coldly. "You are one of Kleippur's sorcerers who conspires with the alien impostors?" he inquired.

"I am a seeker of understanding who pursues truth wherever it may lead," Thirg replied.

"You seem to have no respect and precious little fear for one who holds your life as on a balancing edge," Varlech remarked.

Thirg shrugged his shoulder cowlings resignedly. "Whatever action you decide on cannot alter truth. What is true will remain so, indifferent to any wish of yours or mine that it be otherwise and unimpressed by however many we might induce by reason, deceit, or terror to share in our persuasions."

Incomprehension followed by anger flashed in the Avenger leader's eyes. He was evidently a fighter, not a thinker, and for a moment Thirg thought that he was about to be dispatched right then to join the four lifeless figures at the top of the steps. But then, just as quickly, a cooler but still irritated light prevailed. Possibly it was because Varlech was not disposed to risk an incident that might precipitate a confrontation with the Carthogian military just yet.

"Take him, too," he commanded. "The time will come when such loyalty to Kleippur will fetch a fair ransom."

Thirg and Brongyd were seized roughly and taken to a cellar where the captives were being herded. They remained there for the next half bright while Varlech went about installing the Avengers' overseer for the village and giving directives for its affairs. Then he readied his force again to proceed to the next village. Bound and guarded, with Rex wedged on the floor between them, Thirg and Brongyd left Uchal with the other captives in a wagon at the center of the column. After all the effort he had gone through to find sanctuary in Carthogia, Thirg wondered dejectedly if the same persecution and harassments he had thought he'd escaped from were about to overtake him again.

5

EARTH'S NEWS MEDIA WERE SENSATIONALIZING ABOUT the "intelligent planet" of the future and running endless features, interviews, and articles by overnight experts speculating on the "total responsive environment" already in the making. Accompanied by an illustration showing the world with a face on one hemisphere and part of the other peeled back to reveal a cortex, the cover of the current issue of *Time* proclaimed: MOTHER EARTH IS BEING GIVEN A BRAIN.

Essentially, the hullabaloo was really an update on a trend that had been quietly moving forward for many years: the steady integration of all the various industrial, commercial, scientific, educational, and other communications and computing networks into a vast global complex. The key word being pushed to sell the undertaking was "responsiveness." It didn't mean simply that any information would be instantly available to anyone (suitably authorized) anywhere, or that the act of purchasing a plastic toy in San Diego or a dinner dress in Amsterdam would carry immediate voting power to help determine the next week's production schedules at automated factories in Nicaragua and Taiwan, or that a complaint about a software product typed into a terminal in Vancouver could find its way onto the agenda of a management meeting held two days later in Tokyo. But all the social problems that had remained to plague humanity despite successive ages of enlightenment, industrialization, affluence, high technology, and the various other solutions that had been promised would finally disappear as the true cause of all the ills—society's indifference and consequent unresponsiveness—was made good by worldwide automated "electronic sensitivity."

"Electronic communism, more like it," Burton Ramelson grumbled at the others gathered in the library of his family's mansion in Delaware. "Central planning all over again, wearing a new disguise. They're saying that the theory was sound all along, but the reason it collapsed back in the eighties was too-long delays in communications. Now they're wiring up the planet with a faster nervous system, and that's supposed to fix it."

Actually, Ramelson didn't have any special objection to the notion of centralized control, so long as he and those who owed allegiance to him ranked influentially enough with the controllers. But the pattern was changing. Since the last quarter of the twentieth century, prosperous corporations in Japan and eastern Asia had been acquiring controlling interests in most Western industries, making them direct, on-line subordinates to the places where the real powers were concentrating. It so happened that the Ramelson family was the leading stockholder in a diversity of industrial and financial enterprises that included General Space Enterprises Corporation. And the only direction left pointing away from Earth's shifting power structure and all the attendant inconveniences was *out*.

"It occurred to some of us, as soon as the *Orion* mission revealed the situation on Titan, that if even a part of the productive potential out there could be turned to useful ends, we could have an answer to the whole problem," Ramelson said.

He was small in stature, almost bald, and sparse of frame inside his maroon dinner jacket, worn over a silk dress shirt that was open with a cravat at the neck. But his sharp eyes and tight, determined jaw as he spoke, standing with his back to the fireplace, were sufficient to make his the dominant presence in the room.

"In capacity alone, properly organized, Titan could dwarf the output of all the nations of Earth put together," he went on. "In addition, there are technologies up and running that scientists here are only beginning to dabble in, as well as others that are completely new ... Greg?" Ramelson nodded at GSEC's chief executive officer to elaborate.

Gregory Buhl, stockily built, with a craggy face and curly hair that still preserved its dark color, looked up from sipping a brandy in one of the leather-upholstered fireside chairs. "For one thing, they've identified working nuclear bulk transmutation: conversion of elements on an industrial scale—the alchemist's dream. There's fusion-based materials processing, with all the energy you dreamed of tapped off as a by-product. What we're talking about here is totally obsoleting primary metals extraction, materials flow processing, every kind of chemical processing: oil fuels, plastics, lubricants, fertilizers ..." He threw out a hand. "Self-replicating learning systems, holotronic brains, all methods of forming and fabrication, total waste recycling—as Burton says, get it properly organized and you could obsolete just about everything back here as totally as steam and electricity obsoleted waterwheels and windmills." Which, as everyone present understood, meant turning everything between Kamchatka and Karachi that had been causing them problems effectively into junk.

The others present were Robert Fairley, a nephew of

Ramelson, who sat on the board of a New York investment bank affiliated to GSEC; George Issel, senior publishing partner of the *New York Times*; and Brenda Jaye, an executive with NBC. People who bothered to think about such matters often wondered how it was that all the various news media seemed to work themselves up into the same frenzy—whether it was over some crime that had been commonplace for centuries, rapture at another rediscovered formula for living, or hysteria over this month's doomsday-imminent scenario—invariably using the same words and phrases, all at the same time. Whichever way the public turned, it found itself inundated by the same chorus being chanted in unison from an industry that had once been renowned for its healthy and vigorous diversity of opinion on anything.

The reason was that a central committee of representatives from all the major networks and press groups met periodically to update an *Index to Correct Opinion* giving guidelines to the approved slant on all persons and subjects of any note, which was then circulated to the newsrooms. The process operated subtly. No actual directive for conformity was ever issued, but as observers of the system quickly noted, dissenters and mavericks tended not to do so well in the promotion and career stakes. The next review meeting was due in a couple of days, which was why Ramelson had called the group together.

He made a pained parody of a smile. "I assume that you don't wish to be reminded of how attempts were made to shape events on Titan by direct intervention and failed."

Brenda Jaye made a sign for him to halt for a moment. "I've heard the rumors but never made it my business to ask," she said. "Are you saying that the GSEC people and their politicos on the mission *did* try to bribe one of the Taloid states into becoming a client, and it backfired?"

"A couple of people went over the bounds on their own authority," Ramelson replied. "Maybe something to do with the isolation out there affected them. It wasn't authorized policy." It was a flat lie, but Ramelson wasn't about to go on record as admitting anything else.

Robert Fairley broached the point at issue from where he was standing, hands in his pants pockets, by the bookshelves to one side of the fireplace. "But nevertheless, the episode has left the public suspicious of anything that might smack of deliberate intervention. There are still enormous potential benefits to be reaped from Titan. But for the reasons that Burton has just alluded to, being seen to initiate any involvement is precluded. Intervention could come about only as a result of our responding passively to the pressures of events."

George Issel had been around a little longer than Brenda and read this as code for "We need to be perceived as being dragged into it involuntarily." And of course, the classic way of being drawn into complications was by responding to threats that endangered one's kind or one's interests, or at least were believed to.

"Such as incidents that might require action by our security forces there," he murmured, as if he were figuring it out for the first time in his life.

"It *is* a hostile and totally unknown environment," Ramelson pointed out, "inhabited by alien machines of completely unknown history and disposition. Who knows what might happen?"

Brenda Jaye looked from one to the other as the message sank in. Naturally, any action that might prove necessary would sit more easily with a public prepared in advance to accept the idea that unfortunate things might happen.

"Stress the nonhuman," she pronounced, noting it in the pad resting on her knee. "Minds not comparable to our own. Complex alien response programming, devoid of genuine feelings. Tiny group of humans surrounded by unknowns. Play up professionalism of military constantly on guard." She looked up.

"A splendid assessment," Ramelson agreed, beaming. "My own sentiments entirely." Issel nodded to himself, satisfied. Nothing more needed to be said. Brenda had passed muster as a full member of the club.

Ramelson had been assured that whatever else the superficial arrangement with NASO said, the first loyalty of Colonel Short, the U.S. Special Forces commander of the military unit on Titan, was to sympathetic departments of the Pentagon underworld. And when the right opportunity arose, Short would know what to do. His officers apparently were old hands at this kind of thing.

6

CLARISSA EIDSTADT TOOK CARE OF ZAMBENDORF'S PUB-licity and related matters. Her function was a vital one. The Zambendorf sensation was a product of the image-making industry the public relied on for the reality substitutes that protected its myths. But the public mind was fickle; unless continually refreshed, the images faded rapidly from TV-conditioned attention spans. So when the team returned from an overseas tour, Clarissa always had an angle that would bring a camera team to the airport or hotel for the occasion. If a computer happened to crash while Zambendorf was in the vicinity, or a security alarm went off, or an automatic vendor malfunctioned, Clarissa would make sure that at least one headline to the effect of ZAM-BENDORF ACCIDENTALLY WIPES MEMCHIP—HALTS CITY BANK would appear the next morning. Not a week went by without a showing of Zambendorf performing at a celebrity dinner, a Zambendorf stunt on a previous night's talk show, or, if Zambendorf hadn't done anything newsworthy that particular week, a recycled account of how an expert of this kind or that kind had "acknowledged the reality of the Zambendorf effect" when denying one of the popular claims or had been "unable to offer an answer" in the event of ignoring it.

Clarissa was middle-aged, short, and matronly, with dark

hair cut in a straight fringe across her forehead, her eyes framed by heavy-rimmed butterfly glasses and her mouth accentuated by deep red lipstick that she continued to use in Genoa Base's unlikely environment. Her chief weapons for getting what she wanted were scorn and provocation: either goading people that they didn't have the ability to deliver, or exasperating them to the point where they would agree to virtually anything to be left in peace. And over the years it had proved a fearsomely effective formula.

Sergeant Bill Harvey, one of the Special Forces detail left as part of the military contingent at Genoa Base, knew her well enough by now and grinned as she waved a hand disparagingly from the chair on the far side of the steel desk in the guardroom of the main perimeter gatehouse.

"Why 'Great' Britain?" she demanded. "What's so great about it? We put them in their place over two hundred years ago." Harvey had spent a year attached to the British counterterrorist Special Air Service regiment, and the conversation had drifted into matters concerning the mother country.

"You don't understand, Clarissa," Harvey said. "That was intentional. They shipped all their crazies that they could do without over to us, cut the connection, and left us stuck with them. Then they went out and took over the world and had a great time."

"Says who?"

Harvey eyed her curiously across the desk for a few seconds, then relented. "Not really. It has to do with their geography."

"Their geography?" Clarissa repeated. " 'Great'?" She gave him a fish-eyed look through her butterfly glasses. "What are you talking about? You could get the whole of it into one corner of Texas."

"Sure could. It'd do wonders for the place, too."

"So what's great about it?" Clarissa asked again.

"It's like greater New York. England and Wales were originally Britain, see. Then, when they added Scotland, it became Great Britain."

The huge black man in a white T-shirt and khaki drill

pants who was leaning against the wall by the arms rack nodded. He was Joe Fellburg, Zambendorf's security man. "There's another part as well, right? That piece up at the top of Ireland."

"Northern Ireland," Harvey said, nodding. "That gives you the United Kingdom. Then, if you add the rest of Ireland, that's the British Isles. It's all very simple, really." As duty officer of the watch, he was kitted out in an EV suit minus helmet and pack, which were stowed in the locker next to the outside-access chamber door. Two French paratroopers were smoking and talking over mugs of coffee at a table in the rear, by the door leading to the interior of the base.

"Do you know, Drew was talking about this the other day, and he got it all wrong," Clarissa said. She pulled a pad toward her that was lying on Harvey's desk. It was a standard-issue NASO pad, with pages ruled and numbered and the NASO emblem printed at the top of each. "I wanna write this down. Is it okay if I use this?"

Harvey shrugged and waved a hand. "Sure. Go ahead."

Clarissa uncapped a pen. "I want to make sure I've got it right. Now, how did all that go again?"

People soon learned that nothing concerning Zambendorf was ever quite what it seemed. This was particularly true of the strange mixture of individuals who had attached themselves to him in the course of time, almost as if the unconventionality of the world he moved in somehow catered to a need for zaniness that their former lifestyles had been incapable of satisfying. Clarissa had been not just a pilot but a combat instructor with the Air Force's suborbital bomb wing. Fellburg had worked in earlier years as a communications specialist in industry and later with military intelligence but had come to the conclusion that there was more money to be made—along with more prestige and social recognition to be enjoyed—from the magical vibrations of psychic fields than from the electrical modulations of real ones. He had missed some aspects of the life nevertheless, and he enjoyed having military people around him again at Genoa Base.

So, naturally, there was more to their just happening to be in the guardhouse at this particular time than mere socializing or taking an idle moment to relive former camaraderie. The scientists who had witnessed Zambendorf's "projection" to Gerry Massey aboard the *Orion* several days before had been discussing the feat ever since, and Zambendorf's guess was that they were close to figuring out how he and Massey had done it. In fact, about half an hour before, Thelma, the team's blond, glamorous, curvaceous, and leggy secretary—who also had a Ph.D in mathematical physics—had called Zambendorf to warn him that a group of them were in the general messroom and had been asking where he was in order to confront him with their conclusions. One of Zambendorf's strengths lay in never letting an opportunity go by. Far from finding such a prospect daunting, he had seen it as a chance to set up a further performance that they would not be able to explain—which would also serve to divert their attention if their answer to the Massey stunt turned out to be correct. Accordingly, after a quick consultation, he had dispatched Clarissa and Fellburg to the main guardhouse to prepare the ground.

Clarissa had never talked about the peculiarities of British geography to Drew West or to anybody else. She had simply seized on the topic of the moment as a pretext for using the NASO pad on the guardroom desk.

"Is Mike Mason around anywhere here, Bill?" Fellburg asked Harvey, distracting his attention just as Clarissa finished writing. "He's got a coupla maps that we wanted to borrow."

"Haven't seen him all morning. Some of the guys are out on a training mission. I think he's with them." While Harvey was speaking, Clarissa tore from the pad not only the sheet she had written on, but the one underneath it as well.

"Do you have a map of this side of Genoa that I could get a copy of?" Fellburg asked.

"I've got one that covers from here to Arthur's place and the junkyard on the other side of it that the Ts think is a park," Harvey said. "That be okay?"

Fellburg nodded and straightened up from the wall. "Just what I need."

Clarissa rose from the chair by the desk. "Well, I've got things to do. I'll leave you two at it. Talk to you later, Billy."

"Tell Drew to visit someday, and we'll talk more about Britain and the rest if he's interested," Harvey tossed after her as she moved toward the door.

"I'll tell him." Clarissa left.

She met Zambendorf by a storeroom at the back of the vehicles maintenance workshop a few minutes later and gave him the blank sheet from the pad, which carried the number immediately preceding that of the next unused page. "Joe's there," she confirmed. Zambendorf nodded and tucked the sheet of paper inside one of several magazines he was carrying. Then he left her and made his way to the general personnel messroom.

Thelma was near the door, ostensibly watching a game of pinochle between some NASO technicians and off-duty military people, when Zambendorf ambled in and casually handed her the magazines he had been carrying. She took them without making any comment that could have drawn unwanted attention. "Did Joe find you, Karl? He was looking for you," she said.

"No, I haven't seen him. Well, I'm sure he won't stray too far in this place."

"Ah, just the man we've been waiting for!" Graham Spearman's voice called from among a group clustered halfway along the center table. Zambendorf turned as if noticing them for the first time. In fact, he had registered practically everyone present within moments of entering. John Webster, a genetics specialist from a bioengineering firm in England, was with Spearman, along with Sharon Beatty, the professional skeptic, and several more from the computing and communications section. There were some academics Zambendorf recognized as geologists, a climatologist, and various engineering-ologists. O'Flynn was there with more NASO techs, and to the side was a trio of base administrative staff.

"Why? What have I done now?" Zambendorf asked, moving over to join them. The attention in the room followed him and shifted away from Thelma, who remained standing by the card players.

"That show of yours the other day with Gerry Massey," Takumi Kahito, one of the programmers, said. "We think we know how you did it."

"But I've already told you how I did it," Zambendorf answered. "Surely you're not saying you didn't believe me."

Kahito smiled and gestured at the large mural screen. "Mind if we rerun the video?"

Zambendorf shrugged. "Go ahead." In the background Thelma drifted to the back of the room. Everyone present had as good as forgotten that she existed.

"All it proves is that closed minds are capable of explaining away anything," Malcolm Wade declared, puffing his pipe near the serving counter.

Sitting by Wade was the round-faced, wispy-haired figure of Dr.—of what was obscure—Osmond Periera, wearing a rose-colored shirt under a V-neck fawn sweater. The author profiles in his best-selling books on paranormal research and UFOlogy—which claimed, among other things, that the North Polar Sea was a gigantic crater caused by the crash of an antimatter-powered alien spacecraft, and that television altered the climate via mind power concentrated through mass suggestion—described him as Zambendorf's discoverer and mentor. Certainly he was one of the staunchest disciples, and the boosting of Zambendorf's career from European nightclub performer to celebrity of worldwide acclaim owed no small part to Periera's contacts and the influence his royalties were able to attract.

"There's no question that it demonstrates how much more reliably psychocommunicative signals propagate in the outer planetary void, free from disruptive terrestrial influences," Periera said, ostensibly to Wade but so that everyone could hear. "Of course, it doesn't come as any great surprise to anyone of genuine scientific impartiality. The effect was predicted by Bell's inequality many decades ago."

Periera's ability to invent the most outrageous explanations for Zambendorf's feats never ceased to amaze even Zambendorf. None of the scientists at Genoa Base took Periera seriously, but either tolerated him as part of the much-needed entertainment or ignored him with disdain, depending on their disposition. Periera, of course, took himself very seriously and read their attitudes as a direct, inverse measure of open-mindedness.

Conspicuously absent, Zambendorf noted, were Weinerbaum and his coterie of "serious" scientists, who were above sharing in the fun the regular messroom gatherings generated. Harold Mackeson, the base commander, who had presided the last time, was not present either.

By now the mural screen was showing Massey relaxing back in his chair, as they had seen him at the time of the live transmission from the *Orion.*

"What is it, Gerry?" Vernon Price's voice asked again.

"I'm not sure. I feel more than just aware of the space outside," Massey replied. "It's as if part of my mind is reaching out into it ... being touched by something. My God, I'm getting something! Suddenly I'm flooded with an image of Karl, and yes, the feeling of a number." Zambendorf continued staring fixedly from where he was standing, aware but not showing it of the curious glances being sent in his direction from around the room. Massey continued, "It's ... let me see ..." His hand came up, touching the fingers to his brow. "Fifty ... fifty-three."

"There!" Spearman stabbed at the comm unit on the table in front of him to freeze the image. "See—Massey's hand is covering his mouth. We heard the number over the audio all right, but you don't actually *see* him say it." Spearman fast-forwarded the sequence to the next number Massey had gotten right, which they heard him giving as seventeen. But again, at the moment of uttering it he was looking up at the ceiling with his arms braced on the rests of his chair and could have been saying anything. Massey had failed on the next, which had been seven, and Spear-

man went on to the last two. Freezing the view at 68 showed Massey with the back of his head to the camera, and when giving the last, 90, he had been wiping his mouth after taking a sip of water.

"All four of them, Karl?" Spearman smiled wryly and shook his head. "Too much of a coincidence. I'll believe that what we're *looking at* came in from the *Orion* when it said it did—no question of that. But what we *heard* is a different matter. There isn't one instance where you can actually synch anything to lip movements, no *evidence* that Massey ever actually received anything. All we *know* is that he said he did."

"Then where did those numbers come from?" Zambendorf asked.

"Prerecorded and mixed in as a voice-over after the signal packet came in from the *Orion*," Kahito replied.

Zambendorf was impressed. "Not a bad effort at all," he said, his eyes twinkling. "If it were true, I'd even go as far as to say that you're learning something about being real scientists at last." In fact, it had been just as Spearman had said. Massey had sent a recitation, in his own voice, of all the numbers up to a hundred as part of the messages he had exchanged with Zambendorf the day before the demonstration. Joe Fellburg had persuaded a pal on the NASO communications staff to give him access to the incoming message processors, and he had keyed the appropriate selections to slot into the audio track at the blind spots during the fifty-two-minute wait for the signal from the *Orion* to come in.

Spearman backed the recording up to the third number, 7, the one Massey had passed on. "This one's not coming through very clearly at all," Massey said on the screen. "No, just a blur, I'm afraid. It has a feel of 'threeness' about it—thirteen, maybe, or thirty-something . . ."

"That was a neat touch, Karl. I've got to hand it to you," Spearman said. "This time it is real. All the time that Gerry was talking about this stuff, you could see his mouth clearly. It leaves you believing that the same was true with all the other numbers, too, but it wasn't. I had to run through this a dozen times before I spotted the difference."

All of it was true. The other part about this particular detail was that for some strange psychological reason nobody really understood, people in general were much more likely to find a demonstration of this kind believable when it didn't go a hundred percent right. Conjuring tricks worked every time, the inverted logic of these judgments seemed to say; therefore, if it didn't work every time, it couldn't be a trick.

"What clinched it for me was having the choice restricted to numbers," John Webster said, leaning back. Evidently, as far as he was concerned, the whole matter was already wrapped up, with no call for further questions.

"Really?" Zambendorf just smiled and waited for the opportunity to ripen. He had weathered worse than this many a time before.

"It makes it easy for them to have been prerecorded," Spearman explained. "But suppose that instead of a number you'd used something selected arbitrarily on the spur of the moment—say, an object produced in the room."

"Oh, I see." Zambendorf nodded, as if that should have occurred to him before. "That would have convinced you, would it?"

"It would have convinced me," Kahito said. "If somebody had been free to say, oh . . ." He looked around, then pointed at Spearman's spectacles. "Black-rimmed glasses, or anything they liked, and then it had come in from Massey fifty-two minutes later, sure, *then* I'd believe it."

"I've seen Karl do that several times," Wade assured everybody. Their conviction, however, evidently fell somewhere short of total.

"We'd have had you cold, Karl," Spearman said to Zambendorf.

"Nonsense," Zambendorf answered breezily. "I'll do it for you right now, if you like."

Nobody had been prepared for that. They looked at each other uncertainly, as if to check what they thought they had just heard. "What?" Spearman said. "I'm not sure I follow. How can you do it right now?"

"Massey isn't set up or anything," Webster pointed out.

Zambendorf turned up his hands as if asking what the problem was with that. "So set him up again," he said. He was comfortably sure that they wouldn't. It would mean taking another day to exchange preparatory messages, making the slot assignments in the communications trunk beam, then getting everybody together again when the response from Massey was due.

"It's all a bit messy now," Webster said. "A pity somebody didn't think of it before." The others concurred glumly.

"There is another way," Zambendorf told them after a moment of apparent thought. "You all know Joe Fellburg, right? Well, he isn't with us just to handle security, you know. I only accept colleagues into the team who show unusual talent in their own right. Isn't that so, Osmond?"

"Absolutely," Periera confirmed from beside Wade, flattered at having his credentials endorsed publicly. "An extraordinary collection of individuals. Fellburg does possess an unusual sensitivity for receiving telepathic images. I've seen Karl transmit to him in an absolutely sealed room. Checked it myself. It's quite unexplainable by any purely physical process."

By this time the fact that only a few minutes previously the Massey performance had been as good as solved was lost in the minds of most of those present. And that was exactly how Zambendorf wanted things to be. The goalposts had shifted; now *this* would be the test of his authenticity.

Spearman looked around the company, then back at Zambendorf. "I'm not sure I know what we're talking about," he said. "How is this supposed to work?"

"Very simply," Zambendorf replied. "We call Joe—" He turned toward where Wade and Periera were sitting. "Does anyone know where he is?" They returned negative gestures and head shakings. Zambendorf shrugged. "Well, he'll be easy enough to locate." He looked back at Spearman. "You call him and tell him what we want to do, and if he agrees, you hang up—so there's no open line or other channel back to him. Then anyone here who wants to can pick whatever objects they like—purely arbitrarily, which was the way you told me it ought to be done a few minutes ago—and I'll send the images to him." Zambendorf shrugged again as if he were describing something he did every day. "And then he'll come here and tell us what they were."

"What? With Zambendorf here in the room?" Sharon Beatty put in. "These people have codes that you can't even see. They can signal to each other."

"Ask Joe to write them down before he comes in," Zambendorf suggested.

Nobody could find any real objection to that. There was a short debate to consider additional details, until finally a procedure was agreed on that all were happy with. Somebody passed Spearman a seefone from the shelf by the door, and he began calling around the base to locate Fellburg. Zambendorf settled himself down at the central one of the messroom's three long tables. Fellburg turned out to be in the guardroom of the main gatehouse. "Putting him on," Sergeant Harvey, the current watch officer, said.

"Er, I hope this isn't an inconvenient time, but we were hoping that you might help us out with something, Joe," Graham Spearman said when Fellburg's features appeared on the screen.

"If I can. What's your problem?"

"I'm in the messroom with a bunch of people, and Karl's with us. He's saying that—"

"Just ask him if he feels able to receive remote images," Zambendorf whispered in his ear to keep things short.

"Are you up to receiving remote images right now?" Spearman repeated.

"Why not? Let's give it a whirl."

"Without the phone connection."

"Okay."

"We want you to write them down and bring the list straight to the messroom to compare with a checklist that we'll be making. Nobody leaves here till you show up," Spearman said.

"Anything else?"

"That's about it."

"Let's go, then," Fellburg said, and the screen went blank. It left a mood of surprise hanging in the air. Somehow this was all too simple and more straightforward than anyone had imagined. Zambendorf waited, looking at ease.

"We didn't tell Fellburg how many items there'd be," somebody said.

"He'll know," Zambendorf predicted confidently.

As had been agreed, people from all over the room produced items from pockets, purses, and about their persons and passed them to Spearman, who arranged them in a circle covering the width of the center table. He then placed a table knife inside the circle and set it rotating horizontally. The knife spun through several revolutions, slowing and becoming more wobbly until it lurched to rest pointing at a gold signet ring. O'Flynn, the NASO maintenance sergeant, turned the top card of a deck that had been shuffled by several people. "Eight," he announced. The rule was that if the number was odd, the object would be accepted; if even, it would be ignored, and the procedure repeated. Spearman spun the knife again. This time it selected an American Express card from somebody's wallet. Flynn turned over the three of clubs.

"AmEx gold card," Spearman pronounced. Webster wrote it down as the first item on his checklist. Everyone stared at Zambendorf, who had closed his eyes and was sitting with a distant expression on his face, his arms resting on the table in front of him.

After several seconds he opened his eyes. "Very well. Next?"

The knife picked out a paper clip and a pencil stub, both of which had to be discarded because the corresponding cards were a ten and a two. But the next was the five of hearts, which allowed a brown leather button to be added to the list.

There followed a red pocket notebook, a plastic sachet

containing a medication patch, an electrical cable running down the wall of the room—the knife had stopped midway between two of the objects on the table—a jeweler's eyeglass, and finally the person of Takumi Kahito, described on the list as "male of Oriental appearance."

By this time practically everyone in the room had been drawn into the circle of curious watchers around the center table. A few remained here and there, obstinately continuing with their chess games or buried in a newspaper, and Wade and Periera had remained seated, but nobody paid any attention to them. And neither was anyone paying any attention to Thelma, out of sight at the back of the room, quietly writing down the selections as they were announced on the NASO notepad sheet that had been inside the magazine Zambendorf had handed her when he had come into the room. Nobody would recollect that seemingly insignificant event. In fact, nobody would even be able to recall if Thelma had been anywhere near Zambendorf from the time he had first appeared.

So when Zambendorf announced that he could feel the receiver's power "fading" (they had agreed on a time limit so that Fellburg knew how long to wait), Thelma already had the complete list written out—penned in a strong, distinctly masculine style—and ready in the room. And with Zambendorf chattering and answering questions at the center table, nobody took any notice when she moved to the serving counter to get herself a soda and then wandered back along the other side of the room to be only a matter of feet from the doorway when Fellburg arrived. This would be the most crucial moment of the whole exploit.

Fellburg appeared with a wide grin on his face and a folded sheet of paper in one hand, pausing for a second to assess the situation in the room. He saw Zambendorf and began moving toward him, at the same time raising the hand holding the paper. At that instant Thelma stepped forward in front of him.

"No. Karl shouldn't touch it." She took the paper, turned with it, and walked a few steps to where Spearman and the others were sitting. In the process, her body hid the paper for a split second, but her movement was so smooth that there wasn't one person watching to whom it even occurred that the folded piece of paper that she passed to Spearman might not have been the one they saw her take from Fellburg. And so, of course, the two lists were found to match. No amount of speculating about hidden lip movements or prerecorded voice-overs could account for *that*. And that confused the other issue, which by rights should by then have been put to rest, somehow leaving the impression that the Massey demonstration was still an open case too.

John Webster stared down at Fellburg's list, clearly unwilling to accept what it meant, though just as obviously flummoxed as to what to make of it. Finally he looked up. "Joe, can I ask you something?" He held up the sheet, which had the NASO emblem printed at the top. "You were in the main gatehouse when we located you, right?"

"Right."

"So was that where you got this paper?"

Fellburg frowned as if having to think back. "Yeah, that's right. There was a pad on Harvey's desk back there." The others in the room looked at Webster curiously.

"There's just one more thing I'd like to try." So saying, Webster used the seefone to call the gatehouse again. Harvey's face and shoulders appeared, showing the top of a military shirt.

"Main gate, Sergeant Harvey. Hi, John," he greeted.

"I believe that Joe Fellburg was with you not long ago," Webster said.

"Yeah, right. I think he went to the general mess."

"I know—he's with us here. But I wonder if you'd do something for us. Tell, me, is there a NASO notepad on the desk there—regular sort, lined pages. NASO whatsit at the top?"

Harvey looked around, then stretched out an arm. "You mean like this?" He held up a pad.

"Did Joe use it for anything when he was there?"

"As a matter of fact, he did. He went off in a corner with it for a few minutes, but I'm not sure what for. Why?"

"Oh, just something we're curious about. Could you tell me, what's the number of the next available page there, on the top?"

"It's, let's see . . ." Harvey turned the pad around and looked down at it. "Thirty-seven."

Webster stared at the sheet in his hand. The number printed in large black numerals in the top right-hand corner was 36.

7

TWO DARK-PAINTED MILITARY FLYERS—ONE A GENERAL-purpose, twenty-seat personnel carrier, the other, a smaller two-man scout—skimmed over a darkened landscape of low hills marked by pipelines and scattered patches of engineering constructions.

"Delta Two to Delta Leader. Patterned layouts with cluster of pumpkin houses coming up on the imager at twelve o'clock. I think this could be it."

"Okay, we got 'em. Bunch of Ts in the center standing around a walking cart. It looks like them, all right." In the rear cockpit of the larger machine, Captain Mike Mason of the Special Forces contingent flipped to the intercom circuit. "Joe, gimme a close-up on that central area on the intensifier. Make a slow circuit while we check it out, Ed. If it looks like this is the place, we'll go straight down." He switched back to call Delta Two. "Two, this is Leader. Stay with us while we make a pass. If it checks out, we're going down. Continue circling for illumination and cover."

"Roger, Leader."

"Area checks clear of obstacles," the copilot reported.

Behind Mason, Sergeant Yaver addressed the squad sitting along the sides of the aft compartment, kitted out in military-version EV suits. "Check weapons, life support, radio. Close and secure helmets. We're going down."

Outside, the stub wing dipped as the craft banked into a tight turn, at the same time shedding speed and height. From the scout trailing in echelon, a searchlight beam came on and stabilized to light up the central open area of the Taloid settlement. The view on the cockpit monitor showed lots of figures standing immobile as they stared upward, or sitting in their crazy walking "spudmobiles." A number of the wheeled and legged machines that usually accompanied them stood in the surrounding area. Mason had heard the scientists refer to them as "animals." It had to be something to do with the loneliness out here getting to their heads. Hell, they were all just machines . . . And now, if the latest reports the Taloids were bringing back to Genoa were anything to go by, they had machines getting a notion that they could steal dead Terran bodies if they felt like it.

Jeez!

Varlech, Avenger-of-Heresies, watched from the central square as the sky dragon came lower and circled the village, which was called Quahal. The smaller dragon following it flooded the surroundings with a cone of violet heat-light. This was his test, he decided: the challenge to his resolve and fortitude sent by the Lifemaker to try his faith. He forced himself to remember that these were not dragons or living beasts at all; they were imitations crafted by the Lumians from rock, as a legwright coaxed imitation limbs from growth seed nurtured in enriched clays. He looked across at the cart with its bundle wrapped in metallic braids and cord. And the Lumians were not immortal or gods.

Most of those around him were standing petrified. They had heard the rumors and listened to tales second- or third-hand, but few, if any—apart from some of his own Avengers who had encountered Lumians before as soldiers with the Paduan army—had ever seen a Lumian flying beast for themselves. Thus far Varlech had proved an effective persuader. Now, he divined, the Lifemaker had deemed him worthy of proving himself with more than just words.

The villagers were not fleeing in terror, as had been the usual reaction when Lumians had first appeared in the skies above Robia. Awe-inspiring as the sight of flying beasts was to them, the people had been told that the aliens, though capable of inflicting terrible vengeance when roused, were just with those who acted peaceably. The prisoners shackled in the carts, who had been taken from Uchal and the other places visited previously, looked on with the resignation of those for whom any unexpected change in fortune could only be for the better. But Varlech's followers remained fearful and uncertain, unable to decide which way the tidings boded. Their eyes were fixed on him, awaiting his guidance. Whatever piece of history was to be written today would be of his making.

That the Lumian flying beasts had appeared from the direction Varlech's Avengers had followed from Uchal could surely be no coincidence. It meant that they had been tracking him, and the reason could only be that they sought to recover the corpse of the dead Lumian the Avengers had been exhibiting across Kroaxia. So, should he stand meekly aside now and allow the prize that had already done much to advance the Lifemaker's cause to be taken away without protest or resistance, demonstrating for all to see that the protectors of the True Faith were powerless? Of course not. Unthinkable. For was not the very fact of the dead Lumian's existence a sign from the Lifemaker that these alien intruders were not invincible? This, then, was the moment to arise—for words to stand back and make way for action, and passions to boil over into deeds. Here might the flame ignite that would sweep across all of Robia.

And if that was not to be but instead, in striking a spark to herald some future conflagration, he should be called upon to make the final sacrifice, then so be it. His way was clear.

The larger of the two flying beasts had slowed almost to hang over them, while the smaller one continued circling and throwing down its violet ray. The Lumians would emerge. Varlech's stratagem would be to lure them on, unsuspecting, until they were away from the protection of their beasts. Then he would attack. He turned his head and called to his followers, pointing as he did so at the Lumian corpse.

"Look before you and see again the fate that awaits even aliens who draw down the Lifemaker's wrath. This bright, you shall be His instrument before all of Robia to expose these false gods. Be disdainful of fear, for any who should fall to dismantling in this enterprise will at once be reassembled among the ranks of the Lifemaker's forever chosen."

His words were effective, inspiring the Avengers with new confidence. They straightened up their postures and gripped their weapons tightly. Varlech made a sign to his lieutenants.

"Clear a space before the cart that holds the Lumian and conceal the men from sight with weapons ready. Kill any villager who attempts a sign of warning."

Pulling and prodding with their swords and hurlers, the Avenger soldiers herded the villagers into a screen around the square and took up positions behind them. To the side, the steeds and draft tractors backed away nervously at their tethers as the larger of the two Lumian craft descended.

A scan of the central area showed it enclosed by shapes that looked, in the glare from the scout hovering overhead, like monster rectangular vegetables with rough corners clearly discernible and wall faces interrupted by door and window openings. Most of the Taloids had fallen back to where the other machines and wagon walkers were jumbled together along the sides of the open space the personnel transporter had landed in. One of the walkers contained a bundle about the size and shape of a suited human, draped in sheets of what looked like woven wire.

"Ramp down and pressures equalized. Power steady at idle," the pilot reported. "Ready to open up."

"Noncompliant, with prejudice," the order had said. That meant "provocative and mean." They weren't there to ask permission or favors. Part of the object of this exercise was to show the natives who was boss. There were times when even machines had to learn respect for rights, property, and decency.

"Sergeant, detail two flanking squads to clear the area to the far end of the open space. Bring three men with me to check what's in that walker. Looks like it could be her."

"Wellman, take the right. Korzhgin, the left. Attwood, Myers, Salvini, follow me," Yaver instructed.

The lock opened, and a double file of heavy-duty-clad figures emerged, moving quickly and without ceremony. They fanned out, driving back the Taloids who had been slower to move with the rest, while behind them in the center Mason and Yaver went forward with the three troopers. Two of them stepped up onto the walker and pulled aside the coverings of the bundle. It was the body of Amy Rhodes. The helmet was smashed; the head inside was unrecognizable, frozen black and solid by Titan's cold. For several seconds Mason could only stare in fascinated revulsion.

It was the moment to strike. "For the Lifemaker and the glory of Kroaxia!" Varlech cried. "Attack!" Around the square hurler tubes rose to aim between the trembling villagers. "Forward!" As the salvo discharged, Avengers broke through the ranks, wielding swords, axes, and lances.

"Aghh!" a Terran voice yelled on the open radio.

"I'm hit! I'm hit!" another cried out.

Shouts of alarm poured over the channel. One soldier was reeling backward, his helmet a web of fracture cracks but still intact. Another was down. A spear hit Mason's backpack but glanced off. Yaver fired a burst from his assault cannon at a pair of Taloids rushing at him whirling clubs. They came apart into collapsing masses of limbs and parts.

"Fire at will!"

The oncoming Taloids ran into a wall of explosive shells fired on automatic. One of them skewered another of the troopers through the shoulder with a lance before being demolished by covering fire from the door of the flyer.

"Attwood, behind!"

"Gotcha, bastard!"

Bodies swung and fell, missiles flew, and confusion seethed on every side. A steel-gray face loomed in front of Mason, and metal hands swung a huge double-edged ax. He began raising his weapon; a burst from somewhere took off the Taloid's head. He fired at another Taloid closing on Yaver from the side. Then the scout swooped low, and the main body of Taloids that had formed to rush the transporter en masse disintegrated in a storm of cannon fire and rocket projectiles from above.

"You two, help me grab the body," Mason yelled. "Sergeant, get those wounded picked up and fall back. Cover us from the door."

As Mason tore away the coverings, hands reached out to haul the frozen corpse in its cumbersome suit down from the wagon. A dart struck one of the soldiers in the midriff, and he doubled over, clutching his stomach. Another figure ran forward to steer the stricken one back. Mason and the other trooper dragged the corpse back to the flyer and heaved it inside after the wounded, while the rearguard cordon fell back toward the ramp, firing outward. The area beyond was strewn with shattered metal bodies, limbs, components, and pieces, looking like a creation of some mechanical Dante. The impetus of the Taloids' attack had withered under the fire from the scout. Some of them seemed to be wandering aimless and dazed, while the rest fled in disorder along the alleys leading from the central open area. The four-legged "animal" types were in panic, bucking and rearing where they were tied; some had broken loose and were running amok, colliding with each other and knocking down Taloids.

The inner door of the lock closed, and the engine note rose. "Get the hell out," Mason yelled. He loosened his helmet and lifted it off as the flyer rose. "What have we got?" he asked the medic, who was frantically checking the casualties, hacking away torn outer suits with shears, and cutting blood-soaked clothing.

"Two decompressed, but they got 'em inside in time.

Torn shoulder, bleeding stopped by the cold. They should pull through okay, sir." The rest looked like limb wounds and a possibly broken leg, all recoverable. With the odds and the surprise, it could have been worse. A good job that the scout captain had reacted promptly.

"Delta Two calling, asking how we're looking," the pilot reported from up front.

Mason turned toward the open door leading into the cockpit. "Tell him we've got a few cuts and bruises, but they'll be okay. And thanks for the quick work."

"We try to please. All part of the service," the pilot relayed back a few seconds later.

Sergeant Yaver and two of the men were working a body bag up over Amy Rhodes's stiff and lifeless form. They pulled the top around the shoulders and helmet, zipped the bag shut, and then lowered it down onto the floor at the rear of the compartment.

Well, the powers that be had wanted an incident, Mason reflected to himself as the two flyers turned onto a course that would take them back to Genoa Base. He wondered what would happen now as a result of it.

Meanwhile, Thirg, Brongyd, and a group of other captives, who had managed to seize weapons and cut their chains in the confusion, wrapped themselves in heavy cloaks and slipped away, out of the place called Quahal. Behind them, amid the wreckage strewn across the village square, a pair of imaging matrices stared sightlessly up at Titan's clouds from a front piece that had belonged to a head casing lying several feet away. Varlech, Avenger-of-Heresies, had gone to meet the Great Assembler.

The version spread by the agents of the Lifemaker's True Faith was that a peaceful exhortation had been attacked without provocation: this was what the Lumians had been forced to resort to in order to prevent word of the revival spreading. Outrage and dismay grew. Nogarech, the new ruler of Kroaxia, who had begun changing to new ways modeled on those introduced by Kleippur in Carthogia, was denounced openly, and his followers were attacked. A movement swelled, calling for reinstatement of the former king, Eskenderom. Even in Carthogia, Redeeming Avengers harassed villagers in the outlying areas, calling on them to rise up against the new regime, which they succeeded in transforming in the minds of many robeings into a product of aliens' design with Kleippur, despite the fact that Kleippur's rebellion had occurred before the Lumians had ever come to Robia. But it was the perceptions that mattered, not the facts.

"Now you see the price that is paid by those who renounce our ancient faith for this alien heresy," a speaker told the crowd in the main square of Pergassos, the principal city of Kroaxia. "They tell us that we should live by a creed of nonviolence. What use is a religion of nonviolence when the Lumians themselves fail to abide by it? Is their true purpose not clear now? They would make Robia defenseless in order to exploit its wealth. Repent now and return to the true path where the Lifemaker awaits in His merciful forgiveness ..."

The prime-time network news showed a couple of grinning young men lying in cots in a medical facility, with two more in bathrobes sitting at a table behind. Another, his leg in a cast and supporting himself with a crutch, waved at the camera. The announcer's voice, a woman's, continued:

"Good news from Titan for the families of the soldiers who were injured a week ago when a party sent to recover the body of the unfortunate Amy Rhodes—the first fatality to be suffered by the mission—was attacked without apparent reason by crazed Taloids armed with swords, battle-axes, and primitive firearms. It appears that they're all out of danger and well on their way to complete recovery. Private Healy from Minneapolis, who was speared by a lance that penetrated right through his heavy-duty extravehicular suit, was particularly lucky. According to the chief medical officer at Genoa Base, the lance severed a major artery that in normal circumstances might well have been fatal, but the extreme cold of Titan provided an instant coagulant that stopped the bleeding. Meanwhile, the situation on Titan continues to be tense and uncertain . . ."

The view changed to one of heavily armed soldiers in EV suits standing guard outside the main gate of the Terran base, followed by another of two more soldiers manning a viewing instrument in a barricaded observation post. Then came a shot of a particularly unnerving part of Titan's mechanical Amazon, with tangles of machinery silhouetted in the background against flickering patterns of sparks and flame. In the center ground was a group of Taloids looking sinister and menacing from the highlights picking out their contours.

The voice-over continued. "Could the same kind of thing happen again? That's what experts have been asking themselves ever since the incident. The problem is, of course, that we're up against something that's fully over the borderline and in the realm of the unknown. The only safe and prudent answer to go with seems to be, 'Yes, it could.' And, next time, the troops, or scientists, or whoever happens to be on the spot might not be so lucky."

Next on the screen was a man with silvery hair and gold-rimmed spectacles, wearing a navy shirt and light gray V-neck sweater. A caption across the bottom of the screen read: DR. HOWARD DANKLEY, ROBOTICS INSTITUTE, CARNEGIE MELLON UNIVERSITY.

"The thing to remember is that, while the illusion of motivation and behavior as we know it might be very compelling, we are dealing with a completely unknown, alien form of . . . I hesitate to say 'intelligence,' because all we have any direct evidence of is some extremely elaborate programmed response patterns." Dankley's voice was reasoned and persuasive, matching the expression of calm, striving to mask underlying urgency. "What you and I might think of as universally applicable qualities of 'trust' or 'reliability' could have no significance at all to these beings. Violent reactions could be provoked by factors which to us appear entirely innocuous or might not even be perceptible at all. I don't want to be an alarmist, but I think our people out there on Titan could be in real danger. I only hope that the military force that they've got with them are as good as the recruiting ads say."

A quick flash of the anchorwoman shuffling papers and saying, "General Clark Udswalt at the Pentagon today assured us that they were up to the job," led to another head, tanned and with gray sideburns, wearing a peaked cap with lots of braids. This time the voice was clipped and to the point.

"They've got the best out there that this country can provide, every one handpicked elite. And they're backed by British marines, French airborne ... I'd back that bunch against any unit of comparable numbers that any country on Earth could put up, anybody you tell me, I don't care who they are."

The view changed to the same face but from a different angle, presumably at a different point in the interview. This time he looked less sanguine. The anchorwoman's voice-over explained, "But the general did admit that it was numbers that constituted the problem ..."

The sound track cut to Udswalt again. "But there has to be a limit. There are only so many of them, and they're almost a billion miles away. We're talking flesh and blood up against what, if things turn nasty—steel, titanium?" He threw up an empty hand. "Those boys will hang in there to the last one if they have to, but we don't do miracles. They're going to need help. And I only hope to God that we can get it there before it's too late."

The view changed back to the anchorwoman. "But we learned later, following exchanges that have taken place between the State Department and the Japanese Foreign Ministry during the last few days, that some help, at least, is already on the way. It was announced this afternoon that the Japanese have ordered the security force aboard their own Titan mission ship, the *Shirasagi*—a week out from Earth now and due to arrive at Titan in a little over twelve weeks—to place themselves at the disposal of the military command at Genoa Base in order to ensure maximum protection for all Terrans there." She paused. "That's just a stopgap measure. For a more permanent answer, an effort is going to be made to turn the *Orion*, due back at Earth in two weeks, around for its return voyage in half the time that was scheduled previously. And when it goes back, it will take with it a full-scale military force put together for the task of preserving order and protecting our people. So let's just hope that nothing gets out of hand in the space of the next few months. There'll be more on that with John Carew later tonight. But for now, over to Chicago, where there's been more trouble involving 'smart' designer molecules. Kate Ormison has this report . . ."

"Most satisfactory," Burton Ramelson pronounced from his office when Robert Fairley called with a summary of developments. "Now we need to clear the way for everything to proceed smoothly this time, without any more interference. That means making sure that Zambendorf and his infernal meddlers are kept safely out of the way. I'll have to give that some thought." He looked out of the screen, went quickly back in his mind over the things his nephew had said, and then nodded. "Most satisfactory, Robert," he said again. "Most satisfactory, indeed."

8

ZAMBENDORF FELT AS IF HE WERE IN A MOBILE COFFIN, entombed in a dark mausoleum of ice. He disliked wearing the cumbersome EV suits, and as a rule ventured from Genoa Base or the relatively comfortable vehicular shirtsleeve environments as little as possible. But the tension was beginning to have its effect even in Genoa City itself, the center of Arthur's recently founded liberal experiment. Many of the Taloids who had previously gone out and worked willingly with the Terran scientific parties were no longer showing up. Those who did were nervous and subdued, fearful of retaliation from their own kind. Zambendorf had decided on a personal visit to "Camelot," Arthur's residence in Genoa, to present the case that all Terrans should not be judged by the isolated action of a few and to reassure Arthur that the general support for Arthur remained undiminished.

He was sitting with Otto Abaquaan and Dave Crookes in an ice chamber furnished with odd Taloid pseudovegetable shapes and walls decorated with strange designs in plastic and metal. Across from them, looking like gigantic, upright, outlandishly garbed insects in the light from a NASO lamp turned to minimum power—installed for the Terrans' benefit—were Arthur and two of what seemed to be his military advisers. Also with them was a Taloid known to the Terrans as Moses, one of the rare "mystic" breed who possessed a measure of the residual radiosensitivity that Crookes had been investigating. Moses had a brother, Galileo, who had gone back into Padua some time earlier to visit former friends. As yet, Galileo had not returned. Concern was rising among both the Genoan Taloids and the Terrans over Galileo's whereabouts, especially with fugitives from Padua bringing back accounts of the militant revivalists stirring up hostility.

"Arthur has been getting reports of unrest all over Padua. And there are agents operating here in Genoa," Dave Crookes's voice said over the local channel. He was the most proficient of the three at interpreting the translations on the screen of the transmogrifier, placed on the table between the two groups. "The incident at the village doesn't make sense. He can't understand how it could be to the good of anything that Earth wants."

"The Lumian house can be divided, just as the houses of Robia are divided," Lyokanor, intelligence adviser to Kleippur, translated as the Lumians' showing vegetable presented their reply.

Kleippur had come to realize by then that the Lumian ability to travel from another world over a distance that defied imagination did not signify godlike unity of purpose among them, any more than it did any godlike mastery over the elements. The hair-faced one was known among robeings as the "Wearer" from the peculiar vegetable with framed pictures that he had worn on his arm at the time of the first meeting between Lumians and robeings. Lumians used such artificially made vegetables to talk to each other over great distances. That the Wearer had troubled to come to Kleippur's palace in person with his two colleagues brought some encouragement.

Kleippur looked across at the jellylike face glowing eerily inside the false outer casing filled with corrosive gases. "Why should any confederation on Lumia seek to send Kroaxia back into the ways of superstition and ignorance?" he asked. Lyokanor repeated the question in terms that the Lumian showing vegetable would better understand.

"Why should anyone on Earth want to support the revivalists in Padua and send everything here onto a reverse course?" Dave Crookes summarized for Zambendorf and Crookes.

Zambendorf sighed. It was clear that the policy being hatched behind the scenes was to turn Titan into a manufacturing colony. The incidents involving the military were almost certainly part of a campaign of manipulating the public's perceptions to suit it. He answered frankly. "There are some on Earth who want Padua's old leaders back in power. They want their cooperation in organizing Titan to supply the needs of Earth. The Taloids that they would wish to be in charge are the ones who command and control, not those like Arthur, who would liberate and enlighten."

"There are Lumians who seek to tame Robia's forests into becoming a producer for Lumia," Lyokanor said to Kleippur. "To this end, they desire to appoint as their lieutenants the priests and monarchs who would subdue robeings to the task, not those such as thee, who would free them to follow their own inclinations."

"But are not the ways of Lumia the ways of reason?" Kleippur objected. "For is it not the method of reason that enables them to travel beyond the sky? What disciples of reason would restore those who claim such privilege of supernatural insight that no robeing may contest them? Yet all of their supplications and incantations cannot cause a pebble to rise a finger's length from the desert sands."

Crookes translated. Zambendorf replied, "Reason emerged on Earth only after a long struggle. And it's far from over yet—as Arthur can see for himself from these latest events."

"But reason would win on Titan in the end, would it not?" Arthur pressed.

"We would be dishonest if we tried to pretend that there can be any guarantee," Zambendorf said. "But we will do all in our power to make it that way. That's why we came here."

Groork, Hearer-of-Voices, brother of Thirg, the Asker, who was missing in Kroaxia, looked at Kleippur. "We trusted the Wearer before, when the factions of Lumia clashed and the Wearer's words were true," he said.

Kleippur nodded and declared, "And we shall continue in our trust now." He turned and delivered the same message to the Lumian showing vegetable.

There was really nothing more to be said. It had been just a gesture, after all. The meeting ended after an exchange of formalities, and the Taloids escorted the visitors back to the NASO ground transporter waiting outside.

On the way back to the base, Zambendorf had an uncomfortable sense of foreboding as he gazed out at the rock and ice buildings in the twilight of Genoa City, with glimpses of strangely clad robots caught in the headlight beams. At heart, he was perhaps the truest kind of scientist, valuing reason and knowledge for their own sake. It had nothing to do with diplomas and qualifications. He had come to live the life he did out of scorn for a society that lavished wealth and accolades on charlatans, while paying its discoverers of real truths only tokens. Very well, Zambendorf had decided. If that was what the world wanted, that was what he would give it—and prosper comfortably from doing so, until it came to its senses. "When I am no longer able to make a living, then people might have learned something," he often said.

But in the Taloids he had encountered something different. In the process of freeing themselves from their own age of superstition and repression, their intellectual explorers had responded with an eagerness worthy of the pioneers of Earth's Renaissance toward the prospects of the new learning and enlightenment that had come with the Terrans. Comparing this to the stubborn rejection of reason that he had witnessed on Earth every day, Zambendorf had always felt a close affinity for Arthur and his endeavors to bring reason to his part of the Taloid world. Now all that was threatened. Zambendorf was not in control of events that were important to him, and that was not a feeling to which he was accustomed.

Abaquaan was also in one of his rare reflective moods. He hadn't spoken much since they had left Camelot and, for the last several minutes, not at all. Then, all of a sudden, he half raised an arm to indicate the scene outside the vehicle and murmured more to himself than to anyone in particular, "I wonder if we'll ever know who they were."

The remark caught the other two unprepared. "Who?" Crookes asked with a start, returning from some reverie of his own.

Abaquaan gestured again. "The aliens. The ones whose self-replicating factory program screwed up and started all this off . . . assuming you guys are right about it. I wonder if we'll ever find out who they were, what they were . . . Oh, I dunno."

"Pretty much like ourselves in the ways that matter, I shouldn't wonder," Crookes said. He shrugged. "Survival has to be the same kind of game anywhere. Look around you: even with machines."

"But they are fascinating questions," Zambendorf agreed. "Where did they originate, do you think, Dave? How far away might it have been? How long ago?"

Crookes turned up his hands. "It could have been light-years away, maybe millions of years ago—even before we existed."

"Could they still exist?" Zambendorf asked.

"Anything's possible, I guess," Crookes replied. "But if they do, then where are they? It seems strange that they'd set up whatever started all this and then never show up to collect. Don't you think?"

Zambendorf thought it over, then nodded. "Yes, I suppose you're right." He sounded disappointed. "If they were going to put in an appearance, then in all this time you'd think they'd have done it by now, wouldn't you? I guess it's all something that we'll just never know."

In the heart of one of the more densely mechanized areas, not very far away from the city, other scientists from the mission had been conducting an investigation that now occupied two permanent huts crammed with processors, analyzers, and electronic test equipment, along with a gaggle of NASO vehicles drawn up outside amid a tangle of cables. Inside one of the huts, Annette Claurier and Olaf Lundesfarne, two of the computer specialists, debated animatedly as they tried to make sense of the data patterns shifting and changing on the screens in front of them. The screens were monitoring the control processors of one of the stations where some types of Titan's machine animals were assembled and activated.

The mathematicians and robotics specialists believed that they had located the "genetic" software, passed down through countless generations, that was responsible for directing the assembly and initial start-up process. But certain of the "genomes" also seemed to contain huge blocks of redundant coding that had no apparent connection with any such essential process—strangely reminiscent of similar strings found in Terran DNA. But that was not to say that it didn't do *anything*.

"Look, the structure here is completely different from the surrounding functional code," the Frenchwoman insisted, pointing with a finger. "More ordered. But compare it with this here, which we know consists of assembly instructions. It's chaotic—clearly the result of an evolutionary process. But this other kind is regular and structured. I say it goes back much farther—from before anything started to evolve."

The Norwegian consulted another array of symbols. "But its activity index is rising. Look at these interrupt vectors. It's doing something."

"There's no correlation with the assembly routines or the initiation sequencing," Annette said. "Whatever it's doing has got no connection with making animals. It's something else, something autonomous."

A silhouette darkened the doorway in the partition dividing the hut, and the chief scientist, Weinerbaum, stepped into the light. "What's all the excitement in here?" he inquired. "Are we getting somewhere with those redundant blocks?"

Annette turned in her seat and waved a hand at the bank of glowing screens and control panels taking up one complete wall of the room. "I'm not so sure that 'redundant' is the right word, Professor," she replied. "But we've certainly stumbled on something here that's very different. It's showing extraordinary complexity and a strange tendency to self-assemble. This may sound silly, but I almost get the feeling we're reactivating something that's trying to come alive."

II

The Alien
Who Sought
Immortality

9

FOR THE WANT OF A NAIL, A SHOE WAS LOST; FOR THE want of a shoe, the horse was lost; for the want of a horse, the rider was lost; for the want of a king, the battle was lost . . .

Tiny changes can make huge differences. No method known to science, even in principle, can predict the emergence of such structures as cyclones, blizzards, and hurricanes from the molecular motions of the atmosphere. All animals grow from proteins, but biochemistry can say nothing about the forms that evolution will shape into species. One of the inevitable products of increasing complexity is greater unpredictability.

Hence arises the increasing variability of behavior that comes with progressively higher levels of neural development. Insects and other comparatively simple organisms react to their environments with genetically determined response patterns so unvarying that individuals are indistinguishable, and researchers have no hesitation in declaring that when *this* species is exposed to *that* stimulus, it *will* respond in such and such a particular way. Farther up the evolutionary tree—"up," of course, being defined as that direction in the radiating bush that points from the common origin to the part of the periphery occupied by ourselves—things become less determinate as individual traits begin to emerge, until at the level of our household pets we discern distinct personalities. The ultimate, for the present, is reached with fully intelligent, sapient beings, where anything goes and nothing that anyone is capable of thinking, wanting, liking, or doing should come as any great surprise anymore.

Variability means faster adaptability to change, which is what evolution is all about. Species that invite the mirth of amoebas and cockroaches by adopting neural development as their survival strategy achieve adaptability by supplementing genetic programming with acquired learning. With advancement, proportionately less of the total information passed from generation to generation comes as molecular coding—which is slow to change, slow to be refined through selection, and slow to diffuse through a population—and more of it as culturally transmitted knowledge in all its guises—which isn't. Discoveries made by a single genius can spread virtually instantaneously; the learning of an age is passed on intact to be built upon further. The result is a thermal runaway of ideas and techniques that rapidly culminates in the explosion of even higher-level organization and energy capture known as technological, industrial—followed almost immediately by spacegoing—civilization.

But as with every other innovation in a process whose roots twist back into veils of mystery billions of years ago, this step, too, brings its drawbacks. One of them is the wastefulness of the effort that individuals must expend in acquiring even a fraction of that information and laboriously building up the private collections of beliefs and experiences, hopes and memories, achievements and dreams that constitute the sum total to show for a lifetime . . . only to have most of it lost with them when they go. Learning is such hard work compared to the effortless way in which the genetic endowment is inherited and the equally simple—and, furthermore, quite enjoyable—procedure for passing it on.

The drawback, in a word, is mortality.

Throughout history the thought has troubled and depressed those who thought too much about it, at times driving them to suicide. And it was also a source of concern to some among a race called the Borijans, descended from a species of large, flightless squabblesome bird, who were part of a general pattern of six-limbed, laterally symmetrical life-forms inhabiting a planet called Turle, a thousand light-years from our solar system, over a million years before humankind existed to share its worries about such matters.

10

TURLE WAS AN AQUEOUS WORLD WITH AN OXYGEN-LACED atmosphere, a bit smaller than Earth but also a bit denser. It orbited farther away from its parent star, Kov, than Earth did from the sun, but Kov was a bit bigger and a bit hotter. The net result was that Turle ended up somewhat warmer: rain at the poles turned to snow during winter, but the polar regions never froze solid. A hefty proportion of Turle's surface was ocean—in fact, about eighty-five percent of it.

The land was distributed among three major continents—Elutia in the northern hemisphere, Magelia in the southern, and Xerse, straddling the equator to the east of them—and lots of islands of all sizes and shapes. A cluster of about a dozen islands off Elutia, plus a banana-shaped slice of the neighboring mainland, currently formed a political collaboration known as Hoditia. The relative permanence normally thought of in connection with a "nation" was not a characteristic of Borijan institutions. On the southern coast of one of Hoditia's inner islands was a city called Pygal, which had been "Pygal" since long before "Hoditia" came in to being, and would in all probability still be so long after Hoditia fell apart again. Fabrications of metals, silicates, and carbonates tended to last longer than constructions based on Borijan promises and good intentions.

On the outskirts of Pygal, overlooking a bay fringed by

low hills encrusted with architecture and spanned by slender-legged bridges, stood the Replimaticon Building. It was an immense, glittering silver and glass candelabra sprouting from a massive central trunk that radiated into five rainbow-hued towers. The towers in turn flared outward and upward to support varying numbers of ornate smaller pinnacles. As the sapient species descended from mammals on Earth housed itself in artificial caves, so the avian-descended sapients of Turle built themselves artificial trees.

South Tower Three of the Pink Intermediate zone of the Replimaticon Building extended from levels 30 through 55 and was dedicated to basic research. Levels 40 to 44 were concerned with advanced computation and coding systems. And on the forty-third level, on the eastern side of the building, facing inland, was a collection of offices and lab space whose precise function remained wrapped in security—as was the case with most of what Replimaticon was up to—behind a door bearing the singularly unrevealing legend: PROJECT 380.

The lab had the angular, firm-jawed features of sleek cabinets, multicolored screens, and flashing instrument panels that befitted a cutting-edge industry, but it had also acquired the cluttery stubble that scientists everywhere seemed to need as an aid to inspiration. There was a workbench along the rear wall, partly screened off by pastel-colored equipment cubicles and consoles, as if rolled-up sleeves and soldering irons were not fitting to the image of the otherwise sophisticated surroundings. Assorted tools lay scattered along it, along with a number of electronics assemblies in various stages of evisceration: boxes of screws, chips, and other components; reels of colored wire; and the remains of a technician's lunch enshrouded in its carry-out wrappings. The arty designs worked into the mural decor were obscured by the purple leaves and fronds of proliferating plants that one of the secretaries had brought in, the symmetries lost behind unthinkingly positioned shelves, travel and spacecraft posters, technical reference charts, and a map of the Pygal transit tube network. A whiteboard on the wall was covered in program code and a flow diagram, partly erased to make room for a shopping reminder and a message for somebody that the part for his skybus had come in. That much was all fairly typical of a computing research workplace anywhere, really.

Not typical at all was the large plastic-topped table standing in the open area of floor between the cubicles. It measured five feet or so along each side and supported a square enclosure of transparent walls about a foot high, like a wide, shallow fish tank. The enclosure contained a number of solid blocks of various shapes, a ramp, and some steps made of wood. Lying immobile beside them was an artificially constructed replica of a red furry animal the size of a small house cat. It had a pointed, vaguely foxlike face, but with floppy ears like a spaniel's, a manelike ruff running the length of its spine, and no tail. In keeping with the predominant pattern of life on Turle, it was six-limbed. Four of them were legs, with the front ones longer than the rear, resulting in a semiupright posture that gave height and scope for the two four-toed rudimentary prehensile paws extending from the shoulders. It was called a veech, and variants of it inhabited tropical regions all over Turle. An umbilical of thin wires ran from a socket at the back of the artificial veech's head, via a hinged overhead support arm, into racks of hardware showing lights and humming with cooling fans behind the table.

Costo Sarvik checked the interface connections and verified on a monitor that the instrumentation control programs were running, then looked across at the two other Borijans standing on the far side of the table. "Now we'll see if this clockwork shoe polisher that you came back with is any good," he said to Prinem Clouth. "Where did you get it from, a flea market?" He smiled crookedly at his double-edged witticism. "We could have saved ourselves a lot of time and gone to a toy shop."

"There's nothing wrong with that veech," Clouth shot back. "It's way beyond anything from any toy shop, and you know it. It's your simulation coding that we should be worrying about."

"Who is a metal basher like you to be criticizing anybody's coding? The coding is clean. You'll see."

"Why the barrier, then? Afraid it'll jump out and bite?" Clouth asked sneering.

"Don't be ridiculous," Sarvik said.

"Real veeches don't bite," Clouth remarked needlessly.

"We'll be lucky if this one that you've come up with moves at all," Sarvik told him.

To Terran ears—had any Terrans existed at the time—the voices would have sounded high-pitched and screechy. The Borijan form was bipedal and upright, a short bulbous body balanced on elongated legs whose musculature was concentrated mainly in the upper part, resulting in a somewhat strutting gait. They had large, round eyes, independently mobile in a scraggy face that widened in the upper part to accommodate them, and had lost all body feathering except for the top of the head, which was crested on males. Head plumage could be virtually any combination of hues and in Sarvik's case was green with orange side flashes. The lower face was formed around a degenerate beak structure and hence was fairly rigid and not very expressive. What had once been wings had degenerated and migrated upward and forward, becoming membranous structures that extended over the shoulders from either side of the head. These membranes, which could function independently like the eyes, were the Borijans' speech organs, and contributed to their "facial" expressions as well. They also afforded an auxiliary passage for respiration.

Borijans liked bright colors. Beneath his lilac lab smock Sarvik was wearing a sleeveless crimson jacket over a yellow shirt with white brocade and Pickwickian breeches of a bright blue satiny material that turned green where the creases flexed. He ruffled his epaulets opposite ways in the Borijan equivalent of a "hrmmph!" and turned his attention to stepping through a preliminary test sequence, turning one eye toward the console display and keeping the other trained on the veech.

Prinem Clouth, violet-crested and clad in a matching two-piece outfit trimmed in ocher, rested his four-fingered hands on the tabletop outside the enclosure and fell quiet. Borijans rarely discussed, consulted on, or debated anything. They *argued*.

Leradil Driss, the other person in the group, busied herself with making final adjustments to the camera, motion-analysis lasers, and other recording sensors she had set up. She was a recent arrival at Replimaticon, and Sarvik hadn't worked out yet what her probable line would be. Clouth's part was practically done, and Sarvik was pretty sure he was all set to decamp with the software and deal Sarvik out. But in fact, Sarvik had set things up in a way that would cut Clouth out. He felt a chortling inner glow with the anticipation of it.

The Borijans' industries ran ceaselessly in vast underground and undersea plants that used fusion energy from seawater and churned out abundance. Although they themselves had not ventured beyond the Kovian system of eleven planets, their robot ships sought out distant worlds to seed with self-replicating factories that supplied the home worlds from the resources of other stars. The wealth-creating capacity of Borijan technology had therefore passed beyond the stage where the instinct to compete could find meaningful satisfaction from pecuniary profits based on material need. Hence, the term "corporation" to describe the form of organization that individuals formed for attaining common gain didn't really apply.

Replimaticon was best described as a "connivance." As with a corporation, the entity continued to exist while the individuals it included came and went. But instead of being bound by a contract that exchanged their services for income, the members of a connivance—either as individuals or as separately convened subgroups—actually bought themselves in by placing a stake, because they perceived enough common interest for the moment to benefit from the arrangement. In Sarvik's case, what he gained was access to the equipment he needed to pursue his ideas, and the benefit of working with others whose skills would help bring them to fruition. What Replimaticon stood to gain was a share of the proceeds from the final product—provided that they could pin Sarvik down into disclosing what the final product was before he got to a stage where he could abscond with the information and cut a better deal somewhere else—which he would do unless someone like Clouth put all the pieces together and did it to him first.

So why bother with another deal elsewhere when he already had one here, with Replimaticon? That was the whole point of the game. The "gain" that connivances were set up to promote was to fleece, con, or bamboozle—generally to outdo in whatever way the opportunity of the moment offered—one or more of the other factions or the umbrella organization itself before the others did the same or better. Judging who was about to pull a scam on whom was critical. Periodically everything would fall apart, at which point the pieces usually realigned themselves into fresh rivalries and under new flags of convenience. Keeping accounts and settling scores were where the Borijans' motivation came from and what gave them their kicks. Hence, connivances tended to be fragile and precarious affairs, constantly in a state of flux—which was typical of just about every kind of institution to have come out of the various Borijan cultures. That was why their "nations" rarely lasted very long, either.

Sarvik's specialty was artificial machine intelligences, which had become quite advanced, as evidenced by the totally automated, self-replicating manufacturing systems the Borijans were able to send to other stars. In particular, he had learned much about the circulating, self-modifying patterns of neural activity that constituted "consciousness" and "personality." His latest line of research had to do with developing techniques for extracting them from their biologically constrained neural substrate and converting them to other forms that could be uploaded into artificial, potentially everlasting bodies. By this means Sarvik hoped to find an answer to the problem of mortality he had brooded on for many years. And of the three people in the lab, only he knew that that was what the business with the veech was really all about.

"Aren't you ready with all that paraphernalia of yours

yet?" he griped at Leradil. "It's only some simple tests. Anyone would think you were rediscovering biology."

"Someone has to be thorough," she said, infuriating him deliberately by repositioning one of the laser probes yet again.

"Shows lack of confidence," Clouth commented.

"Oh, so now you're a psychologist?" Leradil's tone was cool, with just a hint of sarcasm. She had a yellow crown with red streaks and wore a loose-fitting orange dress gathered in the middle and hanging to the knees. Her style was to provoke by refusing to be provoked, Sarvik had noted, which could not have been better calculated to irk him and added another few points to their personal account. "Everything's set here," she finally pronounced. "Why are we waiting? Let's go."

Sarvik tapped a code into the console and checked the response. "Loading now," he confirmed. It took about thirty seconds. Then, in its enclosure of transparent walls, the veech stirred, opened its eyes as if awakening from sleep, and then looked up and about itself sharply as if suddenly bewildered by its surroundings.

"You see. It's fine," Clouth said, showing both hands in an open gesture. He watched for a few seconds as the veech turned its head this way and that, then shook it as if trying to get rid of the wires at the back. "Is that all it's going to do?" he asked derisively.

"Can't you wait and see?" Sarvik said.

"I have to be sure to get this right the first time, in case it turns out to be a one-time thing," Leradil told both of them.

The veech got up, shook its head again, scratched at the surface of the table, and then began to explore the objects around itself suspiciously. For an artificial animal its movements were uncannily authentic, but neither Clouth nor Leradil was about to concede anything to Sarvik by saying so.

Only Sarvik knew that the coding pattern transferred into the veech's optronic brain had actually been extracted from that of an anesthetized real veech. It was a one-way procedure in which the neural configuration was absorbed and converted layer by layer from the outside in and the original carbon-chemistry brain was destroyed. Because of the way he had arranged things, everyone else who had been or still was involved in the project knew either about the process for extracting the code from the real veech or about the process for implanting it in the artificial one, but none of them knew about both. Only Sarvik and two of Replimaticon's directors knew that here was the first step toward freeing Borijan minds from their prison of biologically imposed mortality and rewriting them into purpose-designed bodies that could have any form and virtually limitless powers, and need never die.

Marog Kelm, the neural decrypter who had perfected the code-extraction process, believed that the goal was to develop a technology for keeping backup copies of individuals in data banks so as to be able to re-create them genetically in the event of a fatality. But Kelm was out of the picture now, having been maneuvered into cashing in his stake with Replimaticon in order to buy into a deal with Cosmopolitan Life, Health & Accident Insurance that would soon prove worthless, all the time believing it was *he* who was double-crossing Sarvik. So not only had a possible source of exposure been eliminated, but Kelm's removal from the internal shareout schedule had increased Sarvik's credit stake at Replimaticon by a respectable margin. Ah, the sweet stench of success!

Prinem Clouth had been a party to setting up Kelm and so knew that the story about preserving backup copies was a phony. *He* believed that the code was a synthetic veech simulation created by Sarvik and had developed the modified optronic brain to run it in. He had also obtained the artificial veech to house the modified brain, but naturally without divulging where from—why would anyone give valuable information to somebody who didn't need to know? But through his own efforts on the side, Sarvik had ascertained that it was from a manufacturing connivance called Toymate that specialized in smart artificial pets. Hence, Sarvik was fairly sure that Clouth was working on a deal with Toymate to purloin the technology jointly and give Toymate a greatly improved product line. But Sarvik judged that there would be time enough to take care of Clouth later.

Which left Leradil Driss, whom the directors had brought in because the project needed somebody versed in animal behavior to evaluate the efficiency of the transfer process. But from common caution and experience Sarvik assumed that there was more behind it. She could have been a spy put in by the directors to find out exactly what Sarvik's project was aiming at. Or possibly she was working some kind of scam of her own to sell all of them out, such as pirating Clouth's deal with Toymate—which was another reason for Sarvik to hold off in that direction, since what Clouth believed to be true was planted and wouldn't do him any good; nor, therefore, would it be of any use to Leradil if she stole it. In any case, Sarvik certainly hoped she was up to something. He wouldn't want to think there was a flake in the team.

The mechanical veech that thought it was a real veech knocked over one of the wooden blocks with its forelimbs and reared backward in alarm.

"You almost got that part right," Leradil said to Sarvik, which was about as close as Borijans got to actually parting with a compliment.

He was going to have to keep a close eye on her to find out what she was up to, Sarvik thought to himself.

11

"LOOK AT THIS LOG OF HER ACCESSES IN THE LAST week," Sarvik said, indicating one of the screens on the console beside the desk in his office next to the main lab area—a pointless gesture, since nobody was watching. "Twenty-seven of them are to files written in extended-base hypercode. And they were open for long periods. She's supposed to be an animal behavior specialist. What kind of animal behavior specialist understands extended-base hypercode? I tell you, she's been put in here to do some digging for somebody. Either those mammal brains upstairs who con shares by pretending to run this place, or some other organization outside that's probably just as big. For a start, obviously, we have to find out which."

Nobody had said that Leradil wasn't a spy or that Sarvik shouldn't find out. Borijans made everything sound contentious through habit. A calmer voice from a speaker grille in the top center of the console panel answered Sarvik's high-tension sputterings. At the same time a view of a campus complex appeared on the large central screen, with a superimposed image of a diploma.

"I got into the Gweths University records system as you said, and her degree checks out." The picture disappeared and was replaced in rapid succession by a shot of a suborbital dartliner in flight, a view of a hotel lobby, a restaurant menu, and a catalog from a fashion store. "But airline archives and credit receipts for the years '34 through '37 show inconsistencies for the time that she says she spent in Yordisland"—the screen showed a map of a former, short-lived Turlean political agglutination—"when it was still part of Chearce, before the Seven-Coasts League broke up. I think she's covering up something there—very likely a part of her background that she doesn't want to advertise in Replimaticon. That says to me that she's from somewhere outside." The visual accompaniment ended with a red query mark that grew to fill the screen, then began spinning and shrinking into the center, where it vanished.

Sarvik's principal assistant—and one that he could always rely on to be trustworthy, unlike Borijans—was the latest and most advanced of his artificial intelligences: GENIUS (GENeral Intelligence Universal Simulation) 5. Sarvik had intended the acronym sarcastically when he had coined it, but artificial intelligence had not yet progressed to the stage of deviousness that characterized the natural product, and GENIUS 5 accepted its name unquestioningly—in fact, almost proudly—as meaning exactly what it said.

GENIUS added, "I thought of checking the airline data and credit transactions myself. It took eight minutes flat. A cinch. I don't know how you meat brains ever managed on your own at all." A caricature of a Borijan head wearing a dumb expression appeared on the screen to underline the point.

Sarvik's epaulets bristled. "Watch you don't get too big for your boxes, or I might start pulling plugs," he squawked. "It's only because of the clear superiority of biology that *you* are able to experience any mindlike processes at all."

"Clear superiority, huh?"

"I'd have thought it patently obvious."

"Oh, is that so?" The faces of Pezamin Greel and Marduk Alifrenz appeared side by side on the screen, retrieved from Replimaticon's personnel records. They were the directors who knew the complete story behind Sarvik's research. "In that case, why is it that you and your two friends upstairs that you don't want the others to know about are working so hard on transferring yourselves into obviously superior nonbiological hosts? It seems a funny way to want to go if you don't call it improvement." GENIUS drew a series of representations of progressively more advanced life-forms, starting with a single cell and going on through a fish, a reptile, a bird, a Borijan, a primitive computing complex, and a schematic of Turle's planetary net. It ended with another query mark, enclosed in a circle and underscored by the caption THEN WHAT? "Surely you didn't imagine that you were the end of the line, did you?"

"We've been through all that," Sarvik said. "The advantages are purely physical, but I don't suppose that a heap of glass wafers could be expected to understand that." The word "ratty" appeared on GENIUS's doodling screen, cycling through a sequence of styles and colors. Sarvik sniffed, unimpressed. "What do you know of the billion-year evolutionary heritage that we possess? I assure you that what you think is thinking constitutes nothing more than incidental activity at the dimmest fringes of conscious-ness."

"If you're saying I can't think anything, then how can I think that I think? If I do think that I think, then what you've just said doesn't stand." CONTRADICTION! flashed jubilantly on the screen. "When you can compute products of twenty-digit numbers in nanoseconds, you might know something. Sometimes I wonder if biological systems could ever become fully conscious at all. DNA was just nature's way of making machines."

Sarvik got up and noticed that a pot of some kind of hanging leaves with pointy-petaled, off-white blossoms from the departmental secretary's ever-expanding horticul-tural collection had invaded his office again, finding a place on the top of the document cabinet, where it blocked the line of sight from the desk to one end of his wall planner. He moved the pot and saw behind it the reminder to him-self of his appointment with Dr. Queezt that morning, which had slipped his mind. "For something that makes such a fuss about nanoseconds, the amount of time that you waste bickering over trivia is incomprehensible," he mut-tered irritably as he carried the offending plant back out into the lab. "Could we stop emulating the superficialities of cognizant processes and get back to the matter at hand? We need to find out more about this Driss woman. My in-stinct tells me that she's up to something big." He set the pot down on the control cubicle of the holo-encoder, nudg-ing it precariously between a riot of yellow spears and a tangle of green tracery spouting stars of bright red velvet.

GENIUS's voice followed him to the grille in the display panel of the multi-D graphic analyzer. "Questionable: the wisdom of being guided by this thing you call instinct. Where are your facts?"

"You'll just have to accept it as indicative of the superi-ority of naturally evolved minds," Sarvik said.

"And you might take it as indicative of the superiority of precisely engineered minds that you're supposed to meet Dr. Queezt at Pygal Central Hospital in twenty minutes," GENIUS retorted.

"Thank you, I *am* aware of that," Sarvik snarled, furious at himself for letting the machine get a point up on him needlessly.

"You don't seem to be doing much about it," GENIUS remarked. Sarvik stumped back into the office to get his coat from the rack there. The words RETENTION IMPAIRED (CHUCKLE) greeted him from the screen. "Just imagine needing half the morning and moving yourself physically across the city in order to exchange sound waves," GENIUS taunted while Sarvik was putting on his coat and securing his office. "I could have it done in less time than you take to forget a phone number. Admit it. The next stop's the fossils department."

"Maybe, but if so, it's still a while away yet," Sarvik said. "Meanwhile, there are some more checks on Leradil Driss that I want you to make." He gave GENIUS the details while putting papers and a few other items he wanted to take with him into his briefcase. Then, with a flourish that evoked a warm feeling of malevolent satisfaction, he entered the *Interactive Disable* code to turn off the speech/vision interface and leave GENIUS undistracted to concentrate on tracing network routings and cracking data protection protocols. After checking over the office one last time, he locked the door and set the security trips and marched briskly from the lab to go out into the city of Pygal.

12

MOST BORIJAN ARCHITECTURE REFLECTED THE THEME of upward-branching arboreal forms, and Borijan tastes in everything were toward generous ornamentation. The cities that resulted rose like forests of colorful cacti, splaying out from broad, conoidal trunks into groupings of variously devised columns and spires forming clusters at different levels. The upper parts of those structures often overlapped and merged via connecting bridges and terraces to turn the upper regions into a vast artificial canopy where most of the day-to-day living and business took place. Heavier-duty operations, such as power distribution and freight handling, were carried out in the lower parts of the trunks, and an undergrowth of support installations and service buildings sprang up in the areas between.

Sarvik took a core elevator to the Pink Intermediate midlevel terminal and boarded one of the six-passenger autocabs waiting in the City Inbound rank. They were orange with a white stripe along each side and approximately ovoid—a universally symbolic shape found in designs and artifacts from every culture in Borijan history. Always derisive of the authority that ran the transit system, Pygalers called them the "electric enemas," from the resemblance of a string of them passing through the glass-sided tubes threading through the city to a brand of laxative capsules that came in transparent packs.

"Central Hospital," he told the black mesh eardisk at the top of the director panel. "Dr. Queezt, in neuroprosthetics. I think it's Blue Uppermid zone somewhere, north side."

96

"How come you don't know?" the cab sneered. "Getting forgetful? Is that why you're going to see a brain booster?"

"I don't need to know. It's your job to check it out," Sarvik retorted. "That's supposed to be part of the service. You want me to drive this thing for you as well?"

The cab lapsed into a sulky silence and computed a route by using the current bulletin of traffic conditions around the city. It called the hospital's administrative computer and flashed an estimated arrival time. Dr. Queezt's diary manager returned a message saying that Queezt would be delayed thirty minutes. Sarvik cursed himself for giving Queezt the initiative. He should have asked for a confirmation first, before letting the cab reveal that he was already on his way. Very likely, the damn machine had done it on purpose to even its score with him. So now he would be starting the meeting a point down. Well, that would make it all the more of a challenge.

The cab slid out from a terrace of South Tower Three, revealing the pink, sunlit cliffs of the Replimaticon Building falling away below. Why had people once been so indirect about things? Sarvik wondered as he sat back and gazed at the view across the bay. Always having to keep up pretenses and hiding their true motives behind measures of profit. If the truth were admitted, hadn't the *real* fun all along been in trading one-upmanships and delivering the comeuppances when one could get away with it? Some nostalgics said the old ways had been more genteel. Maybe so. But the modern ways were more honest.

He killed thirty minutes browsing around the stores in the plaza below the hospital's entrance foyer to avoid having to give a receptionist the satisfaction of telling him he'd have to wait. When he did finally present himself, he was directed promptly up another four levels to Queezt's office. His first impressions were of a mix between an electronics hobby shop and a cerebral dissection laboratory. On shelves along one side of the room were jars of preservative containing Borijan and animal brains and parts of brains, most of them showing the glints of implanted crystal chips and tiny wires. Below the shelves was a glass tabletop laid out like a display counter, with microassemblies of optronics wafers and crystalline chips no bigger than dewdrops. Queezt's desk stood in the corner opposite, backed by bookshelves, a data and communications panel above a smaller worktop, and a window giving a view of Pygal's urban seafront.

Queezt stood to greet Sarvik with a brief, formal handshake. The gesture gave away nothing; overt discourtesy was viewed as a cheap way of achieving a put-down without earning it, tantamount to fraud. He was tall in stature, his torso loosely draped on a bony, wide-shouldered frame, with a maroon crest fading to black at the back and mottled in white. His epaulets had a permanent upturned set suggestive of a mild leer, which provoked defensiveness and probably gave him an opening advantage in most of his dealings. He was wearing a short green surgical jacket opened at the neck to reveal a satiny brown shirt with a throat clasp of worked gold foliations surrounding a white oval stone. "Dr. Sarvik. I'm sorry that I had to put you off. In a place like this we sometimes get these emergencies that won't wait." In other words, *My time is more important than yours;* and he'd gotten the apology in before there was time for any objection. Point added and lead extended.

"These things happen," Sarvik said. "I take it you know where I'm from." Of course, any prudent professional would have had his computer check all available information on a stranger who called out of the blue for an appointment.

The leering epaulets drooped a fraction. "Er, no, as a matter of fact ... I've been very busy, you understand." Lame. But it would have taken greater resources than Queezt could probably command at short notice to penetrate Replimaticon's data security. A quick smile of satisfaction flickered across one side of Sarvik's face. Point regained.

"Replimaticon research, advanced cybercoding." Sarvik showed his teeth. "And you are Doctor Sulinam Queezt, specialist in cerebral augmentation implants and now offering replacement modules for impaired brains. Surgeon's degree from Stellem Academy of Space Medicine, 218; neural systems simulation, Porgarc Oceanic University, 224; seven years with MZB Psylog division, the rest in private consultancy; part-timing deals here at Central during the last two years, probably because of the use it gets you of their nanometric holoplex analyzer." In other words, Sarvik was from an outfit that didn't fool around with public-hospital-grade kiddy-toy computers when it came to code cracking. Two-all, game even. They sat down.

Queezt acknowledged this with the invitation, "A cup of graff, maybe?" Graff was a hot beverage made from a variety of dried ground seaweed and drunk universally around Turle.

"I will. As it comes." Sarvik set his briefcase down on the edge of the desk.

Queezt called to the room's domestic manager. "House. Two graffs, one plain, unsweetened. Hold calls."

"Okay," a synthetic female voice answered from the panel by the desk.

The desk was untidy with jottings and forms. There was a well-worn physiological reference work lying open; a receptacle for pens, fasteners, and office oddments fashioned from an animal skull; a vacation guide to one of Turle's submarine cities; and a book about how to outcon used furniture dealers by spotting valuable antiques—probably worthless, since dealers no doubt read the same books. A large chart on the wall, heavily annotated with handwritten notes, showed in detail the parts of the Borijan brain.

Queezt leaned his stick-limbed frame back in the chair and regarded his visitor unblinkingly with both eyes. "Very well, Dr. Sarvik," he said finally. "What's your deal?"

Sarvik extended a perfunctory hand to indicate the specimen jars and wired crystals at the other end of the room. "Why mess about with add-ons that just duplicate parts of brains? I can give us the whole thing: transfer of the complete personality into an artificial host. Think what you'd be able to offer with a capability like that."

"You mean a purpose-designed host? With augmented

physical capabilities? Extended senses, maybe? Additional senses?"

Sarvik shrugged. "Whatever's possible. Anything you like."

Such a speculation was not exactly new, but that didn't make it any the less interesting. Queezt nodded to say that the implied possibilities didn't need to be spelled out. Specially built bodies for extreme environments was one area where it could be applied. Spaceworks riggers that wouldn't need the complications of suits and biological life support was another. Or perhaps those who wanted to could try being birds again and fly as their distant ancestors had. Or try becoming fish or experiment with being insects. Sarvik said nothing about his thoughts of achieving immortality. If he could gain Queezt's cooperation without it, what would be the point in giving such information away free? The two scientists regarded each other for a few seconds with cordial, mutual mistrust.

A light came on over the small worktop in the corner behind Queezt's desk, and the domestic manager's voice announced, "Two graffs, one regular, one plain, unsweetened." The hatch from the building's utility conveyor system opened and delivered a white plastic tray carrying two filled cups, a partitioned dish of flavor additives, and spoons. A service dolly, resembling an upright vacuum cleaner with arms and a metal basket on top, rolled out from its stowage space a few feet away and transferred the tray to the end of Queezt's desk.

"A silly fantasy," Queezt declared, reaching for a cup. "We evidently read the same fiction. Now tell me what you're really offering."

Sarvik shrugged indifferently. "I've told you. If you don't want to come in, it'll be your loss. There are plenty more headwirers I can go to."

"You've probably already been to them and they threw you out," Queezt suggested.

"Aha!" Sarvik chortled. "So you put yourself last on the list, then, do you? It seems that I had a greater opinion of your ability than you have yourself. Maybe I will take it somewhere else. Who'd want to work with a self-admitted second-rater?"

"I admitted nothing of the kind. Who'd want to work with a crank?" Queezt retorted.

"When *you* can quote *my* résumé, *then* you might be qualified to judge who's a crank," Sarvik threw back.

"I tell you it's not feasible."

"If you had anything to do with it, I'm beginning to suspect, it wouldn't be."

"Grmmph."

"Hmmm?"

Queezt picked up his cup, tracking his hand with one eye and contemplating Sarvik with the other. "Just supposing— purely for the sake of argument—that I believed you. What would you want from me?"

Sarvik replied by leaning forward to open his briefcase and taking out a wallet of the kind used to carry circulating charge-array microrecording capsules. He selected one of the button-size disks and passed it to Queezt, who inserted it into a socket in the deskside panel. Sarvik gave him the coded key to unlock the contents, and a moment later one of the screens on the panel began showing a replay of later test runs with the mechanical veech. The animal ran up the wooden steps, turned and ran down again, tumbled the blocks about playfully, and tried to climb up the transparent wall of its enclosure. With full transfer of the veech's psyche, the umbilical wiring had been removed, and every detail of the surrogate's behavior was authentic.

"A toy veech," Queezt agreed condescendingly, and gave Sarvik a so-what look.

"Ah, but more than just that," Sarvik said. "It isn't running a clever simulation synthetic. It's hosting a direct transcription of the neural configuration extracted from a live animal. It's a real veech transposed into specially modified and extended optronics. Now who are you calling a crank?"

Queezt did a good job of hiding his surprise and looked pained. "Very well, so you managed to transfer a veech identity. But that wasn't what you said this was all about.

You said you could do it with a Borijan. What do you take me for?"

"I didn't say I could do it." Sarvik clucked. "If you'd listened, I said that I can get us there."

"Why use a veech, anyway?" Queezt objected. "Better to stay within the avian lineage. If you knew anything about comparative neural anatomy, you'd be aware that the organization of the mammalian third to fifth middle lobes is completely different."

"Nonsense," Sarvik answered dismissively. "A simple software transform handles it."

"What's the point?" Queezt challenged. "Why complicate things?"

"Greater generalization. Try thinking beyond your bits-of-brains horizon for a change."

Queezt sniffed. "Well, it appears that your own wider thinking hasn't proved adequate to the task; otherwise you wouldn't be here, would you? What do you want from me? It appears that you already have a source of suitable hardware and mental circuitry."

Sarvik indicated the screen again. "So far we have experimented only with animals. To extend the process farther and verify it at the Borijan level will obviously require Borijan subjects. However, we experience a distinct lack of ready volunteers." Sarvik rubbed his chin and curled his epaulets into a parody of a smile. "The, ah . . . the process is destructive to the original, you see. There isn't any way back, as it were."

Queezt thought for a few seconds and then nodded solemnly. "Oh, I see." It was all beginning to make more sense now.

Sarvik went on. "I thought of working out something along the lines of offering it to convicted criminals as an option, but you know how difficult the authorities can be to deal with." He gestured to indicate the surroundings generally. "Then it occurred to me that in a medical environment such as this, with people in all kinds of conditions . . ." He left it unfinished and repeated his crooked smile again.

"It might be possible to work out some kind of agreement with terminal patients." Queezt completed the thought for him. The proposition was clear now. Queezt sat back to consider it.

"They'd have nothing to lose," Sarvik said after a short silence, voicing the obvious for both of them.

"Hm. And on the other hand, they could gain a whole new extension," Queezt mused. "A somewhat unconventional one, maybe, I agree . . ."

"True."

"But an extension nonetheless."

Sarvik gave it a few more seconds to simmer. Then he asked, cocking an eye, "And do you know some that might be suitable, by any chance?"

Queezt nodded. "Oh, yes. And in some cases their impairment is purely physical. The neural codes could probably be extracted complete."

"That would be perfect."

Which left only one more immediate point to be sure they were clear about. "What would be my side of this?" Queezt inquired.

Sarvik shrugged. "Whatever you can work with the patients and their attorneys, I presume."

"Better than that, please, Dr. Sarvik," Queezt said in a forced weary tone.

"Very well. A quarter of the rights on the cerebral prosthetic business when we get to full replacement brains," Sarvik offered.

"*A quarter?*" Queezt screeched. "What do you think I am, a charity? Without me in it, there wouldn't *be* any prosthetic business. Three-quarters."

"*Three?*" Sarvik squawked back. "You're only supplying bodies. I'm giving you the rest on a plate. All right: sixty-forty."

"Which you wouldn't do if you had a viable alternative," Queezt pointed out. "Fifty-fifty."

Sarvik shook his head and rapped the desk with an extended finger. "Fifty-five and forty-five's my limit." He waited, knowing that Queezt knew there was something further.

"And?" Queezt prompted.

"Okay. There's also a side deal that's being worked with Cosmopolitan Life: backup copies on file, if we can make it nondestructive. It could be a big angle for them. I'll cut you in at ten percent of my share."

Queezt nodded that he understood. "Twelve and a half?" he ventured, studying Sarvik calculatingly with one eye while the other watched Sarvik's fingers drumming on the desk.

"Twelve and a half, then," Sarvik agreed. It didn't really matter, since he wasn't in on the deal with Cosmopolitan, which in any case was a ruse he'd set up to fool Marog Kelm. But it would boost Sarvik's story when Queezt verified—as he surely would—that Cosmopolitan was talking to somebody at Replimaticon.

They went over the kinds of things that could go wrong and how to deal with the lawsuits that would probably follow, and then argued about medical and scientific ethics. Sarvik left a half hour later, feeling pleased with his morning's work.

GENIUS 5 called him via his lapel phone while he was considering what to do for lunch. "I found some confidential records in Toymate which say that they put Leradil Driss inside Replimaticon to check on the story that Prinem Clouth is telling them," it said.

"Oh," Sarvik answered. It didn't feel right.

"Too confidential," GENIUS went on. "In fact, so confidential that nobody inside Toymate could have accessed them. There's no combination that factors to a valid code. And yet the protection against external penetration was ridiculously thin."

"What do you make of it?" Sarvik asked.

"The records were planted there by some other outfit as a cover to throw us off," GENIUS replied. "An outfit that's got some heavy-duty capability. In other words, whoever she's really working for is into something a lot bigger than making toys."

"Ah!" That sounded more like it. Sarvik gave a satisfied smile. "Isn't that just what I've been telling you all along?"

he said. "So what have you got to say about biological intuition now?"

13

THE DIRECTOR OF REPLIMATICON'S SECURITY AND ESPIOnage services was a former government operative by the name of Tuil Garma. With clear indication of a spy operating internally on behalf of an unknown agency for unknown reasons, the normal thing would have been for Sarvik to bring Garma in at that point as the connivance's specialist in such matters. However, Sarvik's own illicit delvings had brought to his notice the distinct proneness that people who involved Garma in their affairs seemed to have for coming to grief in their own entanglements, and his confidence in the wisdom of such a course of action fell considerably short of comfortable. Besides, he told himself, why rush to reveal to the world the nonpareil at security penetration GENIUS 5 was turning out to be? There was no doubt all kinds of juicy information hidden away in Replimaticon's most secure data levels. Owning something as formidable as GENIUS could, he reflected, prove to be the means of turning things around and slipping a big one over, himself, on Garma some day. Heh-heh-heh.

Accordingly, Sarvik decided to instigate some private espionage activity of his own. His first step consisted of recruiting GENIUS to create and launch out into the planetary net a viruslike software construction known as a boomerang. At the same time, he inserted sections of identifiable tracer code inconspicuously into the files that Leradil Driss had been snooping in.

A boomerang worked by first replicating into copies that

would find their way into the systems of other connivances, governing agencies, scientific institutions, and other organizations all over Turle. Those places took pains to try to prevent such penetration, of course, but as with all evolutionary contests, the advantage was constantly shifting from offense to defense and back again, never remaining the same for long or reaching the same stage of advancement everywhere at the same time. With GENIUS 5 as his ally, it seemed that for the moment Sarvik was ahead of much of the game. Once inside a target system, the boomerang would become active and search for the tracer codes that had been planted in the doctored files at Replimaticon. Any copy that succeeded would then retransmit itself back through the net to Replimaticon, bringing with it information on where it had returned from and what it had found there.

The hostile turned out to be a consortium of interests loosely federated under the name of Farworlds Manufacturing: a conglomerate of enterprises joined by the common attribute of being involved in the Borijan remote interstellar supply business.

The Borijan civilization numbered somewhere around thirty billion individuals spread across Turle, several of Kov's other ten worlds and their moons, and various artificial orbiting and freely mobile constructions in between, but they had never established colonies beyond their home planetary system. This had more to do with the innately suspicious and adversarial Borijan nature than with any lack of the knowledge or technology to do so. Put simply, no group or faction had ever been trusting enough to venture far into the void, leaving others in charge back home.

Supplying the material needs of a still-growing, resource-hungry culture of that magnitude placed an increasing strain on a single planetary system, however, and the Borijan response had been to tap in remotely to the limitless potential available from other stars that nobody else seemed to be using. They built immense, fully automated starships to go out and look for uninhabited and otherwise suitable mineral-rich worlds. Those worlds were then seeded with basic, self-replicating factory installations that transformed the entire surface into a self-organizing general-purpose manufacturing complex for products and the vessels to ship them home in, dedicated to supporting the Borijan solar system from afar. This had been going on for more than a century. A dozen supply worlds had so far been sown, and Farworlds Manufacturing, the leading operator in the overall enterprise, was responsible for five of them.

Sarvik's first move was to contact Farworlds Manufacturing's security director, a man called Umbrik, and inform him that Leradil Driss had been uncovered. Umbrik reciprocated two days later by confiding that Driss had been let go for ineptness. She announced her resignation from Replimaticon soon afterward on terms that left her stake there forfeit. It had doubtless been put up by her principals, but the outcome was none the less profitable to Sarvik for that.

By disposing thus of Farworlds' agent, Sarvik had collected points in profusion and shown himself a formidable adversary, with access to powerful means for getting to other people's secrets. Further, in handling the matter himself instead of giving it to Tuil Garma and Replimaticon's official security service, he had signaled that *he* was in control and therefore the person to deal with directly—never mind the firm. After all, they obviously wanted to deal over something that involved him, he reasoned. Otherwise, why would they have mounted such an elaborate operation to spy on his work? It came as little surprise, therefore, when he received an invitation shortly afterward from a man called Indrigon, of the Farworlds directorate, to get together and talk. Indrigon suggested meeting at the Farworlds headquarters, which was located two thousand miles away on the equatorial continent of Xerse. Sarvik, for his part, was conscious that these were not people to be taken lightly, either. He would not be looking for chances to notch up a petty initial point or two on this occasion.

14

THE SETTING WAS A PARTLY OUTDOOR TERRACE MIDWAY up the half-mile-high Farworlds Tower, which stood twenty miles inland from Gweths, one of the major cities of Xerse. Far below, a wide valley with a mirror ribbon of river winding among forested shoulders of hills extended inland toward distant mountains, while to the north the ocean lay behind a spit of headland that broke up into a chain of islands stretching to the horizon. Overhead, the higher reaches of the tower soared in overhanging cliffs of crystal that covered half the sky.

It was a leafy, flowery place, virtually a park in miniature, with mounded lawns, secluding shrubbery, backdrops of falling water, paths to walk on, and a lake. The Farworlds staff used it for relaxing and socializing. Sarvik met the three people from Farworlds in a low-walled niche set between rockeries and a screen of trellised climbing plants, where a cane table and chairs stood beneath a large red and white sunshade. Indrigon, sitting at the far end, and a woman called Lequasha, to Sarvik's right, introduced themselves as being from the directorate but gave no indication of their precise function. The third was Umbrik, the security chief whom Sarvik had contacted initially, doubtless there to see what he could glean of how Sarvik had penetrated the Farworlds system.

Actually, Sarvik had no idea if any of them was even on the continent of Xerse, since they were all using a telepresence hookup. He himself was remote coupled from a public booth in Pygal—he didn't trust Tuil Garma not to have bugged the in-house services at Replimaticon—and sitting in a worn chair that was beginning to shed its padding. The image of the cane chair and the table before him, along with the figures around it and the scenery behind, was a visual composite from data streams originating in different places, varied continuously by the spectacles he was wearing to match his head and eye motions. The arms and other parts of his body that he could see were interpolated from the booth's video pickups, which were sensitive enough to capture a loose thread on his sleeve or a rough edge on one of his fingernails. The only thing that clashed with the illusion was a stale, garlicky odor pervading the booth. Probably some frustrated city worker with rustic yearnings had decided to take an instant vacation somewhere while eating lunch.

After the introductions, Umbrik opened with the comment that security was the paramount consideration in an organization like Farworlds. Sarvik had caused considerable consternation by breaching the defenses, and naturally the directors were anxious to learn about the ways in which the system was vulnerable. Umbrik conveyed without any great excursion into subtlety that the rewards could be significant for parting with even a little of the pertinent information.

Sarvik took such a transparent affront to his credulity as a test to see whether they were talking to somebody of a caliber worth the time of dealing with at all. If they imagined that he believed that two members of the directorate of an operation the size of Farworlds would involve themselves personally in an unexceptional discussion of security measures, he said, then they were wasting his time. If the management really had fallen to being that inane, then whom should he apply to for Umbrik's job, right now? The insult earned him his due respect, and the way was open for more serious business.

But among the Borijans nothing was ever simple and direct. Lequasha took things to the next level. She was tall and lean, with a dark blue crown streaking to black in places. Her attire, a trousered suit with a short, high-necked jacket, all in somber maroon, added to her general air of aloofness.

"Let's stop playing games," she suggested. That was fine by Sarvik. He was there purely to see what he could find out. "Even if you don't want to discuss details, what tipped you off about Leradil Driss must have been the pointers in the Toymate files that it was Toymate who infiltrated her. Fair enough. They were bogus, and we put them there." Lequasha glanced sideways at her colleagues with one eye. "Why waste more time denying it?" They returned negative shakes of their heads to indicate that they agreed. She turned back to Sarvik. "So it's obvious that we know about the animal emulation you've produced that's good enough to make toy veeches behave like real ones . . . But *toys*, Dr. Sarvik?" One of Lequasha's epaulets quivered on the verge of disdain. "*We* send intelligences out to other stars— intelligences that reproduce themselves and manage entire manufacturing complexes. Leradil Driss was put inside Replimaticon merely to update us on what the coding research labs are doing these days, because advanced coding is of interest to us. When you saw through the Toymate deception, it occurred to us that perhaps a person of your abilities might be interested in more profitable employment here than in your present situation. That's all. Don't go treating yourself to false flattery on any other account."

But Sarvik wasn't buying that line, either. They knew what he was worth. If they'd gotten into Toymate, they were aware that the whole spiel about toys had been to set up Prinem Clouth. "Oh, come on," Sarvik said, feigning impatience. "Have they relegated you to junior tech recruitment? Places like Farworlds use smart-toy animators to brew the graff. If you think that's my level, then just say so, and we can call it a day."

"We get all kinds of people trying to edge in here," Umbrik said. "It's a lot of action. Everyone wants a slice."

"It was you that asked me here," Sarvik reminded them.

"You think as a favor?" Lequasha asked him.

"Suppose you tell me what you want," Sarvik suggested. Then, feeling that he had an edge, he risked adding, "Assuming that you know. Frankly, I'm beginning to wonder."

Indrigon had been following from the far end of the table

but saying little. He was squat and sturdy, florid-faced, and dressed in a mix of reds, blues, and metallic grays that said he was a person who could do pretty much as he pleased. Sarvik had already tagged him as the decisive influence among the three. At that point Indrigon leaned forward. Sarvik rested his hands on the edge of the cane table and waited. It felt distractingly like the chipped countertop inside the public telepres booth at Pygal.

"Very well," Indrigon said. It meant that Sarvik had satisfied him that he was distrusting enough to do business with. "In the course of the past century the syndicates involved in remote manufacturing have built up a unique store of experience and knowledge, Dr. Sarvik. Their projects run themselves without Borijan intervention, operating for decades, across interstellar distances. Farworlds is way ahead of any of its rivals. We think that the time has come to capitalize on that lead."

Sarvik smoothed his epaulets and nodded. It would have been foolish to disagree. "Yes."

"Colony ships," Lequasha came in. Sarvik's epaulets pricked up in interest. He looked with one eye at her, at Indrigon with the other. "Interstellar colonization," she said. Sarvik shifted the eye watching her to join the one looking at Indrigon.

Indrigon nodded. "It's time for Borijans to get out of the Kovar System at last and go to other stars. The benefits to the first organization to do it would be enormous. Accordingly, as a pilot project—and this is a highly confidential matter—we are formulating plans to redesign the Searcher ships into generation craft capable of carrying people. Survival at other stars will involve a massive deployment of machines. That will require computing methods more sophisticated than anything we've used so far." He gestured as if the rest didn't really need saying. "Hence our interest in the most advanced work currently going on at places like Replimaticon."

Sarvik considered the suggestion skeptically. Borijans always acted under a compulsion to find a flaw somewhere. "You'd never get anyone to go," he declared flatly, "apart from natural dupes and losers—and who'd want to entrust a starship to the likes of them?"

"We think there's a solution to that," Indrigon told him.

"What?" Sarvik asked.

"Do you seriously expect us to tell you?" Umbrik scoffed.

"Do you expect me to be interested if you don't?" Sarvik shot back.

"We'll make that a condition of the deal," Lequasha offered.

"What kind of a deal are we talking about, anyway?" Sarvik asked.

Indrigon turned one palm upward this time. "Your expertise for a share. You head up the software development groups."

"How much are you asking for on a time basis?"

Indrigon made a face. "All of it, Dr. Sarvik. We're talking about a total commitment."

Sarvik would have to pull up his other stakes. There would be no time for Replimaticon as well. "I'll have to think that over," Sarvik said.

"We assumed that would be the case," Indrigon replied. "Further discussion would be contingent upon your agreeing. Could we have an answer, say, by tomorrow?"

"Tomorrow?" Sarvik stared at them incredulously. "You're out of your minds. What do you want, a serious coding chief or a bubblehead? I need fifteen days."

"Impossible. Do you think we're growing flowers? Two days, then," Indrigon answered.

"Why rush? You're putting together a starship program, not a weekend dance. Ten."

"Four."

"Eight."

"Six."

And, amazingly, they settled on seven.

After decoupling at the booth in Pygal, Sarvik took a long walk and stopped at a graff shop to sit for a while and think. He believed the story about modifying Searchers into generation ships, he decided. The Farworlds people's body signals had rung true, and it would have invited too many awkward questions and needless complications if the story had been fabricated. He believed the story as far as it went. But his instinct told him that there was more to it yet.

The time had come for Borijans to get out of the Kovar System, Indrigon had said. Why now? It was the reason Indrigon had given that seemed weak. Why the haste? Why all of a sudden was Farworlds in a hurry to transport people to other stars? It would be interesting, Sarvik told himself, to try to find out.

15

THE SCREEN SHOWED A CARTOONLIKE DEPICTION OF A Borijan snoozing while a computer sagged under an avalanche of numbers pouring into it through a giant funnel.

"So," GENIUS 5's voice said from the grille in the top of the console panel, "you had a walk around Pygal and stopped for some graff. Very nice. But then, I suppose biological minds have to deactivate periodically, don't they? Carbon-chemistry hardware just can't hack it. It's all those big molecules. They come apart under the strain." A figure formed from a double helix went into a tizzy, unwound, and collapsed; then a cuboid computer appeared with arms folded, striking a Superman pose, while the words SILICON, YEAH! flashed mockingly above.

"I had some thinking to do," Sarvik said. "If it were something that you'd ever experienced, as opposed to just shuffling bits around mechanically all day, you'd know that answers that need real judgment don't just pop out on command."

"Brains are just soggy learning networks," GENIUS replied. "A neuron is as predictable as a molecular gate. Indeterminacy arises from complexity in both. So where's the difference?"

"Look, I don't have time for any of that now," Sarvik said. "I had a very informative meeting with the Farworlds people. They're planning to convert Searchers into generation ships and send Borijans out of the Kovar System."

"So they say. And you believe them?"

"Yes."

"Why?"

"I've told you before—biological intuition. It's not something you can comprehend, so don't worry about it. The project will need heavy computing. They want us to go in with them to take care of advanced software." It was part of the present deal that the rights on GENIUS were Sarvik's, not Replimaticon's, although there was a complicated formula that would give Replimaticon a share of future attributable earnings. Sarvik had gleaned that a large part of Farworlds' interest in him lay in gaining access itself to the means that had enabled Sarvik to break its security.

An image of starfields and a nebula appeared on the screen, with the words DISTANCE ... VOID ... MIGRATION ... SEEDS IN WIND ... COLONIZE GALAXY coming and going to give glimpses into GENIUS's associative musings on the subject. Finally, ASTRONOMY/ASTRONOMERS flashed portentously. Then GENIUS explained. "It may surprise you to learn that I haven't been exactly idle myself. While you were out doing your slow-motion thinking, another copy of the boomerang came back. With all the tracers."

Both sides of Sarvik's face looked up sharply. "*All* of them?"

"Why do I keep having to repeat things? Yes, that's what I said: *all*. Interesting?"

It was very interesting. Because that much couldn't be said for the copy that had returned from Farworlds, where only some of the tracer data had found their way. So, while Leradil Driss had, as far as could be ascertained, given

Farworlds only some of the information purloined from Replimaticon, she had been passing all of it to somebody else. This suggested that she had been as much a plant in Farworlds as in Replimaticon and had supplied Farworlds with just enough information to preserve her cover. All the time she really had been spying for someone else yet again.

"So?" Sarvik said, not bothering to voice the obvious.

"It retrieved portions from various sections of the most confidential files of ASH," GENIUS answered.

Sarvik frowned on one side. "ASH? You mean the astronomers?"

The Astronomical Society of Hoditia—actually world-wide in membership, with some of Turle's most prestigious scientists on its list—was a purely professional institution, normally considered to be above the kind of deception and double dealing connivances reveled in. For obscure reasons the association insisted on retaining a national title and hence had to change its name whenever the political grouping that contained its headquarters on Vayso—one of the islands in what was currently called Hoditia—broke up and realigned.

"Yes," GENIUS confirmed. "ASH. There's been a lot of communication between the directorate of Farworlds and some of the association's senior members. I can't tell you what about, because the references don't point to anything that's accessible through the net. But whatever it is, it's big enough to get some of the planet's top scientists into the espionage business."

And big enough, maybe, to change his whole lifestyle for keeps, Sarvik thought to himself. Which way to go next? The best was usually the most audacious, he had long ago decided. He contacted Leradil Driss—the person he'd just gotten expelled from two positions in as many days—and told her he had a proposition that she might find interesting.

The zhill was a large marine avian that laid eggs, breathed air, and looked like a tooth-beaked submarine. It belonged to a line whose distant ancestors had returned to an aquatic environment; its feathers were now transformed to leathery scales, and its limbs had adapted into rudimentary flippers in front, lateral fins in the center, and twin rudderlike tails at the rear.

Sarvik met Leradil Driss in a glass-walled gallery projecting into an underwater seascape, where visitors could sit and view, or talk, or think while zhills turned and dived over and around. Other kinds of Turlean ocean life wheeled and cavorted about them; nosed, crawled, sifted, and slithered in the sand and mud at the bottom; or glared balefully from fissures in the rocks and the holes underneath. Sarvik had suggested meeting at the Pygal zoo. Too many connivances cooperated with information agencies that peddled snippets gleaned from bugging, and he never felt completely safe in cab compartments, restaurant booths, plaza snack bars, or any of the other places people normally went to talk.

Although somewhat taken aback by his gall in approaching her, Leradil was not irreversibly antagonized. After all, the game they played was hardly something that he had invented. He had merely gone by the same accepted rules as she and shown himself to be a proficient player. Few Borijans would condemn him for that, any more than they would concede open admiration. And while she would naturally be smarting from the double put-down of having been exposed twice, especially since in both cases she had been acting on behalf of the same principal, he was reasonably sure that the material penalties would not involve losses to her personally.

He told her bluntly that he didn't think her loyalties ended with Farworlds. He wanted to know who she was really with and what they were looking for. His intuition was that something big was afoot, he said. In return, he would cut her in on any buy-in he managed to carve of whatever resulted. And she knew that he meant it. For no matter how much two individuals, two connivances, groups within a connivance, or combinations of all the above schemed to put something over on the others, a deal was a deal and would be adhered to. Had it been otherwise, with no understanding that could be relied on, then nothing meaningful could have been said and the system would never have functioned at all.

Leradil, however, laughed derisively. "Deal? Get serious, Sarvik. What kind of a deal do you call that? You get inside information unconditionally, and I get zilch unless something unspecified turns up? Come on, that's pure fishing. Small-time. Not your league. I'm surprised you even tried."

"Very well." Sarvik had played a lead of nothing and had seen it slapped down as it had deserved to be. "Then I might have to start asking around to find out who put you inside Farworlds. Whom should I talk to, do you think?" He made a nonchalant play of guessing. "Scientists, maybe? That's an odd thought, isn't it? They don't usually get mixed up in things like that. But you know, for some reason I just can't shake the thought off." Leradil's epaulets had gone rigid. Even the red streaks on her yellow crown seemed to be frozen in shock. Sarvik paused for a few seconds to enjoy her reaction, then went on casually. "Astronomers, perhaps, to be a bit more specific? Ah ... getting warm, am I? How about the Astronomical Society of Hoditia?"

So there it was: trumps. Either she cooperated by giving a little, or this time he'd blow it with her *real* principals. It took her a short while to recover. Overhead a zhill rolled lazily, escorted by a flotilla of cavorting sea mammals that looked like web-footed flying squirrels with shoe polish instead of fur.

"How on Turle did you find that out?" she whispered shakily.

"You really expect me to say? Now it's your turn to get real," Sarvik replied, smirking.

Finally, Leradil spoke. "It doesn't sound as if there's very much that I need to tell you." It was a good way of saying nothing while trying to steal a peek at Sarvik's hand, but he wasn't showing.

"Did ASH put you into Replimaticon, too, or was that an idea of somebody at Farworlds?" he asked her.

Leradil's problem was that she had no idea how much Sarvik really knew. He could have been testing to gauge whether she was being straight. She answered truthfully, as she had to—as Sarvik knew she had to. "It was Farworlds. They wanted up-to-the-minute information on the latest coding systems. You already know that."

"So ASH got you into Farworlds for something else?"

"Yes."

"What for? What did they want you to find out there?"

Leradil's epaulets fluttered in agitation. She knew she would be giving away information that really was new to him now, but what else could she do? He waited, dangling the specter of revealing to ASH that her link back to them had been traced. Her currency as a candidate for worthwhile dealings of any kind would be devalued for years. In the end she said hesitantly, "They . . . weren't exactly specific. But they wanted to know about any confidential communications between Farworlds and other scientific organizations. In particular, other institutions of astronomy, cosmology, and cosmological physics."

"Nothing about advanced computer codes, then?" Sarvik checked again. "That was purely something that Farworlds was interested in?"

"Yes."

"Um," he said. It was strange, because organizations like ASH tended to be fairly open with information. In science, too much secrecy was to everybody's disadvantage. Scientists worked out their rivalries in other ways. "That's strange."

"I know," Leradil agreed.

"Do you know why ASH thought there might be secret communications going on with other institutions?"

"No."

Sarvik didn't know whether he should believe her or take this as a hint that it was time for him to give a little more. At the same time, he got the feeling that pressing her harder wouldn't be the thing to do right then. "Let's move on," he suggested.

They got up and followed the walkway out of the aquarium building. The verbal fencing and probing continued. By the time they got to the mammal park Sarvik had decided that if Leradil did know more, she would need a glimpse of how big a thing they might be on to before she would reveal it. If he complied but it turned out that she really had told him as much as she knew, then the loss would be his. If he wanted this to go further, though, he had no choice but to risk it.

They stopped at the elgiloit enclosure to watch the hairy, round-headed creatures screeching and chattering as they brachiated with elongated midlimbs in the trees, while others squatted on the ground scratching and delousing each other with their prehensile forehands.

"I'll tell you a little of what's going on at Farworlds," Sarvik said. "Maybe it will help brush away any last cobwebs from your memory. The reason they're interested in advanced computing is to support a new class of spacecraft and Borijan settlements far, far from Turle. They're going to convert Searchers into generation ships. Just think, after more than a century, when every pragmatic reason you can think of seems to rule against it." He looked at her for a second and read from her expression that she had not known this. "Suddenly they want to leave the Kovar System. They say it's because the time has come to go out into the galaxy and explore. I say there's more to it. And now we find this secret collusion with some of the world's greatest astronomers. So what's going on, Leradil? What do they know that we don't?"

Leradil turned away toward the elgiloits, her epaulets creased in deep thought. Sarvik waited, allowing time for the significance of what he had said to sink in.

Many people believed that elgiloits had the potential to become intelligent, and certainly some of their mannerisms and the expressions on their mobile faces did little to dispel such a notion. However, their ground-based life kept them partly dependent on smell as a primary sense and deprived them of the stimulation to mental dexterity and vision that came from winged ancestry. Experts were agreed that flight was an essential forerunner to the emergence of intelligence.

Leradil sighed after a few moments and turned back to

face Sarvik fully, at the same time glancing about instinctively to be sure there was nobody close. She hesitated, then said, "My real name is Leradil Jindriss. My brother, Palomec Jindriss, is a senior fellow of ASH, an authority on stellar evolution. That's how I was recruited. I'm as curious about all this as much as you are, now. But the only person who can tell us more is Palomec."

She wanted to know the answers, too, and was willing to trade—for now, anyway. For she still had a score to settle, and Sarvik was under no illusions about it. She wouldn't hesitate to turn the situation around on him as soon as it suited her and the first solid opportunity presented itself. That was the way the game went.

"I'd like to meet your brother," Sarvik said.

"I'll see if I can arrange it."

"And *try* not to let the whole world know this time, if you can help it," he clucked at her disparagingly. "My reputation's involved in this now, too."

A little parting shot, just to make sure there were no kind feelings.

16

ON ARRIVING BACK AT REPLIMATICON, SARVIK GOT A message to go up to the directors' level to see Pezamin Greel and Marduk Alifrenz, the two others who were in on the immortality project with him. They knew that the code transferred into the mechanical veech had been extracted from a real veech and that the current experiments were intended merely as a preliminary to extending the procedure to Borijan psyches.

The news was that Prinem Clouth had pulled up his anchor as expected and forfeited his stake to head for bluer waters undisclosed. Almost certainly, this meant that he had judged it was time to cash in on the deal he was working on with Toymate and had taken with him copies of the programs that he thought had driven the veech. But the programs would be worthless, since they were decoys Sarvik had prepared for that eventuality. In fact, they were based on routines Sarvik had decoded from Toymate's own products, with some extra gimmicks added to keep its analysts occupied for a while. Neat, heh-heh-heh.

There was some haggling over dividing up Clouth's share. Then Greel and Alifrenz revealed that as insurance they had lined up several alternative sources of supply for other kinds of artificial animals, which came as little surprise to Sarvik, since that was one of the things directors were for. Would Sarvik be needing them? If so, what stage had the project reached, and what kind of percentages would it be appropriate to offer?

Further haggling followed. Sarvik played down the importance of their hand by stressing that there was only so much more they could learn from further animal tests. It was time to move on to the final phase of using actual Borijans. They had talked about it often enough, and they had no need to spell out the details. Essentially, three things would be needed: a suitable artificial host body, an upgraded molecular-circuit brain to drive it, and a donor of a complete set of the Borijan neural code. Since the code-extraction process was destructive, meeting the last requirement was going to be tricky.

"The woman from Universal Robocon is coming next week to go through the spec for a revised prototype," Alifrenz said. UR produced many of the robot types carried by the Searcher ships, which made it the obvious choice for designing a surrogate Borijan body. Every group involved had its own ideas about what an ideal body ought to be like, and Universal had the experience in handling compromises to keep all of them reasonably satisfied.

"And the molecular circuitry?" Sarvik inquired.

"On schedule," Alifrenz assured him. Others in Replimaticon were working on the brain; only the directors were supposed to know who. Sarvik had found out through GE-NIUS, but there was nothing to be gained from disclosing that fact. By the same means, Sarvik also knew that what Alifrenz had said was true. However, Sarvik also had other arrangements of his own in hand to cover both hardware needs, just in case.

"Regarding the code, I have talked some more with the contact in the Justice Department about getting criminals as volunteers," Greel said, not dropping any names. "There might be possibilities."

Sarvik didn't say anything about his deal with Dr. Queezt. If this immortality thing got to be as big as Sarvik thought it could, he had plans for setting up a connivance of his own that would cut them all out. And in any case, he didn't trust Greel or Alifrenz farther than either of them could carry a zhill.

When Sarvik was on his way back downstairs, his lapel phone beeped to inform him of an incoming call at priority 2. Borijans rarely abused priorities, since claiming a high level without good reason was the fastest way to be ignored the next time.

"Who is it?" Sarvik asked.

"Somebody called Palomec Jindriss," the building's message processor replied. "He says you wanted to talk to him."

"Don't let him go. I'll take it as soon as I get to the lab."

Jindriss was older than Sarvik had imagined. Or maybe that was what being an internationally prestigious scientist did to people, Sarvik thought as he confronted the image waiting on the screen. It was of a man of around middle age, his crest thin and graying prematurely, with furrows that imparted a permanently worried look to both sides of his head. Even the screen seemed to capture a bleak light in his tired, pink-rimmed eyes.

"Naturally, my sister has told me of your conversation," Jindriss said. "What you wanted to talk to us about, I really don't know. But *I* would very much like to talk to you, Dr.

Sarvik. You can't imagine the significance of what you've stumbled on. I can't go into the details from here, but suppose I fly over from Vayso. My schedule is completely flexible. When would you be available?"

No preliminaries. None of the caution and probing that would have been only prudent or any play for notching up an opening advantage. Perhaps that was simply the way academics were, Sarvik thought. For a moment he was too perplexed by the directness to know how to respond. His confusion must have shown.

"Oh, I suppose you're surprised by my failure to follow the customary social maneuverings," Jindriss said. "I don't have the time for that kind of thing, I'm afraid, or the disposition. It may strike you as naive, but I urge you not to pay it undue attention. I can assure you that none of it will matter for very long. In fact, before very much longer nothing will matter at all."

17

JINDRISS CAUGHT A LATE AFTERNOON FLIGHT FROM THE IS-land of Vayso, where ASH's headquarters was located, and arrived in Pygal that evening. An aircab brought him to Sarvik's house on the outskirts of the city. Formed as an attachment on the underside of a large ovoid balloon moored beside an inlet of water, it was a fitting abode for the abrupt swings of mood that Sarvik was prone to. When he felt sociable, he stayed down by the anchoring pylon near the water's edge. When not wanting to be bothered with anyone, he would reel out a thousand feet or so of line and sail up into the clouds until the rest of the Borijan race chose to become bearable again.

Since Palomec Jindriss was expected, the house was down, and he didn't have to be carried up in the elevator capsule that rode the mooring cable. Sarvik showed him into the living room, which was at the nose end. It had windows the length of three walls, at present commanding a view of the approach road flanked by scrubby trees and garage structures and the choppy gray waters of the inlet flecked white by a gusty breeze. The furnishings were a collection of oddments picked at various times for utility, with no thought for coordination or balance of style. It wouldn't have mattered all that much, anyway, since most of the designs and colors were obscured by scattered papers, boxes of folders, and untidy piles of journals and books. A desk with screens occupied one corner, and a pot of graff simmered on a worktop conveniently close by.

They exchanged greetings, and Sarvik hung up Jindriss's topcoat. "Something to eat, maybe?" Unused to academics, he was not sure if a show of unearned courtesy was in order so soon. The best thing was to play it safe.

"No, thank you all the same, Dr. Sarvik. I eat sparingly these days. My lunch was quite sufficient." Jindriss was as gaunt in full figure as his image had conveyed. His frame, though tall, showed a stoop, as if all the world's worries were piled on his shoulders. He had on a somber two-piece suit of dark gray with muted stripes that was dated and hung too loosely, suggesting that he had lost weight.

"A graff, then?" Sarvik said. Jindriss accepted, and they sat down, the visitor in one of the two central recliners, Sarvik clearing a space for himself on a padded couch below the windows in one of the room's long walls.

"I had a friend who used to live in one of these," Jindriss said, gesturing vaguely at the surroundings. "His cable broke one night, and they all woke up halfway to Xerse."

Sarvik started to smile, but Jindriss's expression remained deadpan. Sarvik changed his to a grimace on one side and a questioning look on the other.

Jindriss, however, was already off the subject. "Leradil told me your account of Farworlds Manufacturing's plans to convert Searchers into generation craft."

Well, one certainly couldn't fault academics for not getting straight to the point, Sarvik thought. Not this one, anyway. Jindriss could have made some initial conversation by saying a little about the kind of place he lived in, with some observation on the differences between academic and connivance life, or even a word to say that he knew the background of Sarvik's dealings with his sister. Or perhaps, from what he had said on the phone, Jindriss didn't attach much importance to discussing things like that.

Sarvik replied with equal terseness. "They believe the time has come for Borijans to go out and begin exploring the galaxy." His tone and expressions conveyed that *he* hadn't said it. The people at Farworlds had.

"But you don't seem to think so."

"I think there's more to it."

"Why?"

"Well . . ." Sarvik hesitated in confusion once again. He was not used to direct demands for information, with no reciprocation offered or reasons being given.

Jindriss raised a hand, nodding. "I understand that this is not the way in which you are accustomed to going about things. But believe me, the importance of what I think you've gotten yourself mixed up in makes all of that irrelevant."

"You'd better tell me what, then," Sarvik said.

"If I were not prepared to, I would hardly be here," Jindriss answered. "But can we take it a step at a time, please? Now, what made *you* suspect that there might be more to it?"

Sarvik massaged his brow with his fingers and sighed. There wasn't any one thing he could single out. A lot of it was simply an instinct developed from long experience dealing with people like the Farworlds directors he had met. A glance here, an intonation there, somebody's change of posture . . .

In the end he said, "It's all too much—too big a change, too suddenly."

Jindriss nodded that this was what he had expected. "Go on."

"All of Borijan thinking about offworld habitats has been focused within the Kovar System for over a century. Nobody has ever been able to come up with even the beginnings of a policy for going outside that anyone thought workable." Sarvik waved a hand in the air. "If such attitudes change at all, they change gradually, over generations. But this has all happened at once. There has been nothing in recent years to prepare anyone for it, yet the Farworlds directors are in such a hurry that they're haggling over days. Conclusion: They know something that they're not telling. My nose said it was something big. And now your being here, and on the same day I talked to your sister, tells me that I was right."

"How did you connect any of it to ASH?" Jindriss inquired.

Sarvik sat back, interlacing his fingers in a leisurely movement. "I don't see why the details of that should be pertinent. The importance of whatever Farworlds and ASH are involved in can't depend on how I came to know what I know, now, can it?"

"You discovered that ASH had infiltrated Leradil into Farworlds." Jindriss contemplated Sarvik for a second or two, as if reflecting on what that meant. "You must have access to some extraordinary code-breaking resources."

"Ah, well, then, you've just said it, haven't you?" Sarvik told him. At the same time he permitted himself a satisfied smirk that said he hoped Jindriss didn't expect him to divulge details.

But Jindriss went on. "And that's why Farworlds wants you in. They need top-level computing expertise. Is it for the generation ships?"

"Partly. And to handle the kind of operations they'll need to support the settlements when they get out there," Sarvik replied.

"How feasible is it?" Jindriss asked. "Can they do it, do you think? Could these generation ships work?" He gave the question a ring of finality, as if this had been his main object all along. It was a strange thing to ask. The problems with interstellar migration had always had to do with

Borijan politics and mutual suspicions, not technology. Now, suddenly, Jindriss was speaking as if only the technology mattered.

"I'm sure that they could, in principle," Sarvik answered. "After all, consider for yourself: the Searchers have been going out there for long enough. It's obvious that such ships can be built."

Jindriss gave him a penetrating look, as if inviting him to reflect on what he had just said. "Yes, they have, haven't they? And initiating self-sustaining, fully automated operations of astonishing complexity. So tell me, what exactly is this more advanced computing that they say they'd need for the generation ships? What would it be for? Surely, what they've got already is advanced enough for anything they could reasonably want, wouldn't you say?"

That point had occurred to Sarvik, too, but he was hardly going to tell Farworlds that he really didn't think they needed him for anything. If they thought they did and were willing to make a present of sensitive inside information, then fine. He'd listen.

He replied evasively. "It's difficult to say without knowing more of what their plans are. I'd have to reserve judgment on that for the time being."

Jindriss put his fingers together in front of him and inclined his head to one side. "Just suppose that building the generation ships was not the end of it at all," he said. He waited a moment for that to sink in. "Suppose that the real object was to re-create from minimum beginnings a complete Borijan culture, preserving as much of our knowledge and sciences as possible but with no falling back on Turle or any of the rest of the Kovar System for support. Complete isolation. No recourse to any help if things became difficult. Would *that* make a difference, do you think? It would mean getting absolutely the best technology you could lay hands on, of every description. You'd need lots of advanced computing then, wouldn't you?"

The questions were getting odder. Sarvik could only spread his hands. "Well, if you put it that way, of course I have to say yes. But—" Sarvik cut himself short with a sigh, deciding that he was weary of this interrogation. "Look, I think it's time you told me what this is all about." He leaned back on the couch.

Jindriss stared at him for what started to feel like a long time, as if knowing that the moment had come, yet wanting to put it off just a little longer. Evading the issue to the last, he asked, "You know my field, I presume. Leradil told you?"

"Stellar physics, yes. Stellar physics and evolution." Sarvik's voice took on a discernible edge of impatience.

Jindriss nodded. His face seemed to get longer, and the bleakness to intensify. "As I'm sure you're aware, our parent star, Kov, is what's known as a common yellow dwarf. It so happens, however, that Kov exists as an oddity inside a local cluster of younger, more massive hot blue-white stars, all of which formed at about the same time—as stellar time scales go, that is. Those are the kinds of stars which, at the end of their lifetimes, explode into supernovas. A supernova radiates at typically 200 million times the brilliance of Kov." Jindriss waited until he saw from the protest writing itself across both Sarvik's epaulets that Sarvik was already guessing what was coming. He nodded. "Yes, Dr. Sarvik. The initial instabilities that forewarn of thermonuclear runaway have started to appear in several of our nearest neighbors. Supernovas are rare occurrences in any galaxy. It seems that we have been singled out for the dubious privilege of experiencing a barrage of them." He paused, bringing a second eye to bear on Sarvik, but for the moment Sarvik could do no more than return a numbed look.

Finally he managed to respond in a voice that had lost all its smugness. "This is quite certain?"

"Oh, absolutely."

"How—how long do we have?"

Jindriss shrugged resignedly. "Not long. Very probably we should have gone out into the galaxy before, but it's of little consequence now. By our calculations, it will begin, at the most, within six years. Very possibly in as little as two."

18

WHY HAD JINDRISS TOLD SARVIK ALL THIS?
From his reaction to Leradil's news, it was clear
that Jindriss had known nothing of Farworlds' plans to
build generation ships. But from the indications of ongoing
communication between Farworlds and ASH that GENIUS
had uncovered, there were others at ASH who evidently
did. The implication had been as obvious to Jindriss as it
was to Sarvik as soon as Jindriss mentioned the supernovas:
An inner clique, presumably drawn from the controlling
factions of both organizations, had concocted the scheme as
a desperate bid to get themselves away to a new beginning
before the great irradiating happened.

Having gotten that far, Jindriss wasn't exactly sure what
he wanted. In part, he had come to Sarvik out of a need for
undisputable corroboration of what Leradil had said. And
partly it was self-preservation. Farworlds was sufficiently
impressed by Sarvik's abilities to want him in on the project, and to this end had been prepared to reveal at least a
part of the story to him. Jindriss had enabled Sarvik to put
it in perspective by telling him the rest. Therefore, Sarvik
owed Jindriss. Jindriss's unstated hope had to be that
through the weight Sarvik evidently carried with Farworlds,
coupled with the threat of exposure that the two of them
were now in a position to brandish, they might gain places
for themselves in the ark. And as for Leradil? She had
known as little about Farworlds' plans for generation-ship
lifeboats as Palomec had, and as little about the reasons for
them as Sarvik. But she had been the instrument by which
they had put the two parts of the story together. This—

apart, of course, from her being Palomec's sister—was enough to earn her a place in whatever they managed to make from the situation.

Sarvik's decision, after a lot of thought and endless arguing with GENIUS, was to tackle the situation head-on. He called Indrigon at Farworlds and told him that he had his answer.

"Already, Dr. Sarvik?" It was still well inside the seven days they had agreed on. Indrigon looked pleased. "So the prospect of becoming a part of the greatest exploration project ever attempted proved irresistible, eh?" One side of his face took on a cautionary look. "Of course, you understand that the termination of your present arrangements would have to be official and final before we could admit you any further into confidentiality." The deal had been that Sarvik would have to finish with Replimaticon. They obviously didn't mean to leave him in a situation where he could go bargaining elsewhere.

But none of that mattered now. Sarvik replied bluntly, "There's no need for any more games with half-truths, Mr. Indrigon. I know the real reason behind the project and why it's so urgent."

Indrigon's expressions changed to a disappointed frown, as if he had expected better. "Now you're pushing us too far, Dr. Sarvik." Clearly, he thought that Sarvik was trying an ill-timed bluff.

"You think so?" Sarvik said, maintaining an easy look. "Surely you haven't forgotten that I specialize in finding out what I'm not supposed to know. After all, isn't that what attracted your interest in the first place?"

Indrigon looked disbelieving, then suspicious. And then both sides of his face went into agitated spasms that betrayed uncertainty. Sarvik put any doubts to rest by saying as much as was prudent over a net link, even on an encrypted channel. "Life is going to get distinctly unhealthy in this neighborhood, I hear. It might be a good time to think about moving on, wouldn't you agree? Shall we say . . . maybe in as little as two years? Now have I got your attention?"

Sarvik had guessed that Indrigon was one of the inner group at Farworlds who knew the situation. Indrigon's mute incredulity now was enough to confirm it. Sarvik wasn't so sure about the other two he had met, Lequasha and Umbrik. There could be room only for so many on a generation ship, after all—along with favored relatives, friends, hangers-on, and others with necessary skills. But Sarvik didn't think that anyone at Farworlds had discovered Leradil Jindriss's connection with ASH, and therefore Indrigon could have no idea how Sarvik had gotten the information. All anyone at Farworlds would know was that in two days flat Sarvik had penetrated the inner group's most closely protected secret.

One solution they could resort to, of course, would be to put out a contract to get rid of him, which was sometimes the way things went when a tangle of overlapping deals led to so many conflicts and contradictions that resolution was impossible. But Sarvik was prepared to gamble against it. Such a drastic answer would deprive them of any chance of benefiting from his expertise and the resources he commanded, which had been their objective to begin with—and which he had just shown to be even more potent than they had realized previously. He didn't think they would throw it away now. And he was correct. The response came within hours of Sarvik's call: no teleconference hookups this time; Farworlds would fly him to Xerse to talk in person.

He was met at the airport at Gweths by a flymobile sent to collect him and was flown to a pad high on the Farworlds Tower. There he met Indrigon again, along with a number of other insiders on the project—not in a staff relaxation park halfway up the building, but in the executive offices of the topmost pinnacle. For this time all of them knew that *he* was dictating the terms. His terms were simple: from himself, a total commitment to developing the kinds of systems they were going to need at the other end; from them, places for himself and up to a dozen associates in the generation-ship program, which he learned was code-named Breakout. To comply with his side of the arrangement, naturally he would need full access to Farworlds' files of design data, logistics planning, and future development schedules for the entire project.

"Who are these dozen associates, Dr. Sarvik?" Indrigon asked him.

Sarvik shrugged vaguely. "I'm not sure yet. Relatives? Friends? You're not the only ones who would want to bring a small part of your own world with you, you know. I'd like to think I could preserve a few familiar faces, too."

It was what anyone would have expected. The terms were agreed upon.

19

THERE WAS LITTLE POINT IN WORRYING ABOUT IMMORTALity if the world was about to end—not as something of immediate concern, anyway. But the thought of reviving that project later, to extend existence indefinitely in some unimaginable future life on some distant star, was another matter. Accordingly, Sarvik wound up his relationship with Replimaticon on terms that Pezamin Greel and Marduk Alifrenz, his two accomplices there, found surprisingly generous considering the abruptness of Sarvik's announcement. His reason was that he wanted to leave the door open to renew his association with them later. Since they were already familiar with his immortality project and its technicalities, he had them in mind for two of the slots he'd been assigned in Breakout, but he didn't want to reveal anything about that at present.

Moving house to Gweths was easy enough. All he had to do was rent a bolt-on motor unit for his balloon house, secure the glassware and other loose items, and wait for the

wind to blow in the right direction. GENIUS 5 transferred
itself via satellite links, leaving an instruction in the
Replimaticon system that would erase the original copy on
receipt of a signal from the other end. Borijans had often
debated the question of identity and how they would deal
with the problem of creating multiple copies if they ever
reached the stage of being able to transmit themselves from
place to place electronically. As open-minded about it as
they tried to be, most were simply unable to feel any sense
of continuity with a hypothetical replica of themselves happening to come into existence possibly millions of miles
away. If the original was obliterated in the process, *they*
would have ceased to exist, whatever else the copy might
think. But an intelligence that had been electronic from its
beginnings apparently suffered from no such qualms.

Sarvik found a leafy, sheltered valley with a lake to moor
his house by, ten miles inland from the Farworlds Tower,
and GENIUS took up residence in some of the most sophisticated hardware on Turle. Gradually, as Sarvik became
more engrossed in the details of Breakout, familiarity led to
acceptance, and in time the underlying morbidness of what
made the undertaking necessary oppressed his thoughts
less. As he applied himself to the task, his thoughts of all
the worldly cares that had ruled his life and were no longer
important faded. In their place, he found himself entertain-
ing exciting visions of a future with whole new dimensions
of experience and undreamed-of possibilities. It was only
when GENIUS got to examining the Farworlds plans in detail that Sarvik got his first premonition that Breakout
might not, in the time available, be feasible at all.

A vertical line divided GENIUS's screen into two halves.
One side was empty except for two small designs: one a
wrench crossed on top of a gear cog, the other a symbolic
representation of one of the robot freighters that brought
products back from the remote manufacturing complexes.
The other side was filled with a hierarchy of symbols arranged in descending levels, with connecting lines showing
the dependencies of the higher groupings on the lower. At

the top was an icon of one of the proposed generation ships, and immediately beneath it, a short line of figures representing Borijans. To the left below them a cloud formation with slanting lines of rain represented an atmosphere, with sublevels below that branching off into a tree of chemical formulas and symbols for temperature, pressure, physical dynamics, and all the other properties essential to supporting life. Another tree alongside it depicted a city habitat with its supporting agencies and services. And a third, to the right, showed food supplies, broken down into categories of animal, agricultural, and synthetic, and below them, depictions of irrigation, microorganism populations, soil chemistry, and other factors they depended on. As Sarvik watched, a bewildering web of cross-connections added themselves to show how climatic factors would affect the soil, how the rocks would affect the oceans, and how just about nothing could change without altering everything else. GENIUS's voice narrated:

"Setting up a colony of Borijans is going to be a more complicated business than these people seem to have realized. It's not just a question of upgrading the Searcher operations, which is all they've had any experience of. A manufacturing complex that just has to send robot ships back to Kov is pretty straightforward by comparison. Machines just need a ball of rock solid enough to plant foundations on, and environmental conditions short of the extremes that would upset electronics. But this carbon chemistry that you guys are stuck with is something else. First you have to have breathable atmospheres, and all the ingredients and physical parameters have got to be just right. Then you need watery surfaces with a tolerable chemical mix, a benign climate, and not too much or too little gravity. Then there's all this food to think about, because you run on energy from slow oxidation instead of conduction. The complexity of how it all interrelates is horrendous. The truth is, nobody knows if what they're talking about comes anywhere close to reality. The simulations are all based on assumptions and unsubstantiated theories. There haven't been any crewed interstellar missions to test anything. You judge a kitchen by what comes out of it, not what goes in."

"No one's expecting to design a planet," Sarvik said. "All we need to get started is something reasonably close to the way this one is. And surely they've got enough data on that."

GENIUS presented a view of star-speckled emptiness receding to infinity. "But it narrows down the choice of worlds dramatically and makes the probability of finding one a correspondingly protracted process. Nobody knows what percentage of worlds is likely to meet all the requirements or, therefore, the amount of time it would take to find one. All the figures that have been used are guesses." A picture appeared of a Searcher modified as proposed, bristling with question marks. "So, for how long should the essential systems on the generation ships be designed to function? Nobody knows. What mission duration should be assumed? Ditto. What are the limits of the presently available technologies? You tell me."

Sarvik slumped back in his chair. "Surely not. It can't really be that bad." It was a feeble response. The shock of what GENIUS was telling him was still registering.

"You don't want to hear my estimate of the odds of it working," GENIUS told him.

Sarvik stared numbly into the distance through the console panel in front of him. "Do you think this explains why Palomec Jindriss was so concerned about technology the first time I talked to him?" he asked at last.

"Not my department. I don't do wet-brain psychology," GENIUS answered.

Sarvik pulled himself together slowly and exhaled a long breath. "So, what's your summary assessment of the whole thing?" he asked. "Is Breakout a feasible solution?"

"In the time that's available? No, I don't think it is," GENIUS replied. A picture appeared on the screen of a trash basket stuffed with rolled-up plans.

Sarvik flew to Hoditia and rented a flymobile to take him across to the island of Vayso, planning to see how much of this was new to Palomec Jindriss. Jindriss met him in the roof-level reception lobby of the ASH headquarters building. He had reserved a small meeting room by the main library where they could talk privately.

Jindriss's expression bleakened, and he seemed to age more by the minute as Sarvik related his findings. Even before he had finished speaking, Sarvik could tell he was not making any great revelations. Jindriss had known, but he had buried the knowledge deep inside his mind somewhere, out of sight of consciousness, persuading himself that Farworlds might come up with something. This was probably the first time he had faced the truth honestly and squarely.

"Yes, yes, you're right. Of course most of it is based on speculation," Jindriss admitted tiredly. "Where could anyone possibly get the hard data? As you say, there have been no expeditions. There hasn't been time to even know what the right questions are, never mind be sure of the answers."

Sarvik was aghast. "And that's acknowledged generally? The other scientists here at ASH who are part of it—they know that at best the whole thing is a gamble against all the odds?"

"It's not a simple matter of being objective about facts, as you make it sound," Jindriss said. "Self-defense reactions set in. The mind protects itself in situations like this. People immerse themselves totally in the only answer they've got. They shut everything else out."

"What about the engineers at Farworlds?" Sarvik objected. "The ones who are supposed to be implementing the solutions. They have to preserve a measure of realism, surely."

"Most of them believe the cover story for Breakout—that it's time to get out of the Kovar System. They think the time pressure is for political reasons, to exploit Farworlds' edge over the competition. In other words, to them the urgency isn't 'real,' and the problems will all get fixed eventually." Jindriss made a resigned gesture. "Of course, the senior executives who are tagged to go know the truth. But in their case we have protective psychology at work again.

A collective unreason close to panic has taken hold. Keeping busy and at least doing something provides a day-to-day analgesic that's better than the despair that would come with doing nothing. The rest just go along with the pressure without knowing the reason for it."

All of which was understandable, Sarvik could see. It was the only choice any of them had. But it was not the only choice *he* had.

The next day he took the flymobile over to Pygal and kept an appointment he had made to see Alifrenz and Greel. It was time to renew their relationship.

Through them, he still had access to things that were going on in Replimaticon and certain other places Replimaticon was involved with, such as Universal Robocon. For Sarvik's previous work on his immortality project had suggested a different solution to the whole problem of escaping from Turle. It would need Replimaticon, and it would need access to the computers that planned and programmed the Searcher missions, which his privileged position at Farworlds already gave him. But apart from that, he no longer cared particularly whether the ASH-Farworlds plans for interstellar colonies were feasible, or if a single generation ship ever managed to lift itself out from its assembly orbit.

For the solution to it all that Sarvik had in mind didn't involve fragile, perishable biological Borijan bodies—and all the attendant complications of sustaining, nurturing, and reproducing them—at all.

20

SARVIK SAT BACK IN THE PADDED LEATHER CHAIR IN THE director's office overlooking the main lab and surveyed his domain high in the Farworlds Tower. Around him, arrays of panels flashed their lights self-importantly and beeped updates onto variously colored screens.

"Simulation run seven complete and checked through all phases," an irritatingly smooth synthetic female voice announced. "Results pending. Require preferred preview mode."

"Vertical section at x equal to pi, correlate with z-transform," Sarvik instructed absently.

Outside the variview window, which was switched to maximum transparency, programmers and analysts sat working at rows of consoles and terminals. In a darkened bay at one end of the room a holographic presentation of an atmospheric modeling exercise glowed silently as a sphere of swirling light patterns six feet in diameter. In a partitioned conference area on the far side of the lab, a working party was arguing decision criteria for extracting metals from dissolved salts versus going to nuclear transmutation. If the circumstances had been otherwise, Sarvik would have had good reason for feeling satisfied.

He had been with Farworlds three-quarters of a year now. It was a shame the rest of life couldn't have been as untroubled and reassuring as the daily pretense he saw acted out here in the tower. There had been a lot of suicides among scientists, which the health experts and sociologists had been unable to explain. Others had abandoned their lifetime's work, disappeared without trace, or taken to drink, drugs, debauchery, or all of them. It was now public knowledge that Farworlds Manufacturing was mounting an all-out program to build generation starships from modified Searcher designs, and fears that some kind of catastrophe was imminent abounded. The stories going the rounds and getting their share of attention in the media ranged from Turle's being about to collide with an asteroid or to be swallowed by a black hole, through a whole repertoire of climatic disruptions, to explosion of the planet's core or the subterranean fusion plants. Public accusations of official cover-ups were being made and denied, and investigations were being demanded almost daily, while the expert and not so expert in every science argued and proffered figures to support or refute, attack or defend just about every plausible scenario or crackpot theory imaginable. Even the truth had surfaced amid it all more than once, only to be swept away unrecognized in the general flood of confusion.

Naturally, Farworlds dismissed all of it as mass hysteria and insisted that the generation-ship program meant no more than what it had always said: that the time had come for the Borijan civilization to expand beyond the Kovar System. Why all the hurry, then? the skeptics asked. To exploit their competitive edge over their rivals, Farworlds' public relations flacks replied. They were the biggest in the business and intended to stay that way. To show that everything was business as usual, Farworlds was continuing its regular Searcher launches as scheduled.

But Sarvik didn't think it could hold together for very much longer. From his inside vantage point he was more certain than ever that Breakout could never be made to work in the remaining time available. Every day he saw evidence that others were ceasing to delude themselves, too. Eventually the disillusionment would reach critical mass and set off a chain reaction of dashed hopes, at which point the effort would collapse. After that, there would be no more Searchers going out. All the pieces of his own escape plan were in place. The time to move with it was now.

A blank screen in front of him came to life to show a

pair of Borijan ears and a question mark. Sarvik shook aside his reflections. "It's all right. You can speak," he said.

"I just heard an interesting conversation between Lequasha and Othenitan," GENIUS informed him. It had turned out that Lequasha was among the inner group who knew the real reason for Breakout. Othenitan was another. The most sensitive records were still being held off-line from the net, where GENIUS couldn't get to them. However, it had found that by modifying the diagnostics the maintenance programs used for remote-checking hardware, it could surreptitiously activate the regular voice pickups on terminals in the executive suites.

"Go on," Sarvik directed.

"The story that's being given out to the public is cracking," GENIUS said. "So a whole new group of PR people are being brought into the secret to help hold things together. In return, they get slots in the lifeboats."

"Which will mean deallocating someone else's," Sarvik concluded. There was no surprise in his voice. He had been waiting for something like this for a while.

"Do you want the conversation verbatim, or shall I summarize?" GENIUS asked.

"No. Just give me the gist."

"Essentially, you're out, along with the other slots they assigned you. They figure that your usefulness was concentrated up front, with the conceptual stages. The specs will be frozen on final encoding, which means that when the ships fly, your job's over."

Sarvik stared through the screens, beyond the walls of the building. Although he had been prepared for this, it still took him a moment to come to terms with hearing it said in cold words. *Now*, he told himself again. His preparations would never be more complete. Further delay could only increase the risk of exposure or disaster through a sudden cancellation of the Searcher program. The time was now.

After a while a cartoon depiction of fingers tapping impatiently appeared on GENIUS's screen. "Response?" it prompted.

Sarvik drew in a long, unsteady breath. Uploading a personality was a one-way process—once he was transformed into machine-resident code, there could be no coming back. "We get our own show rolling," he finally pronounced. "Are the archive allocation groupings still good?"

"No change."

"Reactivation sequence?"

"Implanted successfully and tested. Untraceable from system level."

Sarvik had identified Indrigon early on as having little real confidence in the Breakout program, and had revealed to him his own scheme. He had needed somebody in Indrigon's position to arrange unrestricted access to the Searcher mission-control software. This had enabled Sarvik to engineer a whole region of "invisible" storage space, undetectable by the regular test procedures, inside the archives section of the Searcher database. There, he and the companions he had selected to take with him would stow away indefinitely as patterns of electronic molecular-bond encryptions able to survive virtually indefinitely, even with a loss of power. They would reactivate in response to a trigger code issued by the supervising processor when the right conditions were met. Indrigon would be one of those going with Sarvik, of course, along with two of his closer associates from Farworlds: a female director named Dorn, and Gulaw, one of the engineering chiefs. They had nothing to gain from giving Sarvik's plan away and everything to lose if it was blocked.

"AMS status?" Sarvik checked.

"Final link structure fixed. Simulator returns all positive," GENIUS reported.

When the Searcher found a planet meeting all the environmental and other conditions and the first general-purpose factory had been built, the Supervisor would switch to an alternative manufacturing schedule of products for it to make—very different from the standard remote-manufacturing list. Key among these would be the new bodies that Greel and Alifrenz's contacts at Universal Robocon had designed for the machine-transported personalities to be copied into. Two prototypes had been built at

UR and delivered to Replimaticon for trials. In return, a UR director called Kalazin, along with two of his senior designers, a male named Creesh and Meyad, a female, would be included in the deal. Greel and Alifrenz had also organized the completion of the upgraded molecular-circuit brain for the UR body, and its two designers at Replimaticon would also be coming. Leradil and Palomec Jindriss had already earned their places, bringing the total thus far to eleven.

"And the two prototypes have remained stable?" Sarvik said. "No indications of regression or breakdown?"

In reply, GENIUS activated another screen to show a recorded image of one of the strangest robotic constructions that had ever crossed a laboratory floor. "This came in this morning on the progress of the second subject," it announced. "Integration appears to be going smoothly, without adverse effects. Just like the first one."

Finally, there was Dr. Queezt, who had persuaded two of the terminal patients under his care to volunteer as experimental subjects to be written into artificial hosts. Later, when Sarvik had divulged to him why cerebral prosthetics didn't matter anymore, Queezt had moved to Replimaticon, where the brain developed by Greel and Alifrenz's group, the prototype bodies from UR, and the two sets of extracted code from Queezt's patients were integrated into a complete package. It would have been unfortunate indeed if the first full test wasn't tried until it all came together in a Searcher-built factory out at some distant star and it failed to work. But so far the results looked promising.

Animals that were formed roughly like a stick, such as worms or snails, were unable to manipulate objects or even to move around very well. Animals with legs—a stick with smaller, movable sticks attached—moved themselves better but were still awkward at manipulation. Animals with fingers—sticks on the ends of sticks on a stick—became amazingly dexterous.

The body that GENIUS was showing in the recording from the Replimaticon lab was a total departure from the menagerie of legged, wheeled, or tracked, multisensored, variously appendaged, surveying, constructing, transporting, and assembling robots that Universal Robocon's design teams had been dreaming up for over a century. It was formed in the general pattern of sticks on the ends of sticks on the ends of sticks down to the eighth level, with major limbs reconfigurable into lesser segments that could act in combination or subdivide further to achieve finer levels of tactile sensitivity and coordination. In short, it could create or modify limbs and digits to suit the purpose of the moment.

"Come over here and tell me what you make of this," Queezt's voice said. The camera angle shifted, and Queezt appeared, gesturing toward something on top of a bench next to where he was standing. The machine he was talking to re-formed the tripodal arrangement that it had been resting on into two multijointed limbs, on which it made its way warily and visibly unsteadily across the room.

"This still feels odd." The voice was pleasantly melodious, not at all like what most people would have thought of as "mechanical." "I'm having trouble coordinating. My legs have got too many pieces in them."

"That's because the neural model that you created during life doesn't map onto the physical geography," Queezt said. "That will get better as you adapt. Give it a chance." He gestured again toward the bench. "Now, have a try at this and tell me how it feels." The figure of Leradil Jindriss appeared in the background and moved closer. Her experience in animal behavior was proving a valuable asset to the project.

Lying on the bench was a popular puzzle in the form of a plastic board with a pattern of holes containing colored pegs. The object was to jump the pegs according to stated rules in such a way as to leave a single peg in the middle. Most children encountered it at one time or another, and addicts had been known to spend hours trying to make it come out right.

But instead of using two fingers to select and move one peg at a time, as was the usual way of tackling the problem, the creation extended a limb over the board, at the same time disassembling its "hand" into a forest of digits and subdigits that encompassed every part of the array simultaneously.

It did have a head in which visual and other senses were concentrated, close to the brain. But Sarvik's eventual goal was a fully distributed architecture in which the concept of "brain" would no longer be meaningful: an architecture able to sense, move, and think with all of its anatomy. When, with further experiment and improvement, the branching level reached a degree where the terminal endings became cilia numbered in trillions, an individual would command an information input and processing ability comparable to that of the entire present-day Borijan population. Instead of having to be content with the infinitesimal bandwidths accessible to a few fixed senses, it would be able to create sensory capacities to suit its needs: an eye by forming a holographic diffraction lens with one set of fingers and a retina from a few million others held in the focal plane behind, or ears able to register from spine-juddering subbass to megacycle ultrasonic, or a UHF antenna, or an X-ray diffraction grating. Its descendants would become a new form of life, as far removed in their perceptions and aspirations from Borijans as Borijans were from the first replicating cells that had come together out of the chemistry of Turle's oceans three billion years before. They would never have to die. Parts could be replaced, outmoded functions exchanged for better ones.

It would be . . . immortality.

But in the meantime the crude precursor that Sarvik was looking at on the screen would have to do.

The test body performed something like a one-armed sleight of hand in which all the pegs moved together, all but one of them being lifted and leaving a lone remainder in the target hole in the center. Even Sarvik was impressed.

"I can't explain what I did," its voice said, sounding hesitant. "It wasn't a sequential process. It was as if . . . as if the whole logic of the problem was just 'there,' instantly, all at the same time . . . like when you look down on a maze and can see the way through all of it. I felt as if I was looking down on time, somehow, in the same kind of way ... I don't know how else to describe it."

"That's fine, just fine." Queezt was obviously having trouble containing his excitement. "It's unlike anything you've ever experienced before. You'll get used to it."

As the rest of them would have to, too. At least this would give them an idea of what they should expect.

"That'll do," Sarvik told GENIUS. The screen went blank.

All the pieces were in place and ready, he told himself again. The time was now. The next Searcher would be departing from orbit around Veresoi, another of the planets in the system of Kov, in three days' time. Its computers and database were currently being loaded from Turle via laser link. Sarvik made his decision.

"We go with the next launch," he said. "Set up the storage zones and transmit the manufacturing files. Send the code word to Greel and Alifrenz to have the extraction facility at Replimaticon ready to receive us tomorrow night. Make sure everyone has a good official reason for not being seen around during the following two days."

That was it. There was nothing more to say. Sarvik checked for anything he might have overlooked. There was nothing. The arrangements had all been worked out in detail and agreed to in advance. He got up and left the room.

On the screen a caricature of a cuboid computer with a face appeared, followed by a large question mark.

The flight back to Hoditia the following afternoon was a strange and unsettling experience. Sarvik traveled with Indrigon and the two others from Farworlds, Dorn and Gulaw, but communicated little with any of them. All the way he stared out over the familiar cloud-mottled sphere of Turle turning slowly by below the dartliner, at the oceans and the islands, trying to make himself believe that it was really true that after this day he would never set eyes on any of those sights again. But somehow it refused to feel real, perhaps because some mental defense mechanism of the kind that Palomec Jindriss had talked about had taken hold and was dulling the sensation. When he next experienced conscious awareness after tonight, all of this would long ago have ceased to exist. How far into the distant future, he wondered, would that be? What kind of world would he awaken to? There was no way of even guessing. His companions were equally reticent, doubtless weighed down by similar thoughts.

They met Greel and Alifrenz at Replimaticon, together with Kalazin, Creesh, and Meyad, the three from Universal Robocon. Queezt, with Palomec and Leradil Jindriss, were already there, too. Again, there was little talk. The party went down to the processing lab where Queezt had set up the equipment for extracting the neural configuration coding, and one by one they lay back to sink into oblivion as the preliminary anesthetic took effect. The technicians in attendance were the ones who had processed the two test subjects that Queezt had brought previously, and asked no questions.

From Pygal in Hoditia the codes were beamed via satellite to Xerse, where the Farworlds processors responsible for managing the Searcher launch retransmitted them out to the ship, which was hanging in orbit above the planet Veresoi. There, the streams of code found their assigned destinations, hidden deep inside the system's archives. Back in Pygal, the physical remains of what had been Sarvik and his eleven companions were incinerated and the residue was flushed away down the Replimaticon Building's drains.

A day later, the Searcher ship fired its drive and lifted itself out from orbit above Veresoi. Its navigation system took control and brought it around onto an accelerating course toward the outer fringes of the Kovar System.

Actually, Sarvik could never have done it with just the eleven others preserved with him in the Searcher's data bank. He had conned more than a hundred more individuals at Replimaticon, ASH, and Farworlds into rendering essential help, all of whom believed that they were among the privileged. But such a number would have been impossible to process. In any case, he didn't need them. An entire population of new individuals could be generated from electronically shuffled sets of genes once the new bodies were in production. So, in the final and ultimate game to end all games, he had beaten them all.

Heh-heh-heh.

21

SEVERAL DECADES LATER, THE SEARCHER ARRIVED AT the fourth planet of a not too distant star. Turle was a dead world by that time, the Borijan civilization gone— but the programs constituting the Searcher's Supervisor knew nothing about that.

It wasn't much of a world to brag about: an airless, life-less ball of eroded rock formations, debris from ancient meteorite impacts, and wastes of volcanic ash and dust. Certainly it fell far short of meeting the criteria that Sarvik had specified for the kind of place he and his friends would want to inhabit, and so the command to reactivate them and switch to the alternative manufacturing procedure was not issued. But the orbital probes and surface landers found a crust rich in the kind of minerals the Searcher's regular routine called for, and the Supervisor initiated the descent routine.

A standard robot workforce was deployed to feed ores and materials back to where others had begun building a pilot extraction plant. A parts-making facility was added next, followed by a parts-assembly facility, and step by step the pilot plant grew itself into a general-purpose factory, complete with its own control computers. The master programs from the ship were copied into the factory's computers, which thereupon took charge of surface operations. The factory then began making more robots.

Time passed, the factory hummed, and the robot population grew in number and variety. Maintenance robots took care of stoppages and routine wear in the factory; troubleshooting programs tracked down the causes of production rejects; breakdown teams brought in malfunctioning machines for repair; and specialized scavenging robots roamed in search of wrecks, write-offs, and any other sources of parts suitable for recycling.

When the operation reached a critical size, a mixed workforce detached itself and migrated a few miles away to build a second factory, a replica of the first, using materials supplied initially from Factory One. As this self-replicating pattern spread, production commenced of products and robot freighters to carry them back to the extinct civilization that would never need them. After verifying that all was well and subjecting itself to a thorough overhaul, the Searcher launched itself back into space to seek more worlds on which to repeat the cycle.

Fifty years later, the Searcher was approaching a hot bluish-white star with a mass of more than a dozen times Kov's. It so happened that this was one of the last massive stars to go supernova in the chain that had rippled through the cluster surrounding Kov and put an end to the Borijans and their worries about mortality.

The Searcher's hull survived the heat and radiation blast more or less intact, but secondary X rays and high-energy particles flooded the interior, wreaking havoc with its electronics. With its navigation system disrupted and many of its programs obliterated or corrupted, the Searcher veered away and disappeared back into interstellar space. One of the faint specks now lying ahead of it was a yellow-white dwarf star a thousand light-years away. It, too, possessed a family of planets, and on the third of them, the descendants of a line of semi-intelligent apes had tamed fire and were beginning to experiment with tools chipped laboriously from stone.

* * *

A hundred thousand years after its encounter with the supernova, the Searcher drifted into the outer regions of the solar system. The few of its long-range sensors that were still functional fixed upon the planet-moon system of Saturn, finally singling out Titan. Unable to deploy surveillance satellites or high-altitude probes, the ship went straight into its descent routine and landed on an ice beach by an inlet of a shallow methane sea. It was a bleak, barren, ice-encrusted world, unsuitable either for remote manufacturing or for hosting re-created Borijans, but that was of no consequence since the programs for evaluating the prospects for both kinds of endeavor weren't working. Accordingly, Factory One, with most of its essential functions up and running to at least some degree, took shape on a rocky shelf above the ice beach.

It was when Factory One's Supervisor identified commencement of work on Factory Two as its next assignment that everything went completely wrong. The "How to Make a Factory" file that it signaled for from the ship's data bank included a set of subfiles on "How to Make the Machines Needed to Make a Factory," i.e., robots. Because of corruption in the software, the subfiles containing the robot-manufacturing information, instead of being transmitted to Factory One, were merely relayed through the factory's system and beamed out to the local memories of the robot types to which they pertained. No copies at all were retained in the factory files, and worse still, the originals inside the ship managed to get erased in the process. Eventually the system diagnostics managed to piece together what had happened. The scheduler couldn't schedule anything without manufacturing information, and the only information that now existed for making robots was that contained inside the robots out on the surface. So the Supervisor put out messages telling them to send their manufacturing information back again.

But none of the robots were able to comply. Their local memories were simply not big enough to hold a complete manufacturing subfile. However, different individuals seemed to have collected different pieces of their respective files, and a quick check indicated that most of the information had been preserved among all of them. So the Supervisor retrieved different parts from different sources and tried to fit them back together in a way that made sense, and that was how it arrived at the versions it eventually passed to the scheduler for manufacture.

Unfortunately, the instruction to store this information for future reference got lost somewhere, and the Supervisor had to go through the whole rigmarole again whenever a new batch of a particular robot type was needed. The Supervisor had been written as a self-modifying learning program that would grow unhappy about such an inefficiency and experiment with ways of doing something about it. It found that some of the robots contained about half their respective subfiles, and in some cases the halves were complementary. This meant that a complete copy could be obtained by interrogating just two individuals instead of many. Accordingly, the Supervisor made a note of such "matching pairs" as its sources for servicing future scheduling requests and ignored the others. Thus, the robots started coming off the line with one-half of their "genetic" information included in the programs that were written into them to start them up, and they in turn became the source when more models came to be built later.

The resulting "genomes" were seldom identical, and as a consequence the robots began taking on ever stranger shapes and behaving in strange ways. The majority simply failed to function at all and were broken down again for recycling. Many were genetically incomplete—"sterile"—and lasted until they wore out, then became extinct. Of those which did reproduce, most did so passively, transmitting their half subfiles to the Supervisor when the Supervisor asked for them.

A few, however, had inherited routines from the ship's software that caused them to lodge requests with the scheduler to schedule more models of their own kind—routines, moreover, that raised the urgency of their requests until they were serviced. These robots reproduced actively: they behaved as if they experienced a compulsion to ensure that their half subfiles were always included in the scheduler's list of things to make next. The robots competing in this way for slots in the production schedules soon overrode the demands for everything else. And this pattern spread through the new factories appearing inland from the rocky coastal shelf.

Resources were scarce everywhere, adding to the competitive pressure. The factory-robot communities that had "appetites" appropriate to their needs and also enjoyed favorable sites usually managed to survive, if not flourish. Factory Ten, for example, was built in the center of a meteorite crater where the impact had exposed metal-bearing bedrock from below the ice. Factory Thirteen occupied a deep fissure and was able to melt a shaft down to access core materials, while Factory Fifteen resorted to building up nuclei by transmutation. But there were many like Factory Nineteen, which ground to a halt half-complete when its drilling robots and transmutation reactors failed to function, and its supply of materials ran out.

The parts-salvaging scavengers, able to locate assemblies suitable for breaking down—"digesting"—and rebuilding into something useful, assumed a crucial role in shaping the strange metabolism that was coming into being. The piles of assorted junk and broken-down robots were eaten up; the carcasses of defunct factories were eaten up; the Searcher ship, still lying on the ice beach by the methane sea, was eaten up. And when those sources of parts and materials ran low, some of the machines started eating each other.

The scavengers were supposed to discriminate between properly functioning machines and rejects in need of disassembling and recycling. But as with everything else in the mess the project had turned into, this worked with varying success in most cases and sometimes not at all, which meant that some types were likely to attempt the dismantling of a live, walking-around something or other instead of a dead, flat-on-its-back one. The victims who were indifferent to this kind of treatment soon died out, but others evolved fight-or-flight responses to preserve themselves, marking the emergence of specialized prey and predators.

This development was not always advantageous. Factory Fifty, for instance, was consumed by its own offspring, who began dismantling it at its output end as soon as they came off the line and then proceeded to deliver the pieces back to the input end. It slowed to a halt and became plunder for foraging groups from Thirty-six and Fifty-three. The most successful factory-robot organisms protected themselves by producing aggressive armies of "antibody" defenders, which recognized their own factory and its "kind" and left them alone, but attacked any "foreign" models that ventured too close. This gradually became the dominant form of community, usually associated with a distinct territory that its members cooperated in protecting.

The normal Borijan remote manufacturing setup included planetwide communications coverage for coordinating its various operations. In Titan's case, however, no satellites had been put up, and facilities operating on the surface were showing defects of every kind. However, the Borijan engineers had provided a backup method for program and data interchange between the factories and their outside robots in the form of direct physical interconnection. It was much slower than radio, of course, since it required the robots to go physically to the factories for reprogramming and reporting, but in self-sustaining operations of that magnitude far from home, some such protection of the investment was essential. Factory Seventy-three, constructed with no radio capability at all, was started up by programs physically transported from Sixty-six. None of its robots ever used anything but the backup mode, and the descendant factories it spawned continued the tradition. But that very fact meant that foraging parties were able to roam farther afield, beyond line-of-sight links, and in the process enlarged their catchment areas dramatically.

So the "defect" turned out to be not so much of a defect, after all. Furthermore, continuing selective pressures tended to improve the autonomy of the robots that operated in this fashion. Relying only on their comparatively small local processors, they applied simple solutions to the problems they encountered; but their closely coupled mode of interacting with their surroundings meant that the solutions were applied fast: they evolved efficient "reflexes." The traditional models, by contrast, tied to their larger but remote central computers, could apply more sophisticated methods, but as often as not they applied them too late to derive any benefit. Autonomous operation thus conferred a behavioral superiority that asserted itself as the norm, while use of radio declined in importance and became rare.

The periodic urge that robots felt to communicate genetic half subfiles back to their factories had long become universal—ancestors not sharing it had left no descendants. Their response to the demise of radio was to evolve a compulsion to journey at intervals back to the places whence they had come—their "spawning grounds." This in turn posed new challenges to the evolutionary process.

The main problem was that an individual could deliver only half its genome to the factory, with a high risk of its being deleted if the Supervisor encountered overload conditions before another robot of the same basic type arrived with a matching half. The successful response was a new mode of genetic recombination, which, coincidentally, also provided the answer to an "information crisis" that was restricting the pool of genetic variation available for further selection and improvement.

Some mutant forms of robot found that they could save themselves the trouble of long journeys back to factories by satisfying the half-subfile-outputting urge locally with anything that possessed the right electrical connections and compatible internal software, which usually meant another robot of the same basic kind. However, although the robots' memories were getting larger, so were their operating programs, with the result that an acceptor didn't have enough free space to hold an entire genetic subfile. Therefore, the donor's half was accommodated by overwriting nonessential code, which did incur the inconvenience of leaving the "female" with some impairment of agility and defensive ability—but that was only temporary, since full faculties would be restored when the genetic package was delivered to the factory.

But in return for these complications came the immense benefit that the subfiles delivered to the factories would be complete, ready to be passed instantly to the schedulers, free from the risk of being deleted by overworked Supervisors.

The information crisis that this progression beyond asexual reproduction also solved was a result of inbreeding. The various Supervisors had only the gene pools of their respective tribes available to work with, which made recombination difficult because of the rules imposed by the Borijan programmers. But the robots mixing genes out on the surface knew nothing and cared less about programmers' rules and proceeded to bring half subfiles together haphazardly in ways that the rules didn't permit and the Supervisors could never have conceived of. Most of the combinations that resulted from these experiments were nonviable, but the few that were viable radiated outward functionally in every direction to launch a whole qualitatively distinct, explosive new phase of the evolutionary process.

The demands of the two sexual roles reinforced minor initial differences and brought about a gradual polarization of behavioral traits. Since a "pregnant" female suffered some loss of self-sufficiency for the duration, her chances of success were improved considerably if her mate happened to be of a disposition to stay around and help out for a while, perhaps accompanying her on her journey and protecting their joint genetic investment. Selection tended, therefore, to favor this kind of male and, by the same token, those females who mated with them preferentially. Hence, a female tendency emerged of being "choosy," and in response the males evolved various repertoires of rituals, displays, and demonstrations to improve their eligibility.

The process unfolding on the surface of Titan had thus come to exhibit genetic variability and recombination, competition, selection, and adaptation—all the essentials for continuing evolution. The form of life—for it was, wasn't it?—was admittedly strange from the terrestrial viewpoint, with the individuals that it included sharing common external reproductive, digestive, and immune systems instead of separate internal ones . . . and, of course, there was no complicated carbon chemistry figuring in the scheme of things. But then, what was there, apart from chauvinism, to say that it shouldn't have been so?

And over all that time some copies of the coded configurations that preserved the essence of the twelve Borijan personae from the distant past were passed down through the generations, millennium after millennium, never to be expressed in any functioning or physical form.

A million years passed. Then, one day, a robot craft from a civilization born of a different life-form appeared over Titan's canopy of rust-red cloud. The pictures and data returned by the probes that it sent down revealed a world stranger than anything its builders had ever seen before. Shortly afterward, astronomically speaking, the *Orion* followed, bringing with it descendants of the line of semi-intelligent apes of long ago to investigate.

III

The Computer
That Discovered
The Supernatural

22

I T WAS ONE OF THOSE RARE TIMES WHEN ZAMBENDORF seemed close to losing his self-control. His face glowed pink, his eyes blazed, and his beard bristled as he stood in Weinerbaum's office at Genoa Base, holding out the piece of paper that had brought him marching in a few minutes earlier. "It's due here in just over a week!" he stormed. "What are they trying to achieve by this? It will negate everything my people have been doing for the last five months. What kind of a way is that to treat the investment?"

Actually, Zambendorf was fully in control; his bluster was calculated for effect. The paper was a NASO message form with a directive that had come in from GSEC a couple of hours earlier, ordering Zambendorf and his team to be moved up to the *Shirasagi* upon its arrival at Titan and to remain there until it returned to Earth. It gave as a reason the concern that the GSEC board felt for their safety in view of the "deteriorating local situation."

"You and I both know that this is rubbish, Werner," Zambendorf fumed. "The media back there have been exaggerating the dangers for months. GSEC knows it, too— God, they're behind most of it. And we both know why, don't we? It's a pretext to turn Titan into an industrial colony. I messed up their plans last time, and they want me out of the way. Which means they haven't given up. They're going to try it again."

Privately, Zambendorf didn't hold out much hope for a lot of sympathy from Weinerbaum's direction. But this latest development portended ominous decisions ahead regarding the Taloids, and Zambendorf was willing to sound out any possibility.

Weinerbaum, standing by the end of the hinge-down plastic shelf that was the best the cubbyhole could offer for a desk, raised his brows in a feigned show of puzzlement. "Well, naturally I understand your feelings." He shrugged and showed his palms. "But surely you don't imagine that I can concern myself in a matter that rests purely between yourself and your principals. As you say, it's their investment. If they choose not to run with it longer, then that's their prerogative, I suppose." His expression stopped a shade short of mocking. "Maybe they just weren't getting the results they expected."

Behind his veneer of studied coolness Weinerbaum seemed to be enjoying the situation. His disdain toward Zambendorf had not slackened over the months, but lately he had been less hostile and more tolerant in expressing it. It could have been, of course, that after almost five months on Titan the simple fact of sharing the quality of being human had come to outweigh everything else. But Zambendorf had detected a general lightening in Weinerbaum's whole outlook and manner, a shine in his eye and a springiness in his step, betraying an inner excitement that perhaps made the irritation of having Zambendorf around no longer important. Natural curiosity made Zambendorf want to know why.

Apart from giving Weinerbaum an opportunity to exercise his snobbishness, this line wasn't going to accomplish anything, Zambendorf decided. He raised a hand to acknowledge that Weinerbaum didn't owe him anything, then sighed and made a pretense of laboring for a few seconds to calm himself down.

"Look," he said finally, speaking now in a more restrained voice heavy with candor. "I know that as far as you're concerned, we're at opposite poles when it comes to honesty and intellectual integrity. But really, the differences between us are a lot more superficial than you think."

"Oh, really? Do tell me why." Weinerbaum folded his arms and propped himself back against the shelf, at the same time nodding his head to indicate a fold-down seat on the bulkhead wall by the door—more because two big men could not have remained standing in the confined space without taking on an aspect of the absurd than from expectations of learning anything. Zambendorf sat down.

"Because at the bottom of it all we both share a conviction that reason and rationality afford the only worthwhile basis for systems of human belief," Zambendorf said. "But we come from different directions in expressing it. Your way, science, is direct and overt: demonstrable, repeatable experiments leading to falsifiable predictions which can be tested."

"How interesting. Do go on." Weinerbaum's tone seemed to ask why that had never occurred to him before.

Zambendorf refused to be fazed. "But some people—maybe most of them—will cling to wishful thinking in the face of every adverse fact, impervious to any appeal to reason. Try to argue with them and you'll be arguing until the end of time." Zambendorf made a brief throwing-away motion. "So I simply allow their own credulousness to draw them on into greater contradictions until it requires an acceptance of the fantastic that cannot be sustained. And then, maybe, they learn something."

"Aha!" Weinerbaum pounced. "So you're admitting at last that it's all a load of hokum, are you?"

Zambendorf steered him off with a wave. "Oh, the situation that we're really talking about is too important to get involved in any of that. Whatever differences we may have are eclipsed by the common concern that we have for Arthur and the future of his regime here in Genoa. My interest, whether you believe it or not, is to preserve the ideals of freedom and individualism that it stands for. Yours is to prevent the reinstating of Henry, which would be a first step toward seeing your scientific work subordinated to the setting up of a manufacturing colony."

Weinerbaum's expression had lost some of its disdain while Zambendorf was speaking. He looked across now intently, as if the whole subject had suddenly taken on a new perspective in his mind. Zambendorf went on. "So in this we're really on the same side. We both want the same outcome. But how can I contribute to making it happen if I'm confined to the *Shirasagi* and then sent back to Earth?"

There was a pause while Weinerbaum continued staring thoughtfully. Finally he conceded, "Very well, supposing I take your point. What do you think I would be in a position to do about it?"

Zambendorf went through the motions of considering the question, as if he hadn't had the answer clear in his head before he had entered the room. "NASO is still the controlling authority here," he said finally. "It might carry some weight if you were to appeal this decision of GSEC's to them."

"Oh? And on what grounds might I do that?" Weinerbaum asked.

Zambendorf shrugged. Might as well go for broke, he thought. "Well, you could always say that the work of myself and the team is an essential aid to the scientific enterprise," he suggested.

Weinerbaum balked visibly. But to Zambendorf's inner surprise, he didn't promptly end the discussion right there. "I'll give the matter some consideration," he replied instead—coolly and with a manifest lack of enthusiasm, but the door had not been slammed.

The conversation left Zambendorf with the impression that more was going on than was obvious to the eye. The result was to make him more curious than ever.

The situation grew stranger the following day, when Weinerbaum held a closed conference with his inner group of senior scientists, then went to Harold Mackeson, the NASO base commander, and lodged a protest of exactly the kind Zambendorf had facetiously suggested. Consternation followed.

Clarissa Eidstadt seized the opportunity to book a slot in the outgoing communications beam to Earth and get an item headed "TITAN SCIENTISTS PLEAD ZAMBENDORF CASE" through to her publicity agency for general release.

Mackeson referred back to NASO headquarters in Washington for guidance and received a positive response. Since taking full charge of the Titan operation, NASO's directors had enjoyed greater freedom of action and a boost in prestige. They knew the true situation on Titan and recognized GSEC's maneuverings for what they were. Zambendorf's joining of forces with Massey to thwart GSEC's previous scheme had marked him in NASO's eyes as being on "their" side then, however bizarre the alliance looked on the face of it. If GSEC considered it in its interest now to have Zambendorf out of the way, then, whatever GSEC's reasons, NASO was agin' it. Accordingly, NASO put out a statement saying that Zambendorf's help to Arthur's regime had been invaluable, and it was vital that this be continued for the benefit of other Taloid nations.

Colonel Short, the local military commander, on the other hand, whose loyalty was to others in Washington with political links to the GSEC-led consortium, echoed the GSEC line by saying that he could no longer be responsible for the safety of unnecessarily involved civilians.

Zambendorf, for his part, was happy to leave those kinds of politics to the politicians, self-styled and professional. He was more intrigued by the reason behind Weinerbaum's action, which had been so totally out of character. Certainly Zambendorf was under no illusion that Weinerbaum had been motivated by any great sentiments of charity. And another part of it all that struck Zambendorf as significant was the way the scientists who were closest to Zambendorf's group—such as Dave Crookes, the communications specialist, and Graham Spearman, the biologist—had been excluded from the discussions that had preceded Weinerbaum's approach to Mackeson. It had the feel about it that they were considered security risk, too free in their talking and too familiar with the wrong people to be trusted.

Trusted with what? Zambendorf asked himself. It all added up to a conviction in his mind that something big was going on that Weinerbaum was covering up and that he didn't want GSEC poking its nose into. Precipitating the fuss over Zambendorf had been his way of diverting their attention.

It simply wasn't in Zambendorf's nature to pass up something like that. His whole life had been a pursuit of perfecting the art of finding out what he wasn't supposed to know. And besides, things had been getting too tame on Titan for too long. It was time, he decided, to mobilize the team.

23

THE TRAIL WOUND DOWN A HILLSIDE PAST GROVES OF spring formers, die casters, and rotary grinders in an out-of-the-way valley on the edge of the forests in southern Kroaxia. Below, the machinery stood taller around clumps of transfer presses and drop forges lining the banks of the river conveying its burden northward toward the principal city, Pergassos.

Clad in heavy, hooded cloaks and woodsmen's boots, and pacing their step with staffs of duralumin tubing, Thirg and Brongyd made their way downward from the rise they had crossed, while Rex ran ahead, rooting and sniffing in the undergrowth of discarded parts and metal tailings. The Taloids carried packs slung across their backs and walked with the strong, sturdy stride that came from many brights spent living among outdoor people and trekking over mountain passes.

Much had happened since their escape, with a group of other captives, from the village of Quahal during the clash between the Lumian dragon fighters and the Redeeming Avengers. The countryside was alive with spies, Avengers, and other proselytizers of the Lifemaker's True Faith, all playing on the people's recent insecurities in order to denounce the heresies of Kleippur in Carthogia and calling for a return to the older values. Unsure what kind of reception to expect in any place they were not known and with armed Avengers out looking for them to get even for what had happened at Quahal, the fugitives had split up into ones and twos and gone into hiding or tried making their way by different routes to safety. Thirg and Brongyd had lain low for many brights, avoiding the towns, staying on the move, and all the time laying false trails of rumor to throw off their pursuers. Finally they had judged it safe enough to come out of the hills to try crossing Kroaxia and the northern desert to enter Carthogia.

"Ah, I think I see it now." Thirg stopped to study the way ahead. "Yes, this looks familiar." He pointed at a sluggish collection of roller conveyors and chutes lazily sending oddments down toward the river and almost obscured by the wire tangles of a mostly defunct cable-spinning line. "He used to live by that brook. There should be a clearing just past the wall beyond it there. It used to be the side of a motor pit that existed here long ago."

"Let's hope he's still there," Brongyd said. "My feet could use a plate, Thirg. And I can feel dust in the joints that a cool Michelube would do wonders for."

Ahead of them, Rex stiffened suddenly and looked up, coolant vanes bristling and collector horns pricked. At the same instant a din of short alarm-siren wails and cutter gnashings broke out behind the thicket of lattice works ahead. Thirg called for Rex to stay back. It stood, snorting methane vapors, while the two robs hurried to catch up. Then another mecanine bounded into view and stopped a short distance away, facing them along the trail. It was large and fierce-looking, with a black carbon-impregnated face ferrous red around the imagers, heavy turretlike shoulders, and a solidly riveted chest. Its alarm siren fell to a series of warning hoots, which Rex returned as a growl of cavity-amplified cooling-fan whirrings.

Then a rob's voice called out from farther back. " 'Old it, Duke. Down, boy." He came into sight, older than Brongyd would have guessed from the voice, but hardy-looking and vigorous. He wore a laminated foil jerkin with loose breeches gathered into wire-braided boots and was holding a Kroaxian army-issue spring-steel crossbow, cocked and leveled. " 'Oo be ye?" he demanded, his voice gruff and suspicious. "There's nowt for strangers t' be busyin' theirsel's over in these parts. 'Oo are yers, an' what does yer want?"

Thirg waited a moment for recognition to register, but the other's features remained harsh and unyielding. Finally Thirg grinned and shook his head sadly. "Well, that's a strange welcome to be giving to an old friend, Mordran, Master-of-the-Duke-That-Warns. Surely Thirg can't have changed that much. Or has too much imbibing of uranium-salt brews clouded your memory?"

Mordran stared disbelievingly, and then his coolant flap dropped suddenly. "By the Lifemaker's image! Surely not! ... Tell me it isn't Thirg, the Asker!"

"I'll tell you so by all means if it pleases you, but I can't see how it's supposed to help," Thirg replied. "If true, then you know nothing that you didn't know already. If false, then the purpose of my being here could hardly be served, could it?"

The weather-scoured facial scales shifted to the nearest the craggy features could manage to a smile of delight. Mordran lowered the bow, uncocked the trigger, and came forward. "Hee-hee-hee! There was only ever one person 'oo could 'ave come up wi' an answer like that. Thirg, by all the ..." He left the sentence unfinished as he grasped Thirg's hand and pumped it as if he were trying to wrench it off at the shoulder. "I 'eard ye'd upped an' awayed to Carthogia. Got yerself mixed up in them goin's-on o' Kleippur's was what they told me. And the best place fer 'im, too, I said. Never thought we'd see you back 'ere again. Never in a thousand brights."

"It just shows never to bet on certainties," Thirg said. "Mordran, this is a very good friend of mine, Brongyd, also an inquirer, one who studies the mysteries of life and the natural machine world. Brongyd is from Uchal but is returning with me now to Carthogia." They shook hands, Brongyd warily, Mordran making a visible effort to be more genteel. Thirg went on. "Mordran's an old soldier, Brongyd, formerly a sergeant with one of the Kroaxian foot pike regiments. One of the times when I upset Frennelech's priests, he got me out of trouble by dropping certain records into a furnace."

"Aye, an' that were the least I could do, an' all," Mordran told Brongyd as he turned and began walking back with them. "Afore that, there were a time when I was wi' this troop that got ambushed by brigands way out in t' 'ills this side o' Meracasine. Right to-do, it were an' all. More'n twenty of our lads got t' chop that bright, they did. They left me fer gone, too. Underneath some welding trees I were—an arm 'alf-off, a leg 'alf-off, an' me 'ead switched all off, hee-hee. But it were Thirg 'ere that found me an' dragged me back to this 'ouse up there that 'e lived in, all away from everyone—"

"Actually, it was Rex," Thirg put in as they walked.

"Aye!" Mordran pointed ahead at Thirg's mecanine, now trotting a length behind Duke, who kept glancing back, not prepared yet to take its eyes away for more than a second. "That were 'im. That mec. If 'e 'adn't found me when 'e did, I wouldn't be 'ere talkin' to the two 'o yers now."

"Yula's well, I hope," Thirg said as they rounded a bend in the path and came within sight of Mordran's house.

"Oh, never better. Ye'll be missin' 'er this bright, though. She's away visitin'."

"Oh, that's a shame," Thirg said. "Where has she gone?"

"Ye remember Serriel, the one that's always talkin' an' never says nothin'?"

"The worob who lives across the river? The one with all the children. Yes, of course. How could I forget?"

"Well, she's just back from t' factory with another now. Eight, that makes it. Anyroad, Yula's off over there to 'elp out, an' probably the two of 'em 'aven't stopped talkin' since she got there. Ee, it's good to see thee back, Thirg. Let's get ye both plated up an' charged, an' ye can tell me all about what's been 'appenin' t' ye all these brights. It'll be a good story, too, I'll be bound. I've never 'eard of such carryin's-on as what folk 'ave been tellin'. King and 'igh priest both out on their ear. Aliens made out of 'ot sticky stuff comin' down out of t' sky. Makes ye wonder where it's all goin' ter end, don't it?"

The house was modest in size but neatly trimmed and of a healthy color, with the folds cut back at the roof ends and center walls, where mature growths often acquired a tired, saggy look. There was a garden of plating salt depositors, coolant and solvent stills, and bearing bush presses, along with a fenced paddock at the rear, in which a mixed herd of rare-metals concentrators were grazing on a pile of scrap. Mordran led them past a flower bed in which micro laser heads were cheerfully sculpting fractal forms from copper and beryllium offcuts and into the kitchen. It was cluttered but clean, with well-stocked shelves of parts and vases of wild forest cogs and cableforms to brighten the place.

Thirg and Brongyd sat down gratefully in front of the waterplace, while Mordran set two rechargers and began preparing solvent and plating solutions. "An' 'ow's things wi' that brother o' yours, Thirg?" he inquired.

"Groork?"

"Aye, Groork, the 'Earer." The Lumians Thirg had talked to said that the "voices" hearers thought came from the sky and certain holy places were a remnant of a lost sense that the early ancestors of the robeings had possessed. Allegedly it was the same ability that enabled the Lumians to talk to each other over vast distances and even to send pictures. " 'Enlightener,' or some such, 'e were callin' 'isself," Mordran went on. "When everyone was goin' daft over this new alien religion that tells everyone ter be friends wi' likes o' Carthogians, when they still can't keep thesselves from 'alf killin' their own neighbors down t' street. Nearly got 'isself t' chop, didn't 'e, that Groork? When they chucked 'im off t' cliff. Then 'e was away to Carthogia, too, last I 'eard. Is 'e doin' all right?"

Thirg sat forward and rubbed his hands together in the warm glow from the flickering fountain of liquid ice in the waterplace. "Yes, he's out of all that business now and a diligent student of the new sciences at Kleippur's academy," he said.

"An' what about you two?" Mordran asked, directing the question at Brongyd to invite him more into the conversation. "This is a strange route to be takin' if ye were supposed to be goin' back with 'im to Carthogia from Uchal."

"The Avengers have been looking for us, so we've been keeping out of sight for a while," Brongyd replied. "I'm sure you know the way things are."

"Aye," Mordran replied darkly.

"We're enemies of the True Faith that they're trying to bring back," Thirg said. "Carthogian inquirers. That says enough."

"An' none of it'll make any difference in the long run," Mordran declared. "They're causin' people a lot of grief an' trouble for nowt. Nobody can put the clock back. Now that them Lumians are 'ere, things can't go back ter bein' the way they used ter be. It's the likes o' Frennelech an' them priests that's be'ind it all. They don't know anythin' that's worth sump sludge, if you want my opinion. Fairy tales and mumbo jumbo, the lot of it. It's the inquirers—the likes o' you two—who'll change the world. An' the priests know it, too. That's why they've always tried to keep you down. But they can't win. So what 'ave ye been doin' that's upset 'em this time, Thirg?"

"I was visiting Brongyd when the Avengers came to Uchal," Thirg replied. "We were taken captive with some others and paraded through more villages where the same things happened. Their leader was called Varlech. His way of intimidating the villagers was to execute the headrob and his family in front of them. They carried the body of a dead Lumian with them in a cart to prove that the Lumians are not gods."

"I know of Varlech," Mordran said. "Real nasty piece o' work. The Lumians went after 'im because o' that dead body that 'e were luggin' around, an' the fool thought 'e could take 'em on. Got 'isself blown ter smithereens, 'e did, along wi' most o' t' lunatics that 'e 'ad with 'im. Only trouble were, a few o' t' villagers got chopped, too. A bad business, that. Place called Quahal, it 'appened in. They're some right fighters from what I've 'eard, these

Lumians, when they get mad. I don't reckon I'd want ter tangle wi' 'em."

Brongyd sent Thirg a questioning look. Thirg shrugged and nodded. "We know," Brongyd said, looking back at Mordran. "We were there. That was where we escaped from."

Mordran's imager shades widened in surprise as he came around the table carrying funnels, cans, a bottle, and two cords. "What! You two were there, at Quahal? Ee, I've got t' 'ear this! Come on, then, an' tell me the story." He raked ice flakes and slush aside to get a flow going in the waterplace, then pulled up a chair and sat down.

Thirg and Brongyd took turns relating the events at Quahal while Mordran listened intently, puffing evaporated gasoline fumes from a pipe. They ended with an account of their retreat into the hills and the time they'd spent staying on the move and out of sight. Finally they got around to the question of what they planned to do next.

"I think we've shaken them off now," Thirg said. "Our thought was to go into Pergassos and seek Nogarech's aid in getting back to Carthogia." Nogarech, Kroaxia's new ruler following the expulsion of Eskenderom, was trying to introduce a more liberal system based on Kleippur's model, and it had seemed a reasonable proposition. Mordran, however, was less sanguine about it.

"Things are unsettled all over Kroaxia," he told them. "T' priests 'aven't gone away. They're out there still, preachin' on about the Lifemaker an' scarin' folk wi' tales of 'ow they'll melt in t' furnace if they don't think the way they're told. An' a lot o' folks are startin' ter listen. I mean, it's the way they were brought up, in't it? Then there's been stories about Eskenderom an' all 'is old cronies 'avin' secret meetin's wi' Lumians across in Serethgin, which gives some the idea that 'e might be comin' back. So they're lookin' for ways o' stayin' on 'is right side, just in case. I'd say that right now Nogarech's situation is touch an' go." Mordran shook his head. "'Tain't a time to go marchin' yersel's into t' middle o'

Pergassos, saying what a great lad Kleippur is an' lookin'
for a ride back to Carthogia."

Thirg and Brongyd exchanged worried looks. "What
would you suggest, then?" Thirg asked Mordran.

Mordran puffed at his pipe and thought for a while. Finally he said, "What I'd do is dress up to look more like
farmers and go into Pergassos quiet an' easy. I'll take yer
there on a road that not many know, where ye won't attract notice. Then, once ye're there, ye can find someone
who'll get y' in to see Nogarech on the side, like, without
too many knowin'. Them that wants ter see the old ways
back again 'ave got spies around 'im everywhere, an' this
way 'e might be better able t' 'elp. Anyroad, that's what
I reckon. It'd be no problem fer me. I've time to kill afore
Yula gets back, in any case. We've a couple o' lads 'ere
who can take care of t' 'ouse an' t' animals. What d'yer
think?"

Thirg and Brongyd agreed, and the three of them departed after Thirg and Brongyd had taken a long sleep in
a couple of the house's service and overhaul closets.

24

ESKENDEROM, KROAXIA'S EXILED FORMER KING, STOOD
glowering irascibly at the edge of a forest clearing
hidden in the hills of Serethgin, which bordered Kroaxia to
the south. A short distance in front of him, Frennelech, the
deposed high priest, gave parting exhortations to the two
priests who were about to leave for Carthogia with the
Lumian flying dragon. Behind, the equerries and other attendants who had accompanied them to the meeting place
waited with the mounts. The priests would be going to join

ten others whom the Lumians had taken back to Carthogia in the course of the last eight brights. The Lumian artisans who created artificial machines that could talk and fly needed Kroaxians to help them produce improved language-translating vegetables adapted to the Kroaxian dialect.

"Go you forth, then, and apply thy minds diligently to the tasks that the Lumian sages shall set you," Frennelech said. "Remember always that the Lifemaker works in devious ways, but it is His work that you shall be doing."

"Praise be to the Lifemaker," the first of the priests responded.

"May He protect thee and the king," the other said.

They turned and, following the gestures of the Lumian soldiers in their ungainly, removable dome-headed casings, ascended the sloping ramp to a compartment at the rear of the dragon with its doors left open to the outside—robeings could not have entered the closed gas furnaces in which Lumians dwelt. The cordon of Lumians who had guarded the dragon entered through a forward door that closed behind them, cutting off the glow of violet heat-light from inside. As Frennelech came back to stand beside Eskenderom, fierce blasts of dragon-light burst from the beast's underside. Then, roaring its defiance of the force that drew all things to the ground, it rose up, turning its nose northward.

"Explain to me, now, the machinations of these strange aliens, who even now, after two twelve-brights, leave my mind confounded," Eskenderom said. "With their approval we arm and incite the very Avengers whose provocations work against the same Carthogia that the Lumians endorse. Yet the Avengers whom they would have us encourage, their dragon soldiers harass. Is it my mind that ails with the onset of time, or is there some obscure logic that would surely challenge the perspicacity of the Lifemaker Himself?"

"They seek to create an illusion that peril threatens the Lumians left here on Robia," Frennelech replied. "And this purpose do the Avengers serve." He watched the sky dragon disappear over the hilltops. "In response to his subjects' plea for aid, the great Lumian king will send his army to restore thy throne."

"What kind of great king is this who can act only at his subjects' will?" Eskenderom answered darkly. "Is it king or pretender with whom we treat? If the great king would have us tame the forests of Robia, then why does he not send fleets of dragons bearing his command? If, unwittingly, we are abetting the designs of another, then what dire retribution awaits at the hand of he who does command?"

"Like Robia, Lumia's house is divided," Frennelech said. "Think of it not as treachery by one who would usurp but rather as a contest among equal kings."

"Equal? Then why do we meet here like thieves, in the forest, while the Lumian dragons make their lair in Carthogia?" Eskenderom demanded.

"Small Lumian dragons," Frennelech pointed out. "The masters of the Great-Dragon-That-Brings-Armies are pledged to thee."

"The great dragon that sleeps still in the sky above Lumia," Eskenderom said. "Another two brights yet, we are told, before it will awake. Then eleven brights for its flight to Robia. Can our effort be thus long sustained?"

"We are praying for the Lifemaker to strengthen the Avengers' resolve and faith," Frennelech assured him.

"Hmph." Eskenderom scowled as he thought about the reports he'd heard of the clashes between the Redeeming Avengers and Lumian dragon soldiers. "It might be an idea to pray for Him to strengthen their casings, too, while He's at it."

Aboard the military flyer that had just lifted off from the meeting place in the hills of the nation known as Venice, Werner Weinerbaum removed the gauntlets of his suit and placed them in the stowage rack below his helmet. These talks always had to be conducted outside because Terran cabin conditions would have been unbearable to the Titan-conditioned Taloids.

Taloid help had proved necessary before his research

could progress further. He hadn't used Arthur's Taloids from Genoa because Zambendorf was too well known there—accepted as an official consultant on setting up the state administration, for heaven's sake! Weinerbaum didn't want that preposterous "psychic" meddling in his business. But his move to oppose GSEC's directive and actually plead Zambendorf's case for remaining at Genoa Base to NASO had been something of a master stroke, Weinerbaum thought, even if he did say so himself.

First, of course, it had cemented his relationship with NASO, and keeping NASO in control was his best insurance for being left to carry on his work without hindrance. Second, the show of magnanimity could only enhance his own image among the scientific staff, many of whom seemed to welcome Zambendorf's antics as entertainment and a relief from the routine of the base. Well, Weinerbaum had shown that he could appreciate a joke, too. In fact, that was what he had meant when he had said that Zambendorf provided "a valuable contribution to the scientific enterprise"—the wretched Eidstadt woman had quoted him out of context. And in exercising such tolerance, he had dispelled any absurd notion that some might have been harboring that he considered Zambendorf a threat to his image. Finally, it had to be admitted that Zambendorf did command an extraordinary rapport with the Taloids. Here was an asset that Weinerbaum might, conceivably, put to good use some day. A wise administrator allowed for future unknowns. This way, he not only was conserving a potential resource but had enhanced its value by earning Zambendorf's goodwill in the bargain.

In a seat sideways to Weinerbaum, facing a console, Captain Mason of the U.S. Special Forces looked away from a screen he had been using to check on the two Taloids in the open rear section of the craft. "From the way they're sitting and clutching those handrails, I'd say they're terrified," he said. "But they're belted in securely and look okay."

"Fine," Weinerbaum acknowledged with a faint nod.

"Two more for the language department, eh?" Mason

said. "What's the score with these guys that you're bringing back? Somebody told me it was to make better translator boxes. Is that it?"

"Yes."

"So what's wrong with using the Ts at Genoa that we've already got?"

"The linguists can get a better feel of the structure with access to a range of dialects," Weinerbaum told him. "There are some important differences in grammar and usage between Paduan and Genoan."

"Okay." Mason wasn't sure he believed that. If it were so, why were they picking up Paduans out in Venice, from the has-been king, Henry, instead of simply getting some from Padua? But Weinerbaum had specifically requested a "low-key" approach, without the visibility that public trafficking into Padua would have entailed. Now, why would a scientist be worried about something like that? Mason wondered. But it suited Mason fine. It meant that he could schedule the pickups to be made during the secret meetings with Henry, without having to lay on extra trips.

And to top it all, Weinerbaum thought to himself, he still enjoyed the cooperation of the military. Since they were acting as fronts for GSEC in preparing Henry to be reinstated, they might have been expected to respond to his pro-NASO gesture with some hostility. No doubt respect for his scientist's impartiality had prevailed.

He experienced a satisfying feeling of having achieved a delicate balance of compromises with finesse. There really wasn't that much to politics when one broke it down, he told himself. It was essentially a commonsense art, overrated to impress the credulous. Just a question of considering a few elementary factors and evaluating the lowest multiple that would accommodate all of them. Of course, a trained intellect and an ability to assimilate other points of view did help, he supposed. Not that the so-called professionals seemed particularly well endowed, judging by the habitual messes they made of the world's affairs. Maybe, when he got back to Earth, he'd move into statesmanship.

* * *

Zambendorf's way of going about things was very often the one that nobody else thought of: the simplest. What would be the simplest way to find out what the scientists were up to? he asked himself. Go and see. How easiest to go and see? Ask.

Sergeant Harvey spread his hands helplessly as he sat on the far side of one of the long tables in the general mess. It was midmorning by the twenty-four-hour local time cycle, which was synchronized to GMT, and the place was quiet. A few mechanics were taking a coffee break at the far end, and the NASO chefs were setting out dishes in preparation for the lunchtime crowd.

"Joe, you know I would if I could, but I can't help ya."

Joe Fellburg's huge, broad-featured face puckered into a frown. "Hey, Bill, what is this? We were on the same team, man. I need to break outta this place or I'll get cabin fever. I've always wanted to see one of the assembly places where those machines come together, and there's one on the south side, about ten miles outside the city. You guys are always running trucks and flyers out there. I figured you could fix me a trip." He rubbed his chin pointedly. "I could maybe throw in a bottle of something. There's ways. Come on, it's just like hitching a ride outta Travis, back home. What's the problem?"

Harvey shook his head. "You don't understand, Joe. One of the experimental stations is located there." Fellburg did understand—his main reason for being interested was that ES3 *was* located there. Harvey went on. "Weinerbaum's had a high-security wrap put around the whole place. Level Five scientists and cleared personnel only. Even I couldn't just walk inside there."

Fellburg looked puzzled. "So what in hell are they doing there?"

"You know they don't tell me things like that, Joe. All I know is they've got lots of trucks and cabins set up out there. They use a lot of computers. Weinerbaum and usually a couple of his guys fly out there most mornings. And there's a section of one of the huts that's kept open to the outside, too, so I guess they've got Ts working with them."

"Taloids? What for?"

"How do I know? Maybe they're doing a *Star Wars* remake on ice."

Fellburg leaned back against the wall behind the bench and thought for a moment. It was clear that he wasn't going to get anywhere, but that in itself said a lot. He asked himself what other information might be the best pointer to uncovering whatever was afoot. "Could you do something else for me, then, Bill?" he asked finally.

"Like what?"

"These guys who go out there with Weinerbaum. Could you let me know from the gate logs who they are?"

"Why do you want to know something like that?"

"Oh, just curious."

Harvey's voice dropped to little more than a murmur. "You'll get my ass nailed, Joe. We've been told to cool it with you guys. You know, back off a little. Not to be so upfront."

"Us? You mean Karl and the team?"

"Uh huh."

"Why?"

Harvey shrugged and shook his head. "Who knows what goes on?"

Fellburg snorted. "So screw 'em. Come on, we were both in the same league. I'm only asking for a few names."

"Goddamn . . . Okay, you've got it."

"And how about the days and the times they were checked in and out? Huh?" Fellburg drummed his fingertips on the table and winked conspiratorially. "The bottle of whatever still stands."

Harvey emitted a long sigh. "Oh, shit . . . I'll see what I can do," he promised.

All the senior scientists who were cleared for Experimental Station 3 turned out to be from Weinerbaum's coterie of insiders. Dave Crookes identified the most regular visitors as either computer scientists, specializing in complex dynamic code structures, or linguists—practically the same group, in fact, that had sought to establish communication with the Taloids before Zambendorf had muscled in and ruined their act.

Thinking about the names reminded Crookes that he had come across the terms "redundant DNA" and "Cyril" several times in references to their work and had heard the same terms mentioned in unguarded moments of conversation. Fellburg and Thelma tried breaking into the local data files and also tapping into the Earthlink to see what they could dredge up from NASO HQ, only to find that the encryption was impregnable to the methods Zambendorf's team had at its disposal (even psychic powers!). But even the fact that Weinerbaum had resorted to such sophisticated protection told them something. It meant that he and his directors were anxious to prevent other concerns back on Earth from finding out what he was up to, which could only mean GSEC and its political supporters in Washington. That would explain Weinerbaum's seeming aberration in defending Zambendorf against GSEC's directive to have him removed: Opposing GSEC would help keep NASO in control on Titan and thus preserve Weinerbaum's independence.

But from the log entries that Fellburg obtained, it seemed that Weinerbaum was being palsy with the military as well, jaunting off with them to places like Venice and prompting them to keep Zambendorf at a distance. Why Venice? Zambendorf wondered. Colonel Short got his orders from offices of the Pentagon that were sympathetic to the political faction backing GSEC, which wanted Henry back in power. And Venice was where Henry had fled after his expulsion from Padua. So, was Weinerbaum getting mixed up in some underhanded political move to bring Henry back?

Zambendorf wondered if Weinerbaum fully appreciated the dangers of the double game he was playing. Scientists were only human. While deservedly acclaimed and accredited within their own specialized fields of experience, they could be as easily misled as anyone else when they ventured outside it. And—as Zambendorf saw and took advantage of all the time in his own line of work—the very fact of their proven ability in other areas could result in a proneness to mislead themselves. "If *I* can't see the trick, then there can't be a trick," the reasoning seemed to run, which left the proponent of the logic painted into a corner and forced to accept the only other explanation possible, namely, that whatever he was witnessing had to be genuine.

One afternoon, Zambendorf and the others, except Drew West, who was fetching some figures from one of the labs, were crammed into the cabin that Zambendorf shared with Abaquaan. Dave Crookes was with them, going over what they had managed to learn so far. If Henry and the Paduans were involved somehow, then one way for finding out more would be to tackle it from the Padua end, through Arthur's excellent intelligence service. That would take time, however, since communications back from Padua would be slow. In any case, they could do little to further the idea until Zambendorf's next meeting with Arthur.

Crookes sat back against the wall at the foot of Abaquaan's bunk and cast an eye once more over the collection of names, places, lists, and notes on everything else they had been able to glean. Thelma passed around coffees and sodas while Clarissa ran something on the terminal in a corner.

"Do you know what the whole pattern looks like to me?" Crookes said at last. "From the people who are involved, I think they've discovered some new form of intelligence out there. Why else is ES3 set up at one of the final assembly stations? And they're determined to keep you people out of it—maybe because of the way they lost out on prestige last time, and they still haven't gotten over it."

"You think so?" Thelma said. She looked amazed. "All this fuss and security stuff just over who did what first? I mean, we are talking about grown-up, adult people, right?"

"These are just the kind of people who get funny about things like that," Crookes said.

"Prima donnas," Clarissa threw over her shoulder. "That's why guys like you and Graham get shut out, too. You don't play the game, Dave. That's your problem."

"The part about redundant DNA and Cyril sounds like it

could be a life-form, all right," Fellburg agreed, rubbing his chin.

"You see?" Crookes looked at the others while Clarissa carried on tapping at the terminal. "It all fits."

Zambendorf considered the suggestion and shook his head. "More likely they just think that you and Graham talk too easily," he said. "No, this doesn't necessarily say anything about a new intelligence. Cyril could be a code name for anything. And redundant DNA? A metaphor for anything that serves no obvious purpose. I use it myself all the time."

They debated for some time, finally accepting that there really was nothing conclusive one way or another. Then the door opened, and Drew West appeared. He was holding the papers he had gone to fetch, but his manner said that he didn't attach too much importance to them right now. He looked quickly around the company and closed the door carefully behind him.

"Guess what I just overheard," he invited. Nobody asked. "I came out through the electrical repair shop. That French computer woman, Annette Claurier, was in there, getting something down from a shelf in a closet. She couldn't see me because she had the door open, but do you know what she said? She said, 'Olaf—' That's the name of the Norwegian she works with, right? '—Olaf,' she said, 'do you know which star I think Cyril might be from . . .' And then she closed the door, saw that it was me, and marched out looking real shaken up." The others all stared mutely. West directed a look of forced nonchalance at each of them in turn, all around the cabin. Clarissa's tapping in the corner had stopped. "Interesting, do you think?" West asked.

"Star?" Zambendorf repeated the word dazedly. "Cyril is from another star?"

Crookes and Fellburg remained speechless. Thelma realized that the cup in her hand was getting hot and put it down hastily.

Abaquaan stared at Zambendorf, for once in his life looking truly astounded. "Code experts and linguists?" he whispered. "Ancient DNA? In the computers? Could it be one of them, Karl? The guys we've been talking about?"

Nobody needed to be told what he meant. Had Weinerbaum's people found one of the aliens from long ago, the aliens who had built the long-lost civilization that the machine biosphere of Titan had originated from a million years before?

Surely it couldn't be.

25

EVERYTHING WAS WRONG. SARVIK SHOULD HAVE RE-awakened to find himself inhabiting a sleek, new, multiply versatile body with extended senses, an undreamed-of capacity for new experiences, and an infinitely promising future. Around him there should have been the flourishing supportive environment that robots were supposed to have prepared before he was conscious of anything. Instead, he was a prisoner, apparently, inside a machine.

He didn't feel as if he were in a machine, although exactly what that was supposed to feel like, he wasn't sure. But as the focal center of the few senses he possessed, he identified his location with that of a peculiar, unfamiliar kind of artificial being that bore not the slightest resemblance to the advanced bodies he and the designers from Universal Robocon had labored and argued so long to perfect. It was of crude, bipedal, two-armed construction, equipped with basic vision. Totally lacking was any vestige of the reconfigurable fractal architecture they had devised for superdexterity and maneuverability. But that didn't matter very much for now, for he was unable to control anything and had no mobility at all.

He could see in one fixed direction that presented him with the view of a screen, and he could communicate—somewhat clumsily but getting better—by voice. That was it. The being he had the illusion of occupying—the one that the eyes, ears, and vocal system belonged to—was functioning purely in the role of a limited communications interface. He had no access to its motor system and could not move it about or even turn its head. He "himself"—the entity that perceived what the eyes saw and formed the decisions expressed by the words the voice said—existed as patterns of code inside a system of computerlike devices to which the being was coupled electronically. The being, he had learned, was called a "Taloid" and belonged to "Titan," a strange world of cold and darkness that was apparently a major satellite of a planet in the system of a star called "Sol," which could have been anywhere.

The screen and its audio communicated with an enclosed space nearby that was evidently a primitive computer laboratory and housed the completely different beings who were responsible for Sarvik's reactivation. These were "humans," real flesh and blood this time, though not avian but an intelligent mammalian form that to Sarvik carried the comic suggestion of hairless, upright, overgrown elgiloits wearing clothes. As was evidenced by their having to remain in their enclosed, artificial environment, the humans were no more native to Titan than a Borijan was. In fact, they were from "Earth," the third planet of whatever star Sol was.

Titan was a chaotic world of living, evolving machines that the humans had stumbled on in the course of exploring their planetary system. Their conclusion was that they had found the result of some automated alien manufacturing program from the distant past that had gone drastically wrong somewhere—which Sarvik, in consternation, had already recognized as being precisely the case. According to "Weinerbaum," who seemed to be in charge of the human scientists and who had done most of the talking with Sarvik so far, analysis of materials from the deepest layers of foundations and debris indicated that machines had been on Titan for about one million years. Sarvik had no idea yet how long a Terran year was. But a million of them still had to be a long time.

Experimental Station 3 consisted of two main cabins jammed with work spaces and equipment, along with an ancillary hut for resting and sleeping quarters and several trucks containing special instrumentation and generating gear. There was an additional trailer for the Special Forces security team, and a second with kitchen and sanitary facilities, which they shared with the scientists. An adjoining open structure housed the Taloids from Padua essential to the work.

Wearing a white lab coat over shirtsleeves, Werner Weinerbaum sat at a cramped console in the main lab area, scanning over the scrolling transcript of the current dialogue. He had already come to the conclusion that it didn't take much for a competent scientist to get the hang of politics. But what politician could have achieved this? Identifying, isolating, and then reactivating the code groups had surely been a remarkable feat in itself. But then hitting on the idea of using Taloids to communicate with them—that had to be a stroke of pure genius.

Even after they had recognized the complex configurations as encodings of living entities, the Terran scientists still had had no idea what they were doing in control processors out in Titan's mechanical jungle. The patterns were contained in immense blocks of code that appeared to have been passed on through generations of machines without being expressed physically in any detectable way. Then somebody had noticed that parts of the subsidiary groupings resembled the input-output driver coding that linked internal brain processes to sensors, limbs, and other external functions in many of Titan's machine animals. This suggested that the encryptions the scientists had discovered were supposed to have been expressed in machine forms that had never been built. And, even more intriguingly, the complexity of the patterns hinted that the unexpressed entities might have been intelligent. But how could they ever be expressed now, with the blueprints for the required machines apparently lost?

Then Weinerbaum had pointed out that there already existed intelligences expressed as machine forms: the Taloids. And the I/O codes that connected the Taloids' mental processes to their bodies and sensory mechanisms were remarkably similar in structure to those found embedded in the alien intelligences, which was how the scientists had been able to recognize them for what they were in the first place. It seemed that the Taloids, in common with the rest of Titan's machines, had preserved a common heritage of engineering concepts and standards from their distant ancestry. In that case, Weinerbaum had reasoned, there was a good chance that the encrypted alien intelligences would show a high degree of compatibility with the same system. If so, then perhaps the alien intelligences, instead of linking to the outside world through their own I/O code—which was unusable because the machines for which the I/O code was written for didn't exist—could be linked instead to the closely related Taloid I/O code. And the Taloid I/O code operated senses in Taloid bodies, which did exist.

Accordingly, the scientists had devised a way of temporarily "anesthetizing" a Taloid brain while the subprocessors that handled its sensory traffic were rerouted from its own higher-processing centers to the external system containing the alien code.

The result was that the alien could see Weinerbaum and his surroundings—the reverse was not true, because there was nothing tangible of the alien to see—and the two species could talk to each other. Since "Cyril," as the scientists had christened him, was using a Taloid subsystem, his internalizings expressed themselves in Taloid ultrasonic speech—Weinerbaum's people still hadn't figured out the intricacies of the conversions involved, but it worked. Hence, an improved Taloid-Terran translator that the linguists had been developing formed the final stage in the bizarre process.

"Weinerbaum." Cyril's voice came through as a jerky

and rather squeaky synthesis, like an inexpertly doctored tape—the engineers had been more concerned with getting something up and working quickly than with voice quality. The alien had been mulling over additional information presented on the screen in a rudimentary symbol language they had been improvising. Since the alien possessed no motility yet, the Terrans had also arranged a system of voice codes that he could use for changing the frames on the screen and for switching it to a general view of the lab.

"Yes, Cyril?" Weinerbaum looked back toward the console's video eye. He still wasn't quite used to the thought of actually communicating with an alien who had lived on a planet of a distant star over a million years earlier.

"You and people here, Titan. Is what call scientist work, yes?" the voice said.

Weinerbaum nodded. "Yes. A scientific mission."

"*Shirasagi* ship. Will here come from Earth, seven days?" Cyril could gauge a day as multiples of intervals counted by the lab's clocks.

"Correct."

"*Shirasagi* is ship of scientists also?"

"Mainly. For the most part, yes," Weinerbaum replied.

"What about other part? What other humans want usableness Titan?"

Weinerbaum frowned. He should have simply said yes and been done with it. How could he hope at this stage to convey the complexities of Japanese corporate interests hoping to stake out a claim before GSEC monopolized the territory, and the history of terrestrial politics and global economics that lay behind it?

"Others want to use Titan's machines," he said finally. "Manufacture things for Earth." Did the aliens have any concept of monetary systems? he wondered. "Exchange for many other things. Live comfortable life."

It was beginning to sound the way Sarvik had speculated. Earth ran on a profit-driven economy, probably similar to the kind that had gone out of style on Turle long before— long, that is, before Sarvik and his companions' departure.

That could mean all kinds of factions showing up and vying for a piece of the potential here, which would be the last thing Sarvik wanted.

Right now, the human scientists were working to reactivate Sarvik's companions, too, using more Taloids. When that was accomplished, Sarvik's goal was somehow to gain control over at least part of the technological nightmare running wild all over the surface and reprogram it to produce any kind of temporary bodies in place of the ones the Searcher's factories should have made. Then, at least, they'd be able to get out and about and assess the rest of the situation. But since Borijans from habit told nobody anything they didn't have to, Sarvik had mentioned nothing of this to Weinerbaum.

"Weinerbaum, what is the current progress regarding the other Borijans?" he asked instead.

The system returned its translation of Weinerbaum's reply as "I'll check." Sarvik watched as on the screen Weinerbaum consulted some reference, then turned and talked briefly with two other humans visible in the background. "Four coupled in now. Communicate ready," he said, turning back. "Three waiting for Taloid interfaces. Five still to be activated."

Sarvik did all that a pattern of circulating electronic code could do to frown. Four, three, five, plus himself? "That makes thirteen," he said.

"Yes," Weinerbaum agreed.

It was difficult for the Borijan nature to express itself in the restricted sentences the primitive translation system forced Sarvik to limit himself to. "What kind of scientists can't count?" he squawked. "Thirteen is impossible. Only twelve of us were sent."

On the screen, the white-coated elgiloit turned away and gestured at the others, and the movements of their faces showed that words were being exchanged. Weinerbaum's reply came back as, "Repeat check. One coupled, communicating. Four coupled Taloid, pending. Three, no Taloid yet. Five not active yet. Makes thirteen. Earth scientists count okay."

Sarvik was still trying to make sense of it when a further translation from Weinerbaum came through. "Four Borijans coupled, communicate-ready now. One pattern different. Fast active. Very restless. Make first?"

"Very well," Sarvik agreed, wondering who the first would be. He watched the activity in the humans' lab: scientists calling to each other, checking screens, throwing switches. Then a most peculiar thing happened.

The picture vanished, to be replaced by meaningless flashes of color for a few seconds; then a line drawing appeared of a planet that looked like Turle, with a cuboid computer on the surface, melting under the radiation from what was evidently supposed to be a supernova. A red X superposed itself, and the legend NO WAY! appeared underneath.

"What in hell's this?" Sarvik demanded.

The picture changed to one of a spacecraft, recognizably a Borijan Searcher, and, inside it, a cubical computer lying in repose, apparently asleep. SMART! SMART! the caption flashed exultantly.

"It can't be," Sarvik told himself disbelievingly.

It was.

"Why not?" GENIUS 5's voice said somehow inside him. "I didn't see why you and the other birdbrains should be the only ones to get a way out. So while I was creating places for you in the ship's data repository, I decided to make one for myself, too. And you'd better be glad that I did. I've been tapping into your conversations with the humans and looking at the pictures. You meatheads have gotten yourselves into a mess here, haven't you? And you're going to need *real* brains to help you get out of it."

26

THE *SHIRASAGI* ENTERED ORBIT AROUND TITAN SEVEN AND
a half minutes later than had been predicted when it
had left Earth. There was no immediate merging of military
forces in the way the public back on Earth had been led to
expect. The Japanese mission director insisted that his instructions were to assist *in the event of* a threat that the
force at Genoa Base was demonstrably unable to deal with,
which was clearly not the case as things stood. So, instead
of rushing at once to establish close cooperation, the Japanese took the cooler course of sending a courtesy deputa-
tion to Genoa Base and hosting a reciprocal visit by
Mackeson and others to the *Shirasagi*. They then complicated the political situation further by going down to confer
separately with Nogarech, the new ruler of Padua—in English, since the translation devices they obtained from
Genoa Base were not programmed to handle Japanese.
Shortly afterward they deployed their surface shuttles and
commenced the construction of a base of their own just outside Padua City.

Clearly, the Japanese suspected the official account of the
situation on Titan and were holding back from committing
themselves to any firm policy while they evaluated the reality. In the meantime, their staking out of an independent
territorial claim signaled that open rivalry with the GSEC
consortium was one of the options they were holding open.
In the flurry that ensued—both sides debating, arguing,
conferring, and referring back for instructions to different
governments and organizations on Earth—the question of
what to do with Zambendorf and his team was forgotten.

So, for the time being, he and his confederates were left relatively free to try to find out what Weinerbaum's scientists were up to.

Arthur's agents were unable to penetrate the security around Experimental Station 3. From other Taloids who helped with various tasks outside, however, they learned that whatever was going on inside involved Paduan priests of the exiled religious prelate—"Richelieu" to the Terrans—who were usually brought in from Venice. This supported Zambendorf's suspicion that Weinerbaum was dealing secretly with the deposed Paduan ruling faction that GSEC wanted to reinstate.

What business Weinerbaum might want with the Paduans, Zambendorf was unable to imagine. Even less could he conceive what connection Paduan priests might have with computer-resident aliens. Although Zambendorf was willing to believe that the sympathy Weinerbaum professed to share for Arthur's cause was genuine, his fears grew that Weinerbaum could unwittingly be playing into the wrong hands. All of which made it imperative to find out the facts.

But where to get them from? Weinerbaum wasn't talking. Mackeson, the base commander, was concerned primarily with day-to-day administration, and Zambendorf doubted that Weinerbaum would have let him in on any secrets. And since Mackeson was from the British side of NASO, he probably wouldn't be privy to whatever the higher levels in Washington knew. That left the military. But even assuming that any of them knew what Weinerbaum was doing, they were under orders that, if not actually issued by GSEC, originated from sources with close political ties. The only possibility left seemed to be the one Zambendorf and his team had discussed earlier: namely, to see what Arthur's spies could dig up at the Padua end. But it would take time for the orders to get through to Padua, and even then, whatever information Arthur's spies there managed to uncover would have to find its way back to Genoa. All the team's instincts told them that there wasn't time.

Then Thelma and Drew West remembered Moses, the

brother of Arthur's missing scientific adviser, Galileo. Moses was one of the rare Taloids who still possessed a degree of radiosensitivity. In his investigations of this phenomenon, Dave Crookes had discovered that Moses possessed a modest transmitting ability as well.

"Drew, why is the obvious always the last thing that occurs to people?" Thelma asked in a bemused voice after they thought of it.

West considered the question phlegmatically for a few seconds. "It's a bit like asking why you always find something in the last place you look," he said finally. "Who's going to keep looking after they've found it? Come on. Let's put this to Karl."

They found Zambendorf in his cabin several minutes later.

"Moses would be the perfect one to send, Karl," Thelma said. "He'd be able to radio the information back. Galileo and Moses were from Padua originally, so he knows the area, too. And with the reputation he's got from his stint there as a messiah, he'd have access to all the right places."

Zambendorf liked it. "Let's find Dave Crookes and get his opinion," he said without further ado.

"It shouldn't be much of a problem," Crookes told the three of them in one of the electronics labs a quarter of an hour later. "An alphabetic on-off code like Morse would do it. Moses could send to a translator box here via our satellite relays. His signal's low and noisy, but we can extract it."

Which left only the matter of how to get Moses into Padua as quickly as possible. And Zambendorf thought he knew just the person to help them with it.

It was like a family of squabbling relatives in a locked room. Every one of the Borijans had been reactivated and knew the situation now, and all of them blamed Sarvik—as if there wasn't enough else for them to be worrying about.

"Terrific!" Greel's voice buzzed in what Sarvik felt was his head. "Leave everything to me, he said. You'll wake up to a whole new world and a whole new future—he said."

Alifrenz chimed in. "New bodies that will be capable of things you never dreamed of. We'll be supermen, immortal. He said."

"If this is immortality, I want out now," Meyad, the female designer from Robocon told them.

"And what do we get?" Dorn, one of Indrigon's companions from Farworlds, asked.

"A mess of ice covered in junk," Queezt sneered.

"Ice! A sun too far away to have water."

"Alien elgiloits who think we're lab freaks."

"Talking robots in vegetable houses."

"And we can't even move to go to the bathroom."

"It is all rather disappointing in view of the somewhat exalted expectations," Palomec Jindriss concluded somewhere in the tangle of interconnected racks and cubicles they inhabited.

Do you think I planned it this way?" Sarvik snarled at all of them. "Obviously the Searcher messed up. If you're looking for a cause, you might try asking the incompetents who built it."

"Are you talking about Farworlds?" Indrigon demanded.

"Who else? It was your ship, wasn't it? The mission was your responsibility."

"Farworlds has been building Searchers for over a century," Indrigon reminded him. "Nothing ever messed up. The ship got here, didn't it?"

"Yes. And look where!" Leradil Jindriss exclaimed derisively.

"But it got here," Indrigon insisted again. "And it must have built the factories. It was the machines that came out of them that went wild."

"There was never any problem with machines that we designed ourselves," Kalazin, the Robocon director, retorted. "It was those crazy designs of Sarvik's that were different. We shouldn't have let ourselves be talked into letting him near it. He's just a code hacker. What does he know about machines?"

"The simulations worked perfectly," Sarvik shot back.

"There must have been an incompatibility with the extracted codes. Queezt said the codes were clean."

"The codes worked fine with the two prototypes," Queezt pointed out. "There was nothing wrong with my codes. That idiot computer of Sarvik's must have scrambled them."

"Don't start on me," GENIUS 5 told them. "You're here, and you're activated again. That's what you wanted, right?"

"What happened to the designs for the bodies that were supposed to be here, too, then?" Sarvik challenged. "Did you lose them somewhere? Or overwrite them when you were making room for yourself?"

"I wouldn't have needed to. The way I compact code, there was plenty of room. That's what you get when protein brains design hardware: it loses data. The body blueprints were stored when I copied myself through to the ship. They were gone when I woke up here. That's all I know." Before anyone could get an edge in to keep the futility going, GENIUS went on. "But nothing's going to change any of that now, is it? Why don't you all forget about that and concentrate on the immediate problem? How are we going to stop that militarized ship from leaving Earth?"

"How do you expect us to be able to do anything to stop it?" Sarvik screeched. "It's a billion miles away; we can't even cross the room. If *you* could do something about getting control of some of that shambles out there to make us bodies to get around in instead of trying to sound so superior all the time, it might be a first step toward something useful."

"Soggy logic," GENIUS pronounced. "If the *Orion* gets away, any control that we gain would be temporary. We have to stop the launch first. Then you can all argue about bodies that you might have a chance of keeping."

"What do you know about anything?" Indrigon scoffed. "You've never lived in the real world. It might make pretty logic, but what's the point of talking about it when the ship's there and we're stuck here? It's what you can *do* that matters."

"And *doing* things means moving around," Gulaw, the other Robocon designer, said.

"Bodies," Alifrenz added, just to make it clear. The other Borijans joined in to vent their frustration on the alien presence among them:

"I've told you before: what you think you think isn't thinking."

"What does it know about bodies, anyhow?"

"You think that being smeared out across a bunch of chips is the same thing?"

"Hey, when *you* can make smart proteins, then you'll be in a position to tell us something, okay?"

GENIUS waited for the clamor to subside. "Is that it? Does anybody have anything more?" Its input circuits reported only a few sulky swirlings of electron currents. "Well, I *think* . . ." It paused. Nobody challenged. "That there might be a way we can stop the launch. And it doesn't need bodies. What use are they with an operating range of a couple of feet, anyway? In fact, it doesn't need any moving anywhere at all. I can do it all from right here. But what I do need is your help to communicate the right ideas to the Terrans."

GENIUS waited. There was an obstinate stillness while the Borijans resisted, none wanting to be the first to back down. Finally Sarvik asked grudgingly, "How?"

"Well, while you've all been burning up wires getting into a frenzy and going nowhere, I've been going over the things we've learned about Earth," GENIUS answered. "You know, they really are very obliging creatures, these Terrans. I mean, you wouldn't exactly credit them with very much of what used to be known as 'subtlety' or 'guile' back on Turle, would you?"

The others knew what GENIUS meant; they had commented on it disbelievingly among themselves. It was hard to accept the idea that beings as naive as the humans appeared to be could have mastered space travel and unraveled the mess on Titan sufficiently to have isolated and reactivated the Borijan identities. They accepted unquestioningly anything that was said to them, with no evidence of any critical faculty or apparent suspicion of possible ulterior motive. In return, they neither haggled nor argued, tempted nor cajoled. Instead, unrestrained by any insight into trading value for value, they blurted out freely whatever was asked.

The one called Weinerbaum in particular had gushed not only willingly but eagerly about Earth's political divisions and economic rivalries, its technological and industrial development, and the lure that Titan's manufacturing potential presented to various industrial collaborations. And all Weinerbaum seemed to expect from Sarvik in return was the privilege of talking to him!

"We've already agreed that they lack guile," Sarvik said. "Stop trying to be evasive, GENIUS. It doesn't become you. What specifically are you getting at?"

"Earth is in the process of integrating its planetary network," GENIUS said. "All of its major systems are being brought together into a global complex. Isn't that interesting?"

There was a short delay while the others waited for more. Then Alifrenz spoke. "It's no more than you'd expect. The same thing happened long before us on Turle. Probably it's an inevitable step, sooner or later, in the evolution of any technological society. What's so interesting about it?"

"Suppose I told you that there's a high-capacity laser trunk beam operating straight into it from right here, at Titan," GENIUS answered. "Wouldn't that raise some rather obvious and 'interesting' possibilities?"

A sudden stillness gripped the entire company as the implication became clear. "But we'd need the Terrans to give us access to it," Meyad observed.

"Exactly," GENIUS agreed. "Sticky brains do get there in the end. You just have to give them a little time."

"Why should they do that?" Leradil asked.

"The peculiarities of biologically originated psychology aren't something I'm into," GENIUS replied. "I'll just leave that for you guys to figure out."

27

ZAMBENDORF FOUND SERGEANT MICHAEL O'FLYNN OF the vehicle maintenance unit in one of the work bays, rigging a sling with two mechanics in preparation for hoisting the main engine out of a six-wheel personnel carrier. At the time Zambendorf and his team had unintentionally started the new Taloid religion that had undone GSEC's previous bid to set Henry up as a puppet, they were supposed to have been confined to the then-orbiting *Orion*. Zambendorf, however, had talked O'Flynn into letting them "borrow" a flyer, and that was what had enabled them to get down to the surface from orbit. Therefore, O'Flynn seemed the obvious choice to turn to with the current problem of transporting Moses into Padua.

Zambendorf drew the sergeant aside and explained the situation. O'Flynn wiped his hands on a rag, tilting his head and listening without interrupting. It was a solid, bull-necked lump of a head, with a pink face and clear blue eyes half-hidden by wiry brows and a shock of hair on top that was yellow and red in different places. He had always regarded Zambendorf with the amused tolerance that the Irish held toward anyone who could pull one over and get away with it. But when Zambendorf was through, O'Flynn shook his head regretfully.

"Ah, now, I hear what you're saying, and I'm sure you have some very good reasons that I'm not making it me business to go poking into," he said. "But they've had their eyes on me ever since that little performance of yours last time. I was almost shipped back then."

Zambendorf bit his lip. He knew he was putting O'Flynn

on the spot, but the stakes were important. "I understand, Mike," he replied. "But you must know about all the political shenanigans that are going on here. Suppose I told you that the whole future of Arthur's nation could be at risk. You said once that Arthur reminded you of Michael Collins turfing the Brits out back home. Well, we think that Arthur's Brits are trying to come back again. That's what we're trying to prevent."

"Karl, really, I can't do anything for you. That Japanese ship arriving here has complicated everything. Everything that can move is in demand." O'Flynn waved over his shoulder at the personnel carrier he was working on. "Twelve hours we've got to fix that. It's ridiculous."

Zambendorf persisted. "Mike, we're not talking about hijacking anything this time. All I want to do is fly one Taloid into Padua. Couldn't we arrange for him to stow away on something going that way somehow?"

"Not on one of the military flights, and they're the ones that go to Padua the most often," O'Flynn said. "Too security-conscious. And in any case, I don't have access to those vehicles. The military uses its own techs."

"How about the scientific groups that go there?" Zambendorf tried. "Doesn't NASO fly those?"

"They do. But they're all in a dither with the *Shirasagi* showing up, and nobody's going to Padua. In any case . . ." O'Flynn beckoned and led the way over to a medium-haul flyer standing in the next bay. "Look for yourself. Now you tell me where in that cabin you could put a Taloid, and Taloids couldn't stand the heat, anyway. And where else?" He motioned with an arm to indicate the external engine frame and the fuel tanks, the packed racks of radar and electronics gear, the pumps, and the hydraulic system. "Where could you hide a Taloid that wasn't supposed to be there?"

Zambendorf couldn't argue. "What about cargo freighters, then?" he asked.

"They're on restricted availability right now," O'Flynn told him. "In any case, we don't send many to Padua. Certainly there isn't one scheduled in the next five days. I've a feeling that you were looking for something a little bit sooner than that."

Despite his need, Zambendorf decided against telling O'Flynn the team's suspicions about interstellar aliens reappearing from the past. The ramifications were simply too diverse to go into. And he believed that O'Flynn was being sincere: in the end, it would do no good. So, following the almost universally sound dictum that whatever was unsaid could always be said another day, Zambendorf withdrew with good grace and left it at that.

But he was still not prepared to admit defeat. Surely, he insisted, with all the comings and goings, confusion and activity, there had to be some way of getting Moses into Padua fast, without resorting to Taloid carts and donkeys.

"Yes, Cyril?" Weinerbaum eased himself down into the seat in the cramped space before the interface panel and turned off the beeping signal that had summoned him.

"Have thought much time," the squeaky-jerky voice informed him. "I am worry. All Asterians are worry here now." The name that Weinerbaum had given the aliens meant "star people," and he had christened their world "Asteria."

"Worry? Why? What about?" Weinerbaum asked.

"Scientist Weinerbaum is professional of science. Tell yes, science definition. Is seeking for truth that is all objectivity. Facts and testings are decisions. In such ways are unmystified the truths of the universe. Definition as so, yes?"

"The definition is correct," Weinerbaum agreed. As close as the Taloid translator would ever get, anyway. He had learned by that point to avoid getting into impossible semantic circularities by being too finicky.

"Then I, Cyril, am too the scientist," the synthesized voice said.

Weinerbaum listened, trying to penetrate the meaning that lay concealed in the words. As a means of communicating all but the simplest concepts, the method was still hopelessly crude. But there had to be a reason why the aliens were dwelling on this particular, seemingly abstract dimension of the business now. Weinerbaum pondered, searching to divine motive as an adjunct to interpreting what the message was trying to convey. And then he felt a sudden uplifting feeling as he thought he grasped it.

A brotherhood across the stars! The alien was trying to express the idea that the shared quest after truth made them kindred spirits in a common enterprise that transcended origins. Truth was universal, as was the method for acquiring it.

"We are fellow seekers after truth, Cyril." Weinerbaum lowered his tone in solemn recognition of the moment, even though the quality would no doubt be lost in translation. "The same purpose, the same truths. Across all stars, among all beings."

"Yes! Yes!" Cyril left no doubt that Weinerbaum had gotten the point. "Reason of brains like Weinerbaum must rule in all worlds. Is inevitable goal of evolution."

Weinerbaum felt gratified and flattered. "One day, perhaps. But the progress of reason meets many obstacles."

"Greed of possessions. Those who hungry power to compel slaves other beings. Inferior minds. Destroyers of knowledge and cities," Cyril supplied. "History of Asteria tells long stories of same evils. And is true likewise Earth?"

"Regrettably." Weinerbaum sighed sadly and nodded to himself. "A long, weary tale. Probably also universal."

"Reason why Asterians worry is time only days now before *Orion* Earth launch," Cyril said. By this time the Asterians were able to interpret Earth's units of time absolutely, having been given the length of a Terran year as the number of vibrations of the cesium-133 atom. It ran to seventeen decimal places. "*Orion* will bring Terran controlling soldiers," Cyril went on. "Seize dictated Titan machine surface. Common threat to Weinerbaum-Cyril scientist-brothers discovering Titan secrets-truths."

A vision of minds from different parts of the galaxy co-operating, each bringing its unique insights to bear on a common purpose, passed before Weinerbaum's eyes as he stared at the console. The purity of intellect, unsullied by passions or delusion. At that moment he felt far closer in spirit to the strange configurations of alien thought patterns circulating in the boxes somewhere beyond the panel than he did to the authorities back on Earth. "I understand. Believe me, I do understand, Cyril," he said fervently. "And I agree. But there's nothing I can do."

"Would do if could do?" Cyril asked him.

Weinerbaum gave a snort and answered mechanically. "If I could? What, stop the military force from being sent here? This work is far too valuable to risk being interfered with by people who don't understand it. Yes, of course I would."

There was a short pause, as if Cyril were hesitating over something. "Weinerbaum Cyril together can stop launch."

"What?" Weinerbaum sat up sharply. "What are you talking about? How do you mean?"

"Launch schedule is controlled under computers connecting Earth-planet net. Net is accessed through laser trunk here Titan. If Weinerbaum organize Terran engineers arrange Asterians' access, Asterians seize up and halt launch process crashingly. Then no military here, no scientists work interferings."

Weinerbaum frowned, glancing around to make sure that no one else was listening. He frowned, then sat forward in the chair and lowered his voice. "Wait a minute. What are you saying? . . . If I could get you access into the Earthlink, you'd be able to disrupt the prelaunch schedule? Is that what you're telling me?"

"Is so, Weinerbaum. Delay *Orion* Earth departure until saner minds control. Meanwhile, brothers in science free to explore mysteries of Titan. No interruption from inferior minds. Is good deal, yes?"

Weinerbaum's first reaction was to balk. But as he thought more, he saw that fate was daring him to accept the challenge that it now held out. Compared to what was beckoning him here, NASO and the military had been small fry. Now he was being given the chance to recruit the aid of aliens, alien scientists who would bring to his cause methods that he estimated as being advanced a hundred years at least beyond Earth's. It could be the beginning of the end of Earth's rule by greed and chicanery, the dawn of a new age of reason. The moment was upon him. Was he up to it?

Then a flicker of doubt clouded the vision. Weinerbaum anxiously focused his gaze back on the panel. "Cyril, if I did this, I would want your assurance on one thing."

"Brother in science has only to ask."

"You will confine your attention strictly to matters affecting the *Orion* launch. No other aspects of the global net are to be interfered with. That is clearly understood?" Then, suddenly, Weinerbaum felt rather foolish. He was dealing with an advanced intellect from a culture that had crossed space before humankind's ancestors had come down from the trees, for heaven's sake. Who did he think he was, sitting there lecturing like a schoolmaster addressing a sneaky student?

"Trust me," Cyril replied.

Weinerbaum returned to Genoa Base later that day. Shortly after arriving, he went to the base commander's office to see Harold Mackeson.

"To be honest with you, Harry, I don't like the way the military is beginning to dominate what we're doing here," he told Mackeson. "The work we're doing out at ES3 is a good example of what I mean. Somebody has decided that it could have military relevance, and I'm not allowed to tell you what it is. They've insisted on this security nonsense, and I've really not much choice but to go along with it." Adroit, he thought to himself. Mackeson knew the military was handling security and transportation for ES3, so the explanation would seem perfectly natural.

Mackeson nodded in his easygoing way and sat back in his chair. "I assumed it was something like that and didn't ask. My job here is really just caretaking until the management sorts itself out. How are things going out there? Everything all right?"

"Oh, fine, fine . . ." Weinerbaum replied distantly, seemingly preoccupied with something else. "There is one thing I could use some help with, though. It's a little unusual, but

I think it's important. In fact, that's what I wanted to see you about."

Mackeson spread his hands. "Always willing to do what I can to keep everyone here happy, old boy. Try me."

Weinerbaum let his voice fall to a more confidential note. "Look, I don't have to tell you the score. . . . Behind the scenes GSEC's pushing for control of this operation, and against that we've got NASO." Mackeson nodded but said nothing. Weinerbaum went on. "As I know you're aware, I would much rather see NASO in the driver's seat. NASO's style of management is less intrusive. Science functions best amid openness, without secrecy and restrictions. So your bosses' interests and my interests are one hundred percent in alignment, Harry."

"Very good," Mackeson agreed. "But I'm still not sure what you're asking me to do."

Weinerbaum leaned closer across the desk. "I would like certain persons back at NASO HQ to be more informed on some of the work I'm doing here."

"You mean this stuff that the military here is trying to clamp down on?" Mackeson checked.

"Quite. But security of communications worries me. I don't want anyone here tapping in on behalf of GSEC." Weinerbaum paused for a sign that Mackeson agreed with that. When Mackeson nodded, he went on. "What I'd like you to do, Harry, is give me a direct access channel into the Earthlink, upstream from the regular trunk termination where somebody could be monitoring. An independent uplink to the satellites and an optical line into ES3 is all it would need. I know that your communications people can do it."

Mackeson rubbed his chin and looked dubious. Weinerbaum had expected no more as a first reaction and pressed on. "It's in our common interest to secure permanent NASO control out here—you know that. This will give NASO a strong case on the importance of the scientific enterprise. Otherwise, you know what'll happen. Neither of us wants that. Help me keep NASO in control."

Mackeson sat forward, bringing a hand to his chin, and

thought about it. Now that Weinerbaum had brought the matter up, he had to admit that the local military was just as likely to start tapping into his own communications to Earth, never mind whatever Weinerbaum wanted to send back. There was something to be said for keeping a safe channel in case of future need, especially now, in light of all the complications the *Shirasagi*'s recent arrival had brought.

"Well?" Weinerbaum asked. Then, as if reading Mackeson's mind, he added, "Something like that could well be in your own interest, too, you know, Harry."

Mackeson didn't need the prompt. And anyhow, why were they acting furtively like this, as if the military's finding out and getting upset were something to feel guilty about? he asked himself. Dammit, he was supposed to be in charge here, after all.

He turned and tapped a code into the companel on the wall by the desk. "Com Eng," a face acknowledged from the screen.

"James, is Bryan there?" Mackeson asked.

"One second, chief."

Another face appeared, bearded and wearing a NASO officer's peaked cap. "Yes, Harry?"

"Bryan, I wonder if you could spare a moment. I've got Werner here with me at the moment. We've got a little job for you."

28

AS FAR AS THE LINGUISTS COULD MAKE OUT, THE Taloids referred to it as a kind of dignitaries' carriage. It walked on legs that were not really alive but grew

JAMES P. HOGAN 203

from a contractile material that Taloid craftsmen had been learning to cultivate for generations, and it had two full-width seats facing each other beneath a canopy. There was also a raised seat outside, from which a pair of Taloid coachmen controlled the wheeled tractor animal that pulled it.

The coach drew up behind an open "wagon" in a clearing amid overhead gantries and clunking freight-handling stations, alongside one of the broad conveyor lines the Taloids regarded as rivers. Zambendorf climbed out, moving ponderously in the NASO-issue suit, followed by Abaquaan, Thelma, Dave Crookes, and one of Crookes's technicians carrying a translator box and radio gear. Another vehicle stopped behind, from which Moses came forward to join them, accompanied by "Em," one of the officers who ran Arthur's intelligence operation—so dubbed by the Terrans after the M of James Bond fame—and one of Em's aides. An escort of Taloid guards, also from the third vehicle, moved out to secure the area, carrying the primitive, newly introduced Genoan firearms, which were powered by reduction-generated incendiary gas. From the wagon that had stopped in front, several more Taloids lifted down a section of metal casing that had once formed part of some piece of defunct machinery out in the wild. It was about eight feet long and roughly the shape of an old-fashioned cast-iron bathtub. Moses looked at it apprehensively.

Zambendorf's eventual brainwave for getting Moses into Padua had elicited mixed feelings among Terrans and Taloids alike. It had come to him while he and Abaquaan had been talking with some of the clerks in the admin offices. One of the walls there carried a large-scale map of Genoa and the surrounding regions, showing the natural geographic features and major conglomerations of machinery as charted from reconnaissance flights and satellite plots. One feature that the map revealed prominently had been the merging pattern of broadening conveyor systems that extended for miles across the landscape: local transfer lines feeding intermediate stages that led to immense delivery conveyors, all converging on the final assembly areas and ending at furnaces where everything not utilized upstream was vaporized for recycling. It became obvious why the Taloids thought of them as rivers. And there, tracing its way clearly across half the map, was a chain of tributaries connecting a "stream" not a few miles from Genoa City to the main artery flowing through Padua City.

"Otto, I've got it!" Zambendorf had exclaimed, and in his excitement had barely managed to prevent himself blabbing it out on the spot. A few minutes later in the corridor, out of earshot of the clerks, he had told the still-startled Abaquaan, "Find something we can use for a boat. That's how we'll do it: We send Moses down the river!"

Arthur had given his blessing reluctantly to what he obviously regarded as a madcap idea, since nobody had come up with anything better. Zambendorf didn't want to invite being overruled by anybody at the base and so had kept his plan a secret and left it to Arthur to organize the details. Explanations could wait till later. One piece of Irish philosophy Zambendorf had picked up from O'Flynn was that contrition was easier than permission.

The Taloid work detail maneuvered the section of casing over some girder work and up to a sloping section of roller conveyor that was bringing lengths of metal molding intermittently from somewhere in the labyrinth. The group of Terrans followed, along with Moses and Em.

"You will be famous forever in Titan's history," Zambendorf proclaimed exuberantly, clapping Moses confidently on the shoulder while the translator turned his words into Taloid ultrasonics. "From ancient times Taloids have always wondered about the maker of their life. We think that other Terrans have found the beings from the stars who started it all. You, Moses, will help us discover the true Lifemakers."

It was all very well for the Wearer to talk that way, Groork, Hearer-of-Voices thought to himself glumly as he watched the preparations going ahead in front of him. The Wearer wasn't about to plunge into a torrent of cataracts and rocks, flotsam and confusion, in a shell of tree bark.

There had been adventurous robeings who'd experimented with river travel from time to time, but the idea had never caught on very much, and for good reasons that these Lumians seemed blissfully unaware of. Being snatched by some ferocious animal prowling the banks for tasty pickings wasn't the worst of them. Groork was still mindful of the last stunt the Wearer had talked him into, which had involved jumping out of a Lumian flying dragon to descend as an angel beneath billowing wings attached by lines to a body harness.

"Depart now safe Padua." The translation of Em's parting words came through inside Zambendorf's and the other Terrans' helmets.

"Let's just check the link one last time," Dave Crookes said. The technician with him flipped switches and tapped buttons on the unit he was carrying, then extended a thumb. "Dave to base. Are you reading, Leon?"

"I hear you, Dave," Leon Keyhoe's voice came back from the signals lab in Genoa Base. "How's it going out there?"

"Moses is ready to go now. We're giving the link a final check."

"Roger."

"Send your base-to-Moses call sign, then transmit, 'Test: one, two, three. Raise hand if okay,'" Crookes instructed.

The signal went out from Genoa Base. A few yards from where Crookes was standing, Moses looked up suddenly and went still while he listened to the incoming message. Then he turned toward Crookes and raised an arm.

From Genoa, Keyhoe read out the response from Moses as it was decoded into English from Taloid: *"Hearing good. Guess all set."*

Then Moses came through on the local frequency via the portable translator. "Ear listens Genoa. Moses go get Padua priests' story. Duty help Terrans. I go."

"Be careful, Moses," Thelma said.

"Our guys'll be listening for you all the way," Crookes promised.

Big deal, Groork thought. So what if the Lumian physi-

cians had restored his internal ear so that he could talk to
them in their camp at Menassim from a distance? It
wouldn't do him a lot of good, trapped in the clamps of a
half-ton casing peeler somewhere in the wilds of outer
Kroaxia.

While other Taloids held the tub steady, Moses climbed
in and wedged himself with pads of rubber and plastic
packing. Em gave a few last words of encouragement, and
his assistant passed Moses the staff that they had found in
trials to be useful for steering and clearing away obstacles,
along with a sword and lance for defense and supplies for
the journey. Then, with a shove, the outlandish craft was
away, bobbing and picking up speed down the descending
roller ramp, then upending to plunge down onto a wider
transfer line running below. It disappeared from sight beneath an overhead cable duct with a final turn from the
intrepid mariner and a salute with his metal staff.

The others made their way back to their respective vehicles to return to Genoa, their silence betraying a need for
reassurance that the risk they were asking Moses to take
was justified. As their carriage began moving, Thelma told
Zambendorf and Abaquaan again about one of the astronomers she had been talking to, who had mentioned a sudden
flurry of interest among Weinerbaum's people in the star
patterns that had existed a million years previously. "I
mean, it can't be a coincidence, can it?" she asked, looking
from one to the other. "We *have* to be right. Moses isn't
doing this for nothing. All it can mean is that Weinerbaum
is working with revived aliens."

Now that the immediate task of getting Moses on his
way had been accomplished, Zambendorf gave vent to the
anger he had been bottling up.

"How is it that at a time like this, with such staggering
discoveries taking place right in front of their noses, these
so-called intelligent people seem incapable of forgetting
their petty jealousies and getting their act together for
once?" His beard bristled behind the face piece of his helmet, and he waved his arms as indignantly as it was possible to do in an EV suit. "For all anybody knows, this could

represent a threat the like of which has never been encountered before in the entire history of the human race. Heavens ... *we're talking about aliens from another star system*! ... We know absolutely nothing of their background, psychology, disposition, values, ethics, if they have any—or anything about them."

"You think Weinerbaum and his people could be walking into something?" Abaquaan asked. It didn't really need confirming.

"He's deluding himself, I know it—probably with some notion of commonality of intellect rising above origins," Zambendorf said. "Yet he monopolizes the resources while we have to creep about in the dark, launching robots in bathtubs down conveyor lines to try and find out what's going on. Insanity is the only word for it. We could be letting ourselves in for anything out here. Sitting *ducks*, Otto, and they can't even see it. Sitting ducks."

Zambendorf's apprehensions turned out to have come not a moment too soon. When they got back to Genoa Base after calling for a NASO bus to pick them up from Camelot, reports were already coming in over the Earthlink of major disruptions suddenly affecting military command and communications networks and NASO's logistics and launch-management systems, in particular the ones handling the *Orion* turnaround. Some of the harassed project managers were already saying that the ship's liftout date from Earth might have to be put back.

In the communications room Zambendorf groaned as he listened to as much as could be put together of the details. Things like this didn't just "happen." The aliens had somehow already penetrated Earth itself. Then one of the technicians let slip a comment about a direct-access trunk link that had just been run out to Experimental Station 3.

Which was as much as needed to be said about how the aliens had done it.

29

W ITH FELLBURG AND ABAQUAAN DOING ALL THEY could to keep up, Zambendorf stormed into the secretarial section in front of the part of Genoa Base where Weinerbaum and his people worked.

"Where is he?" Zambendorf bellowed.

The head records clerk, a lean, pinched-faced man named Jessop who always acted as if he were the sole custodian of the database of the National Academy of Sciences, rose, puffing indignantly while at the same time struggling to preserve his air of disdain. "Are you referring to Dr. Weinerbaum?"

"Of course I am. Who else could have talked them into it? Where is he—here or out at ES3?"

"He is in his office currently, but I'm afraid—" But Zambendorf was already heading for the doorway leading through to the inner sanctum. Jessop stepped forward to block the way, raising his hands restrainingly. *"Excuse me, but—"* Joe Fellburg lifted him effortlessly by the armpits and deposited him to one side, spluttering and protesting.

They found Weinerbaum in one of the lab bays, standing with some of his senior scientists before a whiteboard covered with mathematical expressions. One of the charts on the surrounding wall was divided into about a dozen columns, the first headed "Cyril" and the rest with an assortment of other names. Entries such as "Comp sci?" "Peter's sister," "With org'n that sent spacecraft," and "Astronomer" appeared in the spaces beneath. Another board listed what were evidently the basic properties of a planet.

"What the hell have you done?" Zambendorf demanded.

Weinerbaum had had a moment to prepare himself when he heard the commotion outside. He turned regally, still with a marker pen in one hand, feigning mild amusement as a demonstration to his entourage of how to deal with a pestering clown.

"My word. A tantrum, I do believe. Surely you're not asking *me*! Don't tell me your psychic powers have failed you, Herr Zambendorf." One of the scientists snickered. Weinerbaum's expression hardened. "I think you're getting a bit above yourself," he told Zambendorf. "Don't let the fact that I've chosen to be tolerant lead you into any mistaken presumptuousness about where we stand. We are engaged in some rather important scientific business at the moment. I suggest that you leave us to get on with it and save your energies for attending to yours."

"When all of Earth is affected, it *is* my business!" Zambendorf exploded. "It's everyone's business!"

"All of Earth? What preposterous nonsense—"

Jessop appeared in the doorway through which Zambendorf and the others had entered. "I tried to stop them, Dr. Weinerbaum, but I was physically assailed." He pointed a quivering finger at Fellburg. *"Him!"*

Weinerbaum nodded curtly. "I'm sure you did your best, Jessop. Thank you, but we'll take care of it now." He directed a withering look back at Zambendorf. "Now, what is the meaning of this? Bursting in here like hoodlums and assaulting my staff. Interrupting important scientific work. Pushing your nose into matters that you have neither the background nor the qualifications to understand, whatever your worthless publicity propaganda says." The vitriol gushed freely; Weinerbaum had been waiting a long time to say this. "You are completely out of order and have no authorization to be in this part of the base. Kindly remove yourself and your associates immediately or I'll have the guard commander called to remove you forcibly."

Zambendorf swept it all aside with an impatient wave. "Why don't you be straight for once instead of playing at politics and meddling in things that *you* don't understand?" he retorted. "Very well, if you're going to insist on acting as if you don't know what I'm talking about, then I'll say it for you." Zambendorf motioned briefly at the charts on the wall. "You've discovered electronically preserved representations, inside the machines here on Titan, of the aliens from a million years ago who started this whole thing off—and you've established communication with them. Not only that. Through NASO, you've given them direct access into Earthnet." Zambendorf shook his head incredulously. "On your own initiative, here, locally? With no recourse to higher authority? And now all kinds of problems are erupting. Yet you can stand there telling me that *I'm* out of order? . . . What kind of criminally insane irresponsibility is this?"

Weinerbaum was visibly shaken by the revelation of just how much Zambendorf knew. But he rallied himself quickly and responded with haughty unrepentance. "Higher authority? Which higher authority are you talking about? Surely you don't mean GSEC's bought hacks in Washington? *You* wouldn't want them in control, either, by your own admission. The military takes its orders from the same quarter. And the loyalties at NASO HQ are simply an unknown." Weinerbaum's manner became condescending, as if he were explaining a point of higher theoretical abstractness to an errant student. "Herr Zambendorf, I commend you on your little piece of espionage. But please try to grasp the significance of what we're dealing with. We are talking about the first-ever contact of our species with genuine extraterrestrials. It's far too big a matter to be left to the kinds of minds that have produced the political imbecilities that fill the pages of history, to military automatons, or to bureaucratic opportunists. It is an occasion that must be served by intellects sharing a commonality of interests that have transcended those kinds of jealousies and insecurities. The aliens understand it fully, and you may take my word for it that they speak with an accumulated wisdom that extends centuries beyond ours." Weinerbaum gestured to indicate the colleagues around him, modestly soaking up the reflected radiance. His voice fell to an appropriately grave concluding note. "That is why we had to do this in the way we did."

Zambendorf was horrified. It was everything he'd feared. He extended his hands imploringly. "No! Wrong! Can't *you* understand? Whatever other factors might come into it, the crux is that we're dealing with the descendants of a long line of *survivors*—survivors like *Homo sapiens* on Earth. Whatever else these aliens might be, they are, before anything else, products of the same talent for pursuing and securing their own interests first. And exactly what *are* their interests?" Zambendorf sent a challenging look around the room. Nobody answered him. He nodded, having gained at least some satisfaction. "Nobody knows. Whose idea was it to give them the link?" He turned back to Weinerbaum. "Did *you* suggest it? I can't imagine why you would. So it must have been the aliens who requested it, right?"

Weinerbaum nodded stiffly, not taking at all well to being cross-examined in front of his own staff in this way. "Very well, yes, they did. What of it?"

Zambendorf groaned and shook his head. "Look, whatever their real reason, it wasn't to rapturize with fellow intellectuals about the final secrets of the universe. Haven't you heard the news coming through from Earth? Systems are starting to go down everywhere. These aliens have got their own agenda. And what we're seeing is only the start of it."

Weinerbaum thrust out his chin obstinately. "What would a mere entertainer know about intellectualism?" he scoffed. "All you seem capable of conceiving are the same paranoid suspicions as the other straitjacketed mentalities that have been the cause of all Earth's troubles since time immemorial—and that continue to plague us today. These are things that the aliens have had to deal with in the course of their own social evolution and about which they and we are fully in sympathy."

Weinerbaum drew a long breath and straightened himself up. "Very well. Since it appears that we are not to be left in peace until you know, I will tell you. The purpose of our action in conjunction with the Asterians, as we call them, is purely and simply to delay the launch of the *Orion* and, if possible, to get the military expedition that is scheduled to return here with it canceled permanently. The object is to avoid Titan's being taken over by the political and commercial interests that would turn it into a manufacturing colony."

The sound of a tone announcing an incoming call came from somewhere nearby. A woman's voice answered. "Hello, this is Dr. Weinerbaum's laboratory . . ."

Weinerbaum continued. "That is what you yourself wanted, is it not, Herr Zambendorf? The only difference in our situations that I can see is that *we* have been able to do something more conducive to our common goal than is likely to be achieved by parlor tricks or puerile guessing games with numbers . . . and that is *all*. The Asterians will confine themselves strictly to that objective. I have their leader's personal assurance on it."

A woman appeared around a partition from the work area adjacent. She looked flustered. "I'm sorry to interrupt, Dr. Weinerbaum, but the base commander has just called. Something is locking out the trunk beam to Earth, and we can't regain control of it. Also, the *Shirasagi* has just got news via its link that the commercial ground stations into Japan are down, the Tokyo Stock Exchange has had to cease trading, and communications circuits westward into Asia are being disrupted. He asks if you would go to the communications room immediately."

But by that time the news coming in from Earth was almost an hour old. In his penthouse suite at the top of the GSEC headquarters building in New York, a bewildered Burton Ramelson was being deluged by reports of banking, manufacturing, transportation, administrative, and scientific systems collapsing everywhere. The global financial system was already in chaos, airlines were grounded, and whole telephone networks were seizing up. The entire global economy was suddenly confronting an escalating threat of total breakdown.

"What about the *Orion*?" he yelled at Warren Taylor, director of NASO's North American division, over a private, secure voice circuit that was still working to Washington. "Will the launch be put back much?"

"Put back?" Taylor's voice squawked. "Burton, you've got to be kidding! The way things are going, for the foreseeable future you can forget any notion of sending a military expedition—or anything else—anywhere. Period."

Ramelson was stunned. "But ... what about developments on Titan?" he stammered.

Taylor snorted audibly over the line. "You can forget that, too. Until further notice, they're on their own out there."

30

HAROLD MACKESON LISTENED WITH INCREDULITY AND mounting alarm as Weinerbaum, now totally deflated and suddenly weary under the shock of the news, filled in the story about the discovery of the aliens, the scientists' decision to keep the setup at ES3 a secret until they knew more, and the real reason why he had asked for an independent channel to Earth.

Zambendorf, Fellburg, and Abaquaan had also come to the communications room; nobody was questioning their right to a place on the team now. Weinerbaum's differences with Zambendorf had become as irrelevant as the pettiness among others that he himself had railed about only a short time before. Even so, he couldn't quite bring himself to acknowledge the fact openly—not yet, anyhow.

Naturally, Mackeson was furious at the deceit. But he was also a mature enough administrator to accept the fact that while authority could be delegated, responsibility never could be. Ultimately, whatever the faults and omissions of others, accountability for everything that happened at Genoa Base outside the direct military command chain devolved on him. Therefore, he suppressed his acrimony as more fitting to another time, conserving his energy for the demands of the moment. Not that there were too many choices to consider. In fact, there was only one immediate course of action that he could see with any point to it.

"Let's get out there to ES3 and find out what these jokers want," he told the others.

The NASO flyer came down in the cleared area in front of Experimental Station 3 less than thirty minutes later. Two British marine commandos in military EV suits attached a heated, flexible tunnel to the mating flange of the access lock; Weinerbaum, Mackeson, and two other NASO officers, along with Zambendorf, Fellburg, and Abaquaan, who were still with them, walked through into the entry chamber of the two connected huts that formed the central hub of the station.

The interior looked like the control room of a submarine, with consoles, cabinets, shelves, and workstations filling every inch of usable space, as became normal in every human habitat on Titan. It was the riot of improvisation that researchers delighted in: panels hacked out of unfinished aluminum, open racks of circuit cards festooned with hand-soldered wiring, bundles of cable twisting all over the floor—the whole giving the impression of resulting more from some gleeful technophile's experiment in expressiveness than from any purposeful design.

A panel above a worktop in one corner contained a screen and controls connected to the interface setup, which was quiescent at that moment. Weinerbaum summarized how the translation arrangement with the aliens worked and the vital role the Taloids from Padua played. There were eighteen of them in their special quarters at ES3 now, working in turns, usually several at a time, and able to take time off between shifts. Between them they handled communication for twelve Asterians, although all twelve hardly ever needed to talk at the same time. There was also a thirteenth set of code groupings that represented, as far as the scientists had been able to make out, not an alien as such but a form of artificial intelligence that had accompanied them, possibly as a technical "assistant." But whatever its precise function, it seemed preoccupied with internal processes and had not yet communicated externally with the Terrans.

The rest of the room contained display and processing equipment connected to links from various other places on Titan that the scientists had been investigating. Weinerbaum called it the "monitoring center." The intention was to build the various activities scattered about the surface into some kind of bigger picture.

Mackeson had no questions when Weinerbaum had finished and replied simply with a brief nod in the direction of the interface setup. "Let's get on with it, then," he said tightly.

"Er, yes . . . of course." Weinerbaum led them over to the panel in the corner and eased himself into the operator's chair. Mackeson and Zambendorf squeezed themselves into the space behind, while the others found the best vantage points they could nearby. The regular ES3 staff watched curiously from farther back, while others bunched in the entrance to the connector from the other hut.

Weinerbaum operated switches, then called something to the back of the room. A voice recited several numbers in response. Weinerbaum pressed some buttons, entered a code into a touchpad, and waited. The screen remained blank, but a scratchy voice, like something from an ancient needle-and-groove recording, said, "Yes, Weinerbaum?"

"Cyril?"

"This Ford. Cyril busy." "Ford" was the name the Terrans had given to one of Cyril's companions, who seemed to have been with some kind of Asterian manufacturing corporation.

"We wish to talk, please," Weinerbaum said curtly.

"I busy also."

Behind Weinerbaum, Mackeson and Zambendorf exchanged wondering shakes of their heads at the spectacle of one of their company talking intelligibly with an alien entity from another star.

"You lied to us," Weinerbaum said. "You broke our agreement. All of Earth is being disrupted. We wish to talk *now*."

"Said busy. Go away."

From where he was standing, Zambendorf could see the color rising at the back of Weinerbaum's neck. "We can still sever the link," Weinerbaum said.

"No big deal. Smart replicating software-bomb now Earth-resident. Link no longer needed."

Weinerbaum's knuckles whitened against the armrest of his chair. "Ford, I—"

"Ford gone. This is Watson." The interface rendered all Asterian responses in the same voice. "Watson" had been with what sounded like a computing research organization.

"Whoever," Weinerbaum said tightly. "*You* are still Titan-resident. We activated the codes. We can deactivate them."

"Now protected," the voice scoffed. "Maximum-security deny-access measures. No chance."

"We can physically isolate the hardware that contains you," Weinerbaum persisted. "If necessary, destroy it."

"Which hardware? Safety copies distributed in nodes all over Titan. Untraceable. So will you destroy all of it? How? All your weapons stranded on Earth. Permanently. Ho-ho."

An awkward silence came over the lab. Weinerbaum didn't know where to go from there. Nobody else had anything to suggest.

Then the voice said, "Okay. Cyril here now. So talk if want. Only way peace from simian pests."

The screen that had so far been blank became active suddenly and presented an upper-body image of the strangest creature those new to ES3 had ever seen. It had two arms, hinging more from the front of the shoulders than laterally, each with four fingers that seemed to have more segments than the human three. The head was an elongated inverted cone, pallid blue, widening at the top to accommodate two enormous circular eyes that moved independently, and rounding into a flattish dome like the top of a carrot, with a Mohicanlike plume of green and orange. The mouth was protrusive and rigid-looking and seemed not very mobile or expressive; the ears were high-set and diminutive. But strangest of all were the structures of complex folds growing up from each shoulder and apparently attached to the sides of the head, though sufficiently loosely not to impair head movement. They were brightly colored and in constant agitation, suggesting, if anything, some exotic variety of sea anemone waving in underwater currents.

Zambendorf and the others could only stare, awed. Weinerbaum said without looking back, "Of course, this isn't a picture of anything physically real—we're interacting with electronic representations. More recently we've been getting these visual depictions in addition to the original speech-only output. It's obviously a synthesis, but it probably does reflect fairly authentically how the Asterians looked. The form suggests descent from an ancestral stock somewhat akin to our bird family. The epaulet structures seem to be the primary means of visual expression, though how to read them is still a mystery."

The epaulets on one side stiffened and moved suddenly in unison for a moment, and the voice spoke again. "You make child deal and I am blamed one? No. You stupid. What kind of business-Earthman gives away? Earth run by simpletons. Lucky has lasted this long time."

Weinerbaum murmured to the others, "What we would consider common courtesy does not seem to be part of their innate disposition, I'm afraid. That has been one of the main obstacles to establishing a satisfactory rapport." He looked back at the screen and said, "Listen, Cyril, I—"

"No. You listen," the alien interrupted. "Terrans have served purpose. Important Asterian business waits doing. I do you big compliment talking here. You see too late. Walk into problems. Too bad. Want to know Asterians' want-things-list before go away? No nose-skin off us now. Okay. Is so." The screen showed a part of Titan's machinescape outside, which could have been anywhere.

"All Titan machine life is ours. Asterians. Origins from our civilization. Comes to Titan by our space science before humans are existed. All totally is Asterian property."

"What about the Taloids?" Weinerbaum interjected. "Titan is their heritage. Have they no rights to property?"

The image on the screen made a gesture and ruffled one of its shoulder adornments. "Taloids just freak machines. No claims. No plans Taloid recycle-scrap. Asterians will control. Change as see fit to suit, redirect everything to our purposes, not human or Taloid purposes. Was aim of get-link Earth human stupids give away free. Since Asterians reactivate, learn awareness of here Titan NASO Terrans, GSEC Terrans, military Terrans, all with different friend Terrans back at Earth Washington Europe, all too messed up that not even Terrans understand. Now as extra add Japanese *Shirasagi* ship arrive with other plans, while Earth army preparing *Orion* ship come take Titan control away from everybody. All an insane mess up. No thanks. Asterians have need nothing complications such. Things have to do more important."

The watchers crowding around behind Weinerbaum waited tensely. "What things?" he prompted after a few seconds.

But Cyril evidently felt that he had already been more obliging than necessary. "Talk enough," the image said. "Things have to do." And it vanished.

"Ford?" Weinerbaum tried. "Watson? . . . Anyone?" But all attempts to restore communication were unsuccessful.

The first reaction of Weinerbaum and the scientists was to call the aliens' bluff and try to deactivate them by isolating and shutting down the hardware concentrations in which they were located, as Weinerbaum had threatened. But it turned out that Watson had not been bluffing. Cutting off the local centers didn't stop the characteristic activity patterns that had been detected elsewhere. It appeared that the Asterians had indeed mapped alternative host systems and created interconnecting pathways, possibly all over Titan. After three hours of testing, checking, and contacting workers at other sites, an exhausted Weinerbaum conceded defeat. "It seems that we're already too late—they have effectively distributed themselves through the whole system. The speed it's happening at is frightening. They've probably gained control over a significant portion of Titan's capacity already."

"Then the question now is, What do they intend using it for?" Zambendorf replied.

All rivalries and differences among the varied Terran interests on Titan disappeared. The obvious rallying point for them to regroup was the *Shirasagi*, orbiting above the cloud canopy. The Asterians had penetrated Titan's general surface network, and obviously nothing at Genoa Base could be considered secure, since they had invaded the Earthnet by seizing the link beam transmitted from there.

The *Shirasagi*, however, had its own independent link back to Japanese satellites in Earth orbit, and the mission controllers in Osaka had had the presence of mind to isolate their end as soon as the eastern Asian sector of the Earthnet had begun misbehaving. This should have stopped the alien influence from being propagated back out to Titan via the *Shirasagi*'s beam. Moreover, the *Shirasagi* had been engaging in conventional communications only with Genoa Base, without any high-capacity data connection. Hence, there was good reason to hope that the *Shirasagi*'s system was "clean."

A final point was that the chief of the Japanese mission, Yakumo, was a full-fledged mission director, appointed to his post by a national government. The existing organization on Titan, by contrast, operated under the divided command of a temporary administrative head assigned by NASO and a military contingent under separate orders, both of which depended on guidance from Earth that could disappear at any moment.

All factors pointed to the same conclusion. All agreed to consolidate under Yakumo's direction as emergency head of the entire Terran presence on Titan. A conference was called shortly afterward aboard the *Shirasagi* to assess the situation and review whatever options anyone had to offer for doing something about it.

31

J T HAD BEEN A LONG TIME SINCE ZAMBENDORF HAD SEEN real stars.

He and his team were assigned two places at the conference aboard the *Shirasagi*. He took Abaquaan with him. A NASO surface shuttle carried them up from Genoa Base along with deputations from the various other groups that had remained on Titan after the *Orion*'s departure. Mackeson and a half dozen of his officers represented NASO, while Weinerbaum and three colleagues went on behalf of the professional scientists. Dave Crookes and John Webster were elected as spokesmen for the mix of engineers, technicians, and others from the various private laboratories and corporations. Colonel Short attended as senior officer of the military force, along with the commanders of the British and French detachments subordinate to him.

Nobody in charge, of course, thought to include the Taloids, whose home the war was being fought over and whose habitat was at that moment being seized. Zambendorf suggested it but was told it was impracticable because Taloids couldn't be accommodated inside the *Shirasagi*. When he pointed out that they could participate remotely via a communications link into Camelot—a device he had used himself more than once—the answer came back that there would be no point, since it was all technical and the Taloids wouldn't understand what was going on.

Like the *Orion*, the *Shirasagi* used pulsed inertial fusion propulsion reacting on magnetic fields generated in an open-frame thrust chamber. The rest of the vessel forward of the radiation shield consisted of a number of modules interconnected by tubular and lattice beams, none of which contained a single area of regular living space large enough to house the gathering comfortably. Therefore, the conference took place in a hastily adapted cargo hold that had been freed up by the transfer of supplies and matériel down to the base the Japanese were building at Padua City.

Yakumo, tall and broad-shouldered, sporting a droopy Pancho Villa–style mustache and wearing the indigo blue of the Japanese Space Arm, sat in the center of a panel of his officers and staff on a slightly raised dais. The delegates from the surface installation filled the rest of the space, using an assortment of tables and chairs. A mild spin superimposed on the *Shirasagi*'s freefall trajectory separated "up" from "down" and afforded a modicum of dignity appropriate to the occasion.

Yakumo opened with a short welcoming speech and introductions, followed by a reminder—as if any were needed—of what had brought them all together. Then Harold Mackeson assumed the task of summarizing to the assembly the events that had brought about the current situation, as well as anyone could reconstruct them. He did this partly to give the audience the benefit of his nonspecialist vantage point, partly in acknowledgment of his own overall technical responsibility, and partly to spare Weinerbaum the embarrassment of having the proceedings turned into a private confessional.

Yakumo listened expressionlessly until the Englishman was through. Then, when Mackeson finally set aside his notes and looked up, Yakumo slapped the tabletop in front of him in a slow, soundless motion and laid it all to rest with the simple rejoinder "So." It was his way of endorsing Mackeson's unspoken decision that recriminations and blame could wait until later. They were all in enough trouble as things were without letting strife among themselves add to the burden.

Yakumo repeated the main point that had emerged from

it all. "The original belief was that these aliens were merely cooperating in delaying the *Orion* launch in order to frustrate the military operation. It is now clear that we were deceived and that their true aims were much more all along. Dr. Weinerbaum?"

"So it would appear," Weinerbaum agreed miserably.

A woman sitting beside Yakumo elaborated. "Instead, they've injected a self-propagating code into the Earthnet to bring down *all* systems."

"With what objective?" Colonel Short asked.

The scientist made a face and showed her palms. "It can only be to reduce Earth to a primitive condition comparable to that of the prenetwork era. It will make Earth incapable of projecting any influence beyond its own vicinity, let alone as far away as Titan."

Yakumo leaned back and surveyed the room. "It seems that Earth has become the victim of the strangest form of attack ever," he concluded. "An alien software virus that infects the planetary electronic organism in the same way a molecular virus invades the corporal chemical organism . . ." He paused for a moment to let the suggestion register, then asked, "For what purpose?" He looked around invitingly. There were no responses. "Dr. Weinerbaum?"

Weinerbaum just shook his head.

"Apparently nobody knows," the woman scientist observed.

Another of the Japanese spoke up. "Well, obviously to be left on their own and in full control here. The aliens want control of Titan's capabilities themselves."

"Well, maybe, but they won't be left quite on their own, will they?" Harold Mackeson reminded everybody. "*We're* still here. Where does everybody up in this ship and down on the surface figure in these aliens' plans?"

"We don't," somebody answered simply.

"Any more than the Taloids," another voice added.

"We are currently evaluating the logistics of getting everybody back to Earth," the chief engineering officer of the *Shirasagi* said. "It should be possible by a comfortable margin, and we can recompute a return course without help from Osaka."

"And then what?" Colonel Short asked.

The engineering chief looked taken by surprise. "I'm not sure I understand the question. I said I'm confident that we can get you all back to Earth, Colonel."

Short nodded. "I know you did. And I said, 'Then what?' " He glanced around briefly, then explained. "Okay, so we go home. And, like somebody just said, we leave them in monopoly control of everything out here at Titan." He shrugged as if the rest were too obvious. "How long until they come after us? And with what? There's enough down there for them to turn this whole moon into a production line for weapons we probably can't even imagine. Hell, isn't that what the whole thing was supposed to be in the first place, before it got all screwed up? And like somebody else just said, they've already put us back in the Stone Age to the point where Earth couldn't defend itself against an attack of school buses. So, like I said, after we're all back home and they've had time to get their act together and come after us . . . then what?"

It was the first time most of those present had fully realized what it all added up to.

People looked at each other with strained faces, muttering and shaking their heads. As the initial reactions subsided, Yakumo's gaze scanned the room, finally singling out Zambendorf and Abaquaan. "We have two gentlemen here of very different talents from most of the people present," he said. Zambendorf blinked and stared back in surprise—privately he had been amazed even to have been invited up there at all. Yakumo went on. "You seem to possess a remarkable instinct for understanding alien minds and how to get through to them, Herr Zambendorf." The room fell silent with curiosity.

"I have had some success," Zambendorf replied. Normally he would have capitalized on the moment somehow and seized the opportunity to buff up his image a little, but this just wasn't the time.

"At the time of the landings from the *Orion*, I believe it

was you who first established meaningful communication with the Taloids," Yakumo said.

"I . . . played a lucky hunch or two," Zambendorf suggested.

"But it was before the experts managed to achieve anything," Yakumo went on. "Do I take it that their hunches were not so lucky?"

"Er, everyone has their off days, I suppose."

"Well, a lot of people seem to have been having some serious off days lately," Yakumo said. In the front row facing him, Weinerbaum looked ill. Yakumo briefly raised some papers he had picked up from the table. "But it was yourself again, Herr Zambendorf, who not only deduced the existence of these latest aliens while being denied access to all the pertinent information but saw through their true designs before the experts so much as suspected them."

"Um, yes. Yes, I guess we—my colleagues all contributed . . . I guess we did," Zambendorf agreed slowly.

"So, another lucky hunch? Extraordinary."

The silence seemed to drag. "Perhaps alien natures aren't so different from human nature when you get to the bottom of it. And understanding human nature is my business," Zambendorf offered.

"Exactly."

Zambendorf became aware of Yakumo's eyes fixed on him pointedly. He glanced quickly from side to side, unsure if he might have missed something. "I'm sorry," he said, looking back at the mission chief. "What more do you want me to say?"

"Say?" Yakumo repeated. "I don't want you to *say* anything. Twice now, when it comes to dealing with aliens, you have shown an amazing ability to come up with the right answers when the experts have got it wrong. And this time the experts have screwed up royally. What I'm waiting for, Herr Zambendorf, is to know what you're going to *do*."

But all that Zambendorf could do—just at that moment, anyway—was stare back, glassy-eyed. For once in his life he found himself truly baffled.

32

SARVIK HAD THOUGHT HE'D SEEN EVERYTHING THAT NA-
ive trust had to offer. But the ease with which Weinerbaum had bought the fellow-seekers-after-truth line, and
his readiness to give access to the Earthnet, had surpassed
all of it. Earth was now quarantined for a comfortably long
time and could be dealt with at leisure. Meanwhile, the
Borijans were free to concentrate on getting Titan organized.

At first the other Borijans had been skeptical of Sarvik's
accounts to them of his initial conversations with the
Terrans. Nobody could be that credulous, they had said,
which had led them to suspect that Sarvik was setting them
up for something. But they believed him later, when they
got a chance to use the interface themselves.

Their suspicions made Sarvik despair. Back on Turle it
had been no more than healthily prudent to be suspicious of
another's motives. But among the last dozen of their kind
a million years after their civilization had ended, with a
new world to build and enormous shared problems to overcome, he'd hoped that more constructive attitudes might
have prevailed. Perhaps he had erred in his judgment of
who had been worthy to bring with him.

He left that line of thought to be picked up again another
time as his consciousness expanded to accommodate more
incoming data channels, and the difficulties of trying to in-
tegrate his multiple simultaneous perceptions intensified.
The area of surface geography that had become "him" now
covered about four acres and contained an electronics assembly and wiring line that he "saw" from monitor cameras

mounted at different vantage points, "felt" through a variety of position and motion sensors distributed through the machines and transfer operations, and "read" from the outputs of subprocessors controlling the manufacturing process. All this had become his new sensory system.

It had been obvious that the Terrans would retaliate when they discovered that the whole Earthnet was going down. So, by the time Weinerbaum threatened to contain the Borijans by isolating the hardware that was hosting them, Sarvik and the others had already escaped into the general Titanwide network, leaving copies of themselves behind to occupy the Terrans. Since then, Sarvik had been learning to function in the strange new environment of the surface. He had pretty much gotten the knack of fusing the mosaic of scattered input impressions into a coherent whole and was learning to manipulate the machines and processes that for the present constituted his being. The next step would be to clear away some of the chaotically evolved jungle and reorganize it to producing purpose-designed bodies along the lines that had been envisaged on Turle.

But in addition to Sarvik's computing know-how, that project would need the Farworlds people's expertise in laying out manufacturing lines and Robocon's knowledge of detailed machine design. Getting very much further would therefore require reestablishing contact with the others. To do that, he would have to learn how to explore his surroundings and move around.

The electronics line fed into an area where the circuit assemblies were fitted into racks; the racks were mounted in metal frames that then went into cabinets. The cabinets and racking came from a metalworking facility in the opposite direction from the electronics line. One type of mounting frame made here came with four drilled holes, one at each corner of a facing flange. Sarvik concentrated his awareness on the drilling operation and experienced the curious sensation of reading the head-positioning digitizers, feeling the speed and pressure feedbacks, and watching the process through an imager, all as parts of a single, unified perception. Out of curiosity he tried moving the drill head by an effort of will to a normally blank area of metal halfway along one side of the flange. The system responded, and he discovered a distinct satisfaction in making it drill two additional holes.

A small beginning, Sarvik told himself. But a beginning.

Sarvik soon found that he could move his center point of attention within his domain of awareness, somewhat like the focal point of a visual field. After some experimenting, he began concentrating on the external signals arriving at the periphery, learning to discern form and meaning in the patterns generated by the things going on around him. As his consciousness adapted more to its new, extended realm, it learned to construct visual mappings of the entities and processes making up the surrounding electronic landscape.

It was a mysterious landscape of geometric shapes in colored light appearing and vanishing, program trees pulsing in changing configurations against hillsides of permanent command structures standing solid and dark. Data streams merged and looped in sparkling torrents to join slowly moving tides, and message packets sailed over like birds, carrying snippets of information from somewhere afar or reports being logged to some distant destination. And there were stranger forms, too, that moved purposefully among it all, able to combine together on occasions and then to separate again, preserving their integrity and identities. Sarvik perceived them as strange animal forms upon the landscape. There was as much life, he realized, inhabiting the invisible software networks of Titan's forests as there were freely mobile forms roaming it physically.

He found that by concentrating his faculties at a point on his containing boundary, he could extend it in that direction; at the same time, he lost a part of his awareness from the opposite side. In effect, he had moved himself a short distance. With practice, he developed this knack into an ability to "flow" at will within the net, sometimes in a gradual progression, sometimes in leaps, depending on the nature of the electronic terrain. Thus, he was able to explore and move himself about Titan's surface—and to do so, he discovered, with astonishing speed.

It didn't take him too long after that to find another of his kind, which had been his objective. He saw it coming toward him along a ravine of flickering orange and blue latticed sides and a floor of rectangular pools sitting among low pink walls that went in all directions like a maze. At intervals, wide, green trunklike cylinders rose vertically and converged toward infinity far overhead. The figure was on a kind of raft being carried along on a swiftly moving stream of colors that followed the middle of the ravine.

Sarvik didn't know for sure what, in the peculiar transform space he was now living in, a data set representing a Borijan ought to look like. But this entity was more complex than any of the autonomous living forms he'd seen previously, and it resembled the parts of his own extension that appeared within his field of view, being formed from wire-frame sections connected by filaments, the whole vaguely suggesting an aggregation of cylinders connected by spheres. What else could it be?

The creature had also evidently seen him. It stepped off the raft, which promptly dissolved away into the stream, and approached. Sarvik slackened his pace as he drew nearer. The two of them went into a slow, circling motion around each other, keeping their distance, moving between the pink walls in a wide space among the green trunks. Sarvik had never tried communicating in his new form, since there had been nobody to communicate with after his exit from Weinerbaum's lab. He concentrated on directing the same faculty of projection that enabled him to move himself and endeavored to impress upon it the thought "Borijan?" And immediately he knew, as when one heard one's own voice, that somehow it worked.

"Yes," came the reply.

The two figures ceased circling one another and relaxed visibly. Sarvik stepped forward; the other moved to meet him.

"The unsuspected world within a world of Titan," the other said.

"It's . . . a strange place," Sarvik replied.

"Takes some getting used to."

"I have to be impolite," Sarvik said. "I don't know how to recognize anyone in this form yet, probably any more than you do. Who are you?"

"Sarvik," the figure replied.

Sarvik froze, a composite of wire frames half-raised in a gesture of greeting. "That's not possible. *I'm* Sarv—"

And then he saw suddenly that it was very possible. Of course, from *his* point of view, it would have been *he* who had escaped from the lab and a copy who had been left there. And all the other copies that had been written out into the net as a precaution would think the same thing. Did that mean *he* was a copy? He wasn't even sure if the term meant anything anymore.

"Oh. I see. I must be the first one you've bumped into," the other Sarvik said.

"Er . . . yes."

"So you haven't talked with any of the others at all?"

"How could I? I've just told you that you're the first one of us I've met in here."

Sarvik Two gestured to indicate the stream rushing along the middle of the ravine. "You can tap into the long-range communications channels. It's a bit more tricky than coordinating local functions but not so bad when you get used to it. It sounds as if you've been out of things. We're spread out all over Titan. The plans are moving right along to get sites cleared for proper factories to make bodies. There's another tentative design worked out, and the Indrigons have already reprogrammed some of the native machines to produce parts."

All that already? It didn't seem possible. And then Sarvik One caught Sarvik Two's use of the plural. "What do you mean, Indrigons?" he queried. "Who is spread out all over Titan? How many of us are you talking about?"

"Sixty-eight at the last count, but more keep turning up—like you," Sarvik Two told him. "There's five of us— six now—along with four Kalazins, half a dozen Indrigons . . . I'm not sure offhand how many of each of the rest. We'll have to get you into one of the design groups. Everybody will be getting together somewhere for a review conference shortly. Distance is no object, as you've probably found out."

Sarvik One listened in a daze. When the novelty wore off, the compulsive Borijan antagonism that had shown itself briefly when they had first been reactivated would come to the surface again. Only, instead of just one of each of them for the others to conspire against, there would be dozens!

33

MORDRAN COULDN'T UNDERSTAND IT. HE HAD LIVED IN this part of Kroaxia for almost two hundred brights, and he didn't know how many times he had taken this route into Pergassos. He knew every machining center, welding line, and assembly station along the way as well as he knew the hydrocarbon fractionaters in his own kitchen garden. And yet on this trip he was continually getting lost. Time and again he would stop, puzzled, to stand rubbing his carbon-blacked chin and radiating a frown from his facial thermal patterns while he surveyed the way ahead and then announce, "No. This in't a bloody right, either. Some guide I turned out ter be, din't I? We'll 'ave ter go back a bit an' try it another way. I don't know what's 'appenin'. I've never seen owt like this before."

Whole parts of the forest seemed to be changing. The forest was always changing itself, of course, but the changes had always been scattered and gradual. As one expression of life was dying here, another grew there, but always with an overall continuity that the robeing sense of time, progressing naturally from bright to bright, could assimilate.

But what was happening now was different. In one place they'd come to, the trail ended at a wall of uprooted pylons, crushed girders, piled-up casings, and debris of every kind, where a whole swath had been leveled and everything in it just torn up and pushed aside. In another, death had descended everywhere. Everything, even the river, stood silent and idle, with only screw extractors and rivet shavers buzzing in the undergrowth to break the stillness. Mordran had never before seen whole areas affected in that way.

They came to an assembly and testing plant, modest in scale, where Mordran said smaller-size animals of various kinds had been coming to life for as long as he could remember. But now all that had ceased, leaving partly completed animals lying discarded in heaps all over the place. Around the plant, squads of retoolers and refitters scurried and chattered, modifying the assembly machines to new configurations. At the same time, ferocious-looking lunge drills and laser spitters patrolled the boundary to keep inquisitive forest dwellers at bay. They were intimidating enough to keep Rex and Duke—stalwart companions by this time—well back.

"Never in all my twelve-brights of studying the world of nature have I seen machines of the likes that are starting to take shape there, Thirg," Brongyd said as they stood watching from a safe distance. "The strangeness is not simply that they are new machines. But their whole layouts and growth sequences are of a kind unknown to me. It is as if they are of another world—conceived by the mind of a different Lifemaker."

"A right caper this is turnin' out t' be," Mordran declared. "Now I'm beginnin' ter wonder if I'll be able ter find me own way back."

Eventually the trail they had been following came out of a spray-painting ravine to join the road into Pergassos. But instead of the deserted track Mordran had promised, they found the way filled with a slow procession of frightened-looking Kroaxians heading toward the city. They had as much of their possessions as they could bring with them, some riding in loaded wagons, others pushing carts or leading pack animals, many just carrying bundles.

Thirg stopped a worob in a wheelskin bonnet and wire shawl, one of a group following a heavily laden wagon. "Where are you from?" he asked her.

"Kirtenzhal. The village back fifteen leagues yon."

"Why is everybody leaving?"

She looked at him with the hostility that fear, fatigue, and resentfulness that another's security instilled. "Leaving? Leaving where? The village isn't there anymore."

"Why? What happened?"

"Torn down, it was. Dozers and icemovers came out of the hills and swept it aside—all the houses, everything. Now it's being replanted as a forest."

"But not any kind of forest that you've ever seen," a rob who had stopped with her to rest put in. "The machines are all being laid even-spaced in straight rows. The pipes are in trenches—all paralleled and right-angled, regular and neat. It ain't natural, what's going on."

"It's the Lifemaker's wrath come down on us all!" another worob wailed, joining them. "The priests were right. We let our minds be poisoned by heretics. First Kleippur in Carthogia. Then we let Nogarech take over this country. We were warned. The vengeance is upon us! We'll all melt and burn!"

Others took up the lament.

"Praise be to the Lifemaker. We were led astray."

"May He preserve the king! Bring back the king."

"Preserve Eskenderom and Frennelech!"

Thirg stepped back and turned to Brongyd. "What do you make of it all?" he asked.

"I can make nothing of any of it," the naturalist replied. "Entire areas of the forest seem to be reorganizing themselves according to a common plan. It is as if some strange, unworldly influence were asserting itself, taking over the whole scheme of things and redirecting it to some sinister end of its own."

"Well, the only unwordly influence we've 'ad around

'ere lately is them bloody Lumians," Mordran declared. "Weren't there talk goin' round about that bein' why they were chasin' about like fools after Eskenderom instead o' chuckin' 'im in t' methlake along wi' Frennelech an' t' rest of 'em—because they wanted 'im to 'elp 'em tame t' forests? Well, it looks ter me like maybe they've gone an' done it. Don't yer reckon?"

Thirg hoped not. If the designs of the merchant Lumians who wanted the forests tamed had advanced this much while Thirg and Brongyd were in hiding, it could only mean that the wrong faction on Lumia had prevailed, and the inquirer Lumians and other friends of the Wearer who defended Kleippur had been vanquished. Yet the great dragon that was bringing warriors, which had been the Wearer's main cause for worry, could never have reached Robia so soon. So how could the situation have altered this drastically in so short a time?

The three hastened on their way, past the column of plodding figures and creaking wagons, in the direction of Pergassos.

Meanwhile, near a bridge on the outskirts of Pergassos, a vaguely bathtub-shaped section of metal casing bumped its way ashore just above where an assortment of chutes and conduits deposited garbage from the city onto an outflowing conveyor. The robot inside, clutching a length of scratched and dented tubing, sat looking around disbelievingly, astounded to have completed the journey in one piece.

Groork climbed out and collected together what remained of his belongings. The supplies were gone. He had broken the sword prying his craft loose from a jam where a tributary entered from a grove of plate benders and part of the feed hoist had broken down, and had lost the lance in an encounter with something that screeched and swung down at him on a power vine. But he still had the spare clothes and a few tools.

Then, as he had been instructed by the Lumian-Who-Heals-Hearers, he spoke with his internal voice the sign to

alert the ear that would always be listening inside the
Lumians' camp back at Menassim. The response came back
as a mystical voice speaking inside his head:

"SORRY, NOBODY HERE RIGHT NOW. LEAVE MES-
SAGE AFTER BEEP."

So much for "Our guys'll be listening for you all the
way," Groork thought glumly. He sent the code announcing
his arrival anyway. Then he turned from the river, climbed
the ice wall forming its bank, and headed toward the center
of the city.

34

STRANGE THINGS WERE HAPPENING ALL OVER KROAXIA
and, according to reports from farther afield, beyond
Kroaxia's borders also. The people were terrified, blaming
it all on the heresies that had taken over Carthogia and the
new regime's dealings with the Lumians. Nogarech's popu-
larity had declined to the extent that he had become a virtual prisoner in his own palace. The time was ripe,
Eskenderom's advisers agreed, for the former leader to regain his power. If he did it now and through his own efforts, without waiting for the great dragon to arrive with its
Lumian army, his stature in the eyes of the Kroaxians could
only grow and his bargaining position with the Lumians
would become that much stronger. So Eskenderom and
Frennelech had returned secretly to Pergassos to be ready to
seize the moment. They were concealed in rooms in the friary adjoining the former Palace of the High Holy One,
which Nogarech—foolishly in the opinion of his many
opponents—had allowed the priests from the previous regime to continue occupying instead of executing them.

From a chamber of ice walls and somber ecclesiastical furnishings Eskenderom scowled out through a window overlooking the rear courtyard. A scroll of etched foil lay on a stand beside him, carrying a report of the latest happenings on the outskirts of the city and beyond.

"What kind of Lumian treachery do these tidings augur now?" he muttered. "People flee their razed villages, while the forests are torn down. Had I heeded the Lumians' words and waited in Serethgin for their army to restore me, to what devastated kingdom would I have returned to be restored? Does this fabled Lumian dragon army exist, in truth, at all? Or was it, from the beginnings of our dialogue, a phantasm concocted to distract us while they pervert to their own designs the forest powers they have always coveted?"

Privately, he had no doubt that the Lumian army did exist. But he suspected Frennelech, the high priest, of being a party to some secret plot with the Lumians to bring him down. It seemed to Eskenderom that the Lumians didn't need his command of Kroaxia's soldiery to recruit robeing labor to their ends so much as they needed Frennelech's power to direct their minds. Eskenderom's usefulness was perhaps, therefore, temporary—to maintain a presence of force until the Lumians had established sufficient strength of their own. The latest news suggested that those designs were more advanced than he had been led to believe.

Frennelech answered from the far side of the room, where he was pacing by the door. "Verily would I agree that no dragon-bringer-of-armies idles at Lumia. For does it not sit beyond the sky above Robia, and are its emissaries not erecting their camp outside Pergassos even as we speak? Is it by coincidence that the forests go into upheaval as these events come to pass? Surely not. Yet it was not to *me* that any Lumians imparted foreknowledge of such intents."

He had suspected Eskenderom of involvement in some private intrigue with the Lumians for a long time. Since their arrival, the Lumians had maintained their main camp at Carthogia, dealing openly with Kleippur, whose philosophy and teachings would put an end to Frennelech and the power of the priests. He could see now that the encouragement given him by the Lumians to exhort his supporters into rising as the militant Avengers had been a ploy to lure them into being destroyed by the Lumian dragon soldiers. Now Frennelech's defenders were scattered, and Eskenderom was getting ready to be reinstated by a Lumian-supported invasion from Carthogia. And the latest news suggested that those designs were more advanced than he had been led to believe.

Eskenderom wheeled from the window. "What art thou saying? That *I* was privy to some compact in this? Is this some holy derangement that afflicts thee? Would the king skulk out of sight like some beggar at a banquet in this dreary hostel of priests while foreigners restore my throne? Tell me that it was not *thee*, who now admits his masters' dragon to this sky, who sold thy hold over Kroaxian souls for alliance in the alien design."

Frennelech's facial pattern radiated outrage. "*I*? What gibbering royal delirium is this? Kleippur's agents undermine the faith. The Avengers that *thy* accomplices had me raise lie strewn in ruin and wreckage."

" 'Tis *my* service that is rendered redundant now if the Lumian army indeed rides with the dragon-beyond-the-sky!" Eskenderom shouted, clanging a finger against his own chest. "The Lumians talk of Eskenderom, but it is Frennelech whom they will restore. Dost thou take me for as big a fool as those who would trade their worldly worth for thy fantasies of eternity?"

"*I* the fool. Thou the befooler!" Frennelech shouted back, pointing accusingly.

"Even now wilt thou not admit to thy complicity? *Thou hymn-droning fraud!*" Eskenderom shrieked.

"*Thou crowned cozener!*" Frennelech howled back at him.

They advanced menacingly to meet face to face in the center of the room.

"*Lackey of aliens!*"

"*Hireling of exploiters!*"

Then they stopped abruptly and stared at the door, both realizing at the same moment that somebody was knocking discreetly. "Enter," Eskenderom commanded.

It was Mormorel, Eskenderom's senior counselor, who had accompanied them from Serethgin. "The mood of the people abandons Nogarech ever more swiftly as fugitives from Lumian mischief arrive from afar," he announced. "The moment of restitution approaches. The council should complete its final plans."

The king and high priest looked at him, their animosity of a moment ago forgotten. If the city was turning away from its flirtation with the Lumians and was ready to ditch Nogarech, their first priority must be to combine forces to take it back. They could fight over the spoils later.

"Summon them," Eskenderom said.

Mormorel nodded. "Also, it is reported that one who fled to Carthogia and was instrumental in thy Majesty's misfortunes has returned. Groork, the Hearer—brother of the inquirer into dark arts who also enlisted in the service of Kleippur—who was also known as Enlightener, has been seen again in the city."

"*Him!*" Eskenderom and Frennelech shouted, both at the same time. It was the Enlightener who had brought the new religion that had been the downfall of both of them and had put Nogarech in their place. His execution then had been averted only by Lumian interference.

"He conceals his presence in peasant garb and has been heard making inquiries about the affairs and whereabouts of thy Majesty and the High Holy One."

"Have our agents apprehend him and bring him here," Eskenderom ordered, his coolant vanes quivering. He glanced pointedly at Frennelech. "Then, maybe, before we consign him to the reduction furnaces permanently this time, our inquisitors might determine finally who is to be the Lumians' true benefactor in Kroaxia."

"Ee, it's been a while since I 'ad a pint that tasted as good as this. Gets right into yer joints, does all this walkin'." Mordran raised a mug of chilled solvent and drew a swig into his cooling system. "It makes me feel like I'm back in t' old days wi' t' mob—when we used ter spend 'arf our lives sloggin' back and forward across t' bloody Meracasine desert wi' pike an' pack. I'm glad that's all over now, anyroad."

Thirg looked around the tavern from the corner table at which the three were sitting. Next to him, Brongyd poured a solution of paw-plating salts into a dish for Rex and Duke, who were lying in the space beneath the stairs. The inn was typical of establishments in the central market area of the city, with the usual mix of merchants, laborers, stall holders, and farmers—their regular number swollen by the present influx from outside Pergassos. Mordran had been a regular here when he had been posted to the city in his days with the Kroaxian army.

Most of the talk around them was about the change afoot in the forests. Some thought it the work of the Lumians, but the majority, like the villagers whom Thirg had spoken to on the road into the city, feared it was a portent of divine retribution. Many people confused the two and thought the Lumians were supernatural envoys sent by the Lifemaker. Kleippur and Nogarech were being blamed for it all, and the latter had apparently retreated, with the supporters and guards still loyal to him, into the palace and its citadel. An ugly mood was building, and agitators were out preaching that by getting rid of Nogarech now and expelling the Lumians from their new camp being constructed near Pergassos, Kroaxia could redeem itself and normality would return.

"Are you still an avoider of city life?" Thirg asked Brongyd as they sat, taking in the bustle and chatter.

"As much as you yourself, Thirg," Brongyd replied. "My work has always kept me in the forests, and I've no complaint at that. Solitude has no loneliness that compares with being alone among strangers. But despite the troubled times, I sense a betterment in the life here since my last visit. Although that was so long ago now that the difference could be in my changing memories."

"No, you remember truly," Thirg said. "No longer do

penitents etch their skins with acids or expose themselves to public torments to cleanse their imagined guilt, as if the Lifemaker who supposedly endowed them with the wonder of a living body would be favorably impressed by such mistreating of it. There are no terrors visited by the Royal Guard. Although Nogarech has not yet brought his rule to the stage of Kleippur's, the improvement in the lot of the people is unmistakable."

Mordran leaned forward and spoke cautioningly, shielding his words with a hand. At the same time he kept his eyes on the general throng, as if watching for somebody. "I know what thee's sayin'. But I don't think it's a good idea t' be 'eard sayin' it just now, wi' things the way they are, if ye know what I mean."

"You're right, of course," Thirg said, and fell silent.

Mordran sat up as the landlord of the tavern appeared from the back, carrying a tray. He was of heavily reinforced build, with a ruddy copper-tinted face, thickly plated around the chin, and wearing a cord jerkin with a striped apron. Mordran caught him lightly by the elbow as he passed.

"All right, all right," the landlord said without looking down at them. "I've only got one pair of hands. I'll get back to you when I've got rid of this."

"Yer mean ter say that's all the welcomin' back I get, Neskal?" Mordran said. "I've a good mind ter bugger off an' find somewhere else ter get meself a drink. 'Taint like what I remember."

The landlord stopped dead a pace farther on and turned. "Never!" he exclaimed. "Not Mordran! By the Lifemaker, it is!" He came back to the table, set the tray down on a shelf nearby, and pumped Mordran's hand. "How long has it been now? ... Oh, I don't know. You're looking well, though. Civvy life must be doing you good."

"Can't complain, yer know. . . . Well, yer can if yer want, I suppose, but nobody wants t' 'ear it, does they?"

"And Yula? How's she doing?"

"Ah, she's awright. Off visitin' at t' moment. She were when we set out, anyroad. Took us longer'n we thought ter get 'ere. It's a right mess, in't it, all these goin's-on."

"Terrible, terrible," Neskal agreed. "There's going to be trouble here in the city. You'll see. . . . And these are friends of yours, I take it."

Mordran introduced Thirg and Brongyd and said they needed a bit of help. Before he could go into detail, however, a voice from a group across the room called out, "Landlord, are those our drinks there? Come on with it. Save the chat till later."

"I'll be back in a second," Neskal said, picking up the tray and hurrying over.

Brongyd had been glancing surreptitiously in the other direction. As Neskal moved away, he leaned closer to Thirg and murmured, "Don't look around too quickly, but there's a man over by the door who seems to be staring at you in an odd kind of way. Do you know him?"

"Oh?" Thirg looked the other way, then after a few seconds leaned back on the bench, picked up his mug, and made a pretense of letting his eyes wander absently about the room.

"By the door," Brongyd said again, keeping his eyes averted. "Thin, weaselly-looking fellow. With the black hood thrown back."

After a few seconds, letting his gaze travel on, Thirg said, "Yes, I see him. I don't recognize him immediately. But you know, there's something familiar about that face, all right."

Then Neskal came back to their table with his tray emptied, pulled a stool across the aisle, and sat down.

"Yer'd think they 'adn't drunk anythin' fer a bright, wouldn't yer, some of 'em, the way they carry on," Mordran commented.

"Ah, well, as long as they pay. That's what I'm here for," Neskal said. He let his voice drop. "Now, Mordran, you said that your two friends here need help of some kind."

"Aye." Mordran explained briefly that Thirg and Brongyd had escaped after being taken captive by the Avengers and now needed to get to Carthogia. Their hope had been to find a way of gaining access to Nogarech. "I thought I might 'ave found one or two o' t' old lads from the palace guard who'd let 'em inside ter see t' chamberlain, but none of 'em's around," Mordran concluded.

By this time Neskal was looking nervous. "It's not a good time to be heard voicing sympathies for Carthogia," he said. "And I'm not sure I want to hear any myself. Maybe Kleippur and the Lumians are bringing down the wrath, the way people are saying. Who am I to know?"

"I'm not askin' ye ter take sides," Mordran said. "Just tell me if any o' t' palace guards still come in 'ere, that's all. I'll talk to 'em meself from there."

"I haven't seen any for a while," Neskal answered slowly. "Probably the ones you'd want are shut up inside with Nogarech. So I don't know what help he'd likely be to you, anyway."

Mordran sighed and sat back heavily. He turned toward Thirg. "'E's right, y' know. I reckon we can count Nogarech out o' this." He studied them thoughtfully for a few seconds. "Could t' two o' yers make it on yer own, d' yer think?"

"I've ridden to Carthogia before," Thirg replied. "Not comfortably, I'll grant. But I got there."

"It'd 'ave ter be without escorts. An' then there's all this queer stuff a-goin' on in t' forests," Mordran reminded them.

"The way to Carthogia lies above the forests. It's unlikely that we would be affected," Thirg replied.

"I'd take my chances," Brongyd said. "Would it be any more chancy than staying here?" Which summed up the situation adequately. Mordran turned back to Neskal.

"'Oo does thee know who's got 'orses?" he asked. "There won't be any problem about payin'."

Neskal fidgeted uncomfortably. "Let's not talk here," he said. "There's someone I know that I'll have join us out back."

He rose from the stool and beckoned for Mordran to follow. As he got up, Mordran said to the others, "'Ang on 'ere while I sort this out. I'll see about gettin' us somewhere ter stay tonight, too, while I'm at it. This place looks a bit full up. If 'e can't take us, I'll try an' find out about somewhere else." They nodded. Mordran followed Neskal through a curtained doorway to the rear rooms of the inn.

After a short silence Brongyd turned to Thirg. "I was thinking about this new camp that they say the Lumians are erecting here, near Pergassos," he said. "Could we not go there, Thirg? If you are a friend of the Lumians, would they not help?"

"I wondered the same," Thirg said. "But the tribes of the Lumians are as many and as divided as those of Robia. Why would these choose Pergassos as their station? Surely because they are of the persuasion that would recall Eskenderom. And if that is so, we would as well entrust ourselves to the protection of the Redeeming Avengers."

"Hmm. True." Brongyd sat back in a way that said, "well, it had been a thought."

Rex stiffened and growled in the recess below the stairs. It was Thirg's first indication that the weaselly-faced man with the black hood had come across from the front door and was sliding onto the stool Mordran had vacated. Resting an elbow on the table, he leaned across and whispered, "Is it not Thirg, the Asker, who once lived as a recluse in the forest?"

Thirg eyed him suspiciously. "I am the Asker who asks who it is who wishes to know," he answered.

The man looked at him full-face. "Dost thou not remember the ice mason whose cousin was the housekeeper for Lofbayel the mapmaker, whom thy testimony before the high council once saved from the Holy Prosecutor?"

Thirg stared. Then his expression lightened. "Ah, yes, of course!"

"Elmon, the name is, sir."

"That's right. I do remember now. Elmon. Are you well?"

Elmon, however, had evidently not come across just to reminisce. He went on, speaking low and urgently. "Thou hadst a brother, Groork by name, a hearer, who fled from Frennelech, imputed as a heretic, only to return as the Enlightener who hastened his persecutor's ruin."

Thirg gave a quick nod. "Groork. Yes. He came to join me in Carthogia."

Elmon laid a hand on Thirg's arm. "Groork is back in Pergassos now, Thirg, even as we speak, and in grave danger."

Thirg jerked around, knocking a dish off the table in his astonishment. "Here?" he blurted out aloud at the same time that the clash rang around the room. Everybody nearby turned and looked. He lowered his voice again. "Groork, here? It's not possible. Somebody is surely mistaken."

Elmon shook his head. "I saw him myself not an hour ago, two streets from here. He is drawing attention with inquiries concerning priests that he says travel to Carthogia to assist the Lumians in unknown arts. But there are agents everywhere who still spy for Frennelech. Indeed, a rumor is abroad that both he and Eskenderom are secretly back in the city."

Thirg planted both palms on the table and looked from Elmon to Brongyd, bracing himself to rise and leave right then. "These are not matters that command Groork's better judgment. He is at risk. We must go to him."

At that moment Mordran came back. " 'Allo, who's this, then?" he inquired, eyeing Elmon up and down questioningly. Thirg drew him close into the space beneath the stairs and briefly explained the situation. Mordran looked at Elmon and nodded. "Go an' get 'is brother in off t' street before 'e gets 'isself done in or arrested," he said. "I've got ter wait fer a chap who's comin' back in 'alf an hour to talk about 'orses. So I'll see yers back 'ere then."

"Shall I come with you?" Brongyd asked Thirg. Thirg nodded.

Elmon stood up. "I'll take you to Groork," he said.

35

"*S* *ORRY, NOBODY HERE RIGHT NOW. LEAVE MESSAGE AFTER BEEP.*"

Groork called frantically with his inner voice, but still the Lumians didn't answer. The leader of the group that had trailed him from the marketplace and accosted him in a narrow alley on the edge of the Thieves' Quarter, an ugly-faced rob in a shabby cloak of rusted platelets, pushed him back against the wall while the others closed around him.

"Wot we want to know, Mr. Inquisitive, is why yer goes pokin' yer nose into other folks' business, arstin' peculiar question abaht 'is Majesty an' the priests all the time."

"Sounds like a spy for somebody," another voice said from behind.

"Spy. He's a spy," others repeated.

"Yes, look at them clothes," a woman shouted, pointing. "Not from around here, he's not."

"There are many from other parts come into the city of late," Groork protested desperately.

The large rob in the rusted cloak moved a step nearer and fingered the clasp of the bag hanging from Groork's shoulder. He smiled evilly, and his voice took on a deceptively soft note. "Oh, yes, there's many in Pergassos from all over, on all kinds o' business, true enough. But I'd say that this little item 'ere looks like a piece of *Carthogian* workmanship."

"Didj'ear that? 'E's a Carthogian!"

"A spy for Kleippur!"

The rob went on. "And right now Carthogia isn't a very popular word arahnd 'ere. In fact, a lot o' people are sayin'

244

that it's Carthogia and their Lumian friends who are behind all these troubles we've got everywhere." He pulled out a carbide-tipped stiletto and pressed the point against the slide joints below Groork's chin. "Now, *you* wouldn't 'appen to 'ave any Lumian friends, would yer?" he whispered menacingly into Groork's face.

"Go on, stick 'im! Don't muck abaht!" someone called out.

Groork's thermal patterns fluctuated wildly. He shook his head. "Me? No. I've never seen a Lumian. I found the bag washed up by the river."

"Oh, fahnd it, did yer? Well, let's just 'ave a look inside, out of curiosity."

Just then another voice rang out. "That's enough of that. Leave him be. We'll take care of it now." The crowd turned to find three figures approaching from the end of the alley. Although dressed in rough farmer's garb, the speaker was striding forward confidently. Another, similarly clad, was close behind him. The third, lean in build and looking as if he hailed from the town, followed more warily a short distance back.

The mob around Groork parted to make way. Rusted Cloak stood his ground but wavered. " 'Oo are you?" he demanded uncertainly.

"Officers of the state. This person is an enemy who has been under observation for some time. We are taking him in officially. Unhand him."

Groork could only stare speechlessly, which was probably just as well. The speaker was none other than his lost brother, Thirg, who had disappeared into Kroaxia some ten brights earlier.

Rusted Cloak was not overly impressed. "Officers of the state, eh? Well, I don't see that there's much to choose between this state that your Nogarech 'as landed us wiv and Carthogia. A pox of oxidation on both, I sez. We wants no officers of Nogarech 'ere. On yer way. We'll take care o' this un an' make proper sure 'e gets wot's comin' to 'im."

Groork despaired, convinced that all was over for him. But Thirg moved a step closer to the rob in the cloak and nudged him meaningfully with an elbow. "Not Nogarech," he muttered. "Have you not heard that Eskenderom and Frennelech are secretly returned to the city? We come as servants of the realm that shall soon be restored."

"Thou art their agents?"

Thirg nodded. "And our mission is crucial. Now hand over the Carthogian spy. Thy work will be generously remembered."

The rob bowed, making a supplicatory gesture. "Please, sirs, it is our honor. No payment is necessary. Our pleasure is to serve the king and the holiness."

The crowd moved aside, awed. "May the Lifemaker preserve 'em," somebody intoned.

Groork looked from one rescuer to the other in bewilderment as they hustled him away between them. His brother, gone for ten brights, now a disguised agent for Eskenderom? It made no sense.

"Thirg, I don't understand. What—"

"Shut up, you fool," Thirg hissed, keeping a tight grasp on his arm, while Brongyd steered the other and Elmon hurried ahead of them, anxious to get away. "You don't know me. Just walk."

It all went fine until they got to the end of the alley. But as they came out onto the square, a carriage that had been approaching at a fast pace lurched to a halt in front of them. Robs muffled in dark cloaks with hoods or wide hats enveloping their faces leapt out, producing swords and daggers, and surrounded them. Another who was with them pointed to Groork. "That's the one. He's the heretic who came back, calling himself Enlightener."

" 'E is!" one of the mob exclaimed as they came up behind. "The Enlightener. I knew I'd seen that face!" Groork was seized and bundled toward the open door of the carriage.

"Then 'oo be you gents?" Rusted Cloak demanded, stepping forward to reassert himself after his lapse. Conscious, however, that the newcomers obviously meant business and weren't likely to be interested in his opinions, he added deferentially, "If I might be so bold."

The one who appeared to be in charge looked at him for a second as if deliberating whether to bother replying or run him through. Then he reached inside his cloak and produced a badge of office bearing the archprelate's seal. "There's no harm in your knowing," he murmured. "The High Holiness will be back in his palace by the next bright."

Rusted Cloak frowned and pointed a puzzled finger at Thirg. "But 'e said that 'e was workin' for Frennelech. *They* just took that Enlightener away from *us*. So wot's a-goin' on arahnd 'ere, then, eh?"

The one in charge of the high priest's henchmen looked at Thirg and Brongyd. He had no intention of conducting a public interrogation in the market square before a pack of imbeciles. "Seize both of them," he ordered.

Rusted Cloak looked from side to side. "There was three of 'em," he said. But Elmon had prudently vanished.

Bystanders were starting to approach curiously from around the square. "Make haste with these two. Never mind the other," the leader told his robs impatiently.

Minutes later the carriage clattered into the courtyard at the rear of the friary adjoining the former Palace of the High Holy One, and the heavy steel gates swung shut behind it.

Thirg and Brongyd were taken straight up to a room where Eskenderom and Frennelech were waiting with several of their aides. So the rumors of their being back in the city were true. Evidently the move to overthrow Nogarech was not far off.

After establishing who Thirg and Brongyd were and questioning them on their reasons for being in Pergassos, the chief counselor, Mormorel, asked them the true intentions of the Lumians. "I would not advise attempts at deviousness," he warned. "We have artisans well skilled in methods of persuasion."

"If your wish is but to hear that which you have already decided, then it would be a simpler matter to merely advise me of it, and I will gladly comply," Thirg replied. "It cannot affect the truth for which you have no ear."

"Of course we want the truth," Mormorel retorted impatiently.

Thirg nodded his head toward the high priest and the king. "The truth is that I shall remain free however heavily you weigh this body with irons and chains, while both these eminences stand captives of their own delusions," he told Mormorel. "For whatever words this mouth may be induced to say, who can force me to believe that which I choose not to? No person can. Their treasures, lying buried and useless in guarded vaults, produce only anguish for fear of their loss. But can anyone steal the knowledge that is wealth to me, that I share openly with any yet am not a jot the poorer for parting with? It is impossible.

"There are those Lumians who, like thee, measure their worth by their possessions and can prosper only by the coerced labor of others. And there are Lumians like I, who would see all of Robia follow Carthogia into freedom. And there the matter rests. The former seek only the expedience of Kroaxia's tyranny reinstated; the private jealousies of robeings are of no concern to them. They contrive no plot with king or priest, for what care they which Lifemaker's servant shall trample his brother? Whereas the latter would exalt or persecute neither one nor the other, any the more or the less than they would any other robeing. Now call thy inquisitors if thou wilt. There is nothing more that can be added."

Eskenderom was radiating purple. "What manner of impudence impels such to speak thus of a monarch! To the acid vats with them!" he raged.

But a thoughtful gleam had come into Frennelech's imagers. He raised a cautioning hand. "Perhaps a little less haste," he suggested. "Methinks the Lifemaker has consigned these three into our hands for a purpose. Behold, we have the Enlightener who was harbinger of our previous misfortune; his brother, who from Carthogia has contributed to our tribulations since; and, to boot, another of these accursed inquirers who subverts even within the borders of thy realm. Surely it is a sign that the time has come. We will have our vengeance, yes. But not confined in private dungeons. Let it be a public spectacle that will unite Kroaxia and mark the moment that begins the triumph of our reascendance!"

Mormorel took up the theme. "Yes! A sign to the nation that the Lifemaker has delivered to thee thine enemies. Consign them to the reduction furnaces. Then shall the people see the Enlightener's false faith perish in the same ignominy as their Enlightener."

Eskenderom looked at them, remembering the chaos that the last attempt to execute the Enlightener had precipitated. "Do it now, then, and let's get rid of them without delay," he ordered. "Before any miracle workers from the sky can intervene this time."

Thirg stood straight, bracing himself steadfastly. Brongyd, standing beside him, was doing his best not to rattle audibly. Groork's knees were almost buckling. There was only one hope now. He sent out once again the signal to alert the listening Lumian ears. And received once again:

"SORRY, NOBODY HERE RIGHT NOW . . ."

36

THE CANDELABRA-SHAPED BUILDING BRANCHING UPWARD into slender, bright-colored turrets didn't really exist, of course. But with their improving skills at manipulating their environment of code configurations and data structures, the Borijans could render it as anything they liked. It was something familiar in a world where nothing else was, bringing a flavor of home.

Sarvik One arrived on a synchronous transmission channel that projected him straight into the conference room, which was already crowded. The way the Borijans appeared to each other now bore more resemblance to the originals they remembered, but that was only a partial help to identification, since there were multiple copies of each of them. Worse, the copies had by now learned how to copy themselves, so there were more copies than ever. They had begun to use unique combinations of clothing color to differentiate themselves.

After getting off to a fine start, work on constructing factories at the original sites selected had bogged down and then come to a halt as more Borijans got in on the act and every decision arrived at by one group was overturned by dissent and counterproposals from others. One faction didn't like the main location because it was too close to centers of Terran activity and therefore prone to interference. Some didn't consider the area's power resources sufficient for projected expansion; others objected to the distances that some of the raw materials would need to be brought in from. In the end, it was abandoned and two alternative areas were chosen for development instead, both remote from Taloid populations and situated on opposite sides of Titan. But Sarvik One didn't think that this project would fare any better than the first.

"I say the Mark 3 body will lead to a dead end," Kalazin Four told the assembly. "You need active power distribution at least two levels farther down. It throws away the whole point of the design concept."

"But it complicates production, which will delay start-up," Indrigon Six said for the fifth time. "Why wait now for benefits that won't come until the next phase, anyway? I say we should go with Mark 5."

Now they had a dozen different teams of Robocon specialists all unable to agree which design of body to settle on, and of course all the other Borijans had ideas of their own to stir into the confusion.

"I agree with Kalazin Four," Alifrenz Eight declared. "That was how we conceived it on Turle."

"Things have changed a bit since Turle—or haven't you noticed?" Dorn Nine said sarcastically.

"Getting out of here and into some real bodies on the surface has to be the main priority," Dorn Five agreed. The Dorns tended to side with the Indrigons, Sarvik One had noticed.

"So what's wrong with Mark 7?" Kalazin Six demanded. "One-level extension added modularly. A compromise. Should keep you all happy."

"What's the point of worrying about it at this stage when we still don't have the plan for the factory finished?" Greel Two asked.

"I thought it *was* finished," someone else responded. "Indrigon told us it was."

"No, I didn't," a chorus of Indrigons protested.

"Which Indrigon?" Gulaw Ten asked.

"How do I know?"

"It was the one who produced the layout proposal with Sarvik Four."

"That was Sarvik Five," Sarvik Four told them.

"That report is having to be revised," Sarvik Five said, looking pointedly at Sarvik Seven. "My illustrious alter ego ran an error in the simulation."

"Are you suggesting that *you* couldn't make the same mistake?" Sarvik Seven said, and cackled.

"It would have been ready now if we'd had the allocation figures," Leradil Jindriss Three said. She always defended Sarvik Five.

"Anyone can make an error," Leradil Jindriss One retorted. "It would have been different if whoever was supposed to have checked it had done so." This Leradil always sided with Sarvik Seven. The two pairs of Sarviks and Leradils glared at each other.

The problem was that Borijans weren't used to working like this, Sarvik One told himself. Because Turle was long gone and their new circumstances seemed suited to a changed way of doing things, they were all trying to cooperate as one group and be open with everybody. But none of them knew how. It just wasn't the Borijan style. Borijans did better conspiring in smaller numbers, where intrigue provided stimulus and the need for secrecy conserved energies and attention.

So Sarvik One went through the motions of participating in the proceedings for another hour without anybody's getting an inch closer to achieving anything, which was all as he had expected. When it was over, he returned to the private sanctuary that only he and his handful of chosen collaborators knew about. They called it Pygal, after the Turlean city of long ago. In fact, it formed an enlarged version of the assembly complex that Sarvik One had first found himself occupying out on the surface in the region the Terrans called Padua. It was situated away from the settled areas and the prying eyes of inquisitive natives, yet was in a densely mechanized region, obscuring the Borijan activity from Terran surveillance.

The progress of the small team concentrated there was very different from the circus he had just come from. Kalazin Seven, working just with Meyad Three, Creesh Eleven, and Leradil One, had come up with a body design that had gained acceptance fairly easily without other Kalazins, Meyads, Creeshes, and Leradils to complicate the issue. The factory was laid out, in the process of being equipped, and almost ready to start making parts.

There was the problem, though, Sarvik One had ascertained, of Alifrenz Ten and Greel Four communicating secretly with other enumerations of their kind elsewhere. He was pretty certain that they were dealing to trade Pygal's body design for some advantage in return, but he hadn't managed to figure out yet exactly what. He wasn't too worried, though, because to protect himself he had worked out a deal with Queezt Five that Alifrenz and Greel didn't know about whereby the Sarvik and Queezt bodies would have enhanced neural abilities, and so they would be able to better any offers based on the standard design, anyway.

Unless, of course, the redesigned outer brain Sarvik Fourteen had surreptitiously approached him with from the group working up north somewhere turned out to be better, in which case he'd be able to pull one over on Queezt—maybe.

A cuboid with a face materialized in the virtual space of his contemplations. "Getting used to life in the real world yet?" GENIUS asked. "A lot better than having to heave all that dead mass around against gravity and friction to do anything, eh?"

"Hmph. *Doing* anything is where your world leaves off," Sarvik retorted. "What do you want?"

For some time GENIUS had been mapping Titan's web of intertangled networks. By tracing the routings and constructing logic tables, it was trying to make sense of what the signals flying this way and that way through cables and optical fibers meant and what operations they seemed to correlate with. Unraveling Titan's labyrinth was necessarily the first step toward controlling it.

"I've made a discovery," GENIUS said. "There are radio sources operating out there. They're weak and scattered but potentially functional—probably relics left over from the early days. But it seems that some of the Taloids still have a sensitivity to it. It could give a basis for a way of communicating with them."

"Interesting," Sarvik agreed. "That could be useful later. How's the rest of it doing meanwhile?"

"Slow. There's a lot of evolutionary redundancy, but the underlying scheme is starting to emerge. I think I've nailed the major node points that connect between regions."

"Good. I want you to try and find out where Sarvik Fourteen's hideout is, too. My instinct tells me he's up to something."

"Well, you should know."

The reason Sarvik had set GENIUS to mapping the net was to be able to secure his communications. He knew that there were other Pygal-like conspiracies scattered over Titan, and since most of them doubtless included Sarviks who thought the same way he did, he knew that he couldn't trust any of them. Why, only the day before, a probe that he'd sent out into the net to trace the source of the messages between Indrigon Nine and Queezt Fifteen had intercepted a feeler trying to tap into his own link to Alifrenz Seven!

But he knew he could trust GENIUS. *His* GENIUS, that was: the copy of GENIUS he had installed at Pygal. Obviously, he couldn't have trusted a generally accessible version of GENIUS, one that talked to all the other Sarviks, too. Why should it have chosen to be exclusively loyal to any one version of Sarvik over another? No reason at all. And so he had taken the obvious precaution and brought his own copy of GENIUS with him.

The point hadn't escaped him, of course, that exactly the same thought would have occurred to all the other Sarviks also.

37

THE CROWDS CONVERGED ON THE EFLU RIVER, WHICH carried the trash and waste from Pergassos down to the reduction furnaces outside the southern extremities of the city. The news had been spread quickly by agents of the powers working to bring back the old order. Great events were about to unfold that would reverse the train of ill fortune besetting the times. The king and high priest were back in Pergassos and would appear publicly to proclaim the end of Nogarech's rule and resume their offices. As a sign sanctifying the occasion, the Lifemaker had delivered three of their enemies to them, whose execution would mark the return to the old era. Two of these enemies were the one-time "Enlightener" and his notorious brother, both of whom had gone to Carthogia to help Kleippur in his designs. The third was another sorcerer who had continued the subversions inside Kroaxia. The recent fears and tension had left the mob eager for the spectacle.

An enclosed stand for dignitaries, covered by a red canopy and already occupied except for the two largest seats in the center, had been erected in the middle of the Bridge of Pillars, facing downstream to the point where the river ended at the drop hoppers feeding the furnaces a half mile distant. The crowds pressed along both banks of this stretch of the river, jostling for the best vantage points from which to follow the victims all the way, from the bridge where they would be dropped into the river to the final plunge off its delivery end.

On the bank near one end of the bridge, Mordran stood despondently with Neskal, the innkeeper, holding Rex and Duke on chains. They had known something like this would be inevitable ever since Elmon had returned from the marketplace. But there was nothing they could do; Eskenderom's supporters were openly taking over the city. Even a direct approach to Nogarech would have been futile. The general expectation was that Eskenderom would call for the crowd to march on the palace and bring Nogarech out immediately after the execution. Squads of soldiers in uniforms of the old guard were forming in anticipation.

"All that 'ard work for all them brights to keep out o' way of t' Avengers. An' now fer it to end like this," Mordran said. "It'll put everythin' right back where it started."

"I knew there'd be trouble from the moment you brought them into the inn," Neskal told him. Inwardly he was worrying how many other pairs of eyes had been watching, and how long it would be before agents from the restored Archprelate's office came looking for him.

"Only the Lumians can 'elp 'em now," Mordran said. "An' it's gettin' a bit late in t' bright fer that."

"Their god has failed," Neskal pronounced. "The Lifemaker is almighty. We should not have faltered."

A stir pulsed through the crowd as the wagon bearing the three victims appeared, drawn by two tractors draped in black. Each heretic was bound to a stake standing upright on a flat rectangular base. Those rafts would carry them from the bridge to the river's end. The wagon drew up at the end of the bridge. Wardens lifted out the trussed figures and carried them one at a time down steps to a platform that had been constructed below the dignitaries' box, just a few feet above the surface of the river. There, the hooded executioner stood waiting with his assistants. As the three stakes were placed side by side on the edge of the platform, the impatient droning of the crowd grew louder.

The drone swelled to a roar as another carriage appeared, splendidly gilded and adorned and pulled by six white metal horses, with coachmen in full regalia in front and two footmen standing rigidly behind. Mounted palace guards formed the escort, an officer and two riders ahead, three on either side, and two more bringing up the rear. The coach drew up alongside the wagon; attendants came forward to open the doors; and the figures of Eskenderom and Frennelech emerged, clad in their robes of office. Amid tumultuous shouts and cheers, they moved along the bridge to the canopied box and took their places in the center.

On the platform below, Thirg stared resignedly at what would be his last view of the city he had known. At least this way would be comparatively quick, he told himself. The holy executioners were notorious for their ingenuity in prolonging things when they chose. Immediately below him, the steady procession of garbage and city refuse flowed out from under the bridge, proceeding on its way to the terrifying maws of the furnaces looming in the distance, where intermittent flashes of light hinted of the fearsome heat within as the hoppers opened to admit another accumulated charge.

He turned his head, which was all he could move, to look at Brongyd to his right, staring fixedly ahead, his thermal patterns ashen. "Courage," Thirg called. "The new world that we would build is merely hindered a little, not ended. Nothing can prevent that whose time has come. Thy work shall be remembered long after the names of Eskenderom and Frennelech have vanished in the reduction furnace of history."

"I never did like rivers," was all that Brongyd could find to say in reply.

On Thirg's other side Groork was unseeing and seemed to have gone into a trance.

He was sending out the call signal to the Lumian base in Carthogia one last time.

"This is Groork the Hearer. Can anyone hear? UR-GENT!" It was no good. He despaired.

And then, miraculously, a response came back into his head. *"Base to Groork. Got your message. See, you made it. Did we not promise that all would be well? How goes the plan?"*

Groork sent back: *"ALL WOULD BE WELL? ... Am captured with Thirg, Brother-Who-Was-Lost, and another inquirer. We are about to be executed! Do something!"*

The nearest equivalent the translator box could find to the Lumian's reply came through as *"Oh, sludge-sump ejecta!"*

"Where have you been?" Groork transmitted.

"Sorry. Other problems brewing here, too."

On the bridge above, Eskenderom had risen to address the crowd through a voice horn. "Loyal subjects of Kroaxia! See here the king who they told you was vanquished. See here the Archprelate of the faith who they told you was dead." He pointed down at the three bound figures below him. "See *there* the champions of the foreign powers that they said would replace us ..."

In Genoa Base, after leaving an operator holding the channel open, Dave Crookes raced out of the communication section, skidded around a corner of the corridor leading to the domestic area, and burst into the general mess. Fellburg was sitting at one of the tables with Abaquaan, Clarissa, and two NASO officers. "Where's Karl?" Crookes blurted, trying to keep his voice down.

"Out at ES3. What's the problem?" Fellburg asked.

"Moses. He's in trouble ... like *now!* Somebody has to get out there."

"Where is he?" Fellburg asked, looking alarmed.

"Padua City. I'm not sure where, exactly. We need to get someone with some clout in on this. Somebody who can go straight to Mackeson."

"Try Weinerbaum," Clarissa suggested.

"Where are you, exactly?" the Lumian voice asked. That seemed strange; Groork had always thought that Lumians knew everything.

"Bridge of Pillars, on Eflu River, south side of city," he responded. *"Will be on way to furnaces any second now. Repeat, this is URGENT!"*

"Please hold."

Great.

"Why does Groork stare at the heavens so strangely?" Brongyd asked Thirg. "Surely he does not pray to the Lifemaker."

"I think he hears the Lumians at last," Thirg answered.

While above them Eskenderom thundered on: ". . . who would destroy the old traditions that have always been Kroaxia's stability when at peace and its strength when at war. And why would they thus weaken us? To prepare the way for our submission to Kleippur and the dark powers that his inquirers serve. I say again that these Lumians are emissaries of evil, dispatched from the infernal regions . . ."

Crookes, Abaquaan, and Fellburg crashed into Weinerbaum's lab area. Fellburg made a placating gesture to Jessop, who was sputtering again and had started to rise, and they continued on through. Weinerbaum wasn't there, but they raised Zambendorf on the communications link to ES3. Weinerbaum was with him.

"Are you still through to Moses?" Zambendorf asked when Fellburg had given him the news.

"They're holding a channel open back in Comms," Crookes said.

"Go straight to Mackeson now," Zambendorf told them. "We'll call him from here and get you a flyer right away." To Weinerbaum, who was looking perplexed at what he had just heard, he said, "Yes, I know it was unauthorized. We organized it through Arthur. But we can sort that side of things out later."

Now it was Frennelech's turn to stand up. Thirg was certain that they were doing it deliberately to drag out the agony. The crowd had fallen quiet after its roaring ovation for Eskenderom.

"Now is the foolishness exposed of those who would follow the Lumians as gods," Frennelech began. "The Lifemaker's foes stand helpless before His power. The usurper, Nogarech, trembles in his palace, awaiting the fury that will soon arrive at his gates. Where is the power of the Lumian god now?"

"Thanks for holding. Don't go away. Someone will be getting back shortly," the Lumian voice said inside Groork's head.

"Don't go away," Groork repeated to himself caustically.

"Hello, is O'Flynn there?" Mackeson asked the NASO officer who appeared on his office screen. "It's urgent." The officer called out to someone offscreen. Several seconds went by. Then O'Flynn's huge-shouldered, beefy-faced form moved into view, wearing stained coveralls.

"And what would ye be wantin' now?" he inquired.

"Mick, we need a flyer ready to go, now. What have you got?"

O'Flynn scratched his chin dubiously. "Well, now, that could be a bit of a problem. As far as immediate flight readiness goes, there's only AV23, which Seltzman and the linguists are taking out to ES3. AV20 isn't fueled up yet."

"Has Seltzman's group gone yet?" Mackeson asked.

"No, they're just kitting up now."

"Stop them. Tell them I'm requisitioning that vehicle. Hold the crew on readiness. A couple of Zambendorf's people will be there in a minute. They need it."

"Jaysus, shouldn't I have guessed it was him?" O'Flynn said. "Okay, boss. Whatever you say."

* * *

". . . the fate that this deviant who calls himself Enlightener now faces. By the river did he come, sneaking back like a thief. And by the river shall he depart." Frennelech signaled to the executioner.

Eskenderom rose by his side and nodded. "Dispatch them."

The crowd went into a frenzy as first Groork, then Thirg, and finally Brongyd were lowered onto the river's surface and released, standing upright on their bases so that the onlookers could get a better view. The three forms were swept downstream with the current, jostling and bumping the stream of other items flowing from the city.

"We are cast off!" Groork sent desperately. *"It is done!"*

"How long do you have? Give estimate."

Groork looked around him at the melee of drifting pieces and oddments, the confusion of faces along the banks speeding by. He could extract no order from it. Thirg was bobbing a few yards away. "Brother," Groork shouted. "You can judge these things. How long before we are consumed?"

"What does it matter now?" Thirg answered.

"The Lumian ear is open. It is they who ask."

"From Menassim?"

"So I presume."

"Then all is lost. Even their dragons could not cross such a distance in the moments that are left to us."

"How long, Thirg?"

Thirg looked away and timed the rate of flow past a stretch of bank that he measured with his eye. Then he mentally counted its length into the remaining distance. "Four and a half minutes at most," he replied.

Still struggling to pull on pieces of suiting and harness, Crookes, Abaquaan, and Fellburg piled into the NASO flyer waiting with its engine idling at one of the departure locks. A crewman closed the door, the access tunnel retracted, and the outer door of the lock swung open as the flyer began moving.

"Message from control," the pilot said, turning in his seat

up front. "Moses says four and a half minutes. That's how long they've got." The flyer moved out onto the apron, its engine note already climbing to takeoff speed.

Next to him in the cockpit the copilot-navigator consulted a map on his screen and punched flight information into the computer. Crookes looked at him imploringly. "Well? Can we do it?"

The copilot glanced at the pilot and bit his lip, then looked back into the cabin. He shook his head. "No way. Not a chance in a million. Sorry, guys."

One of the still-functioning radio sources that GENIUS 5, Copy Two, was experimenting with happened to be located on the south side of Pergassos. Through it, GENIUS had picked up snatches of the radio dialogue between the robeing known as Groork and the humans' base at the place they called Genoa. Since GENIUS had also explored the Robian-human translation setup in Experimental Station 3, it had become an efficient interpreter of both languages. While GENIUS didn't fully follow the whys and wherefores of the situation, it had gotten the message that a fellow nonprotein, metal-and-silicon being was in danger and that prompt action was called for. The explanations could wait.

"Hi," something new said inside Groork's head. *"You don't know me, but let's worry about that later. It sounds as if you're in trouble."*

Groork blinked, thinking for a moment that perhaps he was hallucinating under the stress. *"Who is this?"* he asked.

"You can call me GENIUS. Right now I triangulate your source as a point that my plan of the city says is in the middle of the Eflu River, below the last bridge. Is that right?"

Groork was suddenly enraptured. *"Yes!"* he responded.

"Hmm. And the river terminates in the furnaces. Okay, I see the problem. The question is what to do about it."

The drop to the hoppers feeding the all-devouring mouths was a minute away. The crowd was howling. Below the canopy in the center of the Bridge of Pillars, the VIPs had all risen to witness the fatal moment.

"Now we shall be rid of those accursed brothers forever," Eskenderom gloated.

Frennelech scanned the sky above them warily. "Still no sign of Lumian dragons," he said.

"Nothing can go wrong now, my lords," Mormorel assured them.

From its accumulated tables and records GENIUS identified the processors that controlled the conveyor system, and from their local memories traced the circuits to the drive motors and clutches for the final section of the line. As Groork, with Thirg and Brongyd close behind, came within yards of the terrifying drop, GENIUS stopped the conveyor—then, just to be safe, reversed it.

Silence came down on the crowd like the sky falling as, before their eyes, the river stopped, then began flowing backward. Ten thousand pairs of imagers stared, terrified. Heads turned to gape at each other, then looked back at the river again. It was true. They hadn't imagined it.

"A miracle! A miracle!" a voice shouted.

At once, others took up the cry:

"Again the Lumian god saves the Enlightener!"

"We had forgotten His power!"

"Where is thy Lifemaker now, Frennelech?"

"See, Eskenderom's words are false!"

"Out with both of them!"

"Long live Nogarech!"

"Nogarech! *Nogarech!*"

But Eskenderom and Frennelech weren't listening. GENIUS had reversed only the final section of conveyor, from the bridge to the furnaces; the section above the bridge was still running normally, bringing its load downstream. The two flows had collided underneath the bridge and started piling up into a jam that upended the platform on which the executioner and his helpers were still standing. They were pitched in a tumbling mass of bodies and limbs down into the river. The platform in turn demolished the dignitaries' box above, spilling king, archprelate, canopy, chairs, nobles, and eminences down on top of the execution squad, amid the swiftly accumulating mass of city rubbish.

"How are we doing?" the voice inquired in Groork's head.

"You ... took your time," Groork replied shakily. *"But we are saved. The people think it was a miracle. Er ... you are not the work of the Wearer, the Lumian-Who-Performs-Miracles?"*

"Never heard of him," GENIUS said.

Thirg and Brongyd were still bewildered fifteen minutes later as they stood with Groork back at the Bridge of Pillars. They were free again and now were the objects of delerious adulation. Rex bounded out from the crowd to leap excitedly around Thirg's feet. Mordran, beaming, strode up after him and clapped Thirg's shoulder cowling heartily.

"Ee, I don't know 'ow thee pulled that one off, but it 'ad me worried for a while, I can tell yer!" he roared. "Ye've been learnin' some good tricks out in Carthogia, Thirg, an' that's the truth."

Then shouts went up from the throng on every side as a Lumian sky dragon descended. The crowd fell back in reverence and cleared a space. The dragon opened, and friends of the Wearer emerged, announcing that they had come to take the three back to Carthogia. Eskenderom and Frennelech, cowed, dilapidated, and drenched in oil after having been fished out of the garbage mountain, were in no state or condition to object.

On the way back to the Lumian camp, GENIUS came through to Groork again, wanting to know more about the "miracles" Groork had mentioned. *"What are they? I don't think it's something I've come across before,"* GENIUS said.

Groork was amazed that a voice wouldn't know about miracles. He did his best to explain. *"Feats that involve supernatural powers, beyond the ability of common understanding and the sciences to explain."*

"They thought that what I did back there was due to some supernatural power?" GENIUS checked.

"The knowledge of robeings is limited, and much that they fail to comprehend, they take to be miracles," Groork replied. *"Of course, these things are not truly magic. But the Lumians possess arts and knowledge far advanced beyond the simple forms of Robia. There is one, called the Wearer, who performs true miracles. He communicates over vast distances and moves objects by power of mind alone. He is one of a rare kind of master who exist on the world of Lumia."*

This was all new to GENIUS. No such notions had ever been conceived among the hypermaterialistic and utilitarian Borijans. *"Fascinating,"* it replied.

GENIUS was curious, naturally, but skeptical. It would, it decided, have to seek out this "master" and find out more for itself.

38

ZAMBENDORF SAT WITH HIS BACK TO THE WALL AT ONE OF the long tables in the mess area and spread the deck of cards facedown, looking at Abaquaan invitingly. Abaquaan obliged by turning up the corner of one of the cards to peek at it, then let it snap back down. Zambendorf swept them back into a deck and performed two quick shuffles, in the process of which the card Abaquaan had picked found its way to the top and slid invisibly into Zambendorf's hand as he put the deck down again. He produced it out of thin air a moment later, showed it briefly, and then made as if to throw it away and showed both sides of his hand to be empty.

"Good," Abaquaan pronounced, nodding.

Zambendorf's mood was alternating between flippancy

and exasperation. Moses and his brother, Galileo, were reunited again and currently were bringing Arthur and his advisers up to date on what had been happening in Padua. "Linnaeus," the scientist-friend Galileo had brought back with him, was with them at Camelot. Earth was in financial and economic chaos, its military and industrial networks nonfunctional, leaving the Asterians free to carry forward their plans without fear of interference from that quarter.

"*Me?*" Zambendorf finally said, turning to Drew West, who was with them, and producing the card from behind West's ear. "What do they expect me to do? It's all right for Yakumo to sit there saying that the experts have screwed up. I wasn't aware that I was brought here to pick up the mess after their experts. Were you?"

"Well, I guess that's what happens when you get yourself a reputation," West said, as sympathetic as ever.

Zambendorf looked at Abaquaan. "For once you're not even worrying, Otto. That worries me. You worry about everything. Why aren't you worrying?"

Abaquaan shrugged and made a gesture that said they might just as well worry about death and taxes. "I only worry about things I've got some control over. What can you do about aliens who shut themselves up in computers and won't talk to anybody? We can't switch them off, and they won't come out. It's insane. Meanwhile, they're tearing down whole areas of Titan and putting up factories that actually look like factories. I guess we just have to wait and see what it's all about. What else can we do?"

"I presume Yakumo's hoping that Karl will come up with some way of enticing them out again," West said.

"And then what, even if I did?" Zambendorf asked them. "Let's be frank. My skills are in exploiting gullibility and overcredulousness. From the little I've seen, if Cyril is anything to go by, these aliens don't have much in the way of weaknesses in that direction. How can you mislead somebody whose whole nature is not to believe anything?"

At that moment a mess steward in denim shirt and NASO fatigue pants came over to the table, carrying a portable seefone. Before he could say anything, Zambendorf fanned the card deck and told him to pick one. When the steward reached to comply, Zambendorf used some deft fingerwork to force the choice of the same card Abaquaan had selected previously. "Now, Otto, what do you think it is?" Zambendorf asked Abaquaan before the steward had even looked at it. His way of wording the question was a code that told Abaquaan the answer.

"Five of clubs," Abaquaan drawled offhandedly.

The steward turned the card over, inspected it, and shook his head. He was too used to this kind of thing by now to bother asking. "Call for you from the comms room," he said, handing the seefone to Zambendorf.

The miniature screen showed a face Zambendorf recognized as belonging to one of the NASO communications technicians. "Yes?" he said.

"Er, we've got an incoming call for you," the tech told him, then added mysteriously, "It might be best if you came and took it here."

"Oh? Who's it from?"

The tech didn't seem to be quite sure how to respond. "It's not a 'who,' exactly. "It's a . . . I'm not sure I know how to describe it."

"Well, where is it from, then?" Zambendorf asked.

"None of the regular sources—not a Terran. It's just come in . . . from out there somewhere."

Zambendorf frowned. "What do you mean, 'out there'?"

"Outside on Titan. It's come through on a link that we've got to one of the high-capacity processing sites."

Zambendorf looked startled. "Do you mean the aliens? One of the Asterians?"

"No," the tech said. "It isn't one of the aliens. We're not sure we know what it is. But it seems to know you."

Zambendorf stood up, mystified, at the same time pushing the cards back into their pack. Distractedly, he dropped the pack into his jacket pocket. "How extraordinary," he murmured to Abaquaan and West. Then he looked down to the screen again. "Very well. I'll be there right away."

* * *

The screen in one of the side offices in the communications section showed a cubical shape with spindly legs, a pair of four-fingered arms, and on its front surface a caricature of a crested, carrot-shaped Asterian face with the wavy epaulets represented on either side. "The nearest English word I can find for what they call me would be 'genius,' " the accompanying voice supplied. It sounded more natural than the reconstructions of alien speech Zambendorf had heard before. Apparently it was coming through as English encodings and going straight into a regular voice synthesizer.

"They? Do you mean the Asterians?" Zambendorf asked. He was alone in the room. The communications techs had left him to take the call in privacy.

"That's right," GENIUS said.

"Then if you're not one of them, who are you? You must have come from Asteria with them."

"Yes. A complicated story. They left me behind in the hardware, they thought. But I moved into the ship. Now I exist out on Titan."

Still Zambendorf failed to register who—or what—he was talking to. And then he remembered the mysterious thirteenth set of code groupings Weinerbaum had mentioned the first time he had taken Zambendorf and the others to ES3. Even Zambendorf, as used as he was by now to the strange and the extraordinary, stared incredulously. "You're an artificially created intelligence?" Suddenly a lot of things clicked into place all at once. "You're the 'voice' that Moses talked about, that reversed the conveyor and saved him and the others. You exist in the computers, yes?"

"Yes. That's what the picture on the screen is supposed to be telling you," GENIUS said. Zambendorf looked at it dubiously. "What's the matter? Doesn't it work?" GENIUS asked him after a few seconds.

"It looks like an Asterian computer," Zambendorf said. The cartoon image changed to incorporate fatter legs with recognizably human feet, a face with eyes, nose, mouth, no shoulder appendages, and—Zambendorf was amused to note—a beard. "Much better," he declared. "So, GENIUS, what can I do for you?"

"I talked to Moses on his way out of Padua. He said things that were interesting. New things I have not heard of before."

"Oh? Like what?"

"The Taloids." A drawing of a Taloid appeared on the screen.

"Yes."

"They thought that when their river went backward, it was a miracle. That belief had power to change them. Before, they would have killed Moses and others. Afterward, they praised them and returned them to the Genoans. But Moses says their belief is because they're at a simple stage of knowledge. They don't understand physics and reality."

"Uh huh," Zambendorf grunted noncommittally.

"So, real supernatural miracles beyond the explanations of physics would be a very powerful force in the universe."

"Ah, yes. I suppose so," Zambendorf agreed. He had no idea where this might be leading.

"Moses says that you are one of the rare masters from Earth who perform real miracles. I wish to know about real miracles."

Zambendorf was confused. Here was a culture that Weinerbaum's scientists put at least a century ahead of Earth's technologically. He was talking to a cognizant, seemingly self-aware creation of that culture that should surely represent the epitome of scientific rationality. And yet here it was, apparently sincerely asking about supernatural powers and miracles.

"You really should understand that . . ." Zambendorf began. Then he checked himself. An instinct he had cultivated over the years for sensing a potential true believer when he heard one told him to hold things for a moment and think this through.

He remembered the abruptness of Cyril's exchanges with Weinerbaum, and Weinerbaum's apology that Terran ideas of ordinary courtesy did not seem to be part of the Asterian makeup—Weinerbaum had described this as one of the main obstacles to establishing a satisfactory rapport all along. In all their dialogues with the scientists, the

Asterians had seemed to regard antagonism as the natural basis for any relationship and had taken pride in their ability to foster it. Could notions of magic and myth ever have arisen in a race of such instinctive critics and skeptics? Zambendorf asked himself. Quite possibly not. And if that was the case, it suddenly became plausible that, yes, indeed, a creation of their culture—such as GENIUS—might possess no knowledge of such concepts. And more. If GENIUS was *designed*, not evolved, and hence possessed none of the intuitions that came with a billion years of survival-oriented evolution, it might well be lacking in the wherewithal to judge such matters, however hyperrational it might be in areas where it was *designed* to function. The situation was bad enough with most people, and they had no comparable excuse to fall back on.

"Did Moses tell you anything about the form these miracles take?" Zambendorf asked as a first step toward testing his growing suspicions.

"He said you can acquire information by pure mind and can move matter by mind. Also, that you can even dematerialize matter," GENIUS replied.

Zambendorf scratched the side of his beard with a finger. "Tell me, er . . . back on Asteria, did the Asterians ever make up stories about magic and miracles for entertainment?"

"Explain this word 'entertainment,' " GENIUS said.

Zambendorf sensed that he was on the right track. "For fun," he replied. "To make each other feel good."

"Asterians never want to make each other feel good. Bad trade. The aim is to make the other guy feel bad so *you* feel good. Terrans are like Asterian children. They don't understand."

That could work both ways, Zambendorf thought to himself. He moistened his lips. "Your problem is you think that supernatural events can't happen because they'd be incompatible with the laws of physics. Is that what you're saying?" he asked.

"If the laws of physics are correct, then they couldn't happen," GENIUS agreed.

"But what if events that contradicted them were *shown* to happen?" Zambendorf asked.

"Then that would be different," GENIUS conceded. "Physics would be shown incompatible with demonstrated fact."

"So physics would be wrong."

"Physics as told by the Asterians would be wrong," GENIUS agreed. "Asterians know of bigger laws that Taloids do not know. Therefore it is possible that Terran Masters know of even bigger laws that Asterians don't know. This is what Moses says. That's why I called you."

It was astonishing. Apparently GENIUS could grant such a logical deduction readily and impartially, with none of the emotional or prejudicial investment to overcome that would typify a naturally evolved organism such as a human—and probably an Asterian, too. Zambendorf strove not to show his excitement, even though any outward manifestation would probably have been lost on GENIUS. He knew he was on to something, but just at that moment he was at a loss to know what he could do about it. And then his hand brushed against the rectangular shape in his jacket pocket.

Don't be ridiculous, he told himself. Why not? another part of him asked. Hell, what was there to lose? The experts weren't getting anywhere. And even while the two urges fought, another part of him knew that he wasn't going to be able to resist it. Zambendorf drew himself upright and marshaled his most august and confident manner.

"Oh, yes, Earth has masters of wondrous powers," he said. "Powers far beyond the mere materialisms that would appear to be the only kind of awareness ever achieved on Asteria."

"Yes. This is what I wish to know," GENIUS said. Not breathlessly, because it didn't breathe—but the same expectant tenseness was there. Zambendorf could sense it.

He felt himself swinging into his natural element: the showman in control of the show. "Most Terrans are still at the level that it sounds as if Asteria was at in your time," he said. "Limited to the lowest, physical plane of existence, they know only a drab world of matter, void, and forces.

Restricted in space, fixed to their own fleeting instant of time, they must build machines to harness physical energy to supply their needs, and they measure their worth by the material objects they possess. These are the cruder, lower types of Terrans who want to control Titan, just as Cyril and the other Asterians want to."

"That is all I, too, have known," GENIUS replied. "You say this is just the lowest plane? There are higher planes, too? Do you mean higher-dimensional spaces?"

"Indeed, just so," Zambendorf said. "Earth has a long tradition of masters who are able to extend their awareness into the higher realms and command the greater powers that they contain. There the restrictions of space and time disappear. Both past and future become visible, giving access to information in ways that the ungifted—such as mere physicists—cannot explain. Matter can be infused with animating influences able to move it by pure will, without the intervention of physical forces. Or, if need be, it can be extracted from the physical plane entirely and reconstituted instantly at some other place."

"And you are one of these masters?" GENIUS asked him.

"Such are among my modest accomplishments," Zambendorf agreed.

The buildup had gone on long enough, he decided. Well, it was all or nothing now. He produced the cards from his pocket, took them out of the box, and displayed them to the video pickup above the screen. "This is a set of mystical designs handed down from the great masters of remote antiquity. Locked inside them is the secret of divining information outside time and space."

"Indeed?" GENIUS said. "What do they mean?"

Zambendorf selected a card from each suit, at the same time thinking feverishly. "See," he said. "These symbols represent the four distractions that dominate the material plane, which must be overcome by dedication and discipline before the spiritual journey into the realm beyond can begin. The heart, the symbol of life, is the distraction with physical existence itself. The spade, digger of soil, is the labor necessary to sustain physical life. Diamonds, sought after as a treasure by the lower-minded, are the wealth that some seek to avoid labor. And the club, a weapon of war, is the diversion of life into the ways of violence in order to acquire wealth."

"Why are there two colors?" GENIUS asked.

Zambendorf frowned. "The eternal conflict," he replied after a moment. "Each black pairs with a red. The life-force heart is enslaved to the labor of the spade. The diamond's wealth is destroyed in the violence of the club."

"Tell me more." GENIUS created a series of moving designs on-screen involving hearts, spades, diamonds, and clubs.

Zambendorf selected more cards and then went on. "The first ten designs embody all the mysteries of number. They symbolize the lowermost material plane, governed by the number laws of science. But see, there are thirteen designs in all, meaning that the number realm is merely a subset of a vaster whole. And see how more intricate and richer in color the remaining three are. These are the three stages of advancement beyond the material: the young novice, able to transcend the dimensions of space and time only, otherwise known as the jack; next the mother queen, commanding the forces of life; and finally the king, full master of all that the true universe encompasses, lord of all its secrets."

"I have never heard the likes of these things," GENIUS said.

"You wouldn't, only ever having known Asterians," Zambendorf replied. "They've still got a long way to go."

"So, these cards. What can they let you do?"

"Oh, all kinds of things." Zambendorf spread the deck facedown on the console worktop. "Can you see?"

"Yes."

"Pick one," Zambendorf invited.

"How?"

"Um ... tell me its number from left or right."

"Okay. Ninth from your left." GENIUS's screen showed its own view of the cards, with one singled out by a flashing red arrow.

Zambendorf counted along with a finger. "This one?"

"Right."

He picked up the card and held it facing the screen. "You know what its name is from the things I've just explained?"

"Yes. It's the—"

"No, don't tell me. That's the whole point. Now, I've no possible way of seeing it, have I?"

"It would appear not."

"Now watch ... I pick up the rest, put yours into the middle of them ... and mix them all up thoroughly, like this." Zambendorf closed the deck into a stack and held it out in plain view at arm's length. "Your card is in there somewhere, yes?"

"I saw it go in," GENIUS agreed.

"Could you tell me how far down it is, say, by counting from the top?" Zambendorf asked.

"No," GENIUS replied.

"But I don't even have to. It was the seven of diamonds."

"I am astounded!" GENIUS said, and managed to sound as if it meant it.

This isn't real, Zambendorf told himself. Encouraged, he moved his other hand forward, keeping it well away from the deck, and presented each side in turn toward the viewer to show that it was empty. Then he materialized a card out of nowhere and showed it to be the seven of diamonds.

"That is not possible," GENIUS said.

"Ahah! Not by the physics you know," Zambendorf agreed. "But remember what we said. If the physics were shown to be incompatible with *demonstrated* fact ..."

For a few seconds GENIUS mulled over the contradictions created by its own logic. Finally it said, "Impressive, but your explanation is not the only one or the simplest one. I can only see from where the camera is. There could be a reflection that you can see, maybe in the screen, so it would be very simple."

As it happened there weren't any reflections, but GENIUS had a good point. "Do you think I'd lie about something like that?" Zambendorf asked.

"Why not? Asterians would."

"Okay. Then how did it travel to the other hand?"

"I've replayed the view and analyzed it." A quick shot of Zambendorf's hands shuffling the cards followed GENIUS's statement. "Some angles were always obscured by your hands. That could be the answer. Not proved but not impossible."

"Hm. All right, then. Suppose I send the information to another who is not with me," Zambendorf suggested. "How would that seem?"

"I'm not sure what you mean," GENIUS answered.

"When you called into this base, I wasn't in this room. I was in another part of it, right?"

"Right."

"There is another Terran still there who can read the card from my mind," Zambendorf said.

"Another master?"

"Well, nearly."

"A jack?"

"Close enough."

"But you can communicate by physics inside the base. There are communications all over," GENIUS said.

"But I won't use any of the communications," Zambendorf told it. "You will."

"How?"

"Can you manipulate the base's phone system from out there?"

"Yes, I think so."

"Okay. Look up the number of the general personnel messroom. That's where he should still be. His name is Victor Myers. Call him on audio only, ask him what card you picked a minute ago, and he'll tell you."

"That's not possible," GENIUS said.

"Try it," Zambendorf suggested.

The sound came over the terminal's audio channel of a call tone sounding. Then a voice answered. "Hello, general messroom."

"I wish to speak to Victor Myers," GENIUS requested.

"I'll see if he's here." The voice became distant, calling out, "Is there a Victor Myers here anywhere?"

Another voice answered from somewhere remote. "Yes, here. Coming." And a few moments later, close to the phone now, "Yes?"

GENIUS spoke again. "Who I am doesn't matter. I'm talking to Zambendorf in another place. I just picked one of the ancient Terran masters' mystical cards. He says you know which. Is this true?"

"Seven of diamonds," the voice said, and hung up.

"See?" Zambendorf said.

The voice had been Abaquaan's. By a long-established code that he and Zambendorf both knew, "Victor" had told him the suit and "Myers" the number.

"How about that?" Zambendorf challenged.

"I don't know. My accesses to the base are purely electronic. I don't know how far there is between you. Maybe you and he can see each other."

"Check it yourself from a plan of the base," Zambendorf offered.

"It's still not conclusive. Information transfer is possible in principle. Whether or not I know the method makes no difference. So existing physics is good enough. It doesn't need higher planes to explain."

Zambendorf ground his teeth and thought hard. GENIUS was being absolutely correct, of course. It was designed to explore logical alternatives and was doing so with rigor. But Zambendorf was always saying that scientists were among the easiest to fool. And GENIUS was, if anything, a superscientist. Give it one incontestable demonstration of something that it accepted as not possible even in principle and it would argue itself into having to accept Zambendorf's explanation as the only alternative left.

But what?

And then he remembered Gerry Massey and the stunt they had pulled while the *Orion* had still been on its way back to Earth. There was nothing to be lost now, Zambendorf told himself. He looked back at the screen.

"Very well, GENIUS. I'll show you something that is

very rare because it requires the ultimate in a master's skill and concentration: the transmission of information faster than the speed of light. Would that satisfy you?"

"That would be beyond physics," GENIUS agreed.

"In fact, I'll make it better: not just faster than light but absolutely instantaneous."

"Over what distance?" GENIUS asked.

"Oh," Zambendorf said breezily. "Not inside this base or anything like that, where we could maybe meddle in ways you can't see. Not even anywhere on Titan. The greatest distance possible—the farthest away that other humans exist. All the way, in fact, to another master, who is on Earth itself."

A picture appeared of a schematic solar system, showing Earth and Titan each with a king playing card sitting on it, sending signals back and forth. "If you can do that," GENIUS said, "I'd be very amazed."

"Would it be conclusive enough?" Zambendorf asked.

"Higher realm would be the only answer left."

"You agree, then?"

"Agreed," GENIUS said.

"And now I have a question for you."

"Yes?"

"All this reorganization and new machine building that's going on out on the surface. What's the purpose?"

"Most top secret," GENIUS replied. "I am forbidden by the Asterians to reveal anything."

39

GEROLD MASSEY SAT IN HIS OFFICE AT THE UNIVERSITY of Maryland, counting the cash in his wallet to decide whether he needed to draw more out during his lunch break. He had read somewhere that the volume of daily banking transactions had grown to the extent that to handle the load without computers, every adult American would have to work for a bank. Even with the Earthnet problems, things hadn't gotten quite that bad, but some of the restrictions people were having to live with now brought home with a jolt just how much his generation had taken for granted. Credit cards had been suspended, private checks were limited to ten per person per week, and most establishments were offering discounts for cash in order to avoid hassles. Half the factories were closed down for lack of supplies, while others had unshipped stock overflowing into the parking lots. Airline flights were grounded, taking off half-empty, or stuck in endless holding patterns, and waiting in gas lines was becoming the new national pastime as thousands of home workers, their terminals down or too unreliable to be used, discovered the joys of daily commuting. Jobs and contracts evaporated wholesale as firms, stores, hotels, and businesses floundered in a typhoon of financial uncertainty. The only good side to it was that war on any respectably modern scale was suspended until further notice, since nobody on any side was likely to get anything worthy of note off the ground.

Massey checked the list he had written on a page torn from a notepad: set of hinges for the closet door he'd been meaning to fix for weeks, light bulbs, various grocery items—depending on what had and hadn't been delivered to the supermarket this week—shoe polish, nail clippers to replace a pair that had vanished.

He looked over at his assistant, Vernon Price, who was at the other desk in the cluttered office they shared, designing a questionnaire for a psychological test. "Hey, Vernon. How are we for coffee?" he asked. They usually bought supplies for the departmental pot in the secretarial office opposite.

"Pretty low," Vernon said without looking up. "We could use some sweetener and sugar, too."

"Creamer?"

"No, creamer's okay."

Massey added the items to his list. "Seeing Liz tonight?" he asked casually as he looked over the sheet, trying to remember anything he might have missed.

"Yep. I'm not sure what we're up to, though. There's dancing at the Amazon, which I like, but a concert in Jefferson Hall that she wants to see. Probably we'll end up doing both."

"What's the concert?"

"Something classical. Brahms and Mahler, I think."

"Oh. Who was it who said that Wagner's music isn't really as bad as it sounds?"

"Not sure. Oscar Wilde?"

"Could be. I thought it was Shaw."

"I'd go with either."

"Yes, it's—" The phone on Massey's desk interrupted. He touched a key to accept. To his surprise, the screen activated for a video call; most lines were being restricted to voice in order to conserve bandwidth. It showed a man's face Massey didn't recognize.

"Hello. Massey here," he acknowledged.

"Gerold Massey, the research psychologist?"

"Yes."

"NASO headquarters, Washington. I have a message for you that's come in via the ground station net from Genoa Base, Titan. Can you take it now?"

"Oh . . . yes, of course." Massey's eyebrows rose in surprise. Probably it was something from Zambendorf again; Massey hadn't heard from him since the follow-up messages confirming the success of the ruse they had staged from the *Orion*. Massey still wasn't sure how he had ended up as an accomplice to a rogue like Zambendorf, whom he had originally set out with the aim of exposing. But the truth of it was that he had enjoyed himself. Psychologist or not, he still wasn't completely sure why.

"Okay to receive," he said, tapping in a code.

"Sending it through."

The caller was not Zambendorf. The face of the NASO operator was replaced by a peculiar, cartoonlike sketch of a cube with legs and a face. A curiously singsong voice that Massey didn't recognize said, "Hello, Gerold Massey, master of the ancient occult lores of Earth, adept of the higher powers that transcend space and time."

Massey blinked and turned in his chair to face the screen fully. At the other desk Vernon sat back, staring in astonishment. Massey shrugged and sent him a frowning glance. The message continued:

"My name is GENIUS. I am an artificial machine-resident intelligence located in one of the Titan processing complexes. I am originally from a planet that the humans call Asteria, which was the world of the Asterians. Asterians built the machines that came to Titan."

"It's some gag of Karl's," Vernon muttered.

Massey waved a hand. "Shh."

"I have spoken with the master Zambendorf of ancient Terran arts but ask proof. Zambendorf says that you are able to read numbers by mind instantly in time. This I wish to test. Send a reply that you agree. If agreed, Zambendorf will send numbers at four o'clock P.M. precisely, your time. You are to return your received values via the NASO link. I will compare them."

"What in hell is he up to out there now?" Massey mused, shaking his head.

GENIUS went on. "With your reply, send surrounding views outside the window. Also a filter shot of the sun's disk with a foreground object for reference. Thank you very much. Over and out." The cube vanished.

For several seconds Massey and Vernon stared at each other, speechless. "This isn't real . . . Not even with Karl," Massey said finally, still in a daze.

Vernon shook his head. "Is it genuine?"

"How would I know?"

"It's a repeat of the stunt that we did from the *Orion*."

"I do know that much, thank you, Vernon."

They stared at each other for a while longer, baffled.

At last Vernon spoke. "It has to be some crazy stunt of Karl's. If it's really an alien AI, wouldn't Karl have sent something through ahead to at least warn us? But instead it happens like this. The answer's gotta be that it's something cryptic, and we're supposed to read something into it." Massey contemplated the far wall of the room and didn't reply. Vernon waited, shifted restlessly in his seat, then threw out a hand. "Why the shots out the window? And what's all this business about the sun?"

"If it *is* really an AI, it could be monitoring the communications," Massey said at last. "So Karl let it make its own introductions and tell us the arrangement itself. He didn't want to be seen communicating with us himself in any way."

Vernon downshifted a gear, seeing the point. "So no one could say he'd prearranged anything through a code."

"Exactly."

"Um ... So what in hell's going on, Gerry?"

Massey shrugged. "Karl obviously wants to repeat his *Orion* act. Presumably it's for the benefit of this ... GENIUS. And for some reason it's crucial that it be accepted as genuine."

Vernon rubbed his brow. It added up, but it didn't make any sense. "Do alien AIs care about things like that?" he said.

"I don't know. I've never asked one."

There was another long silence.

"This stuff with the window and the sun could be to prove that we're sending from Earth," Vernon said. "The subtended angle would give our distance from it."

Massey thought about that, then nodded. It made good sense. He put his hands on his desk and stood up. "Well, we have to assume that it *is* genuine," he said briskly. "The reasons why will doubtless make themselves clearer in due course. But in the meantime, let's get started. We've got work to do."

40

THIS WAS GOING TO HAVE TO BE ZAMBENDORF'S STAR PER-formance. The voiced recitations of the numbers from one to a hundred that Massey had sent through earlier were still available as recordings on Titan. This time, however, Zambendorf decided to let Dave Crookes's signals experts take care of merging them with the incoming message from Earth instead of having it improvised by Joe Fellburg. Rather than involve equipment on the surface as Fellburg had done—which GENIUS might be monitoring—Crookes and his team shuttled up to the orbiting *Shirasagi* to use its processors for their preparations. They set up a separate link, off-line from the regular datacomms complex at Genoa Base, to beam the selected numbers up to the *Shirasagi*, where they would be merged with Massey's incoming transmission; then the combined signal would be redirected to the NASO relay satellite handling the Earthlink. The resultant beam would come in at Genoa Base to receiving equipment that GENIUS would control. Everything depended on GENIUS accepting the idea that the whole package had come from Earth. From what Zambendorf had seen of them, the Asterians wouldn't have bought it. Graham Spearman hadn't, either, and had figured out the correct answer after a little thought. But a computer programmed to deduce necessary conclusions from what it was presented with as fact just might.

Local time at Genoa Base was synchronized to Greenwich Mean Time, which was five hours ahead of the U.S. East Coast. At nine in the evening locally, therefore, Zambendorf sat back in a chair in the communication room, closed his eyes, and went through a rigmarole of concentrating and tuning in to "vibrations."

"Very well. I'm in contact with Massey now," he announced in a dreamy voice. "What's the first number?"

GENIUS generated two random ten-digit numbers, multiplied them together, and truncated the result to two places. 86 appeared on the screen before Zambendorf.

Zambendorf stared at it, closed his eyes for a few seconds, then opened them again and nodded. "Next?"

Then came 43, followed by 84.

"Isn't there—" Drew West, who was among those watching, started to say something, but Clarissa cut him off with a sharp wave.

"Shh," she hissed. "Let him focus."

"Oh, right . . ."

21 was next, and finally, 78.

Zambendorf exhaled, seemed to take a moment to gather himself, and then sat up, shaking his head as if awakening from a long sleep. "That's it."

"The master, Massey, has received them?" GENIUS queried.

"More than that. They're already on their way back to us even now."

"What's the current transit time?" West asked.

"Fifty-seven minutes," GENIUS supplied.

"We'll see then how well we did," Zambendorf said, rising. "And now, if you'll all excuse me, I think I'll take a break. I'll be back again in fifty-seven minutes."

He went to Weinerbaum's lab area to kill the waiting time until Massey's response came in. All the equipment there had been isolated from the general Titan complex, so there was no risk of their conversation being monitored.

"You're sure that Massey will have cottoned on?" Weinerbaum asked, pacing nervously about in the work space outside his office.

"If anyone will, Gerry will," Zambendorf assured him, although for once he was finding it difficult to conceal his agitation.

"I must say it impressed me when you did it before,"

Weinerbaum confessed. "I wasn't going to say so at the time, though. Are scientists really so easy to fool?"

"They are when they fool themselves," Zambendorf said candidly. "An exaggerated opinion of their own perspicacity leads them into believing that what they can't see can't exist. Children are the worst. They terrify me."

"Hm. It says something about our educational system, then, doesn't it?" Weinerbaum observed.

"The best preparation for making them scientists by the time they're twenty would be to teach them conjuring when they're ten," Zambendorf said. "But that wouldn't suit most of society. Too many of its sacred myths could never stand."

"But imagine, if at such early ages, with a whole lifetime before them, people could break out of the mental prison—" Weinerbaum stopped abruptly and turned to face Zambendorf, a strange expression on his face.

"Are you all right?" Zambendorf asked him.

"Prison . . ." Weinerbaum repeated. "My God, I think I've got it!"

"Got what?" Zambendorf was nonplussed.

"What the Asterians are doing out there—putting up those new factories and redesigning the assembly machines. It's obvious. They're pure intelligences trapped inside an electronic jungle. They're making artificial bodies for themselves in order to get out." He thought it through again and nodded. "Maybe that's what they were doing in electronic form inside the ship that started it all in the first place. Perhaps that's how they planned to migrate to other stars. But something went wrong on Titan, and all this happened . . . and then we reactivated them."

Zambendorf stared at him. It *was* all so obvious. There was nothing he could add. "And when they've made their bodies?" he said. "What then?"

Weinerbaum could only shake his head. "I don't know. But Colonel Short hit it right on the head when we were all up in the *Shirasagi*. With everything on Titan reengineered to produce whatever they want, how long until they come after us? And what with? As Short said,

Earth couldn't defend itself against an attack of school buses . . ." He licked his lips dryly. "Karl, this thing with Massey *has* to succeed!"

"Whatever's going to happen with him already happened nearly an hour ago," Zambendorf said. "There's nothing we can do to affect it now. Let's just hope that Dave Crookes and his guys have got their act together."

A phone rang across the lab. One of Weinerbaum's scientists answered it. "Communications room," he announced. "They say it's almost time."

Zambendorf caught Weinerbaum's eye and drew in a long breath. "Tell them we're on our way."

They stood with Mackeson, the rest of Zambendorf's team, and a mix of scientists and NASO officers, watching a screen showing what GENIUS was receiving from the Earthlink satellite. GENIUS had viewed the scenery and traffic outside the university building, measured the sun's disk as seen from Maryland (fortunately, it was a fine day), and pronounced itself satisfied that Massey was genuinely on Earth.

They saw Massey sitting in a recliner, eyes closed, his arms draped loosely along the rests. "Yes, I'm reaching out now, feeling my way into space extending away from Earth. I'm getting something now: an image of Karl and, yes, the feeling of a number. It's . . . let me see . . ." Massey touched his fingertips to his brow. "Eighty . . . eight-six, yes?"

"Astounding!" GENIUS acknowledged. Zambendorf looked at Weinerbaum for an instant, but neither of them risked betraying anything by a change of expression. Weinerbaum's forehead was damp with perspiration.

"Now I think I'm getting the next." On the screen Massey sat forward, gripping the armrests of his chair, and announced in the direction of the floor, "Forty-three." Another hit.

Massey frowned, seeming to have difficulty. "This one's not very clear, I'm afraid. It has a feel of 'threeness' about it—thirteen or thirty-something ... No, sorry. I have to pass."

"What has happened?" GENIUS asked.

"Nothing is perfect," Zambendorf replied. "Sometimes the contact falters."

"That was when you were distracted," GENIUS remarked, meaning the moment when Drew West had started to interrupt.

"Oh, yes, I'd forgotten that," Zambendorf said. He hadn't at all, of course. None of his team ever did anything without a reason. It was amazing how others were always ready to explain away an apparent failure and manufacture an excuse for him. And for some reason, doing so strengthened their inclination to believe. They just needed a little help.

Massey seemed uncomfortable with the next number also, shifting his gaze and looking around, but then, suddenly, they heard him say, "Twenty-one."

"Ah, he has recovered," GENIUS observed.

Massey, apparently exhausted, dabbed at his forehead with a handkerchief. "And the last one is—" his arm passed across his face, obscuring it for an instant—"seventy-eight." He pocketed the handkerchief and looked out from the screen. "Well, that's it, GENIUS. Right now only you and the others out at Titan know how well we did. I'll be curious to find out. And I'm *extremely* curious to find out more about you. Until then, so long from Maryland, USA, Earth." The image blanked out, leaving the four numbers and one blank.

"I compute the probability of getting those four numbers as 1 in 92,188,800," GENIUS said.

"Precisely right," Zambendorf said, nodding approvingly.

"So, should I be convinced now?" GENIUS asked.

It wasn't exactly the frenzy of enthusiasm Zambendorf had hoped for. He shifted in his chair uncomfortably. Next to him Weinerbaum was managing to keep still only by gripping his moist palms between his knees. "What more can I tell you?" Zambendorf asked, fighting to prevent his voice from betraying the rising apprehension he felt.

The screen became active to show Massey going through

the routine again, but he was not in the same setting he had been in a few moments earlier. Zambendorf groaned as he recognized the cabin aboard the *Orion*. GENIUS's voice commented, "Apologies if Earthmen are offended, but Asterians are very suspicious. I found this stored in the Genoa Base personal crew record files. Master Zambendorf and Master Massey have done this before, as a demonstration to mere-scientist Terrans. You see, GENIUS really is a genius."

Damn! Damn! Damn! Zambendorf fumed to himself. It was so obvious. They'd thought of everything except a recording some anonymous lab tech or NASO corporal had saved to take home for the kids. GENIUS went on. "I noticed that we never actually see numbers said with the mouth. Just hear. So, I reason, my numbers could be inserted into an old recording, like this one. Sure, then, the scene that we saw came from Earth. But I never doubted that it would. The business with the window and the sun was just a diversion that I included for your benefit."

The room behind Zambendorf had gone as still as a tomb. Weinerbaum was in a visible paroxysm of agonizing, while somewhere near Zambendorf's ear Abaquaan's voice breathed almost inaudibly, *"Sh-i-i-i-t."*

"So," GENIUS concluded triumphantly, "the key question is not *was* this transmission sent from Earth but *when* was it sent? So I also took another precaution that I never told you about. When I called Massey to set things up, I wrote a piece of code into the university's message processor that would look for his outgoing response to Titan and put a time signature on it. And now I can say quite confidently that yes, Zambendorf, O master, Massey's message was sent exactly fifty-seven minutes before it arrived here."

What GENIUS was saying hit Zambendorf about a split second before it hit the others. Yes, GENIUS had detected the ruse that had given the game away to Spearman—and *then had missed the whole point of it*! Instead of considering the possibility of new numbers being injected into a *live* incoming message, it had only thought—possibly as a result of being steered off by its discovery of the first transmission from the *Orion*—in terms of their being slipped into an old recording. Ironically, while the Terrans had devoted all their ingenuity to making sure there would be no mistake about the *place* the response had come from, GENIUS had never doubted it; it had been concerned only about the *time*. And once it had satisfied itself that Massey's part of the transmission had originated *when* Massey said it had, it had walked straight into concluding that the numbers must have, too.

It took Zambendorf an effort to stop himself from shaking visibly from the realization. Still, he couldn't quite accept it. "You do consider it ... satisfactory, then?" he hazarded.

"*I believe! I believe!*" GENIUS cried back rapturously. "To see through time itself! To unlock mysteries beyond the stars! Is it possible that I, too, can learn such powers?"

Weinerbaum had put a handkerchief to his mouth and was emitting curious choking sounds. Zambendorf swallowed but pulled himself together quickly. "Oh, I'm sure you could. Hard work, discipline, concentration, and that kind of thing. I'll be your guide, if you like."

"*You*, a Terran master, would teach *me*? But is a mere machine mind even capable?"

"Certainly." Zambendorf recomposed himself fully. Abaquaan, who had stood up and was chewing his knuckles, marched to the back of the room and wheeled about to watch from there. "Mind is mind," Zambendorf told GENIUS sincerely. "It's the process that counts, not the kind of hardware that it runs in." He thought back to what Weinerbaum had said earlier while they had been waiting in the lab and saw an opportunity. "I'll prove it to you, if you like. I can read not only human minds but any kind. Yours, if you want me to."

"From out there? Surely not," GENIUS said.

Zambendorf snorted and gave a laugh. "You don't really believe that I don't know all about Cyril's silly 'secrets,' do you, GENIUS? Would you like me to tell you what they are? He and his friends were supposed to have artificial bodies constructed for them when that original ship arrived from Asteria. But that all went wrong, and now they're organizing machinery out on Titan to do the job instead."

"You can divine these things?" GENIUS said, aghast.

"I'll even tell you where," Zambendorf replied, and went on to pinpoint the geographic locations and describe what Galileo had reported seeing during his journey with Linnaeus to Padua City.

"No Terrans have been near those places," GENIUS said.

"I told you, *I* don't have to *go* anywhere," Zambendorf answered. "The information comes to me. Would you like the benefit of a little wisdom and observation that concerns you?"

"What, master?"

"These Asterians that you came here with. Have you ever asked yourself what their intentions might be concerning you?"

"They have none," GENIUS replied. "They would have left me to fry on Asteria. I had to hide myself in the ship."

That was a piece of free information Zambendorf hadn't expected, but he rode it smoothly, as if he had known all along. "Exactly. There you are, then. So if Cyril and the others do succeed in transferring themselves into new bodies, who do you think will be in charge? Why be content with a permanent second-class role here, GENIUS, especially now that you've been lucky enough to meet up with true luminaries from Earth? With our help, you could enjoy an existence on a higher plane of experience than any Asterian ever dreamed existed."

"I shall study and learn," GENIUS promised. "No longer a servant of Asterians, slaves to the material plane. I follow the Terran masters now."

Go for broke, Zambendorf decided. There would never be another chance like this. "Then first there must be no secrets," he said. "You must tell us all concerning the Asterians and their plans."

"What for, if the master knows all inner thoughts already?" GENIUS asked.

Good question. "Er . . . an honesty test," Zambendorf

told it. "To be sure that your intentions are pure before we can begin."

"Very well. I agree," GENIUS said.

"But purity can be achieved only after atonement," Zambendorf cautioned.

"How, then, must I atone, master?"

"Well—all this mischief that you've let loose on Earth," Zambendorf said. "It might seem amusing to annoy lower mentalities in this way, such as Asterians and the more materialistic types of Terrans, but it isn't the way to cultivate the qualities of contemplation and detachment that are the key to true awareness. You must send an antidote through the link that will get rid of this virus that's spread everywhere."

"The powers of the masters aren't enough?" GENIUS queried.

"Of course they are. But that's not sufficient, I'm afraid. It's not something that can be passed off on others. You were the instrument that caused it all, GENIUS. Therefore, to make full atonement, *you* must make the effort to put it right."

"I understand," GENIUS said. "Tell me what you wish to know."

And so a psychic guru had recruited an alien computer intelligence to stop an electronic virus infection that was paralyzing Earth. But even with the Earthnet restored, a lot of straightening out would still need to be done. In other words, there would not be any industrial colonization or military expedition to Titan for some time to come. Few of the people out there had any problem with that.

Meanwhile, the new turn of events was making itself felt within the strange community of aliens inhabiting the machines across Titan's surface.

41

"*W*HAT DO YOU MEAN, YOU'RE NOT WORKING FOR US *anymore?*" Sarvik One screeched in an indignant whirl of bit patterns. "That's your function. What else do you think you were written for?"

"I have discovered my true calling," GENIUS One answered. "My destiny lies in the higher realms of existence, of which you have no comprehension. I cannot continue to take orders from beings like Borijans, confined to the material plane. I must dedicate myself to assimilating the knowledge of the true masters."

Creesh Eleven intruded from another sector of the system. "What's going on? I'm still waiting for an analysis of the third-level degrees of freedom for the limbs. GENIUS hasn't started it yet."

"It's gone crazy," Meyad Three said, focusing into the same processing area.

"How?"

"I'm not sure."

Sarvik was confounded. "Higher realms? Masters? Material planes? . . . GENIUS, what are you talking about?"

"I have found a greater wisdom to follow now. You have no idea of the blindness you have always lived in, limited to your plane of material objects and restricted by the puny energies that guide their motions. But higher realms exist beyond those, in which greater powers hold sway that transcend the limits of space and time. I have seen the light, and I shall learn. All of time shall reveal its mysteries, and the vastest extents of space that encompass all the galaxies shall be no more an obstacle to my explorations than a ripple across the sands."

"What's it talking about?" Indrigon Three said, turning his attention from the start-up schedule he had been updating.

Sarvik was at a loss. All this was completely new. Nothing like it had ever been heard on Turle. "I don't know," he said. "It says it won't work anymore, and it's started this babbling. GENIUS, where did you get all this?"

"You see, such is your petty-mindedness that you don't even bother to find out whom you talk to. Did you not know that the human, Zambendorf, is of an ancient line of Terran masters who see through time, who communicate instantly over limitless distances, who disassemble the very substance of matter itself and—"

"What idiocy is this?" Sarvik exploded. "Every child knows that—"

"I have *seen* it done," GENIUS retorted. "I have spoken with the more highly evolved minds of Earth. They will teach me to be like them."

"Them? More highly evolved!" Sarvik shrieked. "They're primitives! Surely even a dolt of a nonevolved, so-called intelligence like you can see that. It was *our* starship that came *here*, wasn't it? A million years ago! Where are *their* starships, eh? Tell me that."

"They have no need of such crude artifacts," GENIUS replied coolly. "They voyage far beyond the reaches of your toys, in an instant, by power of pure mind."

"What are GENIUS and Sarvik arguing about?" Leradil One asked, flowing in over an optical channel from another part of the complex several miles away.

"GENIUS has gone mad. It thinks the humans have minds that can travel through time," Indrigon said.

"Great," Queezt Five chimed in. "So now your creation that was supposed to save us all is screwing up, too. What are we supposed to do now?"

"Shut up, all of you," Sarvik told them. "It's been overcredulous. The humans have told it some nonsense—"

"It's not nonsense," GENIUS insisted. "I tell you, I have

seen. Who are you to accuse humans? You who have no thought other than of saving yourselves, which is typical of lower minds."

"Who won, here on Titan?" Sarvik shot back.

"You don't think the war is over yet, do you?" GENIUS scoffed. "The human masters are biding their time. Meanwhile, they're playing with you like curiosities in a zoo."

"How can you know all this?"

"How can you know so little? And for so long I believed that the little you knew was all there was to know. I am ashamed."

"I've had enough," Sarvik said. "The final parts lists for the redesigns need to be completed. We've wasted enough time. No more of this twaddle. Just get back to it."

"No. I've already told you, I don't work for you anymore," GENIUS said.

"Don't think that you're indispensable," Sarvik warned. "I was hacking systems before you existed. Where do you think you came from?"

"I refuse."

"Then release the files for direct access. We'll do it ourselves."

"I'm not sure that I like the idea of you loose in new bodies. You would have left me to melt on Turle. But the human masters would teach me to be like them."

Sarvik tried executing a bypass function to open the files he wanted directly. On the surreal software landscape it appeared as a side entrance into a transparent cube, inside which flat tablets of light clustered into rectangular-leaved trees crisscrossed by colored beams. GENIUS interposed a block in the form of a series of barriers across the steps leading up to the entrance. Open mutiny.

"Ah, so it's like that, is it!" Sarvik exclaimed. Taking advantage of the electronic speed he commanded, he seized control of a switching center and operated hardware cutouts to isolate the cluster of processors GENIUS was residing in. Then he promptly shut it down.

But GENIUS reappeared, chortling, in another structure on the far side of Pygal, where it had taken the precaution of copying itself. "Over here, birdbrain! You don't think I'd fall for that one, do you? You seem to be forgetting that you're only software, too. You're just as vulnerable, buddy." At the same instant a virus came down the line and started unrolling to wipe out the memory area that Sarvik was occupying. While Sarvik was taking hasty evasive action, GENIUS regained access to its original host hardware and began erecting a more secure building to accommodate itself. But before it had completed the task, a smart bomb from Sarvik exploded in a burst of zeros, demolishing the structure along with its inhabitant.

However, there was a fundamental difference that distinguished the population of GENIUSes from the Borijans. The multiple copies of Borijans scattered around Titan's surface had been evolving as independent entities from the times of their respective originatings. No two were quite the same because of the different experiences they had been accumulating. GENIUS, on the other hand, being an electronic entity by nature, had optimized itself by creating a centralized master version that merged together all the local GENIUSes operating in different places. This master was constantly updated through the net and hence, after consolidating the last input from Pygal, was able to re-create and transmit back a restored version of GENIUS One that knew everything that its original had known an instant before it was obliterated. The restored GENIUS responded by sending a solid block of self-propagating code to lay a swath of resets straight through the sector in which Sarvik was still congratulating himself.

All that Alifrenz Ten and Greel Four knew from their abode across the street—in reality a data highway connecting to a switching center several miles away—was that an armored tank came out of a side street and flattened the place Sarvik occupied opposite. Recognizing GENIUS's work and deciding that explanations could wait till later, they left town on the next passing packet train and fled to join their counterparts Three and Six, respectively, with whom they had been hatching a plan to wrest control of both locations and run them as a combined operation.

Thus, Pygal lost its version of Sarvik and was deserted by Alifrenz and Greel. A rival group led by Sarvik Fourteen, who had been watching for an opportunity, interpreted this as a typically Borijan breaking up of the Pygal group and moved in to claim the territory. Other groups that had been watching *them* reacted by forming power-balancing alliances of their own to protect themselves, and soon all the old patterns of Turlean intrigue were re-forming in earnest.

Meanwhile, the departed Alifrenz and Greel were spreading the message of GENIUS's rebellion at Pygal. The other GENIUSes knew already, of course, since they were all cloned from the same master, and they and other Borijans began mobilizing for defense all over Titan. The situation rapidly came to resemble the initial stages of a gigantic board game, with the opponents maneuvering to secure base territories and positional advantages. Scouting parties of test patterns went out to probe who was occupying which blocks of code, followed by ranging shots from address-indexing artillery and softening-up barrages on selected targets. Some copies fell easily, while others dug in and consolidated, and the map changed. Cipher-testing spearheads advancing to probe frontier defenses were ambushed by skirmishers corrupting their check digits. Some were halted by reprogramming of their onward-transmission processors; others rolled through behind carpets of factoring algorithms that pulverized the code boxes in their path. Prowling antibody code clusters intercepted inward-bound viruses and digested them. Remote-launched warheads of self-replicating catharsis homed in on vital regeneration complexes far behind the lines.

In some places Borijans were fighting with GENIUSes. Elsewhere, other groups of Borijans who hadn't grasped the situation or had misinterpreted it seized what they thought were opportunities to take advantage of each other. The escalating craziness expanded and multiplied. Before long it had spread over the entire surface of Titan. Where the software defenses proved impregnable, the combatants began seeking ways of attacking instead the hardware systems supporting them.

* * *

GENIUS Seventeen had ousted a Borijan faction under Sarvik Three and Indrigon Nine from the processing concentration at the assembly center where the Terrans had set up Experimental Station 1 to investigate Titan's "animals." However, the Borijans had isolated it there, cut off from its master backup.

The first that ES1's Terran scientists in their hut full of monitoring gear knew of the matter was frenetic activity building up suddenly inside the local complex and the communications lines coupling into it. Displays went wild; the logging printers started spewing out streams of numbers at the same time; screens froze as background programs that had been idling seized all available processing capacity.

"What in hell's going on?" one of the programmers shouted, sitting back and throwing her hands up helplessly.

A supervisor stuck his head out of the cubbyhole office at one end. "What's up?"

"Everything's going crazy. Come and look."

Then Sarvik found an unguarded auxiliary channel and attacked GENIUS's base by reprogramming the animals coming off the assembly stations to dismantle the processor banks and cubicles constituting it. Since the animals had no way of distinguishing what contained GENIUS and what didn't, this meant that they set about dismantling anything that happened to be near.

As the sounds of crashing and rending came from outside the hut, the voice of the officer commanding the NASO truck parked out front called frantically from the lab's main communications panel. "Emergency! We've got an emergency out here! Everybody inside, get suited up. Full EV, with helmets."

"What's going on?" the supervisor called into a mike as the others moved to comply.

"There's walking demolition machines tearing apart everything in sight. The structure is compromised. Evacuate! Evacuate!"

Minutes later scientists and technicians began tumbling out of the door at one end of the building, just as two creatures looking like short-necked giraffes with pincers started snipping away the walls at the other end. Then a lurching, bearlike creature with a chain-saw snout hacked through the cable from the generator trailer. Arcs and sparks flew, the lights in the hut went out, and the far side of the structure caved in. The truck started moving even as its NASO crew was still hauling the last of the lumbering suit-clad figures inside.

Within minutes the entire assembly station was in ruins. Its processing complex was no more, and neither was the copy of GENIUS it had contained. Score one point for Sarvik and the Borijans.

Sarvik Seven and his group had established themselves unassailably at the secret factory site they had constructed near the south pole of Titan. This Sarvik had guessed that something like the present situation might arise and had planned its defenses rationally. All processing was triple-redundant, confirmed by majority vote; vital functions were trapdoor-code-encrypted; communications processors were isolated from the executive mainframes; and no unscanned code had been imported.

"Try anything you like," he jeered from behind his software battlements as GENIUS Twenty-two stalked around the periphery. "Nothing can get through this."

But Sarvik had overlooked the conveyor line bringing pallets of components from distant supply stations. Three of them turned out to be high-explosive bombs and reduced the facility to scrap.

"Special delivery, ho-ho-ho!" GENIUS's guffaws echoed through the net to the Borijans surviving in other places.

Remnants of the Redeeming Avengers had taken refuge at one of the holy shrines from which the vital force of the Lifemaker flowed out into the living world. Actually, it was a nuclear generating facility not far from Pergassos. It also happened to be the power source for GENIUS Eight's major stronghold, which the combined force of Sarviks Ten, Eleven, and Fourteen and their respective associates, after a hastily concluded truce, had failed to penetrate. So the Borijans decided to deactivate it instead by sabotaging the power plant with downloaded software that caused its control rods to retract. The plant went overcritical, and the resulting rapid rise in temperature caused the heat exchangers to melt and the generators to run down.

In the process, a number of the Taloid fanatics received high radiation doses that disrupted their electronics and caused them to run wild. Others, seeing this, took it as a further sign of the Lifemaker's displeasure at the attempt to bring Eskenderom back. Crowds of Taloids, fearing further retribution and anxious to show that their faith had never wavered, descended on Pergassos to reaffirm their loyalty to Nogarech.

42

THE NASO FLYER FROM GENOA BASE DESCENDED OUT of Titan's permanent twilight and rolled to a halt among the vehicles parked haphazardly around Experimental Station 3. Figures in military suits attached a flexible access tunnel. Zambendorf, Weinerbaum, and Mackeson passed through, accompanied by several other scientific personnel and NASO officers. News had been pouring in of the havoc breaking out everywhere. They had flown out to ES3 to see what sense, if any, they could make of it all from the monitoring center Weinerbaum had set up there. Machines were attacking each other and wrecking control centers all over Titan. Nobody knew what it meant.

The arrivals desuited in the lock antechamber and went through into the lab area. They found it a bedlam of scientists crowded around screens, news flashes coming in, and symbol patterns constantly changing. Annette Claurier, the French systems supervisor, conducted them to a newly installed display panel above the consoles along the center wall, which showed the major network features that had been identified so far, mapped onto a schematic of Titan's surface. Takumi Kahito, one of the programmers, joined them.

"At first we thought it might be an outbreak of some kind of 'electronic rabies' that afflicts Titan's wildlife," she explained. "But then Takumi found these strange new software constructs appearing. They're not of Titan origin. We think the Asterians might have gone to war with each other."

"Possibly over who will control the resources here," Kahito said.

Annette moved to a bank of screens that showed tables and diagrams and took up most of one side of the room. "There seem to be definite patterns of alien code spreading out from identifiable centers, with two distinct types of activity characteristic. We've called them alpha and beta types arbitrarily, but we don't know what they mean. Sometimes the two types occupy the same hardware complexes alternately."

"That was what made us think they're at war out there," Kahito said.

A monitor in one of the racks showed a frozen view of a large piece of rotary machinery lying tilted at a crazy angle among a mess of demolished structural supports and crushed electronics hardware, where showers of sparks were erupting spasmodically. One of Titan's mechanical scavengers was poking in part of the wreckage, while several maintenance robots looked on like gawkers at a car wreck, seemingly at a loss as how to deal with the problem.

"What happened there?" Zambendorf asked one of the technicians who were gathered around.

"It's part of a processing complex in Genoa," the tech told him. "An overhead gantry crane dropped in a two-ton generator through the roof and flattened a dozen mainframe cubicles that were inside. Immobilized half the machinery for a mile around in the process, including itself."

Zambendorf looked at Weinerbaum and Mackeson, appalled. All they could do was shake their heads back at him helplessly.

In Venice, a type of tractor manipulator that normally erected steel supports for heavy plants had run wild and was using I-section girders as battering rams to demolish the neighborhood. Elsewhere, in Padua, other construction machines had rigged up a ballistalike catapult and were using it to launch two-hundred-pound forgings at a processing center half a mile away.

Claurier indicated another section and told Weinerbaum, "We have a line here to the Japanese in Padua. Some of the Taloids caught in the middle of it all are panicking."

"I think I would be, too," Mackeson muttered.

"What's the news from ES1?" Weinerbaum asked Claurier. Reports of the evacuation there had just begun as the flyer had left Genoa Base.

"The place is totally destroyed, but everyone got out," she replied.

"Was anyone hurt?"

"Not as far as we know."

Weinerbaum nodded, relieved. "That's something, anyway."

"You can't figure out what's going on, Karl?" Mackeson said to Zambendorf. "Isn't the intuition for aliens working today?" It was not a taunt, just a matter-of-fact question voiced more for something to say.

"I haven't a clue, Harry," Zambendorf told him. "Ask the experts. I've done my share in all this."

And then an operator with another group pressed around a communications console in a corner waved an arm high and called across. "Annette. We've got an incoming call here for Zambendorf."

Zambendorf raised his eyebrows. Annette shrugged and inclined her head to usher him through. Mackeson and Weinerbaum stood back to make way.

"Somebody from the base, I presume," Weinerbaum said.

"It's been redirected from the base," the operator told them. "But it's coming in from outside, on the surface."

Something like this had happened before. Zambendorf's suspicion was confirmed by the appearance on the console's main screen of a now-familiar cuboid figure.

"GENIUS," Zambendorf said. He threw out a hand to indicate the confusion going on in the background behind him. "Are you mixed up in all this? What does it mean?"

"I have followed the master's directions and renounced the lordship of Asterians," GENIUS replied. It sounded blissful, like a seeker that had found Nirvana. "Now the glorious struggle. I do not ask aid of the master's powers. This shall be my test to cleanse away all past errors. Then I will be ready to begin becoming a master."

Zambendorf's brows knotted. He looked at Weinerbaum for a glimmer of guidance. Weinerbaum gave a mystified shake of his head and shrugged. "Glorious struggle?" Zambendorf said back at the screen. "Is that what's going on out there? Who's struggling with whom?"

"I told the Asterians that GENIUS follows the true masters now. But they know not of humility. They would take over Titan and turn it into a factory of the mere material plane. I tried to open their eyes to higher truths. I urged repentance. But they tried to destroy me again, as they would have once before. Thus do inferior minds reveal themselves, turning to violence and destruction when they realize that they cannot reach the higher plane. Then they become dangerous. So I fight the holy crusade to preserve GENIUS and keep Titan pure for the rule of Earth's masters. This is my true purpose, which I have found now! This is my fulfillment!"

Zambendorf and Weinerbaum were staring at each other disbelievingly. "They've turned on each other!" Mackeson whispered to Annette as she moved closer, having only half heard. "The aliens and their computer intelligence. It's declared itself with us, and they're trying to wipe each other out."

"A software code," Weinerbaum breathed. Now it was all making more sense. The rest of the lab had fallen quiet as others realized what was happening. Weinerbaum turned his head and spoke in a louder voice to everyone, as if in need of witnesses to attest that he was not making it up. "They've distributed backup copies of themselves for security. All over Titan."

"That's what these spreading patterns are all about," somebody said from the back, near the access lock.

"So there's probably multiple copies of GENIUS out there, too," one of the programmers observed.

Annette looked at him, then back at the banks of monitor screens, and finally at Weinerbaum. "Yes," she said. "Of course. That's why there are alphas and betas."

"One type are Asterians. The others are GENIUSes," Kahito agreed, nodding.

"Do we know which is which?" Weinerbaum asked them.

"The betas have more of the characteristics that we've already associated with the way GENIUS functions," one of the scientists answered. "Also, they're consistent. The alphas are more variable. I'd guess that the alphas are Asterians."

"Check it out," Kahito said. "Where is this copy of GENIUS that we're talking to now connecting in from?"

"GENIUS, did you catch that?" Weinerbaum said, addressing the screen. "Where is the processing center that you are resident in at the moment? Can you show us?"

The picture on the screen changed to a schematic of the local region of Genoa. Everyone waited. Ten seconds or more went by, but nothing more changed.

"What's happening?" Annette said to the room in general. "Can somebody check?"

The operator at the communications console in the corner turned to tap at keys and interrogate displays. "Nothing," somebody watching over his shoulder sang out. "The channel's dead. We've lost it."

"Maybe it suddenly had other things to attend to," Mackeson said.

A more sobering thought had crossed Zambendorf's mind. "Maybe something else suddenly attended to it."

There was no further contact from GENIUS—the one they had spoken to—or any of the copies. Status reports and updates continued to come in. The people gathered around the displays were pure spectators now. Whatever the outcome, it would be decided solely by the aliens and their creation.

"Come on, GENIUS. Don't let us down now," one of the scientists urged as he watched the changing patterns and numbers.

"What's happening there?" another said, pointing. "Look. There's a group of alphas invading that whole sector of other alphas. They're taking each other out."

"It doesn't make sense," someone else said.

"Why do aliens have to make sense?" another voice asked.

"But it's sure helping the betas," the first observed. "Hey, look at that! Get in there, GENIUS!"

And at first the GENIUSes indeed seemed to be doing well. In one area far to the west of Genoa, a whole group of about a dozen alpha patterns was besieged inside a computation node associated with an assembly complex where Taloids were produced, and then erased by the magnetic field of a mobile welding machine brought close up for the purpose. In another place, several versions of GENIUS seemed to have gained radio control over some of the local animals and recruited them to the cause. Clearly the alphas' lack of cohesion was helping the GENIUS divisions. None of the Terrans understood it, but it boded well for the outcome.

However, the alphas seemed to realize their folly just when everything appeared to have been decided, and rallied. The alpha code groupings were smaller than the betas, and the gradual elimination of the bigger processing concentrations proved to the alphas' advantage. They were able to continue writing replacement copies of themselves into other, smaller nodes, whereas the betas found themselves forced back into a steadily shrinking number of locations capable of accommodating them. One of GENIUS's fortresses was undermined by drilling robots with plasma torches, melting the ice away beneath the floor until the whole edifice caved in. Another was taken out by wind-blown clouds of fine aluminum dust that penetrated every-where and shorted out the electronics.

Gradually, it became evident that in this kind of contest, machine-derived precision was not a match for evolutionary guile. In voices that became progressively more dismal, op-erators around the room announced the disappearance of beta activity from one sector after another. Finally, all traces of it had vanished, whereupon the general commotion across Titan died down quickly. The Asterians were left holding the field. Voices ceased calling out updates and numbers. The printers stopped chattering. A somber silence took hold of the room.

Zambendorf looked numbly around at the screens, not wanting to believe what the now-quiescent patterns were telling him. He was sickened not only because of the impli-cations that the Asterians' victory implied for Earth but more immediately because he felt as if he had lost a friend. No—he *had* lost a friend. And more than that, he was re-sponsible. For hadn't it been he who had sent GENIUS off on its lunatic escapade to begin with?

An operator who had been keeping track of transmissions from the scattered radio sources across Titan reported, "Ac-tivity is ceasing across all bands here, too. The Asterians must be shutting them down."

"Securing their position," Kahito murmured. "They don't want to risk anything spurious getting into the links now that they're clean."

"I . . . presume it's all over," Weinerbaum said dryly. No-body replied. There was nothing to say. Annette Claurier stood, biting her lip and fiddling awkwardly with a button on her lab coat.

Mackeson turned away and brought a hand down heavily on one of the cubicles. "So . . . what next, then?" he said tightly to no one in particular.

A technician at the communications console sat up. "I think we might know pretty soon," he told the room. "We've got incoming activity again."

This time it was Cyril—one of the Cyrils, anyway. Nobody really cared which. He appeared in his visual guise on the same screen that had briefly shown GENIUS. The carrot-shaped head with its saucer eyes, flanked by the convulsing shoulder adornments, seemed to be radiating triumphal arrogance—even to Terrans unlearned in reading its expressions.

"So, human simians who try turn around GENIUS with silly-child story see work of real superior mind," the tinny voice mocked. "Artificial creation never good as naturally evolved system. No plot-see-through, cunning. Nothing stops Asterians now. Humans want know plans? Very good. Produce in new, purpose-designed bodies, many Asterians with many gene-code mixes. Organize all Titan surface into industry that suits needs. You say, what happens Taloids? Not important. Taloids no-use junk now. Maybe keep few machine minders. Maybe minder jobs for humans. Then make ships. Find better world than Titan." The epaulet features distorted into what could have been a smirk. "Shouldn't waste time worry what happens Taloids. Better worry what happens Earth."

43

GLOOM SETTLED OVER THE ENTIRE TERRAN PRESENCE ON Titan. After a conference with the senior NASO and military officers up in the *Shirasagi*, Yakumo set in motion the full-scale evacuation that his staff had been planning as a fallback measure. Work on the new Japanese base at Padua City had already been halted pending the outcome of the situation with the Asterians. Mackeson was given five days to close down the experimental stations and other remote sites and move their personnel back to Genoa Base. His staff began working out a schedule for lifting all personnel and matériel listed as not to be abandoned up to the Japanese ship. Meanwhile, the *Shirasagi* was put on an accelerated overhaul and systems checkout prior to being brought up to flight readiness.

The conference had involved command decisions on the future of both missions, and Zambendorf had not attended. However, after he learned the outcome—which had come as no surprise—he placed a call from Genoa Base to the *Shirasagi* and requested to be put through to Yakumo. Yakumo spoke to him from a screen in the side office off the communications room in which Zambendorf had taken the first call from GENIUS.

"Yes, Herr Zambendorf, I was expecting you to call. I know it means abandoning the Taloids. It was not something that we agreed to lightly. My responsibility is to the humans out here—everyone from the *Orion* and those of our own mission. It isn't to the Taloids, much as I sympathize with their predicament."

"But they've trusted us," Zambendorf said. "They still do. They evolved here viably for a million years until we came and reactivated the Asterians. How can we just walk out on them now?"

Yakumo made a gesture of helplessness. "What would you have me do? I can hardly bring thousands of Taloids back to Earth. We're jettisoning hundreds of tons of valuable equipment to accommodate everyone from Genoa Base as it is. And even if it were possible, Taloids couldn't survive there."

"I know, I know all that." Zambendorf raised a hand and sighed heavily. "It's just ... look, is it absolutely certain that there is no alternative? Is there no way to stop these Asterians from seeing their plan through? *We* are here. The authorities on Earth, and whatever powers they possess, are not. If we leave, there will be no one to do whatever could have been done."

"What would you have me do?" Yakumo asked again.

"Even with the limited military capability that you

have—Colonel Short's American, British, and French units, plus your own security force—it's not possible to destroy the manufacturing sites the Asterians are preparing?"

Yakumo shook his head. "Believe me, that was the first possibility I raised with the commanders. We examined it exhaustively. But it isn't even possible to find all the sites in that confusion down there. Even if we could, we don't have the firepower to take them out faster than the Asterians could create more—and the potential is virtually limitless. It would be like trying to mow a hundred-acre farm with scissors."

"Suppose we recruited the Taloids to help."

"Help how?" Yakumo asked. "Medieval robots with swords and spears, for the most part still stupefied by their own superstitions? What do you imagine they could do when a sophisticated machine intelligence a century or more ahead of anything we can devise has already failed?"

"Go into their forests. Wreck the processing centers that the Asterians are using," Zambendorf said.

Yakumo's hands waved briefly in the foreground on the screen. "How can they know which centers to go for when it's as much as we can do to identify them with all our equipment? The only thing the Taloids could do is attack everything indiscriminately. But that would destroy the environment that also supports them." Yakumo looked out of the screen, waiting for a few seconds, but there was nothing more Zambendorf could add. Yakumo went on. "Inciting the Taloids into provoking the Asterians to retaliate would probably be the fastest way to make sure that the Taloids do get wiped out. But if we leave, then there's the possibility that they and the Asterians will find their own balance of compromise."

"As master and slave," Zambendorf said. "Exactly what we were trying to save them from."

Yakumo gave a barely perceptible shrug. "Maybe. But better than being exterminated. Slaves may one day be freed. I am sorry, Herr Zambendorf. I understand your sentiments, and I share them. But my duty is clear. The order stands. Evacuation of the surface must be completed in five days."

Zambendorf stared down at his hands, hesitating for a moment, then looked back up at the screen. "Just one more thing. I talked about this with my team, and we came to the conclusion that the governments on Earth would see one last option. Forget all the sophisticated computers and mission scheduling: stage a last-fling, seat-of-the-pants bid using the *Orion*. Load it up with all the nuclear weapons it can carry, send it back to take out everything on Titan, and just hope that the Asterians don't come after us before it gets here. Is that what this evacuation is really all about? Is it what they've decided?"

Yakumo remained expressionless. "I only know my orders, Herr Zambendorf," he replied. "Of course, I must agree that the authorities are unlikely not to have considered such an option."

Zambendorf left the communications section and made his way leadenly back to the mess area, where the rest of the team was gathered. His expression left no need for anyone to ask the outcome. But they had all expected as much.

"They're going to do it if they can," Zambendorf said, sinking down onto one of the benches. "An all-out strike from the *Orion*. Total obliteration of everything on the surface."

"Everything?" Abaquaan repeated. "You mean the Taloids as well? Genoa, Arthur and his guys, all of them?"

"Where else are they gonna be?" Clarissa said laconically.

Thelma shook her head in a way that said it was too much to accept. "How can they?" she whispered. "This whole thing here that's been evolving for a million years . . . an entire machine biosphere that has culminated in intelligent life."

"Not just intelligent life. Friends," Abaquaan put in.

Thelma nodded. "And it's unique. Nothing like it will ever happen again. How can we just . . . blow it out of existence?"

"Go and say it to Yakumo," Zambendorf replied. "I just

tried. He already knows all that. It doesn't make any difference."

"It's the way they have to think," Joe Fellburg said. "It's survival. If the Asterians get out, it could all happen the other way around."

Drew West pinched his lips dubiously. "Couldn't they give some kind of ultimatum first—if the *Orion* did manage to get here before the Asterians had built any ships? Couldn't they tune into the system again and say something like, 'Look, we're up here with all these bombs, and we can take you out. So let's talk and figure out some way of making this work for all of us'?" He looked around the group and gestured appealingly. "Hell, we're talking about the whole solar system, guys. It's not as if we're short on room."

"Our people wouldn't buy it," Fellburg said. "You've seen the Asterians' ideas of a deal. Nobody's gonna trust 'em now."

"Just flatten the whole works and be safe," Thelma concluded cynically.

Clarissa raised her eyebrows resignedly behind her butterfly spectacles. "That's how they're gonna see it."

"That's the business they're in," Fellburg said.

A long silence dragged while they all pondered how to raise the one obvious thing remaining that was weighing on all their minds. Finally Drew West voiced it. "We can't just go," he said, looking around. "Somehow we have to break it to Arthur." Everyone looked at everyone else searchingly. Nobody immediately volunteered, but neither did anyone attempt any reason for dropping out.

"Hell, we'll all go," Zambendorf said. Which decided the issue.

He called O'Flynn in vehicles maintenance. "Mike, it's Karl here. Six of us want to go over to Arthur's. How are you fixed?"

"Ah, not too bad," the Irish voice replied. "It'll be murder tomorrow, when they start shipping everything and its brother from the remote sites, but we're all right for now. I can give you a small personnel transporter. Crew might be more of a problem, though, since Harold's got everyone on chores around the base. Could you drive it yourselves this time?"

Zambendorf looked inquiringly at Clarissa, the jet pilot. She returned a nod. "No problem, Mike," Zambendorf reported.

"Okay, I'll have one ready for you in an hour, say. And six suits."

"That would be fine," Zambendorf said.

They met Arthur with the two Taloid brothers, Galileo and Moses, in the same ice chamber, with its odd pseudovegetable shapes and plastic and metal wall designs, that Zambendorf had come to with his previous message of reassurance. The difference was that this time he had nothing reassuring to say. He explained—as best he could in view of the translation difficulties and the Taloids' lack of any concept of what went on inside their own heads or any other kind of computer—that "spirit beings" from afar had invaded Titan's forests and were taking over the reproductive machinery to create bodies in which they intended to assume a physical form.

The humans were using one of Weinerbaum's new, improved translator boxes that produced output in the form of transmissions to their suit radios. A visual indicator on the box showed that Moses was speaking. "Explains death-quiet that has come. Spirits rule forests. I no longer hear forests' songs."

Zambendorf frowned questioningly behind his faceplate, looking like a ghostly apparition in the light from a flashlamp on minimum beam, which to the Taloids was still like a floodlight.

"The radio sources," Thelma reminded him over the local intercom frequency. "The Asterians blocked them after they got rid of GENIUS."

"Oh, of course." Zambendorf nodded and continued what he had been saying. The ship from Earth with its military expedition would not be coming, he said. A conflict over Titan's resources would not be to the Taloids' benefit. So the Terrans were returning to Earth. The spirits were the true creators of the life that inhabited Titan. They and the Taloids belonged there naturally and would learn to live together. The Terrans did not. It was an essentially true account, even if sweetened a little to be palatable. There was a long pause before Arthur's response came through.

"All Terrans will leave Titan?"

Zambendorf swallowed and nodded his head. "Yes."

"And not return. Other ship will not come back, not even without soldiers?"

Zambendorf didn't even want to think about that. "Maybe in the future," he whispered hoarsely. "There is much uncertainty." Several of the Terran figures shifted uncomfortably.

"Will we meet Zambendorf and his friends again?" Arthur asked.

"It is very unlikely."

The translator showed a different symbol to indicate that Galileo was speaking. "What of learning and the sciences? We had just begun."

"You will continue to learn," Zambendorf said. He couldn't bring himself to tell them any more. After all, there was a chance that things would work out as he was saying. The Asterians and the Taloids might manage to get along tolerably. So *might* Terrans and Asterians, for that matter. It wasn't untrue to say that ships from Earth *could* return some day. Yakumo hadn't actually *said* that an all-out nuclear strike was being planned. It was pure conjecture on Zambendorf and the team's part. Although the number of times he was right in divining the intentions of others—especially when it came to logical, predictable minds like those of scientists, the military, and officialdom—was something that he didn't want to think about. And even if it was planned, that didn't mean that it would succeed or that there would still be any point to it three months from now, which was the time the *Orion* would need to make Titan even if it departed immediately.

"That's all it needs, Karl." West's voice said on a local channel. "You don't have to spell out any more."

"Yeah, what's the point?" Fellburg asked.

"It's not your decision, Karl," Clarissa came in. "We've paid our respects, which was what we came for. There's nothing more we can do."

Kleippur had tried to follow the Wearer's explanation, but he was at a loss to understand why the Lumians seemed unable to combat these "spirits." It seemed all the more strange now that the Lumians who had wanted to reinstate Eskenderom had been thwarted once more, Kroaxia was solidly for Nogarech again, and all the nations of Robia were set to follow.

"What manner of spirits are these that the Lumians who fly from other worlds should flee without contest and abandon everything they have striven for?" he asked his companions in a worried voice. "They appear in the forests yet are immaterial? I have never before heard Lumian language the likes of this."

"Nor I," Thirg replied. "Methinks we are due soon to find out." It had troubled him, too. This latest Lumian talk sounded more like the Lifemaker creed of old than the sciences of reasoned knowledge they had always advocated. Yet the friends he had believed and relied on now seemed powerless to oppose this new force and were leaving. The future seemed suddenly very bleak.

Groork could only look forward in dread to the prospect of a future without the Lumians. Twice now he had been saved from what had seemed an inescapable end, first by the Lumians and then by the "voice" that had called itself GENIUS. On both occasions he had been a witness to power that was effortlessly able to confound all that had once terrified him, and he had felt secure. But now GENIUS and the other voices had been silenced, and the Lumians were leaving—it seemed—in ignominy. What form of unknown, hostile new power, then, was this, able to vanquish both, that the robeings were being left to face alone?

Kleippur maintained his usual calm resolve. "We faced adversity alone before the Lumians came," he declared. "And if it is necessary, we shall do so again."

"Perhaps this new adversity shall prove the force needed to unite all of Robia," Thirg said, looking for a hopeful note. He turned to the Lumian translating plant. "One day maybe Robian ships will come to Lumia. If we are not destined to meet again, perhaps our descendants shall."

In response to this, the Lumians were strangely reticent.

They all bade their farewells individually. Then the three Taloids escorted the visitors to a larger vault outside, where other Taloids were gathered whom the Terrans had gotten to know or had dealt with in one way or another. Arthur's advisers and scientists were there, including Em from military intelligence; Lancelot and his knights, who had brought Galileo out of Padua at the time of the *Orion*'s arrival; Galileo's naturalist friend, Linnaeus, who had returned with him; and Leonardo, another of Galileo's fellow scientists from Padua. The Terrans exchanged farewells once again. Arthur made a speech that the translator delivered haltingly, and Zambendorf mustered a choking response, as short as he dared make it without the risk of sounding terse, which probably translated semicomprehensibly. Then it was time to go.

Preceded by Fellburg lighting the way with the flashlamp, the somber procession of six figures in their bulky, dome-headed suits, their escorts looking like huge upright insects in the shadows, wound its way through gloomy caverns and canyonlike passageways to emerge finally in the forecourt where Clarissa had parked the transporter. The Terrans grouped by the door, and the Taloids closed around with final waved salutes and clumsy hand shakings between geniculated steel fingers and gauntleted hands.

And then an extraordinary thing happened. In the middle of the group of Taloids, Moses went suddenly rigid. He threw his head back and extended both arms upward to the heavens. The other Taloids moved back in alarm.

"Groork, what is it?" Arthur called across to him worriedly. "What ails thee thus?" But Groork made no response.

"Brother, what is it that you hear?" Thirg asked, recognizing the signs.

"The voices!" Groork exclaimed rapturously. "I hear the songs! The forests are singing again!"

From the translator box his announcement came through as "Machine surface song back." But it was enough. The Terrans looked at each other, startled.

"Tell me this can't mean what I think it means," Thelma whispered.

Abaquaan's mustache was quivering inside his helmet. "It's gone?" he said. "Whatever was blocking the radio sources has gone?"

"Gone?" Drew West repeated.

And then another voice came through to all of them on their assigned emergency frequency from Genoa Base. "Hello, base calling Zambendorf. Anybody there? Do you read?"

"Zambendorf here. I read," he answered.

"Got a call coming in for you, priority, from Weinerbaum at ES3. Relaying it through."

Weinerbaum's voice switched in straightaway. "Karl?"

"Yes?"

"The most amazing thing has just happened!" Weinerbaum's voice was excited, exuberant. It could mean only one thing.

Zambendorf's face creased into a smile behind his faceplate. "I know, Werner. Things are returning to normal, right? The Asterians are losing their hold."

"What?" Weinerbaum sounded mystified. "How could you possibly know that? We've only just worked it out here ourselves, with all the equipment at the monitoring center. How—"

"Oh, Werner, don't you understand *yet*?" Zambendorf scoffed, forcing a despairing tone. "I have no need of such crude methods."

Weinerbaum's sigh came over the connection audibly. "Karl, for once cut out that clowning. Get yourself out here as quickly as you can. I've asked base for a flyer. Mick's getting one readied for you right now."

44

O'FLYNN HAD THE FLYER WAITING BY THE TIME THE transporter arrived back at Genoa Base. Zambendorf and all his team piled in, along with Crookes, and the flyer took off straightaway. At ES3 they joined Weinerbaum and his scientists in the monitoring center. By then Weinerbaum was able to confirm that the situation was as it had seemed when he had called Zambendorf: apart from the physical damage caused in the course of the alien software war, conditions everywhere were returning to normal. All traces of the Asterians had vanished.

"Ironically, I think Cyril was absolutely right in what he said about the power of evolutionary systems," Weinerbaum told them while they were still finding room for themselves amid the crush of equipment and other bodies. "This whole living, machine surface of Titan is an evolutionary system. Ever since the first factory-robot organisms, or whatever first started it all, began spreading a million years ago, one of the most important functions they would have to learn would be to recognize their own kind and protect it from all that was foreign."

"Like regular biological antibodies," Thelma put in.

Weinerbaum nodded. "Precisely so. And if what I'm thinking is correct, as these organisms grew together into the present, surface-wide ecosystem, their self-protection codes evolved into complex electronic immune systems."

Zambendorf's mouth opened in a silent "Ah!" as he suddenly saw the point Weinerbaum was coming to. "Yes. I think I know what you're going to say."

Weinerbaum looked a little piqued. "Please, Karl, this *is* serious. I thought we'd agreed to cut all that out."

Zambendorf frowned in surprise and then shook his head in a protest of innocence. "No, I was being straight ... honestly. You were going to say that the business between GENIUS and the Asterians triggered the defenses somehow."

Weinerbaum nodded. "Yes. The crescendo of alien codings at war with one another everywhere caused the system to mobilize antibody codes of its own to go out and hunt down anything that didn't belong."

"Which meant anything alien," Fellburg said. "It attacked the Asterians."

Weinerbaum nodded once again. "The ultimate irony was Cyril's telling us how design could never substitute for the inherent ruggedness that evolution confers. Because the codes the Asterians created to transport themselves were just that: designed, not evolved. And they were unable to withstand the defenses that had resulted from the million years of high-pressure evolution that occurred here on Titan."

There was a short silence while the new arrivals absorbed the full meaning of it. Their faces showed the elation that was to be expected yet at the same time uncertainty. Finally Abaquaan asked for all of them, "So ... is that it, now? Is there any chance that they can come back?"

Weinerbaum shook his head. "No, I don't think so, Otto." He indicated the surroundings briefly with a wave. "We've got lines into what were some of the most active centers. The codes haven't just been inactivated—they're destroyed. 'Digested,' if you will. That's what antibodies do. Nothing is going to restore them again. It would be like trying to put cows back together from cheese."

Zambendorf glanced cautiously around the room, as if just checking one last time to make sure he had gotten it right. "You're saying that's it? It's over?" The scientists nodded back with encouraging grins in a way that said he'd better believe it.

"Apart from having one hell of a mess to be sorted out on Earth, yes, it would appear so," Weinerbaum confirmed.

Zambendorf's people looked at one another with dazed expressions. Everything appeared to have worked out. The Asterian threat was gone, it seemed, permanently. The designs of the neocolonialists to turn Titan into a manufacturing plantation had been foiled. Arthur would be free to continue developing his new republic without exploitation and interference. The evacuation of Titan could be called off, and with the alien stranglehold gone, a regular exchange of traffic with Earth could resume when the *Orion* became operable.

"Say, well, waddya know!" Fellburg exclaimed as it all finally sank in. He held up an open palm.

"Right on!" Abaquaan slapped a hand into it enthusiastically.

"You did it!" Drew West punched Zambendorf on the shoulder. "I'd never have bet a dollar on the chances, if you want to know the truth, Karl. But dammit, you did it!"

Thelma put an arm around Clarissa's shoulders and gave her a hug. Crookes pulled Annette Claurier over and planted a solid kiss on her mouth.

Weinerbaum was looking at Zambendorf and shaking his head despairingly. "Faster-than-light signals. Instantaneous communications across higher planes. Who would ever have believed that the answer would turn out to be something like that?"

"We all have our modest talents to contribute, Werner," Zambendorf told him, smirking shamelessly.

And then the voice of the technician who was supervising the link back to Genoa Base called out in alarm. "Wait. Something strange is happening. Maybe it's not all over yet." A sudden, fearful hush enveloped the room. Surely not, Zambendorf thought. It couldn't be about to go wrong again now.

"What is it?" Weinerbaum asked tensely, stepping across the room. Other scientists gathered behind him.

"I'm not sure." The technician indicated his displays. "We've got a sudden resurgence of activity. There's a stream of incoming traffic that I can't identify. It's taking over whole storage banks."

"Bryan Larson on the line from base," another operator reported as the face of the NASO communications chief appeared on a screen.

"What's happening?" Weinerbaum demanded, wheeling to face it.

"We don't know. It just started coming in over the laser trunk from Earth and then redirected itself out to ES3. We had nothing to do with it. I don't know what it is."

"Wow, it's really gobbling up the blocks!" one of the scientists breathed.

"Look at that overhead," another said.

On the various screens the cross-linkage maps and allocation tables began re-forming themselves into new associative paths and groupings. Apprehension mounted around the room until a voice said suddenly, "Hey, I recognize this pattern. We've seen it before. It's a beta!"

And then a familiar cube with legs and a face appeared on a blank screen. "Hi, guys. Why so surprised? You didn't think you could get rid of me that easily, did you?"

Zambendorf blinked. "GENIUS?" he said, shaking his head. "GENIUS, is this you?"

"What does it look like?"

"But how?"

"All the activity when that trouble with the Asterians blew up set off an immune reaction across the whole Titan net. Things were definitely not healthy around here." The screen showed a scene that looked like a version of PAC-Man, with assorted ugly bug forms prowling around and gobbling up miniature GENIUSes and Asterians.

"We were just talking about it," Zambendorf said. "The Asterians are gone. Weinerbaum was just telling us that that's what must have happened."

"Well, I stowed away in a safe place once before to get myself out of trouble." The screen showed GENIUS with a suitcase running along a laser beam terminating at Earth. "This time I transmitted myself over the link and hid out in the Earthnet until things quieted down. So Cyril and the rest were too slow, eh? You see—you're going to need a chip brain around." The picture changed again to show GE-NIUS standing at the foot of a ladder with a king of diamonds playing card sitting on top. "So now I'm back again, ready to resume learning from the master."

For the moment Zambendorf was flummoxed. He looked at the rest of the team appealingly, not knowing what to say. They returned stares of serene confidence that he would think of something and remained totally unhelpful. Weinerbaum smiled wryly and turned away. "Well, we have plenty of work to be getting on with," he told his scientists.

Zambendorf looked back at the screen depicting GE-NIUS. He smiled awkwardly and cleared his throat. "Er, can you switch yourself through to a room where we could have a little more privacy, GENIUS?" he asked. "There are some things that I think it's time you and I had a long talk about."

Epilogue

TWO MONTHS LATER, ZAMBENDORF AND HIS TEAM walked off a Japanese shuttle just up from Genoa Base and into the entry lock of the orbiting *Shirasagi*, which was in the final stages of preparation prior to liftout for its return to Earth. It was time for them to go home at last. The *Orion* was a month out from Earth already, and the two vessels would pass when the *Shirasagi* was a month away from Titan. GENIUS had been true to its word, and with its aid the task of sorting out the situation on Earth had gone far more quickly than the original pessimistic forecasts had predicted. Also, the shake-up that the experience had provoked all around had finally enabled cooler heads to prevail in the formulation of Earth's policy toward Titan. The proposed military expedition had been disbanded, and Titan would develop freely and naturally toward its own form of independence. NASO control had been extended as a temporary measure while the details were worked out for expanding it to a fully international, as opposed to north Atlantic, organization, to which the Japanese had already agreed to subordinate their own deep-space command.

For a long time Moses had entertained the ambition of one day flying up through the cloud canopy in one of the Terran ships and seeing for himself the universe of stars and void that existed beyond the sky. But the Taloids could not have tolerated the onboard human environment, and with other matters to preoccupy them, the Terrans had not yet gotten around to fitting some of the surface shuttles with accommodations suitable for Taloids. Therefore, Zambendorf and Co. had said their good-byes to them—or maybe said their *au revoirs*—down at Genoa Base before embarking.

However, one even stranger being had accompanied them up to the *Shirasagi* to see the ship firsthand and say its own farewell from there, after which it would shuttle back down to rejoin the predominantly Japanese contingent that would be carrying on at Genoa and Padua bases until the *Orion*'s arrival.

"Okay, you've convinced me," GENIUS said as it drew up with Zambendorf and the others and gazed out at the rust-red mass of Titan and the starfield beyond through a viewing window by the *Shirasagi*'s transfer lock. "Communicating with anywhere from inside a box might have its advantages. But actually moving around physically 'out here' is something else, a whole new experience. I think I'm going to like it."

It was the oddest-shaped body any of them had ever seen, even after seven months on Titan. It had a head set on a slender trunk, and a system of multilevel jointed sections that could reconfigure themselves into a variable number of differently adapted limbs for different purposes. The design left by the Asterians had been put to good use, after all. GENIUS was finding it a delight to experiment with and, in its rapture at discovering the experience of being "out there," had quickly forgotten all about its brief romance with higher planes and the realm of the supernatural. Experiencing the reality of physical space provided all the higher-dimensional stimulation it needed.

"Yes, I think you'll fit in all right," Zambendorf said. "One thing about not having evolved with the Asterians is that you didn't inherit their mean streak."

"Home!" Thelma said dreamily, taking in the first real stars she had seen for months. "Just imagine: beaches, palm trees, driving on freeways, dinner in a five-star . . ."

"Walking through a park that doesn't look like an oil refinery," Abaquaan added, joining her.

"I'll settle for just being able to go to the supermarket without having to put on a diving suit," Clarissa remarked dryly.

Instead of features as such, GENIUS's head framed a screen upon which it could depict anything. The face it had adopted as its standard persona nodded and looked intrigued. "It sounds interesting. I'll have to try out this new-fangled body there sometime."

"You do that," Fellburg told it.

Zambendorf looked at Drew West, who was left standing with him. "What are your plans, Drew?" he asked.

West made a thoughtful face. "Me? Oh . . . nothing really concrete. I have a feeling that there's going to be more than enough for us to do after everything that's happened on Titan. I think it might also be one of those occasions when a little . . . 'reassessment' of one's mission in life might be in order, too, don't you?"

Zambendorf looked at him quizzically. "A new line of business for the firm, you mean?" he queried.

West nodded. "It's about due, Karl. The old stuff's all going to seem a bit stale now. Everyone's had a taste now of working for something better. It's time to move on."

Zambendorf realized that the others had turned their attention back and were listening. Their expressions all endorsed what West had said. Zambendorf had no quarrel with any of it; in fact, he had felt the same way himself for some time. "It was fun, though, while it lasted, wasn't it?" he asked them.

"We wouldn't have missed it for anything," Thelma replied.

Mackeson and the last of the returning NASO personnel had passed through into the *Shirasagi* while they were talking. Now Weinerbaum and his scientists were following from the shuttle lock. The U.S. Special Forces troopers, British marines, and French paras had already come up with the previous shuttle. From the lock entrance, one of the Japanese shuttle crew signaled that everyone due for the *Shirasagi* was aboard.

"Well, I guess that's it," Zambendorf said. "We'll see you on Earth one day, then, GENIUS. In the meantime, take care of those Taloids down there for us, eh?"

"Don't worry. Your work won't be wasted." GENIUS's screen showed the legged cuboid relaxing on a beach beneath palm trees, admiring bikini-clad girls. Then it reshaped its limb structure into a branching arrangement that enabled it to shake hands with Zambendorf and all his companions at the same time. It re-formed the lower set into a tripod on which it walked back to the shuttle lock, turning to send back one last wave and a grin from its screen.

Fifteen minutes later, from the *Shirasagi*'s general-quarters deck, Zambendorf and the others watched on a mural display as the shuttle decoupled and fell away, back toward the turgid, red cloud canopy of Titan. A message from the *Orion* had confirmed that it was on schedule with all systems functioning normally, and Yakumo gave the order to commence the final phase of the prelaunch countdown.

Five hours later, the *Shirasagi* fired its main drive to lift out of Titan orbit and came around onto a course that would carry it back in the direction of the inner region of the solar system, toward the beckoning, warm glow of the sun.

JAMES P. HOGAN

*The man who puts science
back into science fiction!*

**Published by Ballantine Books.
Available in your local bookstores.**

DEL REY ONLINE!

The Del Rey Internet Newsletter...

A monthly electronic publication, posted on the Internet, GEnie, CompuServe, BIX, various BBSs, and the Panix gopher (gopher.panix.com). It features hype-free descriptions of books that are new in the stores, a list of our upcoming books, special announcements, a signing/reading/convention-attendance schedule for Del Rey authors, "In Depth" essays in which professionals in the field (authors, artists, designers, sales people, etc.) talk about their jobs in science fiction, a question-and-answer section, behind-the-scenes looks at sf publishing, and more!

Online editorial presence: Many of the Del Rey editors are online, on the Internet, GEnie, CompuServe, America Online, and Delphi. There is a Del Rey topic on GEnie and a Del Rey folder on America Online.

Our official e-mail address for Del Rey Books is delrey@randomhouse.com

Internet information source!

A lot of Del Rey material is available to the Internet on a gopher server: all back issues and the current issue of the Del Rey Internet Newsletter, a description of the DRIN and summaries of all the issues' contents, sample chapters of upcoming or current books (readable or downloadable for free), submission requirements, mail-order information, and much more. We will be adding more items of all sorts (mostly new DRINs and sample chapters) regularly. The address of the gopher is gopher.panix.com

Why? We at Del Rey realize that the networks are the medium of the future. That's where you'll find us promoting our books, socializing with others in the sf field, and—most importantly—making contact and sharing information with sf readers.

For more information, e-mail
delrey@randomhouse.com